STAR TREK®

STRANGE NEW WORLDS

8

STAR TREK®

STRANGE NEW WORLDS

8

Edited by
Dean Wesley Smith
with **Elisa J. Kassin** and **Paula M. Block**

Based upon
Star Trek® and *Star Trek: The Next Generation*®
created by Gene Roddenberry,
Star Trek: Deep Space Nine® created by
Rick Berman & Michael Piller
Star Trek: Voyager® created by
Rick Berman, Michael Piller & Jeri Taylor, and
Star Trek: Enterprise® created by
Rick Berman & Brannon Braga

POCKET BOOKS
New York   London   Toronto   Sydney

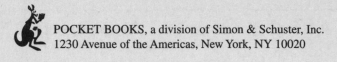 POCKET BOOKS, a division of Simon & Schuster, Inc.
1230 Avenue of the Americas, New York, NY 10020

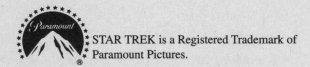 STAR TREK is a Registered Trademark of Paramount Pictures.

This book is published by Pocket Books, a division of Simon & Schuster, Inc., under exclusive license from Paramount Pictures.

ISBN-13: 978-1-4165-0345-3
ISBN-10:   1-4165-0345-5

First Pocket Books trade paperback edition July 2005

10 9 8 7 6 5 4 3 2 1

Cover design by John Vairo, Jr.
Cover art by Doug Drexler

Manufactured in the United States of America

For information regarding special discounts for bulk purchases, please contact Simon & Schuster Special Sales at 1-800-456-6798 or business@simonandschuster.com.

Contents

Contents

STAR TREK
DEEP SPACE NINE®

STAR TREK
VOYAGER®

— STAR TREK —
ENTERPRISE

Contents

SPECULATIONS

Introduction

Dean Wesley Smith

Every year you, the fans, take me on a pleasure ride into the amazing past of the *Star Trek*® universe.

Now, granted, I am a story junkie. I'm a person who loves reading *Star Trek* more than anything else I can think of doing (except writing *Star Trek*). Every October, boxes and boxes of great stories arrive at my doorstep, and every year those stories usher me into the *Star Trek* universe, in ways, and to places, I would have never thought to go by myself.

But besides that, your stories take me into my own past.

The original *Star Trek* series premiered in September of 1966 and was aired on Friday nights in Boise, Idaho. I remember how I would rush home from high school to watch it. I never missed an episode back in the days before videotape machines. I didn't dare—there was the awful chance that the episode might not air again. (Yes, I realize that I just dated myself and told you how old I really am.)

Introduction

The superb *Star Trek* stories you send in to the contest take me back to my high school days. They remind me of my friends and take me back to the nights of worrying about being drafted and the uncertainty of life—deciding if I should go to college or just go skiing.

I did both, didn't get drafted, and years went by. When *Star Trek: The Next Generation*® started, a group of us, all hopeful writers, would gather at Nina Kiriki Hoffman's house to watch it every week. We would talk about the episode that we had just seen, talk about writing, and simply enjoy each other's company. If someone had told me that I would be writing *Star Trek* professionally, I would have just laughed. And wonderful anthologies like this weren't even distant thoughts. Every one of the *Next Generation* stories we receive reminds me of those delightful *"Trek* parties" we used to love so much.

Star Trek: Deep Space Nine® broadcast its first show via satellite, ahead of when it aired on regular local channels. My wife, Kristine Kathryn Rusch, and I lived in the country and had a satellite dish. We had just finished watching the very first show, about three days before almost anyone else in our area would see it, when John Ordover called. At the time, Kris was editing *The Magazine of Fantasy and Science Fiction* and I was editing *Pulphouse Magazine.* Before John started at Pocket Books for the *Star Trek* program, I had bought a story from him, so it wasn't such a surprise to receive his call.

We ended up talking about the new series and how cool it was. The conversation progressed and he asked if Kris and I would be interested in writing one of the first *Deep Space Nine* novels. Well, duh. What a silly question. It came out a year later under our Sandy Schofield name. These are the memories that the *Deep Space Nine* entries trigger in my mind. They remind me of those days out in the country, watching shows ahead of everyone else, and getting the first chance at doing something I couldn't even have dreamed of doing ten years earlier.

Star Trek: Voyager® and *Star Trek: Enterprise*™ both have a similar feeling for me; they lead me to the same place in my memory, even though their starts are years apart. Besides the fact that I love the shows, they bring on a faint recollection of worry and panic, as well as a satisfying feeling of success.

Okay, why such a mix of emotions? Well, Kris and I were hired, for both series, to do the very first original books. When we wrote those books, it was months before the shows aired. We had only a trailer, some still pictures, and a few scripts for guidance. By then, we knew how important getting the characters in *Star Trek* dead-on was for the fans. And we had never seen the characters, heard them speak. Nor had we experienced the life an actor gives to each of the people that we were writing about. Trust me, that sets off a real fear for a *Trek* fan like me—and a lot of pleasure when we realized that we didn't miss by too much.

Now do you see why your stories are like traveling in time for me? My life, especially my adult life, has been tied in and around *Star Trek*. And I consider myself the luckiest person alive for that.

So, send in more stories for the next contest so that I can take new thrilling rides through the history of *Star Trek,* and take everyone else down their own Memory Lane.

Remember, read the rules in the back of this book, read the stories in this book, read previous volumes to really understand what types of stories we are choosing. Then sit down and write a story (or two, or three). Have fun. Take us all to new corners of this vast universe. And send them all in.

Then maybe, just maybe, you'll get a phone call saying we would like to include your story in the next volume of *Strange New Worlds*. Trust me, this is one phone call that will be a unique memory to attach to this great universe.

I hope you enjoy these stories. I sure did.

STAR TREK®

Shanghaied

Alan James Garbers

September 14, 1863

The *C.S.S. Raleigh* was two days west of Liverpool. The blockade runner was headed full sail for Richmond. The sleek cruiser carried enough coal to last eighteen days of steaming, and enough sailcloth to run fifteen knots, fast enough to outrun anything the Yankees had afloat. She was the pride of the Confederacy and a thorn in the side of the Union navy.

Captain Patterson felt like a mother hen on the back of a thoroughbred stallion. Below him was a hold packed with much-needed supplies and, more important, gold headed for the coffers of the Confederate government. While he knew that his ship was the fastest in the Atlantic, he also knew that overconfidence had been the downfall of many of his fellow captains, and when the gold was safe in Richmond he would rest much easier.

It was on the second night that the lights appeared. One moment the *Raleigh* was alone; the next the lights were hovering next to them. Within moments the crew scrambled to their stations to combat this unknown foe. Cannons were rolled out; rifles were pulled from racks and loaded. Captain Patterson commanded the helmsman to bring the rudder hard to port in an effort to lose the bothersome spectacle, but it was to no avail; the lights remained steadfast. Minutes went by. No shots were fired. No boarding party swarmed aboard. Then, as it had appeared, so it vanished.

Captain Patterson was not a superstitious man, nor did he believe in witchcraft, but he was at a loss to explain the phenomenon. The salty captain had seen Saint Elmo's fire dancing from the spars. He had seen glowing swamp gases in his native Louisiana. He had even seen the beautiful dance of the northern lights, but none of them had been as unrelenting as the lights he had just seen.

As he started forward from the helm, Gunner's Mate Vincent McCoy came clambering up the ladder.

"Suh! Gun crew six is missin'."

The captain turned. "Missing? What do you mean missing? Weren't they at their station?"

"Yes, suh." McCoy nodded. "They were . . . and then they wasn't."

The captain scowled. He didn't like cowards. The men on his ship had been handpicked for their bravery and fighting ability. "Find them and bring them to the mast. I don't abide men who leave their posts."

McCoy nodded, then shook his head. "I'm sorry, suh. I'm not explainin' myself rightly. They vanished . . . I saw, uh, it with my own eyes."

The captain looked into the mate's eyes for the first time. Even in the darkness he could see the fear there. "What are you babbling about?"

"God as my witness, suh! The light shone in on them, and then they were gone. It was like the rapture in the Bible."

4

The captain's scowl deepened. "It wasn't the rapture! It was some damn Yankee trick! A hot-air balloon!"

McCoy cocked his head in confusion. "Suh?"

"An observation balloon," the captain explained gruffly. "The Yankees have used them before to spy on our camps. No doubt there's a Union ship nearby. They landed on our ship and captured those men in the confusion."

The fear in the man's face vanished. A rational explanation of an attack was much better than the unknown.

"Yes, suh!"

"Keep the gun crews ready," the captain spat. "If they come back we'll show them some lights."

The gunner's mate snapped to attention and saluted. "Yes, suh!"

On the third night the lights returned. The sharpshooters that Captain Patterson had stationed in the crow's nests put up a blistering barrage of rifle fire. Momentarily the gunfire stopped and the rifles tumbled down to the deck. The lights once again vanished, and with them went seven of the Confederate's finest.

On the fourth night they were ready. Other than the rushing of the waves and slapping of canvas, a ghostly silence hung over the ship as each man wondered if he would be next to disappear. They didn't have to wait long. The watch had just changed when the lights appeared, hanging just off the starboard spar. With grim excitement Captain Patterson swung his sword into the light. "Now, boys! Take that monster down!"

The helmsman gave the wheel a hard spin toward starboard. In response the *C.S.S. Raleigh* bit hard into the sea and lay over so that the port deck was almost awash. The gun crews were ready as the maneuver gave them the elevation they needed. Almost as one the cannons belched flames and smoke. The effect was immediate. The lights went out with a thumping ring. A high-pitched whine started and rose in volume and then ended as the specter crashed into the sea.

A cheer rose from the decks as the *Raleigh* righted itself. "Good

5

work, boys!" shouted the captain. "That'll show them damn blue bellies." He turned back to the helmsman. "Bring us about."

Minutes later the *Raleigh* drifted next to the specter as it bobbed in the cold Atlantic waters. Hissing and clinking sounded above the slap of the small waves. The crew hung lanterns over the side to get a better view. The yellow light gleamed like gold off the shiny metal. The crew murmured among themselves, speculating on what it might be. After a moment Captain Patterson motioned to his officers. "Get that thing on board. As soon as it's lashed down, set sail for Richmond, best speed."

"Sir?" questioned a young ensign. "Why do we want that Yankee trash?"

The captain turned slightly. "That trash took a dozen of my best men. Maybe we can see fit to return the favor."

The ensign smiled. "Yes, sir!"

The fifth day brought a change to the weather. At the beginning of the first watch the seas were running five to seven feet and a fresh breeze hastened the *C.S.S. Raleigh* on her way. By noon the seas were eighteen feet with gale-force winds. During the evening mess, the word came down to stow the sails and prepare for heavy seas. By the midwatch the seas were tossing the *C.S.S. Raleigh* about like a piece of driftwood. The fireman poured coal into the boilers but the ship's screw was chopping air as much as it was cutting the foamy sea.

By dawn of the sixth day the seas were rolling. As the bow plunged into a wave, the crew would pray that the ship would come out on the other side. Waves crashed over the deck faster than the water could drain out the scuppers. Seawater filled the bilges faster than the pumps could clear it. The wind and waves gave the ship a hard list. In desperation, Captain Patterson ordered the masts cut away, hoping the lessened weight would right the ship. Gunner's Mate McCoy and a few others headed topside with axes.

The plan was sound, but too late. With a sickening lurch the *C.S.S. Raleigh* lay over. The cold Atlantic flooded through hatches and doors that were never meant to be under water. Within moments the pride of the Confederate Navy slipped beneath the waves forever. Gunner's Mate Vincent McCoy found himself clinging to a powder keg, alone in an angry sea.

Captain's Log. Stardate 3163.2 We are in orbit over Earth. Starfleet has requested two of my senior officers to help with a classified mission. I don't know what it entails, but we are to meet with a Doctor Bancroft, one of the top archaeologists at the Foundation for Earth Studies. It is rumored that they want my men to investigate the remains of a nineteenth-century sailing vessel that was found off the Avalon Peninsula in Nova Scotia. This is highly irregular, but Scotty and Spock are eager to get a glimpse of history. Doctor McCoy and I are tagging along to keep them out of trouble.

Doctor Bancroft banked the shuttle hard against the ever-present coastal winds and landed on the cracked and weed-infested tarmac. Bancroft tugged his coat tighter and gave them a sheepish grin. "I have to warn you. Winter is coming up here." He passed each of the four guests a coat from a locker and flicked the release on the door. As the shuttle door opened, the bitter cold swept into the cabin and caught the foursome unprepared.

McCoy glared at Kirk. "This is the last time I let you pick my shore excursions." He donned the coat with a grunt. The others followed his lead. When all were bundled up, they followed the archaeologist out into the cold. A large, battered hangar sat on the edge of the field that looked to be a leftover from the Eugenics Wars. Doctor Bancroft must have noticed his guests' expressions as they made for the derelict building.

"The foundation gets very little funding, so we take what we can get . . ."

McCoy gave another grunt. "The next time you call us, make it a Spanish galleon in the tropics."

"Doctor, the foundation didn't call you at all," corrected Spock. "It was the aid of Commander Scott and myself that he requested."

McCoy glared at Spock for a moment. "Just get me somewhere warm."

"I'm sorry, Doctor McCoy," Doctor Bancroft offered. "The hangar does have heat. At least, part of it does." With that he pulled a small side door open and ushered the foursome in.

Doctor Bancroft flipped a breaker on. With a slam the lights snapped on, flooding the hangar bay with warm yellow lighting. For a moment no one said anything as all eyes fell upon the shiny craft suspended in front of them.

"Would ye look at that." Scotty whistled. He forgot about the cold and crossed to the artifact. Ancient compartment doors hung open with cables and components hanging from them like the bowels of a dead animal.

Kirk glanced at McCoy and smiled. "I haven't seen Scotty this happy since the last time the *Enterprise* had an engine rebuild."

Spock adjusted his tricorder and slowly inspected the object. "Where did you find this craft?"

Doctor Bancroft gave a sheepish grin as he glanced from Kirk to Spock. "That's the kicker. . . . We found it about thirty miles off the coast, with the remains of a Civil War blockade runner."

"Which one?" Kirk asked as he glanced about the hangar. "The Eugenics Wars?"

Spock turned to Kirk. "Captain, I believe he is referring to the Civil War of the United States, in the nineteenth century—1861 through 1865, to be exact."

"Very good, Mister Spock!" Bancroft agreed. "You know Earth history very well!"

"But they didn't have this kind of technology then," argued Kirk.

"Could it be a coincidence that the two ships were found together?" Spock asked.

Bancroft shook his head. "It would be so much easier if that were the case, but we found the spacecraft lashed to the remains of the deck. The hawser dates to the same time as the ship timbers."

McCoy pulled the hood of his coat back as he slowly walked over to the craft. "It was the *Raleigh,* wasn't it?"

Doctor Bancroft's jaw dropped. "How did you know that?"

"My great-great-great-something-grandfather was aboard her," McCoy replied.

Bancroft slowly shook his head. "I saw a McCoy on the crew roster when I was researching her, but I never made the connection."

"I was told stories about it as a child. I think he even wrote a journal about his adventure."

"Do you still have it?" Bancroft pleaded.

McCoy shrugged. "Don't know. I'll have to check with some of my relatives."

"The craft has been badly damaged," Scott commented. "It looks like someone took a giant hammer to it."

McCoy smiled. "I think you'll find those dents match the size of a Confederate cannonball."

Spock raised an eyebrow. "It would be highly unlikely that weapons of that era would be accurate enough to take down a spacecraft."

McCoy glared at Spock. "It's highly likely that you underestimate the marksmanship of the Confederate Navy, Spock."

"I would say he's right, Mister Spock," added Scott. "I canna think of anything else that'd do that."

"Do the controls look like something you can figure out?" asked Bancroft.

"I don't know, laddie, but I would sure like to try." Scotty grinned.

Spock stepped up to the craft and studied the hieroglyphics embossed on the metal. After a moment he recorded them in his tricorder.

"Have you ever seen characters like that before?" Bancroft asked.

Spock was silent for a moment. He raised an eyebrow. "I believe I have; however, I will need to consult the computer on board the *Enterprise*."

McCoy nodded agreement. "I might be able to track down that journal, but I can't do it from this frozen wasteland."

Kirk grinned. "Too cold for you, Bones?"

"Damn right it's too cold. I'm a doctor, not Admiral Byrd!" he snapped back.

Bancroft looked crestfallen. "I'm sorry, Doctor McCoy. I can take you back right now."

"Captain, I would like to stay and see what I can figure out," Scott pleaded. "I might even be able to get this lassie working."

Kirk scowled. "I would have thought the salt water ruined everything."

Scotty shook his head. "It looks like all the seals and gaskets held against the water. Other than the damage from the cannonballs, she looks to be in prime shape."

Bancroft's face lit up. "Everything you should need is here in the hangar. I even have a surprise for you in the cabinet in the office," he said, referring to the expensive bottle of liquor that he had personally bought for the engineer.

Scotty gave him a sly grin. "And what might that be?"

Bancroft's face blushed. "Um, let's call it a bit of 'hospitality.'"

Scotty raised his hands in supplication. "See, Captain, I have to stay and partake of the foundation's hospitality."

Kirk eyed him skeptically. "Are you sure you'll be all right, Scotty?"

"Sure, I'll be as snug as a bug," replied Scott.

Kirk nodded. "All right, but contact the *Enterprise* if you need anything."

"He said he'll be fine, Jim," McCoy chided. "Now, let's head for someplace warmer."

Bancroft opened the door to the hangar and motioned the trio outside. "This way, gentlemen. I'll have you back to civilization in no time."

Scotty watched his friends for a moment, and then turned back to the spacecraft. "Now, where were we?"

Six hours and a hospitable bit of Scotch later found the damaged panels and equipment removed. Scotty had figured out the basic circuitry, including the power system. With a click, he shoved what he assumed to be a switch inward. There was no explosion, sparking, or even a puff of smoke. He was, however, rewarded with the steady hum of power. Somewhere deep within the craft there was a series of clicks, and the craft moved with a sharp upward motion, like Gulliver testing his bonds.

Scotty took a tentative step back. "Easy there, lassie. I'm your friend." Scotty took a reading with his tricorder and analyzed it. Making an adjustment, he heard a slight change in the pitch of the hum.

"Are you singing me a tune, lassie?" Scotty chuckled. "Let's see how you like this." He pushed another switch home. The pitch changed once more. Scotty took his readings and found them not to be what he expected.

"What the . . . ?"

Suddenly he was bathed in light. Now realizing what the circuitry was designed for, he lunged for the control switch, but it was too late. The hangar bay turned to white and Scotty knew no more.

The spacecraft computer scanned the area and found it to be devoid of any other life-forms. Following its programming, it took the next rung of logic and lunged upward against its bonds. The cradle was meant to hold the craft off the floor, not keep it from flying away, and the small straps separated with little resistance. Sensing a weak spot in the hangar roof, the craft continued its ascent, puncturing the rusty sheet metal like tinfoil.

Free of the hangar, the craft rose rapidly until it was past the interference of the planet. Within a blink of an eye the computer had its celestial bearings. It aligned itself as programmed and, gathering all its power reserves, transmitted its cargo into the darkness of space.

*   *   *

Kirk was heading for the bridge when he got the call from Uhura. Within moments he strode through the doors. Spock was at his station, monitoring the progress of the computer.

"What is it, Lieutenant?" he asked.

Uhura turned. Her face was a sea of concern but her voice was steady. "Sir, Starfleet has monitored an unauthorized vessel leaving Earth." Uhura's voice choked for a moment. "It came from the Avalon Peninsula, sir."

"Spock, is there anything on sensors?"

Spock turned his attention to the sensor readouts. "Sensors show a small craft in high orbit over Nova Scotia."

"On screen," Kirk ordered. In a flash the screen held a small golden dot.

"Magnify," he commanded. The image jumped to the craft that they had left only scant hours before.

"It would appear Scotty is a miracle worker," Kirk said as he turned to Uhura. "Contact Mister Scott."

Uhura shook her head. "That's just it, sir. I've been trying to raise him since Starfleet contacted us."

"Spock, do you get any life-sign readings aboard the craft?" Kirk asked.

"None. Nor do I detect any in the hangar," he replied.

Kirk punched the com button and called sickbay. In a moment he had an answer.

"McCoy here. What do you need, Jim?"

"Bones, meet me in the transporter room," Kirk barked. "Spock, you're with me. Sulu, get a tractor beam on that ship and bring it into the shuttlebay."

Kirk spun on his heel and hurried out the bridge doors. Spock followed.

The three figures in Starfleet arctic gear materialized in the hangar. Two immediately started scanning the hangar with their tricorders. The third gazed at the mess. It didn't take long for his patience to run out.

"Is there anything on sensors?" Kirk demanded.

McCoy pulled his hood back and pursed his lips. "Jim, I don't see a body, dead or alive."

"Spock? Anything?" Kirk pleaded.

"My readings are the same as the doctor's," Spock said as he searched the hangar.

"He couldn't have just vanished into thin air!" growled Kirk.

"Maybe Doctor Bancroft came and got him," offered McCoy.

Kirk shook his head. "No, Bancroft had some business at Starfleet to attend to before heading back—" Kirk noticed Spock's sudden increase in tricorder activity. "Spock, did you find something?"

Spock kept studying his tricorder. "I am picking up traces of energy consistent with molecular transport activity."

"He transported out of here?" Kirk questioned.

"Possibly, but to where is the question," Spock replied. He turned a dial on his tricorder and then crossed the hangar. "I'm getting another weak energy pattern from here." Spock shoved bits of tin aside to reveal a tricorder. Picking it up, he played back the recordings. His eyebrow rose slightly as the data passed before his eyes.

"Fascinating."

"Dammit, Spock!" McCoy snapped. "Don't be coy! Where's Scotty?"

"Possibly aboard the spacecraft," Spock answered calmly.

"Spock, you said there were no life signs aboard the vessel," countered Kirk.

"There were no life signs as we know them. I believe that Mister Scott may be held in transporter stasis within the vessel."

"What are you talking about?" McCoy demanded. "Are you telling me that a four-hundred-year-old derelict craft kidnapped Scotty?"

"In a manner of speaking, yes," replied Spock. "According to his tricorder, Mister Scott was able to get the vessel operational. It recorded the power buildup and transporter function." Mister Spock placed the tricorder in his coat pocket. "It is highly likely that Mister Scott is in that craft, in one form or another."

Kirk flipped opened his communicator. "Then we need to get up there now and get him out. *Enterprise,* three to beam up."

In a twinkling they were gone.

They wasted no time getting to the shuttlebay. The spacecraft hovered, suspended in the tractor beam.

"Spock, are you getting any readings?" asked Kirk.

Spock held out his tricorder and studied the readings. "Minimal. The craft seems to have expended all its reserves. However, I am getting similar residual energy readings to that which I found in the hangar . . . but at a much higher density." Spock lowered his tricorder. "That would indicate that the craft has emitted a narrow, high-strength molecular transmission."

"Cut the mumbo jumbo, Spock!" snapped McCoy.

Kirk held up a hand. "Hold it, Bones. Spock, are you saying this thing has transported Scotty into space? That would take a transporter of immense power."

"It would take a transporter with power unlike anything in recorded history," replied Spock. "Yet, there is a ninety-nine point three percent chance that it has occurred."

"Where did he beam to?" Kirk growled.

Spock raised his eyebrow. "Unknown at this time. It would be safe to assume to another vessel or planet. Judging by the power involved, it could be anywhere within a hundred light-years."

"That's like a needle in a haystack," Kirk spouted.

"Dammit Jim, we can't just give up!" cried McCoy. "This is Scotty we're talking about!"

Kirk spun as if stung. "Doctor, I have no intention of giving up, Scotty or no." Kirk hammered his fist on the spacecraft. "Spock, can we find out which direction it transported to?"

"I will check on its original heading before we brought it aboard. If we could narrow down our search, the sensors might be able to pick up the residual transporter pattern, and indicate its direction."

Kirk nodded. "Do it." The three headed for the bridge. "Bones, did you have any luck finding that journal?"

McCoy gave Kirk a grim smile. "Yes, I did, for all the good it will do."

"Why do you say that?" Kirk asked.

"Well, I read the part about the attack on the *C.S.S. Raleigh.* I didn't see anything that would help us get Scotty back."

"What was the information?" asked Spock.

"Why waste time with that, Spock?" McCoy asked angrily. "It's old news now."

"Indulge me, Doctor McCoy. It might provide us with clues on the situation we are now in."

"Tell us, Bones," Kirk said. "At this moment, anything might help."

McCoy sighed. "Something otherworldly came three nights in a row. The first two nights that it appeared, there was a blinding light and men would turn up missing—five the first night, seven the next. There appeared to be no feasible explanation."

"That would be consistent with what we know. It would appear that the craft transported men off the *Raleigh.*"

"But why come back each night?" Kirk wondered.

"Judging by the state of the vessel currently, it takes a full day to regenerate enough power to transmit the prisoners to wherever they were headed," replied Spock.

"So you're saying this machine came in every night, like the boogeyman, stole away with some of their best men, and sent them to who-knows-where?" McCoy asked.

"I would not have used those words, but you are essentially correct," replied Spock.

"Bones, what else did the journal say?" Kirk asked.

McCoy shrugged as he thought. "They were ready for it on the third night. They had the cannon ready and did some sort of maneuver that pointed the guns right at it. They fired. The spaceship fell. They caught it."

"What about the wreck?" Kirk asked.

"There wasn't too much. They got caught in a hurricane, the ship sank. My ancestor, Vincent McCoy, was the only survivor." McCoy added.

15

"That explains why the alien vessel was found with the *Raleigh*, but it doesn't explain where it came from, and why," murmured Kirk.

"I am researching those questions now, Captain. There are some obscure texts that are stored in the Vulcan Ministry of Ancient Alien Cultures—"

"Imagine that, something obscure coming from Vulcan," McCoy said dryly.

Spock ignored the dig. "I am waiting for the data to be transferred to the ship's computer. I believe it might prove useful on this subject."

"Useful, Spock?" Kirk jibed. "Knowing you, I'll get a road map to Scotty."

The turbolift stopped at the bridge.

"Chekov, I want the alien vessel's last location and bearing transferred to Spock's station."

Chekov nodded as he flicked a switch. "Aye, Captain. Coordinates have been transferred."

Long moments ticked away as Spock adjusted his station controls. Kirk's patience was limited and his voice mirrored it. "Spock. Is there anything to go on?"

"Sensors have picked up a trail," Spock replied. "The computer has calculated a course, and I am transferring it to the navigation computer."

"Chekov, lay in a course. Helm, as soon as you have the course, go to warp factor six."

Sulu nodded. "Aye, Captain, warp factor six."

The *U.S.S. Enterprise* leapt past the speed of light, and in a flash was gone.

Sixteen hours later, the *Enterprise* was in orbit of a small, barren planet. Kirk stared at the viewscreen in disbelief.

"Are there any life signs?" Kirk asked.

Spock wasted no words and shook his head swiftly instead.

"Are you sure this was the right trajectory, Spock?" he asked.

"There is a ninety-seven point six percent probability that this is the intended target of the transmission." Spock replied.

"There's nothing there but rock," snipped McCoy.

"Nonetheless, sensors detect trace molecular-transport residue."

Kirk smacked his fist into his palm in impatience. "Spock, can you pinpoint the location?"

Spock bent over his console and scanned the scope. In a moment, he adjusted a slide switch. "I have traced it to a complex in the southern hemisphere. Readings indicate an energy buildup."

Kirk leapt from his chair. "We're going down there. Sulu, you have the bridge."

When the turbolift doors opened, Kirk, McCoy, and Spock stepped in, leaving Sulu staring at the closing doors.

Minutes later the trio materialized inside an ancient chamber. Dust covered everything but didn't stop the soft illumination of a thousand lights and indication meters. A soft hum reverberated throughout the chamber.

Spock wordlessly wiped away some of the dust on a display and scanned it with his tricorder.

"Somebody must have fired the maid," quipped McCoy.

Kirk ignored him. "What is it, Spock? What's happening?"

"A transfer relay. I believe it is building power to a point at which it will send the transport signature to the next destination."

"Can you stop it?" Kirk cried.

"That would be unwise. I believe Mister Scott's signature is held in memory. Any interruption might purge the contents."

"Dammit, Jim! We have to do something!" shouted McCoy.

"Bones, don't you think I know that?" Kirk shouted back. "Spock, can we direct the signal to the *Enterprise*? Maybe we can send it to the transporter there."

Spock shook his head. "The technology is too dissimilar to try it. Perhaps, with time, I could figure out how to adapt this equipment to our own."

"Time is something we don't have," Kirk growled. Then his face lit up with hope. "Can we send him to a transporter chamber here?"

Spock wiped away more dirt from another display. "We may have a chance, if I could read the inscriptions, but randomly redirecting power without knowing the consequences could be fatal to Mister Scott."

Kirk waved his fist in the air, as if looking for a target to vent his frustration on. "I've never felt so helpless. If it was reversed and I was in there, Scotty would find a way to get me out."

"Mister Scott's expertise would be most valuable. However, he is in there, and we are out here," commented Spock.

McCoy spun on his heel. "I think he just said that, Spock."

"I realize I have failed to release Mister Scott, but I am doing the best I can under the current circumstances."

Kirk's face softened. He placed a hand on Spock's shoulder. "I know that, Spock. There's no one else I'd rather have here, now, to help me out."

"Sorry, Spock," McCoy offered. "It's just that Scotty is a good friend to me."

Spock nodded. "To all of us, Doctor."

Just then, the hum changed pitch. Indicators jumped to maximum. The chamber reverberated for a moment, and then stopped. The humming plummeted to a whisper.

"What just happened?" Kirk demanded.

Spock checked his tricorder. "I believe Mister Scott was just sent to the next relay site."

Kirk hung his head and slapped his hand against a panel, knocking some of the dust loose. "And we did nothing to stop it."

Spock inspected the panel next to Kirk. "Captain, I think you may have just uncovered a very important key. This appears to be a chart of the relay stations. We should be able to transpose it upon our star charts and find where Mister Scott is headed."

"Spock!" Kirk shouted. "I knew you could do it!"

Spock raised a cautious eyebrow. "I have done nothing yet, sir. If we can get to the next station before the transmission arrives, I might be able to figure out how to rescue Mister Scott."

"How can we do that?" McCoy demanded. "It's traveling as fast as we are."

"Not exactly, Doctor," Spock corrected. "By my calculations the transporter beam is traveling at warp factor five point eight—"

Kirk looked up from the display. "If we went maximum warp, we could get there before it does."

Spock nodded agreement. "Precisely."

Kirk opened his communicator. *"Enterprise,* three to beam up."

When they got to the bridge, Uhura was waiting for them. "Mister Spock, the information you requested has arrived by subspace communication."

"Thank you, Lieutenant." Spock went to his station and downloaded the chart from the relay station. Within moments it was on the viewscreen. "This is the chart from the station." Spock punched another button. A star chart was imposed over the relay map. "This shows its course."

"The last station is in an uncharted region of the quadrant," Kirk murmured.

"But the next one is not. We can arrive there in fourteen hours if we push the engines."

"And that won't give us any more time than the last station. Helm, lay in a course, maximum warp." Spock raised an eyebrow, but said nothing. He turned and analyzed the data from Vulcan.

It took them ten hours to reach the next relay station. As with the last one they had visited, it was on a secluded, barren planet, devoid of life. As soon as the trio beamed down, they realized something was very wrong. The equipment was damaged. Part of the chamber had collapsed, smashing into the network of panels. Kirk and McCoy stood dumbfounded. Spock started scanning the remains with his tricorder.

McCoy was the first to break the trance. "Spock, tell me we can do something about this. Tell me we can save Scotty."

Spock scanned the readout on his tricorder before answering. "There are several incoming molecular-transport receiver relays feeding into the final transporter transmitter—"

"Dammit, Spock!" growled McCoy. "Speak English!"

"I thought I was, Doctor," replied Spock. "This relay station is like an old Earth railroad station. There are multiple tracks leading here, and one track leaving. The track Mister Scott is on is damaged. Since there is no way to switch him to another track, we will have to replace the damaged track with undamaged track; otherwise Mister Scott's signature will derail, and he will be lost forever."

"Can we do it?" asked Kirk

Spock nodded. "There is a ninety-eight point three percent probability of success."

Kirk breathed a sigh of relief.

"However—"

"Spock!" moaned McCoy. "We don't want to hear any 'however's!"

"We will not be able to route Mister Scott's signal to the transporter pad."

The growing hope drained away like sand from an hourglass.

"Why not?" Kirk asked.

"The transporter emitters are destroyed." Spock said bluntly. "But I have learned enough from the data I received to decipher the rest of the controls to send him on to the final station. However—"

"Stop with the 'however's, Spock!" shouted McCoy.

"—I will need time to make repairs," continued Spock.

"How much time?" Kirk asked.

"Unknown. Being able to read their hieroglyphs will help, and I have the readings from Mister Scott's repairs to the spacecraft to aid me."

"How soon until Scotty gets here?" McCoy asked.

"Three hours, thirty-one minutes, forty-two seconds."

Kirk nodded with grim determination. "Let's get to it."

The three worked with clocklike precision, removing components from one panel and placing them in another. It was hard, dusty work in tight areas, but because they knew that a dear friend's life was at stake, there were no complaints.

Three hours, fourteen minutes later, the work was done. The room was filled with a soft hum.

"All circuits are functioning," Spock commented. "Mister Scott should arrive in seventeen minutes."

Kirk nodded and sat down next to McCoy. "Tell me what else you learned about the creators of this mess."

Spock gathered his thoughts for a moment. "It was recorded that there was a race called the Carthians. They were an imperial society that ruled by constant conquest. However, their boundaries grew too large for their troops to hold, so they started recruiting outside their region."

"You mean they started shanghaiing people to do their grunt-work," McCoy sneered.

"However you want to say it, they started adding to their ranks with alien races, people who didn't hold the Carthians' beliefs in conquest."

"This sounds familiar," Kirk said. "I think the Roman Empire tried to do the same thing."

"With the same results," agreed Spock. "The Carthians were overthrown in an uprising. Their empire fell into chaos. Nothing is known of their fate." The pitch of the hum suddenly changed. Spock turned to the displays.

"The sensors have picked up the incoming transport," Spock said. "Power is starting to build."

Kirk stood up. "Spock, correct me if I'm wrong, but wouldn't it stand to reason that the next station, the last station, is on the Carthians' homeworld?"

"That region is uncharted, but I can only assume you are correct."

Whatever Kirk was going to say next was forgotten as equipment that had been dormant for hundreds of years commenced its sequencing.

"The transport is coming in," shouted Spock over the din. "The signature is stacking in memory." The hum increased an octave. "The transmitter is resequencing the data." The whine reached a deafening pitch, and then died.

"What happened?" asked McCoy. "Is everything all right?"

Spock placed his tricorder at his side. "Everything is fine, Doctor. Mister Scott is on the last leg of his journey."

Kirk flipped open his communicator and nodded. "No matter what awaits him, let's make sure we're there for him. Three to beam up."

The final transporter station was titanic. Hundreds of transporter receiver relays were arranged in an amphitheater facing skyward. When functioning, it had been a monument to the technological advancement of an empire. When the rebellion came, it was a symbol of slavery to be destroyed. Now, four hundred years later, it was an empty, crumbling ruin.

Rivulets of sweat dripped down the despaired group's faces. Kirk gritted his teeth as he leaned against a wall in fatigue. "All of them. All of them are smashed. All of them are ruined, useless." Kirk looked to Spock for some sort of hope. "Spock, is there any way to repair just one of them?"

Spock was logically blunt. "Not in the time remaining."

Kirk hung his head in defeat. "Then we lost. Scotty lost. After everything we've done, we failed."

"Dammit, Jim!" McCoy blasted. "We can't give up now! Scotty's life depends on us."

"You don't think I know that," Kirk spat. "Tell me what to do, and I'll do it! But right now I don't see any options."

McCoy's eyes blazed, but he said nothing. In a moment he turned away in frustration.

"Captain, I have a hypothesis," Spock offered. "There may be a way."

Kirk spun around. "What is it?" he demanded.

"With the data I have gathered we might be able to integrate the spacecraft's modules to our own equipment."

"I thought you said it couldn't be done."

"Circumstances have changed. I believe I can gather the signal with the navigational deflector and redirect it through the Carthian vessel's circuits and into our systems."

Kirk straightened with hope. "Is there time?"

"Since we have no other options, time is irrelevant."

"You and your damn logic will be the death of us all, Spock," McCoy shouted. "If there's something we can do, then let's not waste what little time we have."

"I do not intend to waste time, Doctor," Spock calmly replied. "I am already making the necessary calculations."

McCoy's expression changed from anger to expectation. "Then, what are we waiting for? Let's get back to the *Enterprise* and start hooking the relay transporter thing to the integration module thing."

Spock raised his eyebrows in surprise. "Doctor, perhaps you should leave the process to me."

With the glimmer of hope Spock had given him, and the antics of McCoy, Kirk had to smile.

Kirk strode onto the bridge and sat in his chair as if it were a pincushion.

"Time remaining, Mister Sulu," he asked.

Sulu checked the chronometer. "Sixteen minutes, sir."

"Mister Chekov, plot a course to the coordinates directed by Mister Spock."

Chekov nodded. "Course already laid in, sir."

"Mister Sulu, take us in and hold her steady," Kirk ordered. "We need to be in exact alignment with the transporter stream."

Sulu nodded. "Aye, sir."

Kirk softly hammered the arm of his chair solemnly. "It's all up to Spock now."

*　　*　　*

The transporter engineer watched Spock's adjustments with a helpful eye. Adapting the circuitry of the Carthians' equipment to the Federation transporter modules was taxing, even for Spock's wealth of patience.

Each connection required redundant components, multiple terminations, and countless shunts and conductors. Any small error or defect could result in failure. Failure was not an option.

After hours of tedious work, Spock and the engineer stood before the transporter control panel. Preliminary checks proved satisfactory, but there would be no time for a full diagnostic. Time was up.

The transporter room doors opened as Doctor McCoy entered with his medical kit.

"If everything goes as it should, Doctor McCoy, your services will not be needed," Spock commented.

"If everything went as it should have, we wouldn't be here right now," he replied dryly.

Spock raised his eyebrow and nodded. "You are correct, Doctor."

McCoy gave a smug grin. "Of course."

Spock hit the communications switch. "Captain, the transporter beam should arrive in three-point-two minutes."

Kirk's impatience flooded back over the speakers. *"Think you could have cut it any closer, Spock?"*

The remaining minutes ticked away like hours. Then indicators started lighting up. Spock opened the com channel to the bridge to allow Kirk, and the rest of the bridge crew, to hear what was happening.

"The transporter beam is approaching," Spock droned. "Compensating for deflector angle—"

Whatever else Spock was saying was lost in the whine of electronic components screaming in overload. Sparks shot out from board after board as they failed under the strain. Then, as it had started, the whine diminished, only to be replaced with warning buzzers. Spock and the transporter engineer worked frantically.

"*Spock!*" Kirk's voice shouted over the din. "*What's happening?*"

Spock's hands flew over the console as he tried to coax a little more life from the unit. "The molecular sequencers are failing!" he shouted back. "Switching to backup!"

The image of Scotty faintly appeared on the transporter pad, and then faded.

McCoy watched in horror, and then turned to Spock. "Spock, he's dying! Do something!"

As if responding to McCoy's demands, Spock shoved the slide switches forward. Then, as if a miracle had happened, Scotty materialized on the pad.

Scotty straightened up and looked around him in bewilderment and then frustration. "Mister Spock, ye dinna have to pull me away from the hangar. I had everything under control."

McCoy tried to run his medical scanner over Scotty, but he shoved it away. "Doctor McCoy, I'm perfectly fine. Now, I have critical work to do, so send me back."

McCoy glanced at Spock in disbelief. Spock returned the gaze with an upturned eyebrow. McCoy threw up his hands. "Do it, Spock, but send him back the way he came!" McCoy turned on his heel and stormed out of the room, only to be replaced by Captain Kirk.

"Scotty!" Kirk grabbed Scotty's arms and shook him. "You had us scared to death!"

Scotty looked from Kirk to Spock and then to the transporter engineer, "Laddie, can ye tell me why they've all gone daft?"

Kirk started to laugh. In a moment the transporter engineer hid his face as he followed suit.

"What?" Scotty asked. "What's so funny?"

*   *   *

Captain's Log, supplemental. The Carthians' spacecraft has been turned over to Starfleet for further study. We have resumed our mission, seeking out new life, new civilizations, hopefully not in the manner we just encountered. Kirk out.

Assignment: One

Kevin Lauderdale

The swirling blue smoke opened like a miniature wormhole, and Gary Seven stepped out of it into his office.

"Report," Seven demanded, as the door to his teleportation chamber—a steel-reinforced safe—closed behind him and shelves of vintage 1960s barware slid in to conceal it. He had maintained many bases of operations over the years, but he always came back to this, his first one. He had not changed the office's furnishings since his arrival, more than three decades before, no matter how much Roberta had complained. He liked the orange shag rug, the abstract art, and the vaguely Asian design to the tables specifically because they were so different from the aesthetic sense of the world where he had been raised.

"Probability of events now set at ninety-two percent," replied the computer in a brisk tone as it swung out from its hiding place behind a bookshelf.

Seven nodded gravely. Earlier that morning, the Gamma-3 computer, along with Seven's own highly trained intelligence, had plotted the events with only an eighty-nine percent confidence rating. The FBI and FAA memos, the field reports of various governments (unread by anyone but him, he feared), and his own clandestine reconnaissance all added up to just one thing. Seven shook his head. *No, it only adds up to that if you yourself are the result of an alien breeding and training program and you have a G-3 at your disposal.* Realistically, he doubted that anyone else on Earth could have taken the shards of evidence and assembled anything coherent from them.

"Evidence," said Seven, and the G-3 began to spell out the details of several bank transactions and driver's license applications from months earlier that it had just identified as being related to the next day's attacks. In and of themselves, they would not have set off any alarms. But when added to what Seven and the computer already knew . . . .

Seven walked over to a window and looked out. The view from the twelfth floor on East Sixty-eighth was outstanding. The first time he had looked down on the street and its people, he had not appreciated it. He had actually found it appalling that people could exist in such crowded, primitive conditions. It was only after years of living here that he had grown fond of the world, its people, and especially this city.

Eight million people lived in the five boroughs of New York, one and a half million in Manhattan alone. *So many people, so many lives,* Seven thought. He knew that it was fashionable to refer to Earth as being a "small planet." People had been calling it "Spaceship Earth" since he had first arrived. By now Seven had seen most of the world, and to him it was huge. And its six billion people led very full, very individual lives. To him they were not masses or numbers. They woke up every morning, went about their days, and dreamed at night. They were what he fought for. He wouldn't stop tomorrow's events any more than he would have stopped the bombing of Pearl Harbor or Hiroshima. Things would get a lot worse before they got a lot better. But they would get better.

Roberta had certainly done her part for that. Over the years, the two of them had spoiled the plans of more than their share of would-be world conquerors and high-tech criminals.

But this was different.

Seven couldn't blame his partner for retiring the year before. He had been selectively bred for the demands of his tasks, yet even he was starting to feel the toll on his body. Along with whiter hair and more wrinkles had come slower reflexes and a tendency to tire more easily. After a strenuous twenty-four straight hours spent racing around the globe to make sure that the Y2K changeover happened without a hitch, fifty-two-year-old Roberta had announced she was "giving up the whole enchilada."

In a way, he was glad Roberta wasn't there to share in this particular assignment. She might have tried to talk him into stopping the planes themselves. Saving thousands of lives rather than just one. It had always been hard to explain to her why, when their job was to stop things from going wrong, they occasionally had to allow them to go wrong. Sometimes Seven wasn't sure himself.

It was one thing to sacrifice oneself—as Isis had done a few years earlier to protect him and Roberta from a madman threatening to release Ebola into Tokyo's water supply—but quite another to sacrifice others to a higher good. Seven turned away from the window. He missed them both.

Glancing at the G-3's monitor, Seven could see circles of probability, graphic representations of the computer's statistical analysis, radiating like the proverbial ripples in a lake after a stone has been tossed into it. Tomorrow's events were a turning point in the planet's history. They were . . . Seven hesitated to consider them "necessary," but they were decidedly "important."

Seven thought of the people who would die or whose lives would be changed the next day as characters in a story that they were unaware was even being told. He wanted to tell the people of his adopted city that he was still looking out for them, even though it might not seem like it. He really would do everything he could for them: he was their supervisor. Not that that thought alone would help them or their families.

Seven looked out the window again and down to the teeming population. Earth was his protectorate; his life was devoted to looking after it. The Eugenics Wars weren't even a decade in the past. There would be more wars to come. And diseases. And natural disasters. It would be a long time before Earth made contact with intelligent life from other worlds.

Seven's director at the Aegis had told him a few things about Earth's future when he had been permanently reassigned here, replacing Supervisors 201 and 347. He knew that, eventually, Earth and Vulcan would form an alliance. He also knew that there would be a devastating nuclear war, though he had been told that it would occur after his tour of duty. (Seven's job was just to make sure humanity survived long enough to be able to pull itself together after that happened. He did not relish the task of the supervisor who had to let that happen—or, rather, *ensure* it happened.) And he had been told to watch several people especially.

How the directors knew these things, Seven did not know. He himself was, after all, merely human. Perhaps the directors could see into the future. Or were from the future. Or perhaps they and their computers were just better at predicting.

Shaun Geoffrey Christopher was one of Seven's cases. He was a scientist and astronaut. Why Seven was supposed to protect him above, for example, the three Russian and seven American astronauts who had died since his arrival in 1968, he did not know. Though, as he followed Christopher's career, Seven suspected that the young man would soon be traveling farther than Earth's orbit.

Christopher was currently in Boston attending a conference on microgravity materials science. He was scheduled to return to Los Angeles the next day and continue on to Edwards Air Force Base, where he was stationed.

The G-3 had already located his hotel and room number. But Seven couldn't just kidnap Christopher tonight and hold him for a day. Seven's mandate was to do things as clandestinely as possible, leaving as little effect on individuals as possible. No, the best solution was to transport in and then just put Christopher to sleep for a while. All he had to do was make the astronaut miss his flight.

Seven lay down on one of the low, sloping couches he favored and began to plan his next day's actions. Christopher would have to be at the airport one hour before his 7:49 a.m. flight. Subtract another hour to travel to the airport, and that meant he would probably be leaving his room between 5:30 and 6:00. Seven estimated that he would have to visit Christopher's room at around 5:00. He would set his servo's immobilizer at maximum, and Christopher would be knocked out for a couple of hours. He would "oversleep" right through his plane's takeoff. Checkout wasn't until 11 a.m.; no one would miss him, nor come looking for him, until it was too late . . . and Christopher would be safe.

The G-3 beeped and said, *"Information update."*

"Report," said Seven.

"Probability of events now set at ninety-seven percent."

The blue fog of his transporter thinned, and Seven appeared on the fourteenth floor of the hotel. He looked both ways. There was no one else in the hallway. Why would there be, at this time of the morning? Though his transporter always placed him in as large an empty space as was practical, Seven never knew exactly where the device would deliver him. It was like the thing had a mind of its own. He was pleased to find himself only a few steps from room 1405.

Seven removed his silver, pen-shaped servo and activated it, releasing two tiny antennae from its sides. Carefully bringing the device down to the door's lock, he twisted the servo's lower half. The door popped open, and Seven quickly slid in, closing it behind him.

Seven had been bred for, among other things, excellent eyesight; his eyes instantly adapted to the darkened room.

The bed was a mess and there were towels on the bathroom floor. The closet doors were wide open, but there were no clothes hanging inside. There were no suitcases or garment bags anywhere.

Christopher had already left.

*   *   *

Shaun looked at his watch. The lady at his hotel's front desk had been right. With the "Big Dig"—the mammoth turnpike extension that Boston was working on—the traffic was worse than ever. He was glad he had taken her advice and left a full three and a half hours before his flight. As it was, he had just arrived "on time": one hour before his flight.

He put his laptop computer on the X-ray machine's conveyor belt and slowly stepped through the metal detector. This time the metals on his uniform didn't set off a round of alarms—which they sometimes did, depending on the airport.

He picked up his computer and headed for a stand selling giant pretzels.

"Lieutenant Colonel Christopher, isn't it?"

Shaun turned. The speaker was an older man. About his father's age, Shaun guessed, and with the same broad shoulders and tall, straight stance. He wore a simple, dark suit. Shaun didn't think he knew him. Was he someone from the conference? He met so many people at those things.

"Look," said Shaun, "I'm sorry, but I've got—"

The man pulled a photo ID out of his jacket pocket: Colonel Gary Seven, NASA. "It's about your next mission."

"Mission?" Shaun knew he was on the fast track for the Mars mission. Maybe even the Saturn project—unless Roykirk and his buddies convinced Congress that robot missions were the way to go for the in-system planets as well.

"Come with me. It's not far, and it won't take long."

Shaun looked at his watch. *What the heck*? He was always happy to make time for NASA, and he was better off without the pretzel's calories anyway. Seven led him around the corner, and they were soon facing a door with the stylized image of a mother and baby embossed on it.

"The child-care station?" asked Shaun.

"It will have to do. I don't think we want to have this conversation surrounded by software marketers in the Ambassadors Club."

Shaun nodded. There was a number pad next to the doorknob. He looked at Seven expectantly.

"Hmm," said Seven, pointing over Shaun's shoulder and through the plate-glass window behind him to the tarmac. "Is that an SR-71?"

Shaun spun around. "A Blackbird! Where?" He hadn't seen an SR-71 in a long time. Hadn't they retired them all a few years back? Their black, sleek frames were the coolest-looking planes ever.

"Just to the right there."

Shaun craned his neck. "I don't see—"

There was a click and the sound of a door opening. Shaun turned to see Seven holding the door open for him.

"Must be here for an air show or something," Seven said, gesturing for Shaun to enter.

The room was cramped. There was a sink, a fold-down diaper-changing table set into the wall, two chairs and a table for adults to sit at, and a knee-high plastic castle. Shaun and his wife, Debbie, had one of those castles at home for their three-year-old daughter.

Shaun slid into a chair, and Seven closed the door. "Can I see your ID again?" asked Shaun. He wondered why the colonel wasn't in uniform.

"Certainly," said Seven, reaching into his pocket and handing Shaun the plastic card.

The image was certainly Seven's, and the NASA hologram logo looked authentic. Shaun turned the card over. The magnetic stripe on the back even showed signs of wear. Fakes were usually pristine.

"Fine," said Shaun, returning the ID.

Seven pulled out a silver pen and said, "I'll just need to take a few notes." He flipped the pen with his fingers, and Shaun felt very happy and relaxed. Yes, he could use some sleep. . . .

Shaun slowly became aware of the pain in his right side. It was a dull pain, but it grew, and that was what finally woke him. Discomfort aside, he felt remarkably well-rested and refreshed. He opened his eyes and stretched.

He was alone in the child-care station. The pain in his side turned out to be one of the plastic castle's towers. Shaun had slid off his chair and was now propped up against the thing. He was alone.

Shaun remembered . . . what? Colonel Gary Seven of NASA, something about a mission, and coming into this little room.

Shaun climbed back up onto his chair. No, there was something else. Seven had taken out his pen to take notes. . . .

Shaun shook his head. That was all; he didn't remember anything after that. Where had Seven gone? Shaun hoped he hadn't left to find medical help. He sure didn't need an unexplainable blackout on his record. That was the sort of thing that could ground him for the rest of his career.

Sean's laptop was still on the table. At least Seven wasn't a thief.

"Well," muttered Shaun, "there's no point just sitting here." He grabbed his computer, opened the door, and stepped outside. The waiting area was a lot brighter than he remembered it being when he had arrived. As he walked, he noticed that sunlight was now pouring in through the huge observation windows. Shaun checked his watch. It was almost 9:30. He'd been asleep for two hours. He'd missed his flight!

Shaun sighed, thinking that he'd better go over to the gate and see if he could get on the next plane out. Then he'd call Colonel Barquero back at Edwards. . . .

Shaun noticed a large crowd standing facing a TV monitor tuned to CNN. It was showing the World Trade Center in New York City. Smoke was coming out of one of the towers. Shaun heard something about a plane crash. *Whoa. Some accident.* He recalled that in the 1940s a plane had once crashed into the Empire State Building. A dozen or so people had died.

His cell phone rang. He pulled it out of his jacket and flipped it open. The screen read HOME. It would be 6:30 back home in Mojave. Debbie and the kids were up early, as usual.

"Hi," said Shaun.

34

"Oh my God! Shaun! Where are you?! *What's going on?!*" Shaun could hear panic in Debbie's voice and was shocked. Debbie never panicked. \

"Huh? No, I'm still at Logan. I was . . ." On the monitor, Shaun noticed that the lower part of the screen had an overlay reading RE-BROADCAST. Then he saw another plane crash into the second tower.

Unbidden, his mind flew into action. One crash was an accident, but two—especially in clear weather (the television screen displayed that New York's sky was a particularly bright blue)—was some sort of an attack. Hijackers! It was like something right out of a Tom Clancy novel. Had he been presented the scenario as a training exercise back at the Academy in Colorado, he would have laughed because it seemed so improbable.

As if far in the distance, he heard Debbie yelling. "Shaun! Shaun!"

He shook his head to bring himself back to his wife. "Yeah, Deb. I'm here."

"We just turned on the TV. . . . So, you're *not* on a plane?!" She sounded like she was going to cry.

"Right. I'm not even at my gate."

"Oh, thank God!" Now she was laughing and crying.

He probably wasn't going to be getting on a plane anytime soon, either. If *he* was in charge of the FAA, he'd probably ground all nonmilitary aircraft and scramble some F-117As with instructions to shoot down anything not squawking the proper ID codes.

"Yeah," said Shaun. CNN was showing the second crash again. "Yeah, I, uh, missed my flight. I . . ." He looked around. Crowds in other parts of the airport stood still, all eyes trained on TV screens. Families held each other. A few people were crying. Many were on cell phones. Shaun turned slowly, scanning the crowds.

Where the heck was Colonel Seven? Not a single dark suit to be seen. What had that been about? Did he really have a mission for Shaun?

Debbie gave a deep sigh. "I'm glad."

Shaun nodded. "Don't worry, Deb," he said. "I'm still here." He took a deep breath. "I'm still here."

Demon

Kevin Andrew Hosey

Opening his eyes, James T. Kirk glanced around the bridge of the *U.S.S. Enterprise*—and wondered what the hell he was doing there.

"Captain . . ."

Swiveling in his command chair, Kirk faced his first officer. "Mister . . . Spock?"

"Based on the original position of the Klingon vessel and its estimated speed, we will be within range in five-point-seven minutes."

And then he remembered. A Tellarite merchant ship reported seeing a Klingon vessel deep within Federation territory, and *Enterprise* was en route to investigate. Based on the description, it sounded like a D-7 dreadnought-class battle cruiser.

The Tellarites also reported that the vessel was traveling at impulse speed only, not warp. Kirk had found that odd. Not only that; they weren't using a cloaking device either.

Even stranger, Spock had been scanning for the vessel for the past hour with no sign of it. The logical answer was that it had altered course. If so, it could be anywhere. As a precaution, Lieutenant Uhura was monitoring communications in surrounding sectors in case the cruiser was spotted by another vessel.

"Thank you, Spock." Feeling tired, Kirk rubbed his eyes. His temporary loss of memory a moment ago worried him. They were about to confront a potentially dangerous adversary, and he knew he must stay alert.

His current physical condition didn't help either. He had a constant throbbing in his temple. A hangover. One hell of a hangover, actually.

And it was all Mark Offutt's fault.

Kirk had run into Mark—an old friend from the Academy, now first officer of the *Kennedy*—the night before at a small cantina on the promenade of Starbase 9. *Enterprise* had docked at the base three days earlier for much-needed repairs and supplies.

It didn't take long for the two of them to catch up on old times. The next thing he knew, Kirk was drunk. Not something he liked to be, since a captain has to set a good example. But the alcohol seemed to hit him out of nowhere, like a phaser on stun. *What the hell were we drinking, anyway?* wondered Kirk. *Something . . . green.* The last thing he remembered was Mark checking him into a starbase hotel to sleep it off.

This morning Kirk woke with the worst hangover he'd ever had. So he returned to *Enterprise* and went directly to sickbay. There Doctor McCoy injected him with something he called Scotty's "private stock," a remedy the chief engineer, Montgomery Scott, made use of after virtually every shore leave.

Then he received word from Starfleet Command regarding the Klingon vessel. All major repairs had been completed, so *Enterprise* left in record time.

"ETA is two-point-three minutes, Captain." Spock's voice snapped Kirk back to the present.

"Take us out of warp, Mister Sulu," ordered Kirk. "Go to half impulse." Then he nodded at Uhura. "Yellow alert."

As *Enterprise* dropped out of warp, the streaking stars snapped back into place like rubber bands—and the viewscreen suddenly filled with the sight of a Klingon battle cruiser dead ahead.

"Sulu!" Kirk yelled.

Sulu's fingers flashed across his console and the *Enterprise* veered starboard just in time to avoid slamming head-on into the cruiser.

"Red alert!" Kirk ordered. "Shields up! Sulu, bring us about and put us right in front of them."

"Aye, Captain."

"Mister Chekov." Kirk turned to his young, brown-haired navigator. "Have they armed weapons?"

"I . . . can't tell, sir," Chekov replied as he made adjustments on his console. "I'm . . . not picking them up on sensors."

"He is correct, Captain," Spock confirmed. "Sensors are not reading the Klingon vessel. We can see it, but the sensors cannot."

"Captain," Sulu interrupted. "We're directly in the path of the vessel. It's moving at full impulse and shows no sign of slowing."

"Reverse engines. Match speed and maintain distance." Kirk turned back to his first officer. "Spock, why aren't we able to scan that ship? Sensor malfunction?"

"Negative, Captain." Spock turned to face the cruiser on the screen. "It appears that something on the Klingon vessel may be preventing us from scanning it."

Kirk rolled that around in his head. "As far as we know, the Klingons don't have anything that'll prevent scanning while the ship is uncloaked, correct?"

"As far as we *know.* That doesn't mean they do not have such technology."

That's all we need, thought Kirk. *Technology like that could shift the balance of power between the Federation and the Klingon Empire dramatically.*

"Uhura, open a channel. Let's find out what's going on here."

"Channel open, sir."

"Klingon vessel." Kirk spoke toward the screen. "This is

Captain James T. Kirk of the *U.S.S. Enterprise.* You have entered Federation territory. Please state your intentions immediately."

The bridge fell silent as every ear tuned to the hidden com speakers. But there was no reply.

"Klingon vessel, I repeat, state your—"

"Captain," Chekov cried out, "I read three Klingon vessels dropping out of warp dead ahead!"

Onscreen, three bursts of light flashed behind the Klingon ship, heralding the arrival of three more dreadnought cruisers. Before anyone could react, the ships overtook the first cruiser, then soared past the *Enterprise,* so close that Kirk could read the Klingon characters imprinted on each ship.

"Klingon cruisers are coming about, Captain," warned Spock.

Chekov slammed his fist against his console. "It's an ambush!"

"We don't know what it is, Ensign," Kirk stated. Then he faced Uhura. "Open a hailing channel to those ships. I want . . ."

"Captain," Spock interrupted. "Although sensors still cannot detect the first Klingon vessel, they *are* displaying the other three. And they are powering weapons."

Spinning back toward the screen, Kirk watched the trio of cruisers approach them in a triangular formation. As he watched, each cruiser launched two glowing projectiles.

"They have fired six photon torpedoes," Spock stated calmly, eyes never leaving his viewer. "Time to impact: twenty-point-three seconds."

Kirk cursed silently to himself. "It *is* an ambush! Sulu! Evasive action! Now!"

"Hold on!" Sulu warned. "This isn't going to be pretty!"

Kirk felt his stomach slide into his throat as the *Enterprise* rotated on its axis and the bridge literally dropped beneath them. The inertial dampers practically screamed in protest as the *Enterprise* angled downward, then dropped away like a submarine performing an emergency crash dive. The torpedoes passed between and on each side of the two warp nacelles, barely missing them. Everyone watched the screen as the photon torpedoes continued on and struck the first vessel.

Chekov whooped in excitement. "Nice move, Sulu!"

"Prepare to go to warp on my order, Sulu," Kirk ordered. "We—"

"Captain," Chekov cut in, eyes wide, "look at the Klingon vessel!"

Kirk watched in stunned silence as the cruiser, struck by the energy of three photon torpedoes, slowly emerged from the fading explosions—totally unscathed.

"Spock," Kirk asked, "why the hell wasn't that ship destroyed?"

The Vulcan wore his usual mask of nonemotion, but Kirk could tell he was taken aback. "Unknown, Captain. Besides being undetectable to our sensors, it appears to possess superior shielding."

"Sulu." Kirk turned back to his helmsman. "Get us out of here, maximum warp, before all four ships regroup and come at us again."

"Fascinating," Spock stated calmly as he stared into his viewer. "Captain, the second group of Klingon cruisers is ignoring us," —he looked at Kirk—"and they are continuing to fire on the first vessel."

"Belay that last order, Sulu." Kirk turned and watched the battle raging between the four cruisers. *What the hell are they doing?* he wondered. "Sulu, put some distance between us and the Klingons. I want to see what they're up to out there."

"Aye, sir," answered the helmsman as the ship moved off.

Resting his chin on his right knuckles, Kirk studied the main viewer. "Looks like we weren't the target in the first place. Apparently they were aiming at the other battle cruiser and we were just in the way."

Spock stepped down onto the command level and stood next to the captain's chair. "It would appear so."

"But . . . why fire on their own ship?" Kirk mused. "Could the original vessel be a deserter? What would make a Klingon vessel risk entering Federation space?"

"Or, more pertinent," added Spock, "what would compel three

more Klingon vessels to enter Federation territory to intercept the first one?"

Kirk turned to Uhura. "Lieutenant, contact Starfleet and inform them of our situation. Request reinforcements, and tell them we're staying put to determine what we're facing." He then turned back to the main screen. "All right, Spock, as you are so fond of saying, without hard facts our sitting here and guessing is just a waste of time. Right?"

Spock cocked his left eyebrow. "Not exactly how I would phrase it, Captain, but essentially that is correct."

"Well, let's see what we can do about acquiring some hard facts. Uhura, hail the other Klingon vessels. Let's see if one of *them* is willing to talk."

"Channel open, Captain."

Taking a breath, Kirk began. "Attention, Klingon vessels, this is Captain James T. Kir—"

"Federation vessel!" A deep, growling voice suddenly erupted from the com. *"This is no concern of yours! Do not interfere!"*

Both Kirk and Spock raised their eyebrows that time. The captain began to reply; then the channel went dead.

"Well . . . that was rude," commented Uhura.

"And very interesting," added Kirk. "They're totally focused on that other cruiser and ignoring us. What the hell is *on* that ship?"

"Fascinating." Spock pointed toward the screen. "Captain, the three cruisers are all suffering substantial damage, yet the original vessel is still unharmed."

Kirk watched the group of Klingon cruisers circle the first vessel, continuously firing disruptors and torpedoes. Spock was right. The first vessel continued to move forward without so much as a scratch. He must have been correct about the advanced level of their shielding.

Then Kirk noticed something else odd. "Spock, most of their shots are missing entirely."

"I noticed that, too, Captain. It appears the vessel may be invisible to *their* sensors as well."

41

"Their targeting computers can't lock on," Kirk said as he realized it, "which means they're aiming weapons manually. The way those ships are circling wildly, it's amazing they're hitting anything at all."

He was about to comment on the fact that the first cruiser had yet to retaliate when it suddenly opened fire on the other ships. Yet, rather than standard Klingon-issue weaponry, it launched what looked like glowing cerulean spheres of energy—and they were having no problem at all finding their targets.

"What . . . is . . . *that?*" asked Sulu.

A sphere struck one of the attacking cruisers head-on. Its shields held, but judging by the violent way the ship vibrated, Kirk imagined it must have suffered considerable internal damage.

"Unknown," Spock answered after returning to his station. "Sensors cannot detect the weaponry either."

Chekov turned to them. "Could this be some kind of test run for a Klingon prototype vessel?"

"Not likely," replied Spock. "I do not think even the Klingons would destroy three of their own cruisers for the sake of a test."

Kirk nodded. "They also wouldn't be testing in Federation space. It could still be a prototype, though. Stolen by someone else, perhaps? A defector . . . or an ally of the Federation attempting to deliver the ship to us."

Spock arched his eyebrow as he considered the suggestion. "Perhaps. It is logical the Klingons would prefer to destroy the ship rather than let Starfleet take possession of it."

Chekov suddenly adjusted his sensors. "Captain, one of the attacking vessels has lost its shields!"

All eyes turned to the screen as a Klingon cruiser veered away from the battle, arches of energy cascading from its nacelles.

"They have just lost their warp-containment field," warned Spock. "A warp-core explosion is imminent."

"Back us off, Sulu!" ordered Kirk. "Full impul—"

A blinding flash of white light filled the main viewer. Kirk covered his eyes until the screen dimmed automatically to compensate for the sudden brightness.

"The cruiser has exploded," announced Spock, "and it has destroyed the other two Klingon vessels as well."

"Shock wave approaching, Captain!" Chekov warned as he grabbed the edges of his console.

Kirk slammed his fist against his armrest console, activating intraship communications. "All hands! Brace for impact—"

Then it hit.

Like a monstrous hand slamming against the hull, the shockwave literally pushed the *Enterprise* sideways. Everyone, including Spock, was thrown to the deck. Sparks erupted from various points around the bridge as the ship's systems overloaded. Immediately the automatic fire-containment system kicked in and extinguished any flames. The bridge lights suddenly dimmed, then brightened again as emergency systems took over.

Finally, everyone managed to climb back into their seats. A moment later, Spock reported that the shockwave was dissipating.

"Damage report," called Kirk.

Before anyone could reply, Chekov cried out, "Captain, the Klingon vessel has fired on *us!*"

Kirk watched as another powerful sphere of energy sped toward them. In the milliseconds it took Kirk to formulate an order, it had already filled half the screen.

Surrounded by the red handrail, Kirk sometimes felt like the center of the universe. At that moment, he felt like the center of a target. "Evasive, Mister Sulu!"

But the sphere hit faster than Sulu could react—and it was worse than the shockwave. Once again, everyone on the bridge fell to the deck.

"All right," said Kirk, climbing into his chair, "that answers the question of whether or not they're allies. Sulu, fire phasers. Best guess on targeting."

Twin shafts of phased energy cut across space toward the Klingon vessel—and missed. Immediately, Sulu fired again. That time he struck the ship, but the beams merely deflected off the hull.

"Arm photon torpedoes," ordered Kirk. "Fire!"

The moment the torpedoes left the ship, Chekov called out, "Vessel is firing again!"

Kirk watched as another deadly sphere shot from of the cruiser. It enveloped and destroyed the photon torpedoes, then struck the *Enterprise* head-on. Chaos erupted as sparks flew from several consoles.

"Shields at nineteen percent, Captain," reported Spock. "One more hit and we will lose them."

As if on cue, the Klingon vessel fired again. The cruiser had managed to move closer to the *Enterprise,* so the weapon struck before the crew could prepare itself.

This time Kirk was thrown over his left armrest, and he let out a grunt as his head struck the deck. Ignoring the pain, he pulled himself to his feet.

Spock, somehow still in his seat, turned to Kirk. "Shields are down, Captain."

Suddenly, the science station went wild as the computer beeped and lights flashed at an incredible rate.

"What's happening?" asked Kirk, moving to his first officer's side.

Spock quickly entered several commands. "Someone has accessed the main computer."

"Who? And how?"

"Unknown. They are attempting to take control of it. If they do—"

"—they'll have total command of the ship!" finished Kirk. "Shut them out!"

"I am attempting to do so," replied Spock, "But, I am not—"

"Captain!"

Kirk turned at the urgent sound of Sulu's voice.

"Impulse engines have just shut down. We're drifting."

Jumping down to his chair, Kirk punched the com button. "Kirk to engineering . . ."

This time Chekov interrupted. "Captain, the Klingon cruiser is still moving forward, and we are directly in its path! If we do not move—"

"Scotty!" Kirk yelled as he watched the vulture-like vessel on screen looming closer. "What happened to the impulse engines? We need power up here—NOW!"

"Captain," Scott's burly voice boomed from the com, *"everything's gone to hell down here! Nothing's responding to our commands! It's as if the ship is acting on her own!"*

"Can you get shields back up?"

"I can't do anything *until computers are back online."*

"Keep working on it, Scotty. Kirk out." With a single step Kirk moved next to Chekov. "Can we fire torpedoes?"

The young Russian lifted his hands in frustration. "No, sir. I can't arm phasers or torpedoes."

Kirk straightened and watched the cruiser as it drew even closer. Another few seconds and they would be nothing but tiny pieces of debris floating in space. "Well, if anyone has any suggestions, now would be the time to—"

The bridge suddenly shuddered as a sphere of cerulean energy shot forth. Not from the Klingon ship—but from the *Enterprise* herself.

"Did that just come from *us?"* Kirk exclaimed.

Seconds later it struck the Klingon vessel—and the battle cruiser exploded. The explosion blossomed outward toward *Enterprise.*

"Brace for impact!" Kirk warned. But rather than with another bone-jarring collision, the shockwave hit with barely a tremble. Confused, the captain looked at Spock.

What he saw was the science console explode—or rather, a swirling tendril of cerulean energy as thick as a man's arm suddenly erupt out of the panel and envelop Spock.

Immediately, Kirk ran toward his first officer but was forced to stop a few feet away, held back by the heat emanating from the energy. He stared in horror at Spock, who was surrounded by a cocoon of electrical energy. It was the same type of energy launched by the Klingon ship.

"Spock!" Kirk yelled.

Spock couldn't answer. His entire body spasmed violently, his face a mask of sheer pain. Barely a minute passed, when the Vulcan was thrown over the handrail and across the bridge. With a sickening thud, he hit the deck to the right of navigation.

Chekov and Sulu, already on their feet, quickly bent down to help. A moment later Kirk was there, as well. Behind him he heard Uhura say, "Bridge to sickbay! Medical emergency!"

The captain knelt by Spock's body. He was shocked to see his eyes were open. Spock was *alive.* Barely, but still alive. His face and clothes were burned. Kirk could tell he was still in severe pain, but true to the Vulcan way, he refused to show it.

"Captain . . ." Spock gasped, his voice hollow.

"Save your strength. Help is on the way."

"No . . . time . . ." the Vulcan insisted, his left hand grabbing Kirk's right arm. "Listen . . . to me. The energy . . . that struck the ship . . . is a . . . *living . . . being.*"

"Living? How do you know, Spock?"

"I . . . felt it . . . in my . . . mind. It is . . . sentient . . . but hostile. . . . It craves only . . . death and . . . destruction." Spock erupted into a fit of hacking coughs. Drops of green blood spewed from his mouth and speckled the front of Kirk's gold tunic. "The . . . entity . . . has taken control . . . of . . . ship. . . ."

"Why?"

"It needs . . . warp engines. . . . Klingon cruiser was . . . damaged. . . . No warp. . . . Entity . . . needs . . . starship . . . with warp to travel . . . vast distances."

Kirk understood what was happening. "So it left the Klingon vessel and entered the *Enterprise.*"

Spock seemed to nod in confirmation, but Kirk wasn't sure if it was a nod or a shudder. "Now . . . it has . . . warp . . . and . . . access to our . . . database . . . and . . . the location . . . of . . ."

Eyes widening, Kirk whispered in alarm, "Earth . . . and other planets in the Federation. With its power it could tear a path through the galaxy. Is there anything we can do to stop it?"

Spock shook his head. "It is . . . too powerful. . . ." More coughing. Then his eyes widened slightly and looked off. Staring, yet not seeing.

"Spock, what is this thing?" Kirk asked. "What has control of my ship?"

Leaning closer, the captain heard his friend utter one final word: "Veqlargh . . ."

Then with a subtle gasp, Spock slumped in his arms. Kirk stared at him in shock. "Spock?"

Seconds later the turbolift doors whisked open and McCoy rushed out, followed by a medical team.

"My . . . *God,*" McCoy whispered when he saw Spock's torn, beaten body. Kneeling, he waved his medical tricorder over him, but it was too late. He was dead.

Sighing deeply, he lowered his head in a moment of respect and loss. Then he gently placed his hand on Kirk's shoulder. "Jim . . . what happened?"

Kirk lowered Spock's body onto the deck. "We've been invaded by something from that Klingon vessel. It attacked Spock . . . and killed him." He slowly rose and stared down at his friend. "Take good care of him, Bones."

"You know I will, Jim."

The captain took a deep breath and stepped away as the medical team carried Spock toward the turbolift. Once the doors slid shut, he squared his shoulders and cleared his throat. "I know Mister Spock meant a great deal to everyone here, just as he did to me. But we still have a job to do. Everyone . . . back to your stations."

Sulu and Chekov, eyes hollow, sat at their consoles. Uhura seemed to have a harder time holding back her grief, but soon regained her composure.

Kirk walked over to the communications station. "Uhura, Spock said something . . . a word I've never heard before. 'Veqlargh.' Is that Vulcan?"

"I've heard it before, sir. It isn't Vulcan. It's Klingon. Roughly translated it means . . . *demon.*"

"Demon?" Kirk repeated, then shook his head. "Sorry, that

damn thing is no demon. It's probably just a term it heard from the Klingons when it took over their ship."

"Captain!" cried Sulu. "We've changed course—and we've just increased our warp speed!"

Rushing to his chair, Kirk saw the stars streaking past onscreen. "Heading?"

Chekov looked toward Kirk, eyes wide. "Earth."

Nodding gravely, the captain reached to press his com button, then stopped when it whistled. He punched it. "Kirk here."

"Captain." It was Scotty's angered voice. *"Some kind of . . .* force *appeared in engineering a moment ago and blocked us from our consoles. A few seconds later we jumped to warp."*

"I know, Scotty. We've been boarded by a hostile alien entity. We're no longer in control of the *Enterprise*. It's set course for Earth, but we can't let it get there. Is there any way you can shut down the warp engines?"

"Shut them down?" Scotty cried out, his brogue more pronounced than usual. *"Sir, we can't even get near them! Two of my men were killed trying to access the computers!"*

Kirk gritted his teeth. More deaths. "All right, you and your men get out of there. I'll get back to you." He clicked the com button. "Chekov, how long until we reach Earth?"

"Twenty-point-five hours, sir."

"Uhura, can we still send subspace messages?"

"No, sir. All outgoing communications are down."

Damn, Kirk thought. *No helm, no weapons, and now no communications. That means we'll hit Earth without any warning. And no telling what kind of damage the alien can do once it gets there. It's powerful, invisible to sensors, and indestructible.*

"Sir, last reports stated that the *Kennedy* and the *Potemkin* are docked at Earth," said Uhura. "When Jupiter Station sensors pick us up, they'll send a standard greeting. If we don't answer, they'll know something is wrong and intercept us long before we reach Earth. Can't they stop us?"

"You saw what the entity did to the Klingon cruisers, Lieutenant. I don't imagine it would have much trouble fending off Starfleet vessels as well. Or worse. What if it possesses them like it did *Enterprise?* It would have three starships under its control."

"Captain," said Sulu, "we don't know if it can possess more than one ship at a time."

"And we don't know that it *can't,*" Kirk replied. "We don't know *anything* about it . . . except for what Mister Spock told us." He paused, fighting the urge to glance at the destroyed science station. "So, it's up to us to stop it *before* it reaches Earth."

"But how, sir?" asked Chekov.

Kirk hesitated. He knew exactly what they had to do. It was the only thing they could do. He just hated saying it. "We have to destroy the *Enterprise.*"

The others stared at him silently, then nodded in agreement.

"But, sir, how can we order self-destruct without the computer?"

"Simple, Mister Chekov . . . we don't use the computer." Before anyone could reply, Kirk pressed his com button. "Kirk to Scott."

"Aye, Captain?"

"Where are you now?"

"In the corridor outside engineering."

"All right." Kirk nodded. "I've got an idea on how to stop this thing, but I'll need your help."

"Anything, Captain. I'm itching to get that thing off the ship so we can get her home for repairs."

Kirk took a breath and frowned. "No, Scotty . . . if my plan works, the *Enterprise* won't be going anywhere . . . *ever* again."

There was a deep pause on the other end, and Kirk could almost hear the sound of Scotty's heart shattering at the thought of losing the ship. *"Aye, sir . . . I understand."*

"Good. Here's what I need. . . ."

The bridge crew listened as Kirk explained what he had in mind. When he finished, Scotty acknowledged the orders. *"I'll get right on it, Captain. Scott out."*

"Captain," cried Uhura, "life-support is being shut down on all decks!"

That thing is trying to kill my crew, Kirk thought. "Uhura, order everyone to abandon ship!"

Sulu looked at the captain. "Sir, launching escape pods while the ship is in warp is extremely dangerous."

"We have no choice. Order the evacuation, Uhura." Kirk contacted Scott again. "We're abandoning ship, Scotty. Once you've completed my orders, get your people to escape pods. Understood?"

"Captain, I can't just leave—"

"That's an order, Scotty. No arguments." Then Kirk cut communications before Scott could say another word.

"Captain," said Sulu, "you'll need help and we volunteer to stay behind."

Kirk smiled. "Gentlemen, I appreciate your devotion, but I want you all out of here as soon as possible." He turned to look at Uhura. "You've done everything you can. Now follow me."

Kirk led them to an emergency access hatch. He felt it was a safer way to travel in case the turbolifts suddenly malfunctioned. After popping open the hatch, they crawled down a narrow ladder.

On deck four, Kirk bid the others a final good luck and stepped into the corridor. As he jogged off, he noticed his breathing was harder. The physical exertion coupled with the thinning oxygen made it difficult to breathe. The air was much colder, too. Rubbing his hands together for warmth, he hurried on—and almost slammed right into a crewman wearing an environmental suit.

"Captain?"

Kirk peered into the large translucent faceplate and saw Mister Scott staring back. "Scotty—" he began, then stopped to catch his breath.

Grabbing Kirk's arm to support him, Scott held up another environmental suit. "Here, sir, you'll be needing this."

Nodding, Kirk donned the bulky garb and activated it. Fresh oxygen filled his mask and he took a deep, welcome breath.

"They're ready for you, sir," proclaimed Scott.

"And how do I activate them?"

"With this." Scott handed him a tricorder. "Just enter this code—" He indicated the sequence. "—and you have ten minutes to get off the ship."

"I don't want ten minutes. I want a reaction to occur the moment I enter the code."

"But, sir," Scotty looked horror stricken, "how can you get off the ship if—?"

"I won't be leaving the ship, Scotty. We only have one chance at this. If it doesn't work the first time, I need to be here to reprogram the tricorder for a second try."

The chief engineer stared at his captain for a moment; then he nodded. "Aye. In that case, you'll be needing someone who *knows* how to reprogram it, sir . . . and that would be me."

Kirk was about to argue, then stopped and sighed. "Thank you, Scotty. Now let's go check out your handiwork."

The two officers moved as quickly as the suits would allow. Soon they reached a large doorway at the end of the corridor. It slid open and Kirk examined the bay inside. Secured racks lined the walls as far as he could see. And each was filled with large, black cylindrical objects.

Photon torpedoes.

Just one was powerful enough to destroy an unprotected starship—and Kirk planned to detonate all of them.

Steeling themselves for what was about to come, they stepped into the bay and the doors slid shut behind them.

"I've reprogrammed the tricorder," said Scott, handing it to Kirk. "Once you enter the sequence, the torpedoes will detonate immediately."

"Good." Kirk nodded. "Everyone should be safely away by now . . . so let's do it!"

His fingers hovered over the tricorder a moment; then he turned to the man beside him. "Scotty . . ."

A silent message passed between them. "Aye, Captain, I know. It's been an honor for me, as well. Now . . . let's send this beastie back to hell—"

51

And then the doors exploded inward. They hit Scotty full force, slamming him against the bulkhead. Kirk wasn't hit, but the explosion knocked him back several feet, and knocked the tricorder from his hand. If not for the strap wrapped around his wrist, it would have scattered across the deck.

Shaking his head to clear the ringing in his ears, Kirk turned toward Scott. But he could tell by the way the engineer's body was bent that the man was dead.

With a flash of anger, Kirk turned to see a sphere of cerulean energy filling the damaged doorway. The alien.

A glowing tendril, like the tentacle of some hellish sea creature, snaked toward him. Quickly, he tugged hard at the tricorder strap and pulled the unit to him. Then he held it up, entered all but the last number in the code—

The alien reached him.

Kirk screamed as every nerve in his body seemed to rupture. The entity held him against the deck as a tremendous energy bombarded him relentlessly.

Suddenly, he heard a voice—or something like a voice—inside his head. It told him that he had failed. The ship belonged to it—and his entire crew was dead. Over two hundred people were now dead, because the alien had destroyed the escape pods right after they launched.

McCoy. Uhura. Sulu. Chekov.

Everyone . . . dead!

"NO!!" Kirk screamed.

The voice told him that he, too, would die, and it would continue on to his homeworld. Images of more death and destruction flooded Kirk's mind. Billions of people suffering and dying.

As if the being could read his thoughts, the alien told him that there was nothing he could do to stop it.

Then, even through the excruciating pain, Kirk remembered the tricorder. He was *not* going to fail. His crew was gone, but he would do everything in his power to prevent the loss of Earth.

Somehow he willed his trembling thumb to move to the tricorder. With one final defiant cry, Kirk completed the destruct code—

—and his entire world vanished in a flash of light.

Opening his eyes, James T. Kirk looked around—and wondered where the hell he was.

All he could make out were blurred images and a very bright light. He raised an arm to shield his eyes, and one of the blurred images moved toward him. It was a humanoid . . . with pointed ears.

"Spock?" he whispered weakly.

"No, Captain," replied a deep, calm voice. "Please rest. It will take a few moments for the effects to wear off."

Kirk blinked and the figure came into sharper focus. It *was* a Vulcan. But not Spock. Spock was dead.

His entire crew was dead.

But . . . why aren't I dead?

He realized he was lying on some sort of reclining chair. Gathering his strength, he sat up. Swallowing, Kirk tried to moisten his dry lips. "Effects? What effects?"

"Here, drink this."

The Vulcan gave him a cup of water, which he sipped slowly. Looking around again, Kirk saw that he was in the center of a dark room. The only illumination was a lamp somewhere above, surrounding him in a circle of light.

"Where am I? Is this a Starfleet vessel? Did you beam me over before my ship blew?" And then he added anxiously, "Did you manage to rescue anyone else?"

"Don't worry, Jim," a different voice said. "The *Enterprise* is fine . . . and so is your crew."

Squinting, Kirk tried to locate the source of the voice. "Who . . . ?"

A man stepped into the circle of light. A man Kirk recognized immediately. "Commodore Wesley? . . . Bob?"

"Jim. It's been a while."

The last time Kirk saw Wesley was during the M-5 fiasco. The

Federation's "ultimate computer" had taken control of the *Enterprise* and attacked three other starships, including Wesley's own, the *Lexington*. The irony of the similarities between that situation and this one was not lost on Kirk.

"With all due respect, Commodore, what the hell is going on? Why am I not dead?"

"Perhaps you should rest before—"

Kirk stood up. "I'm ready to talk *now*."

The commodore could tell by the edge in Kirk's voice that it was more than a request. "Fine. Follow me."

As Wesley turned and stepped away, the room was suddenly filled with light. Kirk blinked a moment as his eyes adjusted, then surveyed his surroundings. It didn't look like a starship cabin. It looked more like an office on a starbase.

Wesley walked behind a single desk and motioned to a chair in front of it. "Have a seat."

Kirk took one more sip of water and turned to set it down; then his blood ran cold when he realized exactly what he had been sitting on. It was a large metallic chair with two circular appendages rising up from the top and positioned on both sides of where his head had been. He had seen a chair like it only one other time in his life, on the Tantalus V penal colony when Doctor Tristan Adams used it—to try and empty his mind.

"I see you recognize our equipment," said Wesley as he sat down.

Kirk nodded. "A neural neutralizer." He turned and gave Wesley a cold, hard stare. "Exactly where am I, Commodore? And what is this thing doing here? I thought it was destroyed."

"The original was destroyed, yes, but not the technology. It was too valuable to discard."

"Valuable? For what?"

"To do exactly what we just did, Jim. Determine whether or not you have the psychological strength we need."

Kirk walked over and plopped the cup of water on the desk, ignoring the fact that a good deal of it splattered on the surface.

"You're not making any sense, Commodore. I want to know *exactly* what happened to my crew, and I want to know *now!*"

"Of course," Wesley smiled and motioned to the other chair again. "Please. . . ." After Kirk finally sat, Wesley leaned back. "It's actually pretty simple, Jim. What you just experienced wasn't real . . . it was a test."

Kirk frowned. "A . . . *test?* You aren't making any sense. I told you I wanted to know what happened to my crew."

"That's exactly what I'm trying to tell you, Jim. Your crew is fine. They're right here with us."

"Where is 'here'?" Kirk asked.

"Starbase 9."

"We were brought *back* to the starbase?"

"You never left."

During his years as captain of the *Enterprise,* Kirk had made first contact with dozens of alien life-forms, some speaking the strangest languages he had ever heard. Yet every single one of them had still made a hell of a lot more sense to him than Wesley was making at that point.

"I can understand how confusing this must be, so let me start from the beginning." Leaning forward, the commodore began, "I was recently assigned to a covert-operations group known as Section 31."

"I've never heard of Section 31."

"Very few people have, and that's the way we want it. Our organization handles very . . . *special* assignments, Jim. Assignments that fall *outside* Starfleet parameters. Assignments that deal with problems that can't be resolved by following the standard rules and regulations the rest of Starfleet must follow."

"You're a shadow-operations group."

Wesley shrugged. "You could say that."

"Commodore," Kirk said, rubbing a knot in his neck, "this is all very interesting, but what does this have to do with my ship and crew?"

"I told you, Jim, your crew is fine. As I said before, what you experienced wasn't real. It was all part of an evaluation. Think of it as a variation—albeit a far more advanced variation—of the *Kobayashi Maru* scenario, designed to determine how you'd react to a no-win situation. Only, you can't *fix* this one, Jim, not like you did at the Academy. After all, how can you change the outcome of a test . . . if you don't know you're taking it?"

Kirk shook his head. "That was no test, Commodore. I saw—"

"What you saw . . . was all in your mind."

"My—?" Kirk's eyes darkened as he suddenly understood what Wesley was implying. He turned and stared at the neural neutralizer. "You used *that* . . . on *me?*"

"Yes. But not just that . . . it was a combination of the neutralizer *and* a Vulcan mind-meld."

Kirk saw the Vulcan standing to the right of the neutralizer, arms resting behind his back. He was older than Spock, with a streak of gray in his jet black hair.

"This is Doctor Syral," said Wesley. "He's a civilian member of my team. A brilliant psychologist."

The Vulcan merely nodded.

"We've improved upon the technology behind the neutralizer," explained Wesley. "It's much more advanced than the one you saw on Tantalus V."

Kirk turned to face the commodore. "You mean the one that almost *killed* me?"

Wesley ignored the comment. "We programmed it with what we call the 'Demon' scenario, in which an indestructible alien being takes over your starship. Then we enter psychological profiles of your crew so that their reactions will seem more natural. The program is then actually run within your mind. It's much like a dream, though you think it is real, and we can adjust and control the outcome. At the same time Doctor Syral performs a mind-meld to control the direction of the scenario and monitor your reactions."

Kirk couldn't believe what he was hearing. "How *long* have I been here? When did this scenario of yours begin?"

"Right after you had drinks with Commander Offutt," answered

Wesley. "Bumping into your old friend wasn't a coincidence, Jim . . . Mark Offutt works with us."

Kirk was silent, yet the look on his face betrayed his feeling of shock.

"It's true," said Wesley. "You'd be surprised to learn who works with us. Anyway, the commander slipped a sedative into your drink—"

"A sedative?" Kirk frowned. "That explains why I got drunk so fast."

"Correct. But rather than taking you to a hotel, as you 'remember,' he brought you to us."

Kirk gritted his teeth. The more he heard about Wesley's test, the more it angered him. *"Why* did you do this to me?"

"Your five-year mission is about to end," explained Wesley, "and when you return to Earth in two months, we know that Starfleet Command will be promoting you to rear admiral once you relinquish command of the *Enterprise.*"

"Rear admiral?" Kirk shook his head. "I'll be damned if I'll spend the rest of my career wasting time behind some desk."

"We agree," said Wesley. "It *would* be a waste . . . of your talent and experience. That's why we wanted you *with* us, Jim, to join our organization as head of a task force. But before we offered you the position, we needed to know if you were psychologically fit to handle it."

"I experienced the death of every member of my crew," Kirk stated slowly, "just so you could determine whether or not I was ready to join your team?"

"Exactly."

Kirk stood and leaned over the desk, fury igniting his eyes. "Who the *hell* do you think are, Wesley?"

The commodore's face darkened. "I am your superior officer . . . *Captain!* And you will give me the respect due that rank. Is that clear?"

Kirk fought the urge to tell him what he could do with his rank. Clenching his fist, he forced himself to sit.

"The test is necessary, Jim. As a task-force commander you would encounter dangers worse than anything a standard Starfleet officer faces. Not only that, but you would be utilizing weaponry and technology only we have access to. We can't allow them to fall into the wrong hands. That's why you must be willing to sacrifice your crew and your ship at a moment's notice. So we had to know if you are capable of doing that—without hesitation."

"I've been in more than one situation where I've ordered the self-destruct of my ship, Commodore," Kirk retorted. "So why subject me to this test of yours?"

"Because you've never actually followed through with it," replied Wesley. "You've always managed to find another option so the self-destruct order wasn't necessary. That in itself is a quality we're looking for, but we had to know that if you truly faced a no-win scenario, you would actually push the button, so to speak."

Kirk had had enough. He stood again and stared at Wesley. "Dammit, Commodore, using this type of technology to play with people's minds was wrong on Tantalus V, and it's wrong now! It's a violation of my rights *and* my mind!"

"I'm not here to debate the ethical use of the neutralizer, Captain. I'm here to decide if you're the right person for Section 31. To see if you live up to our ideals."

"Then don't waste your time, Commodore," Kirk spat out. "Or mine! I'm not interested in you or your group. Anyone who would treat me or anyone else like this doesn't live up to *my* ideals. I want nothing to do with you!"

The commodore raised his eyebrows. "And what makes you think you actually passed the test?"

Kirk blinked. "What?"

"To put it bluntly, you failed." Wesley stood to face Kirk. "Oh, we were *very* impressed with your performance, but Doctor Syral informed me that you have a few character flaws that disqualify you."

"Flaws?"

"Basically, you have too much compassion for your crew."

Kirk shook his head. "You consider compassion to be a character flaw?"

"In our line of work, yes," explained Wesley. "Instead of detonating the photon torpedoes as soon as you had the chance, you paused to say good-bye to your chief engineer. That hesitation almost prevented you from stopping the entity. That moment you became a liability to us."

Raising his hands, Kirk sighed. "Fine. If that's a character flaw, then it's one I'm proud to have. Now," Kirk looked around impatiently, "how the hell do I get out of here?"

"Oh, you can't leave just yet, Jim," stated Wesley as he stood.

Irritated, Kirk faced Wesley again. "Why not?"

"You know too much. And we can't afford to have non–Section 31 personnel walking around with knowledge of our existence."

Kirk frowned at the commodore. "So, what happens now? Is this where I disappear, never to be seen again?"

"Excuse me?"

"How far are you willing to go to protect your existence, Wesley? Would you kill me?"

The commodore laughed. "Really, Jim, we aren't the Romulans. Do you think we'd terminate our own people just to keep us a secret?"

"Based on what I've heard so far . . . in a heartbeat!"

"I'm sorry you feel that way. But you can relax. No one's going to harm you. We have other ways of preventing information from getting out."

Kirk frowned, immediately wary. "And what are they?"

Suddenly, he felt the pressure of two fingers against the base of his neck. *The Vulcan,* he thought, as he lost all feeling in his body and slumped back into his chair.

In the few seconds of awareness before the nerve pinch took full effect, Kirk heard the commodore say, "Nothing you need concern yourself with, Jim. . . . You won't remember it anyway. . . ."

*   *   *

Opening his eyes, James T. Kirk looked around his hotel room—and wondered what the hell he was doing there.

And then he remembered. He'd checked in the night before with a beautiful woman he met in the cantina. Shiana was her name.

Sitting up, he checked the time. The chronometer read 1730 hours, which meant he'd slept through the entire day. Not something he did normally. He must have had a bit too much to drink the evening before.

Standing, he paused as his head began to throb. *Yes,* he thought, *I definitely had too much to drink.*

After a quick shower, Kirk walked through the hotel lobby. He wanted to get back to *Enterprise* as soon as possible. And if they didn't have plans yet, maybe he could convince Spock and McCoy to join him for dinner.

Glancing around, he noticed an older Vulcan gentleman with a streak of gray hair standing in the hotel lobby. For a brief moment he looked familiar. *Very* familiar.

And then the feeling vanished.

Shaking his head, Kirk entered the nearest transporter station. Repairs should be completed on *Enterprise,* and he was anxious to get back into space. There were only two more months until their five-year mission was officially over . . . and he wanted to spend every minute of them among the stars.

Don't Call Me Tiny

Paul C. Tseng

"Now get outta here, ya half-pint runt!"

Hikaru hit the pavement and felt the sting of a skinned knee through his pants. Eric Monroe—the class bully, who stood a head and a half taller—pulled him up by the collar and slammed his back up against the schoolyard fence. Eric's buddies looked on and laughed.

"And next time, tell your mother to pack some beef teriyaki for lunch!" Eric shouted as he threw a half-eaten apple straight into Hikaru's face. It was the apple Hikaru's mother had packed in the lunch bag, which Eric had just ransacked. He wanted so desperately to wipe the spit from Eric's cruel words off his face. But he didn't dare. Hikaru just stood there, eyes wide open in fear, and didn't flinch.

"See you later, Tiny!"

Hikaru felt the wind knocked out of him as Eric slammed his elbow into his gut. He waited till they were out of sight before he allowed himself to groan audibly and fall to the floor. It was the first day of middle school, and Eric Monroe, Hikaru's worst nightmare, had somehow been promoted to the sixth grade along with the rest of the class. He had prayed all summer that Eric's poor grades would force him to repeat the fifth grade, in their old primary school. But instead, Eric, who had already been bigger and taller than most of the other kids, not only had graduated and come to the same school as Hikaru, but had grown even more in height and formidableness. Of course, Eric had repeated the fourth and fifth grades, making him two years older than Hikaru, but that was beside the point.

The real problem was that, while all the other boys had begun to grow, as boys did when they became adolescents, Hikaru still retained his diminutive stature. He felt left behind on the growth trail. It wasn't any fun being the school pipsqueak, especially when Jenny Faulkner, the secret love of his life since third grade, had caught Eric's fancy.

Hikaru peeled himself off the schoolyard floor and noticed Jenny in the corner of his eye. She quickly turned and walked away. Hikaru wiped the spit, sweat, and tears from his face, gathered his padds, and limped off to class just as the late tone chimed. It was going to be a long day, and at this point all he wanted to do was to run home and lock himself in his room until he was ready for college!

"Hikaru. Come on, son, open the door!" his father called, gently knocking on the door to his bedroom. "Whatever it is, we can talk about it."

"Go away!" he shouted back. "I don't want to talk!" Hikaru tried his best to sound upset, but the truth was that he rather enjoyed the attention and concern he solicited from his parents, especially from Dad. While his father kept pleading with him to open the door and talk, Hikaru posed before a mirror, bare-chested, and pretended to be a *kenjutsu* master. He wielded a toy samurai sword that Dad had given him for his tenth birthday.

His mother, however, could see right through his wiles. A single, heavy thump on the door jolted Hikaru out of his fantasy.

"Hikaru Sulu!" she said sharply. "You open this door right now!"

He quickly dropped the sword and rushed to put his shirt back on. As loving as she was, his mother was not one to be trifled with; he knew that full well. Running to the door with one arm still not inside his sweater, Hikaru tripped over his backpack.

"Are you all right, son?" Dad called out.

"Stop fooling around and open the door!" Mom shouted.

Still on his scraped knees, Hikaru reached up to turn the shiny old brass doorknob to his room. He didn't even bother to fix his mussed hair or his left hand, still dangling out of the bottom of his sweater.

"Hi, Mom. Hi, Dad," he said as nonchalantly as he could while he stood up and finished getting dressed.

Dad had always been soft on Hikaru, his only child and beloved son. Mom was the stricter parent. He loved and respected her for her strength and consistency.

"Come on, Karu," Dad said, using his childhood nickname. "Tell us what happened. We're your parents and we care."

Mom folded her arms in front of her and gave him a stern look. "I've just finished making dinner, and it's getting cold. Your poor father has been trying to talk with you all afternoon. Don't play these games!"

"Sorry, Dad. I didn't mean any disrespect," Hikaru started. "I just . . ."

But before he could finish, Dad came over and wrapped his arms around him. "It's okay, son. You seemed so upset after your first day at school; I wanted to know what happened."

Dad was very different from all the other Sulus he'd known in his life. None of his uncles were as openly affectionate to their children as his father was to him. At times he found it embarrassing, but deep down it comforted Hikaru to know that he meant that much to him.

"Aw, Dad . . . come on!" he said, still muffled in his father's arms.

"Well, you talk to your father, but I expect you both down to eat in ten minutes," Mom said, pragmatic as always. "Whatever the issue is, don't try to hide from it. We can always find a solution, because . . ."

"I know, Mom. Sulus don't run. They fly," Hikaru recited, as if for the millionth time.

Mom nodded her approval sternly and walked out of the room. His father sat down on the edge of Hikaru's bed and looked at the toy samurai sword on the floor. He smiled and looked at his son. "So, tell me all about it."

Hikaru sighed and sat at the chair by his desk. He fidgeted with a toy replica of an old twenty-first-century F-16 fighter jet, pretending to fly it in the air.

"You know, Dad, it's the same old story," Hikaru answered. "Eric Monroe's still picking on me at school. He stole my lunch and roughed me up in front of everyone!"

Hikaru saw his father's jaw and fists clenching. He didn't speak at first; perhaps he was trying his best to set an example by keeping his cool despite his fury. Finally, he let out a breath of exasperation.

"Maybe I should have a talk with your school director about this Eric boy. I'll not have anyone bullying . . ."

"No, Dad! It's embarrassing enough as it is. Please, don't come to school!" He still couldn't shake the memories of his father holding his hand and walking him to school every morning. Finally, in fifth grade, he had insisted on walking by himself, like the rest of the kids. It had broken his father's heart, which made Hikaru sad, but he was too busy fighting for his independence at the time to be concerned with anyone's feelings but his own.

"I understand, Hikaru," Dad said with a kind smile. "You are becoming a man. You must fight your own battles, eh?"

"Dad, I just need to. . . . Yeah, I need to handle this on my own."

Hikaru's father scratched at his whiskery gray beard. The sound annoyed and comforted Hikaru at the same time. It annoyed him because the sound was darn irritating to the ears but it comforted him because he still remembered, as a little child, loving to rub and make scraping sounds with his little fingers against his daddy's beard. Sometimes it had been the only way he could fall asleep, on those stormy, thundering nights when he could actually see from his window the lightning illuminate the Golden Gate Bridge.

"So what do you plan to do about Eric?"

Hikaru considered many possibilities. None of them fit well with the Sulu mantra of flying and not running.

"I really don't know," he replied. "Gosh, Dad, Eric's like six feet tall, and me? I'm just barely five!"

"So you are thinking about fighting him?" Dad asked, leaning forward with curiosity.

They both laughed, but Hikaru's laughter was more out of anxiety than finding the proposition humorous. Dad's countenance then became more severe.

"Karu, I have always taught you to be brave, to be fair, and to be right, haven't I?"

Hikaru nodded.

"There is a time for all things. Sometimes you have to fight, even though you know you can't win—because it's worth fighting for, even dying for."

Hikaru gulped. He had heard this speech before and was hoping that Dad wasn't telling him to fight a bully who seemed twice his size.

"But you have to ask yourself if what you are fighting for is worth dying for. Just what *would* you be fighting for . . . with Eric?"

The question hit its mark and sank in deeply. Hikaru didn't know how to answer. *I'd be fighting for . . . my lunch? My dignity? My pride? Are those worth dying for?*

"I don't know, exactly," Hikaru answered. "I just hate getting picked on every day. I want him to stop."

Just then, Mom's booming voice echoed through the hall. "Dinner's ready! Hikaru, wash up and help me serve the rice!"

He jumped to his feet and called back, "Coming!"

"Remember, son, you will have to fight the battle in here first," Dad said, pointing to Hikaru's heart. "When you have won, then you will know what the next step is."

The next morning, Hikaru felt a spring in his step as he walked to school. It was September in San Francisco; he could feel it in the cool brisk air and the warm sunshine on his back. He had left the events of yesterday behind him, hoping that today would be a peaceful—day; one without Eric Monroe.

After dinner the previous evening, Hikaru had helped load the dishes into the sonic dishwasher while his mother had cleaned the rest of kitchen. She didn't ask what he and his father had spoken about. In fact, she didn't say much of anything at all, except just before he had finished his chores and left the kitchen.

"Listen to your father," she had said. "His words will guide you, years from now."

He wasn't certain what that meant to him today, but it was good enough for him to have gotten it off his chest and to know he didn't have to suffer through this in silence.

About one block from school, he spotted Jenny Faulkner walking with some of her girlfriends. They were all giggling as Hikaru approached; all but Jenny. Maybe that was a good sign. She gave him a look of sympathy—or was it pity?

"Hi, Jenny," Hikaru said.

"Hi."

"So how do you like our new school?"

Jenny seemed a bit distracted, if not apprehensive. She kept looking over Hikaru's shoulder, while the other girls continued to giggle. It made him downright antsy.

"You should go, Hikaru," Jenny said, her brow furrowing.

"Go? Why?"

The next thing he felt was an elbow in his back, and before he knew it he was flat on his face on the floor again.

"Whoops!" snorted Eric. "Sorry, Tiny. You're so small, I didn't even see you!"

From Hikaru's perspective, with his lunch, books, and limbs sprawled across the ground, Eric looked like a giant. He watched helplessly as the bully bent down and rummaged through his lunch container.

Eric tossed aside a metallic, rectangular box. Its lid popped off and all the steaming rice inside fell into the dirt. Eric took an apple and chewed on it, as he had the day before. With his mouth full of half-masticated fruit, he said, "Damn! . . . I thought I told you to have your mom pack beef teriyaki today, *Rice Boy!*"

Hikaru would have slashed the bully to pieces with a samurai sword, if there had been one there for him to use—and if he had the courage to do it. He also fantasized about knocking Eric's lights out with judo chops and karate drop-kicks. He had never worked up the nerve to ask his parents to send him to martial-arts classes, for fear of having to explain why he wanted to learn. After today, however, maybe he would ask. Then Hikaru thought of his strong, yet gentle, father. He wouldn't approve of learning any form of art to use for violence or aggression.

"You'd better get up, Tiny," Eric scoffed. "You'll be late for math class!"

Then to Hikaru's horror, he saw Eric put an arm around Jenny as they walked off to class together with the other girls. Hikaru wanted so badly to die right there on the floor that he didn't notice that Jenny had turned back and looked sadly at him before disappearing into the school building with Eric.

"He what? What did you eat for lunch, then?"

Hikaru was disconcerted that the most important issue for Mom, after learning what had happened in the morning, seemed to be the rice.

"I just ate it without the rice! But you don't understand! It's Jenny Faulkner!"

Mom sighed and shook her head. "Why don't you just find a nice Japanese girl, eh?"

"Mom!"

The anger on her face softened. She smiled and walked over to Hikaru with open arms. Unlike with Dad, Hikaru didn't mind her displays of affection, because they were so rare. He let her hug him and even hugged her back.

"Listen to me," she said. "I know that your dad is a very philosophical and wise man who hates violence. But there are times you really have to defend yourself."

"But Mom, Eric's huge! He's a monster!"

"Well then, why not just wear a sign that says 'Beat me up, take a number'!"

Nothing incensed Hikaru more than when his mother got "smart" with him. The worst part of it was that she was always right. He hated that.

"You just don't get it, Mom. Eric's right, I *am* tiny!" And to culminate the self-pity, Hikaru frowned, looked out the window, and sighed. "I bet even Jenny thinks I'm nothing but a little bug to be squashed by him."

Mom grabbed him by the shoulder and spun him around to face her. "Now, you listen to me. We Sulus may not be physically very tall, but we are *not* little people!"

"Mom, look at me! My feet don't even touch the ground when I sit at the cafeteria tables!"

"No one can look down on you without your permission, Hikaru!" She grabbed his hand and yanked his arm so hard that he let out an embarrassing yelp. "Now, you come here, boy! I'm going to teach you how to fight!"

Hikaru followed his mother to the center of the living room and stared in disbelief as she pushed all the furniture aside. *My God, she's serious!*

Mom put her two fists up and began shifting from side to side. "Come on! Give me your best shot!"

Mom was even tinier than he was, by at least two inches. Hikaru almost laughed, but he knew she was serious.

"No way, Mom!"

Then she approached him and took a swing, just nicking his chin.
"Ow! Hey, that hurt!"

"What's the matter," she said, taunting him. "Afraid of a girl?"

Rubbing his chin, Hikaru couldn't understand why she was antagonizing him like this. Sure, she had never been one to baby him when he was upset, but this was simply adversarial.

Mom began circling him again. "Come on, fight!"

"No! You're crazy, Mom!"

She nailed him with a punch in the gut.

Hikaru could tell she was pulling her punches, but damn, that one really hurt. *What's gotten into her?* He couldn't believe it; now he was actually trying to run away from her. She came in close again and stared him straight in the eye.

"Come on, Tiny!" She then planted a firm, but restrained punch onto his nose.

That did it. Hikaru didn't care that it was his own mother, or that perhaps she had gone temporarily insane. Who was *she* to call him Tiny? He let out a gut-wrenching scream and charged his mother, posed in a defensive posture. Just as he got close enough to tackle her, she grabbed his arm, and in one swift move flipped him flat on his back.

The floor shook as Hikaru's body smacked down against the wood parquet floor. He was starting to get used to having the wind knocked out of him.

"Get up, Tiny!" Mom yelled.

"Don't call me that!" Hikaru yelled as he got up and lunged at her again. This time, Mom juked to the left and with one quick sweep of her foot under his, dropped Hikaru square on his rump.

Hikaru glared up at her, trying to catch his breath. He was beyond confusion now; he was downright angry.

Mom stood above him with one fist drawn to her chest and the other poised to strike. "That's right, get angry! Use it to make you do something besides sitting on your butt feeling sorry for yourself!"

Angry. Yes, that's what he was. Hikaru was angry; not so much at his mother—he knew there must be a lesson for his benefit in all this madness—but at feeling like a victim. It finally dawned upon him that he was most angry with himself, for allowing Eric to make him and others believe that he was a worthless, helpless little Japanese boy. He took all that pent-up rage and aimed his eyes at his mother, who had now moved across the room to the doorway. She was smiling, nodding her head and taunting him. Hikaru wiped the sweat from his brow and gave his mother a menacing look. Then he charged her with all his might.

Just as he was about to make contact, she pulled out of the way and he went flying through the open doorway. He would have surely hit the wall in the hallway had his father not shown up.

"OOF!"

Dad caught Hikaru's head right in his midsection and they both fell to the ground. Hikaru could hear his mother laughing out loud at the sight of them lying on the ground.

"What is going on here?" Dad demanded.

Mom casually fixed her hair and walked up to the heap that was her son and husband. She smiled and patted them both affectionately on the head and answered, "Just a little life lesson." And with that, she walked down to the kitchen to prepare dinner.

It took some effort, but Hikaru finally managed to get up, with his father's help.

"What was *that* all about?" Dad asked.

Hikaru rubbed his sore back. "I'm not sure, but Mom nearly killed me! I thought Sulus were philosophers and artists, not fighters!"

"Sulus, yes. But your mother is a Tanaka by birth," Dad answered, patting his son's neck.

"Where did she learn to fight like that?"

Dad answered while examining Hikaru's face and body to see if anything was broken or bleeding. "Let's go out to the backyard and I'll tell you all about it."

The sky was filled with so many stars that Hikaru imagined he could just scoop up a few hundred and keep them in a jar. Sitting in a lawn chair next to his dad, he watched shuttles rise up across the bay from Starfleet Command and disappear into the heavens. Since he was a little boy, he had found the occasional sparkle of a starship warping out of the system more exciting than spotting a shooting star, which everyone knew was, in fact, just a meteorite skimming the atmosphere.

"So what *else* don't I know about, Mom?" Hikaru asked, taking a sip of hot tea.

Dad looked up into the sky and sighed. "First of all, being the only girl in her family, she learned martial arts from her brothers."

"Tell me about Grandpa Tanaka," Hikaru said. Mom rarely spoke of him and this always puzzled him.

"Well, Karu," said Dad. "It's hard for your mother to talk about him, because it makes her sad."

"Mom? Sad?" Hikaru could hardly imagine her being anything but tough as duranium.

"Her father served in Starfleet not long after the Federation was first formed. He was rarely home. In fact, when she was born, he was on a deep-space assignment near the Romulan Neutral Zone."

Hikaru's eyes widened like ancient silver coins. "Wow, Starfleet!"

"He never got to meet her until she was four years old. And then he was only home every few years for a short time. He died defending a Federation outpost during the First Klingon War, and his body was never recovered. For that, she always hated Starfleet. To this day, I'm not certain she's forgiven him for leaving her."

"Why didn't you guys ever tell me any of this?"

Dad turned to face him and put his hands on Hikaru's shoulders. "There's more—more she didn't want you to know about. But we think you are old enough to know and understand now."

These revelations were both exciting and frightening to Hikaru, who desperately wanted to know everything about his parents' mysterious past.

"Come on, Dad! Tell me!"

The look in Dad's eyes betrayed pride in his son, yet there was a melancholy that Hikaru didn't quite understand.

"I was also in Starfleet."

Hikaru leapt out of his lawn chair, mouth gaping wide open. "I knew it! The model ships you built with me, all the history lessons, your old friends who served in Starfleet . . ." He pulled a fist down, excitedly. Hikaru grabbed his father's arm and shook it eagerly. "Were you a captain? Did you fight Romulans too? Come on, Dad, you gotta tell me!"

A nostalgic smile spread across Dad's face. "No, I didn't do any of that. When I just graduated from the Academy, my commanding officer, who was an old friend of your mother's family, introduced me to her. To make a long story short, we got married."

"Well, what ship did you serve on?" Hikaru begged. "Did you ever fight Klingons?"

"I was a shuttle pilot and about to be posted on the *Lexington* . . ."

Hikaru's mouth simply hung open, as the word "wow" silently floated out.

"But your mother refused to marry me as long as I served in Starfleet. She didn't want to become a 'Starfleet widow.' So I resigned my commission and became a civilian." Dad exhaled in such a way that Hikaru could detect regret and relief. "You see, Hikaru, she didn't want you to know all this when you were a little boy, because she didn't want your head full of dreams of joining Starfleet."

Hikaru's heart sank just as quickly as it had taken flight. "But . . . but why?"

"Try to understand, son. She'd already lost her father; she couldn't bear the thought of her baby flying off to the ends of the galaxy."

"So what's changed your minds? Why are you telling me this now?" Hikaru then felt a warm hand on his shoulder. When he turned around he found his mother there, eyes shimmering with tears—something he'd rarely seen from her.

Paul C. Tseng

"You're growing up into a fine young man," Mom said. "But when we saw how broken your confidence was, by a foolish bully like Eric Monroe, we decided that you had to know who you truly are, before you could confront him." She turned to her husband. "I've already robbed one Sulu of his destiny and greatness. I'll be damned if I do that to my son!"

Dad held her tenderly. "You did no such thing. I gladly gave it up to be with you and to raise our Hikaru."

The awe that filled Hikaru's heart seemed to make his breath short. As long as he could remember, he had dreamed of exploring the galaxy like his hero, Jonathan Archer. And while his parents never outright discouraged him, their lack of enthusiasm or response to his daydreaming had always meant that it wasn't something to be considered. Hikaru felt a weight lifted from his chest; he was so happy that he felt he could surely fly into the heavens! Suddenly, thoughts of Eric Monroe and Jenny Faulkner seemed to shrink in significance.

Over the next few weeks, his father began taking Hikaru to Point Reyes with his old hovercar for flying lessons. Of course, Dad knew Hikaru was still a few years shy of getting a permit, but that was what made it all the more exciting. He looked forward daily to being regaled by Dad's Academy stories.

Mom spent the afternoons teaching Hikaru martial arts and how to use his slight stature to his advantage by means of maneuverability, agility, and stealth.

But Hikaru's heart was in the stars. He managed to duck out of Eric's way at every confrontation. It didn't bother him the least bit now when Eric, winded from repeatedly swinging and missing, would call him "chicken" for leaving the scene of a fight with him. Hikaru could tell that Eric was frustrated by the other kids' giggling at his inability to catch him. All he could think about was getting home and taking flying lessons. He took the karate lessons from his mother seriously, but Hikaru's first priority was becoming a pilot—something Dad was all too happy to help him with.

The end of the school year had arrived, and Hikaru had finally grown two more inches. Practicing had gotten him to the point where he could take his mother on in a sparring match. And Dad called him a prodigy, because in a few short months he'd become very adept at piloting all kinds of air- and spacecraft. Hikaru would never forget the midnight joy ride he took with Dad to the Lunar Station and back in Uncle Yasu's shuttle. Uncle Yasu, a veteran Marine Corps pilot and a MACO, affectionately referred to Hikaru as "Cadet Sulu"; he loved it.

Eric Monroe had all but given up on harassing Hikaru. And though it mattered very little to Hikaru now, Jenny had long since broken up with the bully because of his cruel ways.

But on this, the last day of school, Eric had broken from his routine of hurling insults at Hikaru from across the street and started following behind Jenny and her friends instead. Hikaru didn't want to care about what might happen, but he overheard some of the commotion and turned back to look.

"Let go of me!" Jenny shouted.

Eric gripped her arm firmly as he yelled back. "You never return my calls! What's the matter with you?"

"Don't you get it, you idiot? I don't want to see you anymore!"

Eric didn't let go. He tightened his grip even harder, causing Jenny to cry out in pain.

"You're hurting me, Eric!"

"And your ignoring me is supposed to tickle me?" he yelled. "Nobody treats me like that! Nobody!"

All of Jenny's girlfriends ran away, leaving her with Eric and struggling to break free. Hikaru wanted to turn his back and leave as well. After all, if she was stupid enough to get involved with someone like Eric, didn't she deserve this? This wasn't Hikaru's problem, was it?

It amazed him to see dozens of other children walk away from the scene, trying to pretend they weren't seeing Eric hurting the girl Hikaru had been enamored with for as long as he could remember. Just as he began to judge them for turning a blind eye, and deeming them cowards, he heard his father's words in his heart, clear as the day itself:

Sometimes you have to fight, even though you know you can't win—because it's worth fighting for, even dying for.

So far, Hikaru was confident in his ability to evade and avoid Eric Monroe, but having to fight him was an entirely different story. Why did he have to deal with this, on the last day of school?

Once again, Hikaru heard Jenny squeal in pain as Eric twisted her arm and shouted more insults and threats. Hikaru wanted so much to turn away and pretend this wasn't happening. But then he thought of Grandpa Tanaka, who died defending innocent people he never knew. What kind of Starfleet officer would he ever be if he turned away from a call for help?

"Hey, you big pile of *targ* crap!" Hikaru called out as he walked toward Eric.

Eric turned toward Hikaru and sneered, still gripping Jenny's arm. "Well, well. If it isn't the little flea himself."

Hikaru tried his best to appear unafraid, but in fact, he was trembling. Seeing Jenny afraid and in pain, however, caused his blood to boil. He focused on that anger and it seemed to calm his shaking.

"Let her go."

Eric snorted. "Or what?"

This was the moment of truth; the next words from Hikaru would commit him to the first real fight of his life.

"Why don't you let go of her, and find out?"

Eric threw Jenny to the ground, and she let out a pained grunt. He then started for Hikaru, beating his fist into his other hand, making sure to corner him as best he could.

"Okay, Tiny! I'm gonna give you a chance to tuck your tail between your legs, and run like the little rat that you are."

Hikaru stood unflinching. He knew that if he ran, Eric would keep bothering Jenny all summer. And Jenny would lose what little respect she might have had for him.

Eric was nearly upon him. "Go on, Tiny. Run!"

Hikaru remained where he was and fixed his eyes upon Eric's, which seemed to make Eric uncomfortable. The bully turned slightly to avert the steady gaze, just as he threw his first punch at Hikaru's face.

Jenny let out a startled shriek, but Hikaru quickly moved just out of Eric's reach and shuffled behind him. He gave Eric a swift kick in the rear.

"We don't have to settle it this way!" Hikaru said tensely.

Eric spun around swinging, but was unable to land a solid hit because of Hikaru's stealth. "Oh, so you wanna talk this over, huh?" He took another swing, but Hikaru slipped past his punch and struck Eric square on the jaw with his palm, pulling his punch.

"Trust me," Hikaru said. "It's better than fighting!"

"Hold still, so I can hit you!" Eric let out a primal grunt and lunged for Hikaru.

But Hikaru simply stepped a couple of inches to the side and winced as Eric ran headfirst into the trunk of a tree. He looked over and saw Jenny, now joined by a growing crowd of kids from school, cheering him on.

Eric took advantage of that momentary distraction and grabbed Hikaru in a choke hold. Hikaru tried to call out, but he realized that the air wasn't able to flow in or out of his lungs. He saw Jenny's smile turn into fear.

Eric began laughing madly. "You think you're fast, but you're still just a little flea, Tiny!"

Hikaru tried with all his might to pry Eric's arms off from around his neck. But even with both hands pulling, Hikaru could not free himself. His vision began to blur and he thought he might black out in a matter of seconds. Hikaru felt his two arms fall and dangle flaccidly. Eric was not very smart, but he *was* strong. In the last couple of seconds of consciousness Hikaru knew he had left, he considered the fact that his hands and feet were still free. So in a split second he took all he had learned from his mother about fighting, and combined it with all he had learned about the laws of

physics, from flying with his father. He wrapped his two feet behind Eric's legs and pulled quickly, collapsing them by bending
them at the knees. Both boys fell backward onto the ground, and
upon impact Hikaru drove both elbows into Eric's midsection.
Falling on his back with all his and Hikaru's weight, as well as the
impact of Hikaru's two elbows, winded Eric.

Hikaru's vision then became clear. He realized that he was
breathing again and that Eric had released his grip. Hikaru got back
on his feet and noticed that Eric was also getting up, though he was
holding his gut and panting heavily.

Looking around the floor at his feet, Eric spotted a fallen tree
branch, about the size of a baseball bat, and picked it up. Before
Hikaru had a chance to consider the new threat, Eric charged him,
brandishing the wood stick.

"You are so dead, Tiny!"

Hikaru realized that one blow to the head with that tree branch,
and Eric's threat would become reality. He could see by the madness in his eyes that Eric was well beyond reason. How could this
be happening? Hikaru had come so far, since that first day his
mother had taunted him into standing up for himself. He recalled
that day with clarity and used the lessons to his advantage.

Just as Eric came within striking distance, Hikaru grabbed the
arm wielding the branch. He swung the branch into Eric's face, and
then used his attacker's own momentum to throw him forward,
flipping him over onto his back. Hikaru grabbed the sharp end of
the branch, pointed it at Eric, and thrust it down, stopping just short
of his opponent's throat.

"Stop . . . please . . . I give up . . ." a dazed Eric sputtered, as his
head dropped back onto the ground.

Jenny ran to Hikaru's side and held him tightly, as they both
looked down to an utterly defeated Eric.

"If you ever touch Jenny again . . ."

"I won't, I promise . . ." Eric groaned, holding up his hands in
surrender.

Hikaru turned from Eric and motioned for Jenny to start walking ahead of him. He then turned back to Eric, who was stunned and motionless on the floor, save for his exhausted breathing.

"Oh, and one more thing," Hikaru said, as he lifted the stick over his head and thrust it down so that it impaled the ground, millimeters from Eric's head. Eric's eyes widened in fear as he looked up at Hikaru, who spoke in a cool, even tone.

"Don't call me Tiny."

Morning Bells Are Ringing

Kevin G. Summers

To: *Captain Jean-Luc Picard*, U.S.S. Enterprise, NCC-*1701-D*
From: Marissa Flores, U.S.S. Chamberlain, NCC-*56810*
Subject: Scared

Dear Captain,
I'm not sure if you remember me. My name is Marissa Flo-
res. My father is Lieutenant Peter Flores; we used to live on
the Enterprise *until about a year and a half ago. Anyway, I'm*
writing you today because I don't know what else to do.
There's been a terrible accident on the Chamberlain. *Every-*
one is frozen. Not frozen cold; it's like they're frozen in time.
I don't know why or how, but I'm the only person who can
move around or do anything. Really. I walked right up to my
dad and poked him in the ribs, and he just stood there, staring
at nothing.
I've been wandering around the Chamberlain *for two*

days now. She's an Excelsior-class starship, not as nice as the Enterprise, *but Dad says she's a classic. I don't know about that, but I do know that most of the ship's systems are still online—the replicators and the artificial gravity still work, anyway. It's a good thing too. We ran an antigrav program on the holodeck one time, and it made me pretty sick.*

I'm assuming the external communicators are still working, but I really have no idea. I could be writing this letter and you'll never see it. I don't want to think about that, though. I'm going to hope for the best.

So, Captain Picard, I hope you get this letter, and I hope you can help me. I'm scared, and I don't know what to do. I'd raise a distress call if I could, but I don't have that kind of access to the ship's computers. So please help me, if you can.

Sincerely,
Marissa Flores
"Number One"

P.S. I was trapped in a turbolift with you when the Enterprise *passed through a quantum filament, and you gave me two of your collar pips and made me your acting first officer. Do you remember me?*

Jean-Luc Picard looked up at the sound of his chirping communicator. *"Bridge to Captain Picard,"* Data's familiar voice said into the captain's ready room.

"Go ahead."

"There is an incoming message for you, sir."

"Route it in here." Picard marked his place in the book he was reading and moved behind the computer terminal on his desk. Scrolling through color-coded menus, the captain of the *Enterprise* located the message. He read it.

"Number One," he mouthed silently, recalling the incident that the girl was referring to. *She must be, what, fourteen now*? Picard remembered the shy little girl who had almost certainly saved his life by refusing to leave him behind. He had given Marissa the moniker normally reserved for Commander Riker as a means of getting her and the other children trapped in the turbolift to calm down. They were pretty upset, as could be expected; they were in some real danger that day. Now it seemed that Marissa was in trouble again.

Picard tapped his communicator. "Captain Picard to Commander Riker." Riker answered a moment later. "Number One, track the last known location of the Starship *Chamberlain*."

On the bridge, Picard could hear Riker tapping at his computer console for a moment before he responded. *"The* Chamberlain *reported finding a spatial anomaly near the Cheron system. That was five days ago, sir."*

"Can we pick her up on long-range sensors?" asked the captain.

"No, sir."

Picard paused, scanning back through the letter. *"There's been a terrible accident on the* Chamberlain." He thought about the little girl who had performed so bravely when the ship was in trouble. She was a frail little thing, with bright blue eyes and blond locks pulled back in a ponytail. Pretty, but that wasn't the first thing he noticed; she had seemed somehow troubled.

"Captain Picard?" Riker's voice broke into the captain's thoughts.

Picard made his decision. He hated to act on instinct alone, but that was practically what he was doing, ordering the *Enterprise* halfway across the quadrant over a child's letter. His instinct was warning him that Marissa was telling the truth, and if her letter could be believed, the *Chamberlain* was not going to be emitting a distress signal.

"Set coordinates for the *Chamberlain*'s last known position," Picard ordered. "Maximum warp."

"Captain?"

"Engage."

The *Enterprise* turned in a large, sweeping arc, and then disappeared into subspace.

To Captain Jean-Luc Picard, U.S.S. Enterprise, NCC-*1701-D*
From: Marissa Flores, U.S.S. Chamberlain, NCC-*56810*
Subject: Theory

Dear Captain Picard,

I've been trying to figure out why everyone else on board the Chamberlain *is frozen and I can still move around. We've never covered anything like this in my science classes, but I did find some of my dad's journals on a padd in our quarters, and I've been developing a theory.*

My dad is the Chamberlain's *science officer, you see, and he let me hang out in one of the research labs right before the accident happened. He was on the bridge, but since I could see everything that was happening from the lab, I stayed there. It was a great opportunity, he said, because the ship had picked up some kind of spatial anomaly on the sensors, and we were checking it out.*

I was thrilled, of course. I haven't really decided what I want to do when I grow up, but I've narrowed it down to two choices. I want to be the captain of a starship or science officer. Both seem like great jobs and it's just so hard to decide. Anyway, the prospect of being there when a new spatial phenomenon was discovered was just too good to pass up. I mean, this is what Starfleet is all about, right?

It didn't turn out so well though.

As soon as the Chamberlain *got close to the phenomenon, the thing opened up like a giant flower. I've seen some pictures of the Bajoran wormhole; it looked kind of like that, except that it was yellow on the inside. It was beautiful. My dad launched a probe into the wormhole (I'm pretty sure it was a wormhole) to see where the other end came out. The probe was sending back all sorts of data . . . it was awesome!*

I'm not exactly sure what happened next, because I was still looking at the readouts from the probe, but the ship suddenly started shaking really badly. I wanted to run, but I know that to be a Starfleet officer you have to be brave, so I stayed put. Captain Brown gave an order to back off, but I could feel the ship moving forward. I think we were being sucked into the wormhole.

The next order I heard over my linkup to the bridge was the captain screaming for us to go to warp. The engines were really straining, and I was scared that we were going to explode. Just then, a conduit did explode right next to me. I was thrown from my chair, and I passed out. When I woke up, everything was frozen, and it's been like that ever since.

All right, here's my theory: When that conduit exploded, I think I was covered in some kind of subatomic particles. Maybe even chroniton particles. And those particles are making it possible for me to move around when everyone else is standing still.

I know it's just a theory, and it's pretty stupid. I'm sure Mister La Forge could figure it out in about five seconds, but he's not here. I wish he were.

I wish you were here too, Captain. I know you could make everything all right.

You know what I've been singing a lot today? "Frère Jacques." Remember, we sang that when we were climbing out of the turbolift?

I hope you get this letter, and please, help me if you can.

> *Sincerely,*
> *Marissa Flores*
> *"Number One"*

P.S. Ding, ding, dong.

When Picard received Marissa's first letter, the *Enterprise* was four days away from the Cheron system at maximum warp—four days away from the last known location of the *Chamberlain,* and from Marissa Flores, who had saved his life when she refused to leave him behind in a damaged turbolift. She could have left him; she should have, but she didn't.

"This is mutiny," Picard recalled saying at the time. He supposed it was, but that didn't change the fact that the turbolift broke free from its moorings just minutes after they escaped out of the roof. The captain of the *Enterprise* smiled. A moment later, his memory turned sour when he thought about Marissa, frightened and alone on board the *Chamberlain.*

"Captain?" Riker asked.

Picard jolted back to reality. He hadn't realized he'd been staring dreamily at the stars zipping past outside the conference-room window. Staring dreamily while his senior staff stared at him like he'd gone mad. "Number One," Picard said, wiping away the last vestiges of his smile. "What is our current status?"

"We're still two days away from Cheron," Riker said. "Did you get another letter?"

Picard nodded. "Computer, read aloud the text of file 'Marissa—2.'"

"Dear Captain," said the melodic voice of the computer. It narrated the letter, causing Geordi and Data to nod their heads when it recited the part about the chroniton particles.

"Geordi," Picard said when the reading was complete, "is something like this even possible?"

"It's possible," answered the engineer. "Chroniton particles are difficult to predict, and there's a lot we don't know about wormholes, an awful lot. There's no way of telling how a wormhole might react if it came in contact with chronitons."

"Perhaps," Data interjected, "the spatial phenomenon the *Chamberlain* discovered is not a wormhole at all."

"What do you mean?" Picard crossed his legs and leaned back in his chair.

The android looked up at him with lifeless yellow eyes. "Perhaps the phenomenon is actually a temporal hole," he said.

"A temporal hole?" Worf asked in his humorless voice.

"It is like a wormhole," Data explained, "except it is shaped like a cone. There is no exit."

Geordi seemed to light up. "I've read about those," he said enthusiastically. "It's possible that if a ship entered subspace inside the temporal hole, it would be moving forward in time at the same rate the phenomenon is moving backward. Thus, it would be standing still."

"Why is it called a temporal hole?" Riker asked.

"Theoretically, a temporal hole moves backward in time, from the moment it opens into regular space-time until it reaches the apex, which is the moment of its formation," Data clarified.

"If that's the case," Picard interjected, "where is the *Chamberlain* now?"

"It is most likely still inside the phenomenon," Data expounded. "However, I should note that a temporal hole has yet to be discovered. It is only a theory."

"But a good one," Geordi added. "At least it makes some sense. If Marissa were exposed to enough chroniton particles, she might not be affected by her environment."

Picard stared at his senior staff, men and women who, in his opinion, were the finest in the fleet. "Data, Geordi," he said, "I want you to compile everything we know about temporal holes. When we get to Cheron, we may not have a lot of time." He turned to Counselor Troi. "Deanna, are you able to sense anything?"

The counselor gazed at him for a long moment before speaking. "Fear," she said simply. "Fear and guilt."

Picard was taken aback. "Guilt? What do you mean?"

"I don't know," Deanna said. "I can tell Marissa admires you very much, but there is something hidden beneath her feelings, something she thinks will make you very upset if you find out."

Picard nodded. Sometimes it still felt strange to rely on an empath, but the captain had grown to trust Deanna Troi over the years. A few minutes later, he dismissed the meeting. Staring out the window once more, he watched the stars racing by.

To: Captain Jean-Luc Picard, U.S.S. Enterprise, NCC-1701-D
From: Marissa Flores, U.S.S. Chamberlain, NCC-56810
Subject: Guilty Conscience

Dear Captain,
*   I've had a lot of time to myself these past few days—a lot of time to think. There's been something on my mind, and I think I ought to tell you about it. Just in case, you know?*
*   Remember that science fair I won back on the* Enterprise? *The prize for the winner and two runners-up was a tour of the ship given by you—which was how we ended up in the turbolift when everything went crazy. Anyway, what I want to tell you about has to do with my science project.*
*   My dad says that it's best to just tell the truth and let the pieces fall where they may, so that's what I'm going to do.*
*   I cheated on my project. That's why I was able to win the science fair. Before the turbolift broke down, you asked me what my project was about and I never answered. That was why; I was ashamed.*
*   I'm really sorry, Captain Picard. I know you're probably terribly disappointed in me, and you have every right to be. You could even hate me. But I hope you'll still come and try and save the* Chamberlain. *Captain Brown is really nice, and this is a good crew. Please don't turn your back on them just because I'm a stupid kid. I only did it because, well, never mind. It's dumb.*

*   Regretfully yours,*
*   Marissa Flores*
*   "Number One"*

The *Enterprise* dropped out of warp as the *Galaxy*-class starship reached the Cheron system. Several light-years away, the dead planet for which the system was named hung in space like a rotting tangerine.

Picard had once again assembled his senior staff to assess the situation. *The finest crew in the fleet,* he found himself thinking again. *If anyone can come up with a solution, they can.* The conference room doors whooshed open, admitting him. His senior staff were already seated around the massive table. Beyond the window, the stars seemed stationary once more.

"Report," Picard said, taking his seat.

Geordi shot Data a nervous glance, and then began to speak. "Data and I have been researching temporal holes. There's not a lot out there, but there is a widely accepted theory among most physicists."

"Go on."

Data spoke up, the tone in his voice as dispassionate as if he were reading the menu in Ten-Forward. "The theory suggests that any object trapped within the temporal hole would eventually be crushed as it was pulled toward the apex of the cone."

"If the *Chamberlain* is moving fast enough," Geordi continued, "she would eventually escape. If not, time would catch up to her sooner or later and . . ."

He let his words trail off, something for which Picard was eminently grateful. It was bad enough to think about that innocent child and her shipmates being crushed to death; there was no need to say it out loud. "Do you have any theories on how we might get them out of there?" Picard asked, tearing himself away from the dark thoughts.

"Actually," Geordi said, "we do."

"Well?"

"If a photon torpedo detonated at the apex of the phenomenon," said Data, "the temporal hole would, theoretically, begin to collapse."

"Wouldn't that trap them in there for certain?" Picard asked.

"It would not," said the android. "The phenomenon would begin to collapse in the past, and work its way forward to our time."

"The *Chamberlain* is moving at warp speed," Geordi said. "She would break free from the phenomenon's gravimetric pull, which would decrease as the temporal hole became smaller."

"There is one problem I see," Picard said. "If we fire a photon torpedo into the temporal hole, we run the risk of hitting the *Chamberlain*."

Data and Geordi looked at each other for a moment and then turned back to the captain. It was the android who spoke, his tone as pleasantly curious as ever. "Not if the torpedo were fired from the *Chamberlain*," he said.

To: Captain Jean-Luc Picard, U.S.S. Enterprise, NCC-1701-D
From: Marissa Flores, U.S.S. Chamberlain, NCC-56810
Subject: Science Fair

Dear Captain,

I know you probably hate me because of what I told you in my last letter, and if you do, I can't blame you. But if it's all right with you, I'm going to keep writing. It's so lonely here, and I've been getting pretty bad headaches since this morning.

I'm really worried about my dad. I'm worried about the rest of the crew too, but my dad especially. No one's eaten for like four days now. That's not healthy. Do you think they'll be okay, if we ever get out of here, I mean?

I wasn't going to tell you why I cheated on my science fair project, but I was thinking maybe I should. My dad says it's best to get everything off your chest, so that's what I'm going to do.

My mom, Elista Roth, is a professor at Starfleet Academy. You may have noticed that her last name is different from mine; that's because my mom and dad are divorced. Anyway, my mom is a science professor, and she's really busy. Sometimes I don't hear from her for eight or nine months at a time. When she does send a transmission . . . well, we don't have a lot to talk about.

I'm pretty good at science, but probably not good enough to win a science fair. Still, I desperately wanted to win, because I thought my mom might contact me. So, I cheated. And I won.

My mom did send me a note. It was only two words long, and she didn't even sign her name. It said, 'Good job!'

I'm not telling you this to justify what I did. I can still remember how I felt when I was on the bridge of the Enterprise. *I was so ashamed; I couldn't even look at you. And you were so nice and understanding and patient. I heard a rumor that you didn't like kids, so I was kind of afraid of you. But that rumor was obviously just something somebody made up. I think I would have died of fright if it hadn't been for you.*

There's one more thing I want to say, and since this might be my last letter, I'm going to say it now.

I've felt a whole lot better about myself ever since that day in the turbolift. I never knew I could be strong before. I'd always had my dad to protect me, and I was pretty frightened of doing anything on my own. But now I'm not afraid anymore. I mean, I get scared sometimes, but when I do, I think about how you called me 'Number One.' You had faith in me—something I'd never had before in myself.

So, I want to thank you, Captain Picard. No matter what happens now, I'm glad I got to meet you.

Sincerely,
Marissa Flores
"Number One"

P.S. I hope you're not mad at me.
P.P.S. My headache is getting worse. I had to stop writing several times because my vision got blurry. If you're coming, PLEASE COME SOON.

"Found it!" Riker exclaimed as the sensor chirped on his console station.

"On screen," Picard ordered.

The *Enterprise* had been scanning for the temporal hole for three hours before finally locating the phenomenon. Picard was beginning to wonder if they would run out of time, so he gave out a great sigh of relief when the swirling mouth of the anomaly opened up on the viewscreen.

"It's beautiful," Riker whispered.

"Beautiful and deadly," Picard observed. His first officer nodded accordingly.

Data turned around in his chair, his yellow eyes shining dispassionately. "Captain, we have located the *Chamberlain*. She is four hundred eighty-six point three kilometers inside the temporal hole."

"Can you lock a transporter beam?" Picard asked.

"Aye, sir."

Picard rose to his feet, straightening his uniform top. Tapping his communicator, Picard said, "Captain Picard to Doctor Crusher."

"Doctor Crusher here."

"Do you have the chroniton injections?"

"I do."

"Meet me in transporter room two in five minutes," ordered the captain. He turned to Commander Riker. "Number One, you have the bridge. Data, Geordi, you're with me."

"Captain, I must protest . . ."

Picard stopped his first officer with an outstretched hand. "I know what you're going to say; you may as well stop."

"Captain," Riker persisted. "This mission is far too dangerous. You need to stay on board the *Enterprise*."

Picard's eyes met the eyes of Commander Riker. For a moment they locked, and in that moment, something like understanding passed between the two officers. "Number One," Picard finally said, "do you recall the time the *Enterprise* passed through a quantum filament?"

"I do."

"My ankle was broken, if you recall, and I was trapped in a

turbolift with the little girl who wrote those letters." Riker nodded; Picard continued. "I ordered Marissa to get herself and the other children out of there, but she refused to leave without me."

Riker said nothing, but Picard could see the argument diminishing in the commander's eyes.

"She saved my life," Picard said. "And now she needs me to return the favor. I'm sure you can understand why I intend to go on this mission."

Riker sank silently into the captain's chair; Picard said nothing more as he stalked across the bridge toward the turbolift.

To: Captain Jean-Luc Picard, U.S.S. Enterprise, NCC-1701-D
From: Marissa Flores, U.S.S. Chamberlain, NCC-56810
Subject: Dizzy

Dear Captain,
  I think this is probably my last letter. Headache   much worse and feeling pretty dizzy.
  I've been staring   at the computer screen   for I don't know how longnowandI

Marissa slumped over her computer console, her head throbbing. The past couple of hours were so terrible that she could barely keep her eyes open. The end was coming. She sensed it, but she wasn't ready to admit defeat. Marissa knew that if she closed her eyes, she would most likely never open them again.

Voices in the corridor.

Marissa sat up, listening intently. *Silence.* She laid her head back on the desk, embracing the darkness.

"According to the ship's manifest, her quarters should be right over here." The voice was vaguely familiar, but Marissa was unable to place it.

"Get down to engineering, Geordi. Data and I will take care of Marissa." *Could it be? That sounded just like Captain Picard.*

"Impossible," Marissa whispered. "I'm probably hallucinating." The thought was confirmed when the doors to her quarters slid open and two figures in Starfleet uniforms stepped inside.

"Marissa, are you . . ."

Before the apparition could finish, Marissa toppled out of her chair. She tried to lift her head, but she was just too exhausted. The last thing she saw before she slipped into unconsciousness was Captain Picard's concerned face staring down at her.

Marissa awoke to a stinging pressure on the side of her neck. She turned to the android administering the hypo.

"Chroniton particles," Data explained. "Your exposure was deteriorating. That is why you were experiencing discomfort."

"Chroniton particles?" Marissa asked. Her head ached, but the pain was nothing compared with what she had been experiencing before. "Like in my theory?"

"Your theory was only partially accurate," said the android. "The *Chamberlain* is not trapped within a wormhole. In actuality, the ship has entered a temporal hole."

"A what?"

As Data explained the situation to Marissa, Captain Picard led them into the corridor. He navigated their way toward the bridge, and as Data's story drew to a close, the party reached one of the ship's turbolifts.

"Well," Captain Picard said, turning toward Marissa. "Here we are again." Marissa smiled, her blue eyes shining bright. They stepped into the turbolift. "Bridge," Picard stated. It came out like an order.

"I suppose you got my letters," Marissa said. "About my science fair project . . ." As the turbolift began to rise, Marissa dared to speak. She was thankful to see her former shipmates, but terrified just the same. If Captain Picard was here, it was because he had received her letters. That meant he knew the truth about her: She was just a no-good cheat.

She was about to continue when Picard stopped her with a stern look. "This is not the time," he snapped. "The ship is in serious danger, and it is our duty to try to save her."

Marissa silenced herself. Captain Picard was right, of course. It seemed like he was probably always right.

As the turbolift doors opened onto the bridge, Picard, Data, and Marissa spilled out into the spacious blue-carpeted room. Annie Brown, captain of the *Chamberlain,* sat poised on the edge of her chair, one hand clenched on the armrest, her eyes fixed on the viewscreen. The bridge crew stood at their posts, frozen like a holosuite program on pause. Her father was poised over the science station, his gaze locked on a display that had not changed in days.

Data approached the captain, placed the hypospray against her fleshy neck, and injected her with chroniton particles. Captain Brown blinked three or four times, and then looked around.

"What's happened?" she demanded. "What are you doing on my bridge?"

Picard and Data exchanged glances. "Captain Brown," said the android, "the *Chamberlain* has become trapped in a temporal hole."

As Data went through the explanation one more time, Marissa stared fixedly at the man who had come to rescue her from fate. Picard had placed his faith in her the day the *Enterprise* was nearly lost, and she had betrayed that faith. *Can he ever forgive me?*

Once the situation was clarified, Captain Brown was prepared to enact Data's plan of escape. Picard himself took the armory console, squeezing his way in front of Lieutenant Walden Taylor, the *Chamberlain*'s security officer, who stood like a statue.

"Lock torpedo on the apex of the temporal hole," Annie Brown ordered.

"Torpedo is locked," Picard said. "Geordi, are the engines ready?"

"Ready, sir." La Forge's disembodied voice spoke through the ship's communications system.

"Mister Data," said Captain Brown, "are you ready?"

"Yes, Captain." The android stood over the conn officer, reaching around the frozen pilot to reach the console.

Marissa was seated next to Captain Brown, in a chair normally reserved for the first officer. She was just trying to keep out of the way, and so she was pleasantly surprised when Brown turned to her with a warm smile on her face. "Marissa," she said, "give the order to fire."

Marissa looked from her current captain to her former. Picard gave her an emotionless nod. In a small, quiet voice, Marissa gave the order.

"Fire."

A photon torpedo tore across the sunflower landscape of the temporal hole, growing smaller and smaller as it approached the apex. For a long moment, it seemed as if nothing would happen. Then the torpedo detonated, and the phenomenon began to collapse. The *Chamberlain* started to move, slowly at first, but with greater velocity as the temporal hole's gravity weakened. A moment later, the ship was vomited back into normal space, coming to a stop alongside the *Enterprise*.

Marissa burst into tears as soon as the doors to her quarters slid closed behind her. She threw herself onto her bed, sobbing uncontrollably. The engines were humming belowdecks, and Marissa knew the *Chamberlain* was moving away from the *Enterprise*.

He hates me. He doesn't forgive me and now he hates me. Marissa's shoulders rose and fell as another round of weeping took her.

Almost as soon as the *Chamberlain* reappeared into normal space, her crew resumed the activities that they were doing just before the ship entered the temporal hole. There was a great deal of excitement as the *Enterprise* crew filled in their *Chamberlain* counterparts about what had happened. Marissa had rushed to her father, throwing herself into his arms before he even had a chance to understand what was happening.

"Marissa," he said. "What are you doing here?"

It was Captain Brown who answered. "Lieutenant Flores, your daughter's bravery saved the ship."

Peter Flores looked from Captain Brown to Marissa, a mixture of pride and confusion in his eyes. Their reunion was short-lived, however. The ship's security had to be addressed, and, savior of the *Chamberlain* or not, a teenager had no place on the bridge.

Before she returned to her quarters, Marissa attempted to speak with Captain Picard about her letters, but she couldn't even get close to him. With her emotions swinging wildly between joy and regret, Marissa slipped away from the bridge.

The tears dried up eventually, leaving Marissa with a headache almost as bad as the one she had had in the temporal hole. She drifted toward sleep. As the blessed darkness threatened to engulf her, she heard her computer chirp.

Marissa dragged herself out of bed. She moved to her desk, slipped into the chair, and tapped the computer controls. There was an incoming message for her; she opened the file.

To: Marissa Flores, U.S.S. Chamberlain, NCC-56810
From: Captain Jean-Luc Picard, U.S.S. Enterprise, NCC-1701-D
RE: Guilty Conscience

Number One,
*   You disappeared before we had a moment to talk, so I'm writing you this letter. First, I would be remiss if I did not mention my disappointment to learn that you cheated on your science fair project. That said, I believe you've learned your lesson.*
*   Second, I want to commend you. Without you, the* Chamberlain *would have been lost. You kept your head when others would have been wild with panic. I'm proud of you for that, and you should be proud of yourself.*

You're going to make an excellent Starfleet officer someday, Marissa. You have more than earned my forgiveness; you've earned my admiration.

Take care of yourself, Number One.

Sincerely,
Jean-Luc

P.S. Whenever I hear someone singing "Frère Jacques," I can't help but think of you.

Passages of Deceit

Sarah A. Seaborne

The electrical shock was slight, like hitting a nerve, but the sudden realization of what was about to happen dropped him to his knees. His portable light source shattered against a rock, and two miles below the planet's surface, Jean-Luc Picard collapsed in complete darkness.

"*Enterpri . . .*" he whispered as a great pain stabbed through his brain. A second pain, exponentially more painful than the first, sent him into a fetal position on the newly carved floor of the mine shaft. A split second before his mind exploded into broken images, one word echoed through the crumbling pathways—*No!*

"Mister Data, are you almost finished with the scans?" Commander Riker asked, leaning back in the captain's chair and frowning at the forward screen. He tried to look attentive, but in fact he was bored. The *Enterprise* had been in orbit over a small moon since shortly after dropping off her captain for an archaeological survey of mines that were being opened for the first time in eight hundred years. He could well imagine Captain Picard having the time of his life crawling over ancient mining equipment and through small crevices while Riker stared blindly at a floating rock for five hours.

"Scans will be finished in twenty-eight minutes, thirty-six seconds."

Riker looked at the white and gray sphere displayed on the forward viewscreen. Visually, it looked like a thousand other moons they had studied over the years. The reports he had glanced at four hours ago indicated that it was composed of the same elements and minerals as most of the other moons in this sector. Why Starfleet wanted so much time put into this particular moon was beyond him. He shifted in the chair and stretched. *In twenty-eight minutes, thirty-six seconds,* he thought, *I'll be snoring.*

"Commander," Data said, turning and looking at Riker. "There is a subspace message from Ka'Tral."

"The captain can't be ready to come home this soon." Riker smiled, sitting up straight and nodding to Data. "Put it through."

The image of a gray-green face filled the viewscreen. Riker knew little about the inhabitants of Ka'Tral, but he guessed it was the face of a young man. Briefly, he wondered if the long, brown line down the right side of his face and neck was a normal physical characteristic. There was a long pause, then the young man began speaking in a flat, monotone voice.

"I am Glorell. Interpreter for the Ka'Tral. There was an accident in the mines. Captain Picard requires medical attention."

Riker jumped up and approached the viewscreen, pausing beside the communications console. "How long before we can get back to Ka'Tral, Data?"

"At current speed, about, three hours, forty-eight minutes."

"Do we have that kind of time?" Riker asked the viewscreen, feeling adrenaline surge through him as the young man looked away.

Glorell looked back at Riker. *"We do not know. We have not been able to ascertain what happened to him."*

"We're on our way. My chief medical officer will need to speak to you as soon as possible to assess the captain's condition."

"*I understand. I will leave this frequency open.*" A starfield view replaced the green face on the screen.

"Data, contact Starfleet. We need to go faster than warp five. Tell them it's an emergency. Send all the information you have on Ka'Tral to the captain's ready room. I don't like the sound of this." Riker hit his combadge. "Doctor Crusher, meet me in the captain's ready room. Now."

Captain Picard twisted against his restraints. Glorell closed his eyes and relaxed, trying to mold his thoughts around the captain's broken pathways. The doctors had already given up. The breaks were too severe. But Prime Minister Sebridge told him to try again. And again if necessary. They had to know what the captain knew before they could release him back to his people. *Pain.* Glorell clenched his fists. The human's images were almost too intense for him to grasp. *Burning.* Glorell's arms were on fire. *Screams.* Long, agonizing screams that evoked images in his own mind of being tortured beyond what he could endure. Trying to hold on to the captain's broken mind, Glorell wondered how long any man could endure this deluge of painful images.

Beverly Crusher paced back and forth in the transporter room. "Come on, Data," she said, tugging on her lab coat.

The interpreter had told her so little. They knew as little about human physiology as the Starfleet database knew about theirs. The Ka'Tral was an isolationist species who had begun to interact with other planets only thirty years before. Deanna said they communicated telepathically. The interpreter, Glorell, had been specially bred to communicate with nontelepathic species. The long scar down his face and neck was evidence that, even with a Betazoid mother, surgery had been required to create functional vocal cords.

She called the bridge. "What's taking so long? We've been in orbit for almost ten minutes."

Riker's voice filled the transporter room. *"The Ka'Tral don't want Data to beam down with you. They don't allow anyone access to their planet whose mind they can't read, and they're not willing to make an exception."*

Doctor Crusher stepped onto the transporter pad. "I know Data insists on examining the mines where they found him, but the captain can't wait. Send me now and work it out."

Minutes later, she found herself in what reminded her of a twentieth-century Earth hospital waiting room. *All it needs is a few slick magazines,* she thought, looking at the cushioned benches and square tables.

"It's funny what you think of at a time like this," Glorell said quietly. He was standing in the corner of the room where he knew she wouldn't see him when she first arrived. He needed to assess her unguarded thoughts. He smiled as he approached her, vaguely remembering that the curving of the lips was a calming signal for humanoids. "Instead of jumping directly to the point, we notice small, inconsequential things."

"You read my mind," Beverly said.

"In my culture, it is simply part of life," he replied, motioning her to follow him.

"It is on other telepathic planets we visit too," she retorted, surprised at how angry she felt. "But they have rules of etiquette so they don't offend other species."

Glorell stopped and turned to her. "I apologize, Doctor Crusher. The Ka'Tral are only beginning to have contact with outside species. On our world, almost everything is common knowledge. If we have something we want kept secret, we have the ability to shield our thoughts. I take it this is not something humans can do."

"Not being telepathic, we don't have the need," Doctor Crusher said. "Now, where is the captain?"

Glorell began walking again. "He's in a room at the end of the hall. As you know, our doctors have attempted to treat your captain telepathically. So far, they have been unable to produce a single clear, complete thought. It's as if your captain is drowning in a sea of disconnected images. Here we are."

Glorell stepped aside as they entered the room, and Beverly Crusher gasped.

"What have you done to him?" she demanded, staring at the thin, almost naked figure writhing on a narrow bed. His shirt was gone, and deep scratches crisscrossed his chest and moved down his arms. His arms and legs were bound to the edges of the bed with thick straps, and the skin around the straps was raw and bleeding. She rushed toward the bed, almost gagging on the overwhelming smell of feces, blood, and urine that filled the small room.

"He has been restrained for his own safety," Glorell answered calmly. "He was scratching himself until he bled."

Shaking her head as if to clear away the image before her, Beverly placed her hand on Jean-Luc's arm. He screamed and tried to roll away from her.

"Touching his skin burns him," Glorell informed her.

Doctor Crusher pulled her hand back. Then, pushing her emotions away, she pulled her tricorder out of her pocket and went to work.

Do you sense any duplicity, Glorell? Sebridge asked telepathically. He was in his office, a few blocks from the hospital, but his mind was focused on Doctor Crusher. He would normally pick up any signs of deception, but this situation was difficult. The Federation had never sent humans to Ka'Tral before, so Sebridge didn't know enough about them to know whether or not they could shield their thoughts.

No, Prime Minister. The human's horror and concern are genuine. She is frightened and doesn't know what has happened to her captain.

So the chief medical officer is unaware of any conspiracy to obtain information the Ka'Tral are not willing to share, Sebridge thought, *that is a relief. But what about this android they want to send down? Do we let him beam down to the mines? Captain Picard collapsed near the north shaft. He shouldn't have been anywhere near that area. So the question is, did he foolishly wander off, or did he seek out that area for some other reason.* Sebridge frowned. He wanted Ka'Tral to be accepted into the Federation. Once it was a member, its access to other worlds would expand exponentially, and with that access, their trade.

What do you want me to tell the Enterprise? Glorell asked. *They want an answer.*

Very well, their android can inspect the cave, Sebridge responded. *But I see no reason why he should examine the exact place where the captain was found. Tell the guards to escort him to a location near the south entrance, where the captain should have been.*

Data walked behind the guards, constantly moving his tricorder back and forth as they passed several intersecting shafts. His readings indicated that most of the shafts were indeed almost one thousand years old, their mineral and alloy content consistent with that of other planets in the sector. There were a few shafts, however, that had been constructed within the last five years, and those were the ones that produced the readings that Data found interesting. His tricorder, like the one Captain Picard had taken into the mine, was specially calibrated to detect chemicals used in all known biological weapons. Many of these chemicals were present, but in amounts so small the Ka'Tral could easily explain them away. Suddenly the men stopped and pointed at a place on the ground. Data looked at the tricorder.

"Am I to understand this is where Captain Picard collapsed?" Data asked into a small communicator Glorell had given him. The interpreter had instructed him to say what he wanted into the communicator. Glorell would either respond the same way or instruct the guards to do as Data requested.

After a moment, the men nodded and pointed again. Data adjusted the settings on the tricorder. They were clearly not telling him the truth. Captain Picard had never been near this location. He stooped and picked up the tricorder the captain had taken with him. It was pressed against a rock. Data quickly confirmed that the memory had been erased. If it was a normal tricorder, they would never know what the captain had found before he collapsed. This one had been modified to store information in two locations, and Data had confirmed that both were in working order before giving the tricorder to his captain. What he had been unable to check, but had obviously worked, was the overload feature. When the readings on the tricorder reached a level that could be produced only by the presence of substantial amounts of the designated chemicals, it shorted itself out, separating the two memories and activating the nanites that had been stored in the captain's mechanical heart.

"I would like to see Captain Picard now," Data said, looking around to confirm nothing else had been planted for him to find. No one moved for several seconds; then the guards motioned for him to follow them.

A few minutes later, he stood before his captain. As he looked at the shrunken, trembling man on the bed, Data acknowledged that it was a good thing he was not human. If he had human emotions, he would have been overwhelmed with guilt and anguish over his role in the mission.

"It's like he developed full-blown Irumodic syndrome," Doctor Crusher said. "All the symptoms are there. But it just doesn't happen like this. It takes years to develop. And he only had a predisposition to developing it anyway."

"Perhaps he should be transported to sickbay."

"I've told Glorell that, but he says the prime minister must okay the transfer. We're waiting for a response from him."

Data looked at the captain, his internal clock telling him that Picard had only two hours and twenty-seven minutes before the effects of the nanites would be irreversible. It was his responsibility to save the captain's mind if at all possible, but he could not endanger the mission in doing so. He turned back to Doctor Crusher.

"I will beam back to the *Enterprise* with the captain's tricorder. Perhaps we can retrieve something that will tell us what happened to him." *And,* he thought, cognizant of the fact that the internal dialogue of his positronic brain was safe from telepathic minds, *the sooner I can send Starfleet the readings, the sooner I can try to save the captain.*

Agony. Blood. Dark. Burning. Death.

Glorell turned his thoughts from the captain and watched Doctor Crusher. He had been reading her mind as she examined Captain Picard and was impressed with her ability to separate herself from her emotions. It was only when the thought of Irumodic syndrome came into her mind that fear overtook her for a moment. He had quickly contacted Sebridge and requested information on the condition.

A defect in something called the parietal lobe, Sebridge had informed him shortly after the android left. *There are many resulting disorders, and most of them have the same symptoms as Captain Picard. It usually takes years to reach this stage, but perhaps one of the chemicals in the mine triggered it.*

So you believe this is what he has?

Sebridge sighed. *I don't know. You're there, what you do think?*

Glorell closed his eyes and searched Doctor Crusher's mind. The captain's lack of response to anything she had done was alarming her. Frustration was growing. He found what he was looking for and withdrew. He didn't need to read her thoughts to know she and Picard had a relationship in addition to the one they shared as chief medical officer and captain.

It doesn't matter what I believe, he told Sebridge. *She believes he has it.*

It took almost an hour for the prime minister to approve the transfer and for Captain Picard to be beamed to the *Enterprise*'s sickbay. Doctor Crusher put him directly into stasis. It wouldn't help his condition, but she needed to buy some time to figure out what had happened.

Immediately upon his return to the *Enterprise,* Data had begun retrieving the data from a second memory capsule inside the tricorder. While he waited for the information to complete downloading, he sent a subspace message to the *Vortex,* a medical ship that only he knew was hiding on the other side of the moon he had been scanning earlier in the day. Starfleet Intelligence had determined the moon was out of the Ka'Tral's telepathic range, and one of the scientists waiting on the *Vortex* was the woman who had designed the nanites that had incapacitated Captain Picard. She had also designed the nanites that could cure him.

When the captain's transfer was approved, Data had hurried to supervise the transport, specifically looking for indications that a biological weapon might have been planted somewhere on either Captain Picard or Doctor Crusher. He was unaware of anything happening that might have made the Ka'Tral suspicious enough to risk killing the crew of the *Enterprise,* but the chemicals the tricorder had detected were identical with those used on several of the planets on the Ka'Tral's trade route. If word got out the Ka'Tral were trading in biological weapons, they had more to lose than just membership in the Federation. They therefore had strong incentive to make sure that kind of information never left the planet.

Once the captain was in stasis, Data requested to speak privately with Commander Riker and Doctor Crusher.

"This better be important," Beverly said as the door swished open and she entered the captain's ready room. "I should be down with the captain."

Data waited until she sat down to recite the dialogue lines he had been given almost a year earlier. "The medical ship *Vortex* is in the vicinity. Doctor Toby Russell, who is a leading expert in Irumodic syndrome, is aboard. I believe . . ."

"No," Beverly said, shaking her head. "We've encountered her before. She's too willing to experiment on her patients. She almost killed Worf."

"But ultimately, she saved his life."

"Ultimately, his Klingon anatomy saved his life," Beverly argued.

Data turned to Commander Riker, who returned his look in silence, and suddenly realized he had a decision to make. Starfleet had given him a script to follow, but it had not provided the script to the other two key players. If he simply tried to press the issue of taking the captain to Doctor Russell, their arrival there might be too late. He could not endanger the mission, but he found himself unwilling to sacrifice Captain Picard.

He tapped his combadge. "Bridge, what is the distance between the *Enterprise* and Ka'Tral?"

"Data," Commander Riker said from behind the captain's desk. "What is going on?"

Data waited for the response from the bridge before speaking. "The Ka'Tral is the most powerful telepathic species Starfleet has ever encountered. At our present rate of speed, your minds will not be safe from them for another twenty-seven minutes."

"What does that have to do with Captain Picard?" Riker asked.

Data paused, uncertain how to proceed. Finally, he said it as simply as possible. "I cannot answer your questions for another twenty-six minutes, thirty-eight seconds. In the meantime, I must recommend that we go to emergency warp and take the captain to Doctor Russell."

Riker sat back and looked at Data for a long moment. "You're asking me to blindly trust you, Data? No questions asked?"

Doctor Crusher looked directly into Data's face. "Are you telling us that the captain's best chance at recovery is with Doctor Russell?"

He nodded.

Beverly turned back to Riker. "Glorell was reading my mind as I beamed in. I didn't like that. And while I don't trust Toby Russell, I trust Data. If he says we need to do this and he can't tell us why, then as chief medical officer, I recommend we do it."

Riker drummed his fingers on the arm of the chair and looked at Data. Finally, he rose and walked around the desk. "Data, I'm going to be down in sickbay with the captain. You have command of the *Enterprise*. For the next twenty-six minutes, nineteen seconds anyway."

Data almost sprinted onto the bridge, barking out commands and hurrying to the captain's console. Within seconds, he created an encrypted message to Starfleet headquarters listing the biogenic components the tricorder had detected in the mines. It was an impressive list by anyone's standards. The Federation had been trying for months to get definite information regarding several allegations that the Ka'Tral were creating biological weapons and selling them to the highest bidder. Unfortunately, Ka'Tral telepathic abilities were so strong it was virtually impossible to send an informant into their midst.

Then the Ka'Tral had announced the reopening of mines that had been sealed for almost eight hundred years. In an unusual move, they had invited several archaeologists from the galaxy to be the first visitors into the mines. Starfleet, of course, had wasted no time in obtaining an invitation for Jean-Luc Picard. Not only did he have a solid reputation in the archaeological community, but he also had a genetic predisposition to develop a terrible disease that would render his mind unreadable. That was where Doctor Russell had come into the equation.

Data contacted the *Vortex*. Even though the seven scientists on the *Vortex* knew about Captain Picard's condition, he spoke as if they did not, keenly aware that other people on the bridge would hear the conversation. "Doctor Russell, Captain Jean-Luc Picard has developed symptoms of severe Irumodic syndrome. I will have Doctor Crusher send you all the data we have at this time. We should be able to transport him to your ship in twenty-five minutes."

"How long since he collapsed, Data?" Doctor Russell asked.

"According to the captain's tricorder, five hours, eighteen minutes ago."

Doctor Russell gasped. *"Five hours, eighteen minutes. He's almost out of time."*

Data did not reply. In twenty-five minutes, the captain's chance of full recovery would be less than thirty-three percent. Reflecting on the events of the last five hours and eighteen minutes, he did not see anything he could have done to minimize the amount of time necessary to recover the captain and the tricorder.

"Optimize your transporter beam and get him over here," Doctor Russell ordered.

"It would not be one hundred percent safe, but I believe we could narrow . . ."

"I'm a neurogeneticist, not an engineer," Doctor Russell said. *"And quite frankly, we don't have time for this lesson. Just do what you can to get him here. His life . . . or at least a life worth having . . . depends on it."*

Doctor Beverly Crusher sat at the computer terminal in the *Vortex* sickbay studying the test protocols and results on the nanites that had been injected into Captain Picard—both the instigators and the retrieval nanites. Once the *Enterprise* had reached the moon, she, Riker, and Data had met again in the captain's ready room, and Data had told them everything. *Everything he knew,* she corrected herself. He didn't know about a late-night talk she and Jean-Luc had had a few months after tests had shown that Irumodic syndrome might well be in his future. It was the one and only time Jean-Luc had opened up to her about the fear that woke him up in the middle of the night. The fear that he would become a frightened, delusional old man who could not remember the extraordinary life he had led or the extraordinary people he had encountered along the way. *He was so afraid of losing himself, of becoming little more than an animal,* she thought, *and now he has.*

She forced herself to begin reading again. *If there is any hope of saving Jean-Luc, it has to lie in these records.* But the more she read, the more upset she became. The studies were well done, what there were of them. The nanites were nowhere near ready to be implanted in a human. No legitimate scientific study would have allowed it. *Clandestine,* she thought. *The only reason they were used prematurely was because this was a clandestine operation. And Jean-Luc Picard gave his consent.*

"He was so excited to be among the first to view those mines," Crusher muttered. "How could he have been so excited when he knew this might happen?"

"He didn't know," Doctor Russell answered. "He was given the least amount of information possible so that when the time came to use the nanites, his mind would not give him away beforehand."

Doctor Crusher turned from the terminal and looked at the captain. She wished she could see the new nanites at work fighting the old ones. If the retrieval nanites won, the *Enterprise* would get her captain back. If the instigator nanites won, Jean-Luc Picard would almost certainly spend the rest of his days in a life-care facility, unaware that his sacrifice had saved the Federation from welcoming into its fold the makers and distributors of highly advanced biological weapons.

"When he comes out of this," Crusher said, refusing to even consider that he might not, "I want you to tell me all the instigator nanites were deployed or destroyed. That there are none left in his system that can be used against him later."

No one answered her.

"Just what I expected from you." Crusher stood and looked at Doctor Russell. "You don't know the answer, do you? Starfleet gave you a puzzle to solve. A toy to play with. And you ran with it, unwilling or unable to look at the consequences of your work."

"Your captain chose the assignment," the younger woman said, looking directly at Doctor Crusher for the first time since the three *Enterprise* officers had beamed over. "He could have turned it down, but he didn't."

"But did he have all the information he needed to make an informed decision?" Doctor Crusher asked. "According to your own notes, you don't know if using nanites to cause the instantaneous onset of end-stage Irumodic syndrome, even if the retrieval nanites do exactly what they're supposed to do, will cause him to develop

Irumodic syndrome later in his life. Before today, that was only a possibility. You may have made it inevitable."

"Let's save the arguing and recriminations until after we know he's all right," Riker said, stepping closer to the biobed. "Data estimates that we missed the safe zone by at least eighteen minutes. How long until we know exactly how important those eighteen minutes were?"

Doctor Russell ran a tricorder over the captain's sleeping form. "We should have picked up something by now. In the simulations, we had a return to baseline brainwave function within eight minutes."

"But this wasn't a simulation," Riker said. "And the Ka'Tral didn't alert us to the problem until three hours had passed. So we were behind the proverbial eight ball from the beginning."

"I don't know the reference." The young doctor glanced up at Riker. "But if you mean this assignment was problematic from the start, I would have to agree with you. However, now Starfleet has the information it needs to reject the Ka'Trals' request to join the Federation, and we have discovered the source of biological weapons that have devastated several planets in this sector. Not a bad day's work."

"But what about Jean-Luc Picard?" Beverly Crusher asked.

Doctor Russell blushed. "I didn't mean to minimize what he's going through, but the mission was always to get evidence that the Ka'Tral were creating and distributing biological weapons. We got that information, thereby saving millions of lives."

"And what about Jean-Luc Picard?" Beverly Crusher repeated.

The red in Doctor Russell's face darkened. "All we can do now is sit back and see if the retrieval nanites do their job."

"And keep running your tests," Beverly said. "Collecting more data about your nanites. You had an unqualified success with instigator nanites. I'm sure Starfleet will give you a commendation for that. So the failure of your retrieval nanites to bring him back will be just a footnote in your paper."

Doctor Russell said nothing.

Doctor Crusher pushed the young scientist away from the biobed. "If you can't do more for him here, then I'm taking him back to the *Enterprise*. Data can run your tests for you. I'm going to try to help him. Because he's *my* patient. He's *my* captain! And dammit, he's my friend."

"Doctor," Data said, reaching for Beverly Crusher's arm.

"Don't, Data." Beverly turned on him. "I can't even look at you right now. The idea that you did this to him . . ."

Riker gently pushed Beverly away from the biobed.

"*Enterprise,*" a hoarse voice whispered.

Everyone in the room stopped and turned toward the captain.

"Did he just . . . ?" Riker asked.

Doctor Russell ran her tricorder on the captain in silence. Several minutes passed before she lowered the tricorder and smiled. "The retrieval nanites are working."

"Will he be all right?" Riker asked.

"We can't be sure for a few more hours, but the scans look good."

There was an awkward silence, then Beverly Crusher spoke. "I apologize for my outburst. It was unprofessional."

Doctor Russell shook her head. "Don't apologize. I'm well aware of your feelings toward me. You expressed them quite well the last time we met. And you are correct when you say there's nothing we can do for him here that you can't do aboard the *Enterprise*. Data can monitor the nanites. I think the captain will recover more quickly in a familiar setting."

Doctor Crusher stepped closer to the biobed and touched the captain's arm, relieved when he didn't jerk away from her. At least her touch didn't burn him anymore. She nodded at Riker.

"*Enterprise,* four to beam directly to sickbay," Riker said, pausing when Doctor Crusher held up her hand. "On my command."

Beverly Crusher looked at Data, her hand still touching the captain's arm. "I should apologize for my outburst at you too, Data.

I'm calm now, and I know you were following orders. I also know that you retain the knowledge of what kind of shock is needed to activate any nanites remaining in the captain's system. And I'm telling you here and now, if you use that knowledge, I know where your off switch is."

Final Flight

John Takis

He can see it now: the Scimitar. *It drifts into view, wreathed in smoke and sparks from damaged conduits. The corridor in which he stands is ruptured, terminating in empty space. Gases and debris spill out into the Rift. Geordi is behind him, watching, protected from the vacuum by a forcefield. Geordi, tender and warm-hearted . . . Geordi, his closest friend.*

Geordi, who must now be left behind.

He runs.

His speed is tremendous, especially given the fact that he faces essentially no air resistance. His artificial legs move as fast as they ever have. Yet his mind is faster. He notes the pitch and yaw of the deck beneath him. He calculates and adjusts as he runs. The whole time he keeps his optical sensors locked on to the Scimitar. *The Reman warship is not entirely visible, being partially obscured by a cloaking device. He fills in the missing data based on prior observations. He follows the ship's movement, calculating its trajectory*

115

and creating a mental projection in three dimensions. There can be no margin of error in his calculations. He will have time for only one jump. He considers that no biological being could make this leap with confidence. But he is confident.

He is nearing the ragged lip of the deck now. The starfield grows continually more visible. It is an arena of battle, and his superenhanced vision can pick out every twisting fragment of shrapnel. Mercifully, there are no bodies in his field of vision. The space outside the breach is lit by a soft green glow. Clouds of particles cast off shimmers of reflected starlight. Electromagnetic distortion creates flashes of staggeringly complex energy patterns, invisible to human eyes—but not to him.

It is beautiful. The thought breaks over him, and in his mind he seems to stumble. The shock of the emotion is powerful; he has not had an active emotion chip in some time. His forward motion seems to cease. The stars become frozen, two-dimensional . . . for a moment they swarm with guessed-at constellations. Then he is moving again. He consults his chronometer; no time has passed. His feet pound forward, oblivious of his mental goings-on. It is a strange experience, but he has little time to wonder before the critical moment is upon him.

His boots grip the rim of the sheared-off deck and send him launching into the void. . . .

For a 152-year-old man, Leonard McCoy had an amazingly steady grip. He took a sip of tea, grimacing somewhat at the heat, then set the cup down without a hint of a tremor. Age had not dulled his eyes, evident by the way the retired admiral peered at Picard from within a network of cobwebbed wrinkles. They were piercing eyes, intelligent, and not lacking in compassion.

"I'm sorry for your loss, Jean-Luc," McCoy said. "I've said my final good-byes to more friends and shipmates than I care to remember."

"It never gets any easier, does it?" Picard asked.

McCoy shook his ancient head. "Nope."

Picard took hold of his own Earl Grey tea, allowing the warm china to settle against the cusp of his hand. It was a wonderful feeling. The admiral had insisted that authentic, handcrafted china made all the difference—"None of that modern replicated crap," had been his exact words—and Picard was beginning to believe him.

"I appreciate your sympathy, Admiral."

"Doctor," McCoy broke in, with a dry cackle. "Always hated being called 'Admiral.' They haven't revoked my certification yet, so you can call me "Doctor." Or how about 'Bones'? You're the captain of the *Enterprise,* I s'pose you've earned it."

Picard shifted awkwardly in his seat. "Perhaps 'Leonard'?"

McCoy shrugged, and Picard could see indentations rise beneath the fabric that covered his shoulders, where an exoskeletal frame was mounted. "I appreciate your sympathy, Leonard," Picard continued. "But I'm not sure I'm quite ready to consider him lost."

"Oh?"

"That's actually the reason I requested this meeting with you. As you know, the *Enterprise* is still undergoing repairs, and it's given me some time to reflect."

McCoy took up his cup of tea and settled back into his chair. "Go on, Captain."

"You are familiar with the unusual case of B-4, an android of Doctor Soong's who is apparently an early prototype of Lieutenant Commander Data."

"Yeah, I've read the reports."

"What you may not have known is that before Data's . . . before he saved my life, he transferred his memory engrams into B-4 in an attempt to unlock his brother's potential for growth . . ."

McCoy did not let him finish. "You're going to ask me about Spock."

The bluntness of it startled Picard, and his jaw hung open momentarily. After a moment, he composed himself, sitting straighter and tugging at his tunic. "My position in Starfleet has given me access to certain classified files, including the private logs of James

Kirk regarding the Genesis incident. I was struck by . . . certain parallels. You acted as host, for a time, for Spock's *katra*—his life-force, his inner being—until the regeneration of his body, when his *katra* was restored to him."

"The *fal-tor-pan*." McCoy shook his head. "I'm still a bit fuzzy on all the ritual details, Captain. I can't tell you how it was done, or if it would work on androids. To the best of my knowledge, no non-Vulcan has ever managed to accomplish it. Doesn't even work for all Vulcans, so I'm told. They don't even all *believe* in it. Anyway, it sounds as though the transfer has already taken place in your case. Did it work?"

Picard frowned. "It's impossible to say at this point. Data himself believed the experiment was a failure. I have reason to believe it may have had some effect . . . but if the Data I knew is in there, somewhere within B-4, he has yet to concretely express himself. I wonder if it's even possible . . ." He trailed off, at a loss for words.

"Captain," McCoy said, "are you asking me if an android has a soul?"

"Oh, no," Picard said, shaking his head. "If any of us has a soul, Data did—of that much I am certain. Whatever it is that makes us human, that drives us to be more than we are, he possessed in abundance."

McCoy snorted. "Wouldn't have thought it the first time I met him, just before they launched your *Enterprise*-D."

"Yes, I remember."

"Of course, I didn't think there was anything human about Spock the first time I met *him*, either. So I guess the question's not did he have a soul, but rather, does it still exist?"

Picard nodded slowly. "I have always tried to remain open to extreme possibilities."

"Wise," said McCoy. "Remind me to tell you about the incident at Sigma Draconis."

"I suppose what I'm looking for . . ." A small, weary smile formed on Picard's lips. " . . . is hope."

"That's not a bad thing to look for," McCoy said. "But I'm

afraid I'm not going to be of much help. Never was much good with figuring out machines, sentient or not. You'll have to look up Scotty if you want any high-tech voodoo done." He abruptly broke into a massive yawn, then blinked his eyes. Very suddenly, he looked his age. He sagged in his chair. "Dammit, Jim, we never used to get this tired this fast," he muttered.

"I appreciate your taking the time for me," Picard said softly, a heartfelt smile on his face. "It was certainly very good to speak with you, and I didn't really come expecting anything more than that. I'll let you return to your rest now." He made as if to stand, but McCoy reached across the table and grabbed his wrist with surprising force.

"Listen to the voice of experience, son. . . ." McCoy's wizened voice was slow and deliberate. "I've been where you are. Cosmic thoughts. You're looking for answers, asking the big questions." His bright eyes gleamed. "Go ahead. Ask. Petition God Almighty if you want to. Just remember . . . it doesn't matter what the religion or what the planet: sometimes the answer you get back isn't the answer you wanted, and there's not a damn thing you can do about it but accept it and move on." He paused. Beneath his shirt, his exoskeleton flexed and he drew in a breath. "But if he was your friend, you have to take every chance, explore every possibility. The human conscience demands nothing less."

Picard's smile faded and his gaze became distant. "Is there reason for optimism, do you suppose?"

McCoy laughed. "There's never a *reason* for optimism. But don't let that stop you!"

He flies free, traversing the space between the Enterprise *and the* Scimitar. *His arms and legs flex, adjusting his balance in order to maintain the necessary course. It is a relatively simple act for his positronic brain to perform, which leaves him ample time to reflect that the situation in which he now finds himself is his own fault.*

He thinks back to the moment when the captain had declared his intention to beam over to the enemy ship. Everyone had seemed to understand that it was a probable one-way trip. Everyone had understood the risk. Data himself had thought he had understood it. His duty had been clear—he had volunteered to go in his captain's stead.

But had it been only duty that led him to volunteer—a product of his Starfleet programming? Examining his memory, he found a curious lack of data . . . as if experiences had passed through him without leaving any record. How to account for this mental gap—the inexplicable sluggishness on the part of his positronic network? Unknowing exposure to Thalaron radiation, perhaps? Normally, he would file the conundrum away for later analysis . . . perhaps in consultation with Geordi or Counselor Troi. But he is not sure he will have that opportunity. And in the face of possible deactivation, the question seems unusually significant:

How to account for the fact that he had forgotten about the Emergency Transport Unit?

Of course he had not "forgotten" it, precisely. . . . Soong's children were incapable of forgetting even the smallest detail; even the prototypical B-4 exhibited this characteristic. The real puzzler was: Why had he not thought of the ETU before his captain's departure? One of the most highly advanced computers known to science, he experienced millions of thought processes per second. He had engaged the problem. The ETU would have been a logical response to the scenario . . . had he thought of it. Perhaps there had been an error . . . unlikely, but not impossible. Whatever the root cause, the impulse to offer himself in his captain's place had been so powerful—and had seemed so logical at the time—that it had assigned itself maximum priority, overriding all other considerations. The implications were striking: there had been mental processes taking place of which he had not been consciously aware. He had been . . .

Preoccupied.

Distracted.

What a triumph this would have been under other circum-

stances! He recalls experimenting with dreams, his consultation with a holographic representation of Sigmund Freud. But if this is a breakthrough, it brings him no pleasure now. There is, after all, a very good chance that his all-too-human error will be responsible for the death of his captain . . . his friend. This thought loops continually through Data's mind, and he finds that he cannot subdue it. It resurfaces again and again, replicating itself across his neural net, clogging positronic pathways. Realizing that his processing ability will become compromised in short order, he scans his subsystems for any trace of a virus or defective code. He finds nothing. Is this the experience which humans classify as guilt? *he wonders.*

Ultimately, it is the urgency of the approaching hulk of the Scimitar *that breaks the discomfiting thought loop. As the moment of action draws near, his rigorous calculations kick in. As he predicted, his grab at a spar of wreckage is insufficient to halt his momentum. Instead, he uses the brief contact to modify his trajectory, allowing his body to go limp. Now he must trust to his memory engrams. Given his recent self-questioning, it is something of a leap of faith.*

Seconds later, he slams forcefully into an invisible section of hull. Grabbing tightly, he climbs along the invisible surface. Microsensors in his fingers assess the metal beneath him, probing for resonances and electromagnetic fluctuations that will give some indication of what lies underneath. It does not take him long to locate an access panel; it takes less time to rip it open with his bare hands.

He is inside the ship now, standing in a corridor that he will follow until he can find his way to the bridge. On impulse, he turns and takes one last look at the stars. He has calculated the odds; he does not think he will ever see them again. A raw and inexplicable energy courses through his positronic pathways. This sensation . . . is it . . . fear? Gratitude? There is no emotion chip to consult for reference. He has noticed that humans sometimes speak to themselves when they believe that no one can hear them . . . acts of vocalization, Counselor Troi once told him, that are reassuring

of themselves. The gesture seems appropriate. "Thank you," he
says aloud, *to no one in particular. And then,* "I am frightened." *He
suspects this is true.*

Then he is running again.

"The life-force survives the destruction of the body. This is testi-
fied to by the unyielding traditions of numberless worlds. You bear
witness by your own science. For—is it not so?—transporting me
here to your ship, you destroyed my physical form and created in its
place an exact duplicate. Yet I know that my *katra* is unbroken. You
also sense this fundamental truth, or you would not have sought me
out. Is this not so, Captain?"

The speaker was male, slightly taller and thinner than Picard. He
sat facing Picard across the ready-room table. He was draped in
elaborate, overlapping sand-colored robes that were inscribed with
strange symbols and characters. His face was thin, his gaze hyp-
notic. His eyes shone with passionate intensity. His name was
Symek.

He was Vulcan.

Picard considered his response carefully. "I do not wish to debate semantics," he said. "You are certainly entitled to your meta-
physical beliefs."

"Then you're not a believer?"

Picard took a deep breath. "That depends on what you mean by
'believer.' I do not wish to remove possibilities out of hand. You
see, I owe a great debt to my friend. It was his . . . quest, I suppose
you might say, to grow beyond himself. I have learned to look beyond myself in order to survive on a number of occasions. I have
learned to respect that my own beliefs about what is possible and
what is not possible are not always correct."

"A hard truth."

"I had some hard teachers."

Symek spread his hands in a gesture of receptivity. "Where
should you like to begin?"

Picard ran a hand over his chin. "To begin with, you were a

difficult person to get ahold of," he said. "Even for a man with my connections. I know very little about you, other than the fact that you're one of the few Vulcans still writing publicly about the practice of *fal-tor-pan.*"

Symek cocked his head slightly to one side in a pedantic fashion. "The Order of Sybok prefers to remain out of the headlines, Captain, as I'm sure you will appreciate. Vulcan society, in its 'enlightenment,' shows little patience or toleration for our way of thinking." He pursed his lips. "They are . . . shall we say, *selective* in their reading of the Scrolls of Surak. In his day, Sybok, our own noble patron, was driven away in disgrace."

"My point being," Picard said, "that I still have relatively little idea what it is exactly that you do."

"Individuals, when confronted with mortality, often experience unique traumas and psychological disorders. Rather than attempting to avoid the emotional consequences of such inner devastation, as with the damaging and ultimately futile suppression techniques of the Vulcan majority, we advocate facing emotion head-on. Only in facing one's pain can one conquer, and thereby remove, one's pain."

"And to that end you employ holotechnology?"

"The original technique, pioneered by our patron, was accomplished without the aid of technology. Unfortunately, few Vulcans possess his remarkable gifts. Today, we employ the most sophisticated holograms known to science. Realistic—and effective—enough that our methods have been deplored by many supposedly 'reputable' schools. You may have heard stories, Captain, disseminated by our unscrupulous detractors. I urge you not to take them at face value. Our treatments are consensual and fully within the boundaries of Federation law."

"If I suspected otherwise, Mister Symek, I assure you I would never have allowed you aboard my ship. I am satisfied with Doctor Zimmerman's report and the Federation's assessment of your institute. But having spoken to you in person, I'm not entirely sure what you have to offer me."

Symek steepled his fingers. "Tell me, Captain, what do you think about death?"

"Death." Picard looked aside and sighed. "I've seen far too much of it, but I have learned to accept it. It does not prevent me from engaging in sincere relationships with loved ones, and it does not prevent me from moving on with my life. Now I find myself faced with a dilemma . . . I find myself wondering if death has actually taken place, or if life has merely entered into . . . some kind of suspended state, waiting to be reclaimed." His voice became strained, powerful emotions beginning to show through. "And I cannot trust myself! I cannot trust that my inability to resolve this issue is an honest grappling with the facts, or a mere product of my own feelings of guilt and sorrow."

Symek slipped into an expression of sympathy with the practiced ease of a man stepping into a pair of well-worn boots. "Sometimes the spirit slumbers, and will not awake until the conditions are right. In this case, the spirit that lies dormant within the android B-4—and I concede that an android may have a spirit; the Order is not prejudiced against so-called artificial life—this spirit was cut off from its host body prematurely. There is a disconnect between the Data who gave up his *katra* and the Data whose body was destroyed in the destruction of the *Scimitar.* This disconnect also exists in the *fal-tor-pan* . . . it is why the ceremony requires a mediator; someone to bring the detached *katra* back into harmony with the new experiences which the host body has accumulated—an outside agent, or guide, who makes complete integration possible, you see?"

"Yes, but androids do not register with biological empaths or telepaths," Picard said. "How can you provide such an agency?"

"We are presented with a unique opportunity, Captain—one that will take full advantage of both the Order's knowledge of the *fal-tor-pan* and our experience with holographic technology. Working closely with you and your ship's computer, we will meticulously build a comprehensive holoprogram that re-creates in exact detail the hours between the *katra* transfer and the moment of death. You and the android B-4 will be placed into this scenario, the program itself will act as the agent—a technological mediator for a technological mind. Simplicity itself."

Picard's hesitation was plain. Symek continued, his tone growing more compelling. "The Vulcan race has a credo which many have perverted, but which we retain and affirm: Infinite Diversity in Infinite Combinations. In such a universe of infinite possibilities, is it not conceivable that this course of action is the one which will lead to the resuscitation of your comrade? Are you ready to rule out that possibility, without the benefit of an honest and open-minded effort?"

Picard reflected. He did not like this idea—did not like the thought of exposing the android B-4 to such a confusing and intensely private scenario. On the other hand, Data had freely and willingly shared everything with B-4. Perhaps it was he himself, Jean-Luc Picard, who was afraid. He did not know how he could find the strength to stare into those eyes again and watch them dissolve into nothingness.

And then there was the question of Symek's motives. Had the Vulcan anything to gain, any ulterior agenda? Picard suspected that such a dramatic vindication of his order's philosophy—something he could write up and trumpet before his peers—was motive enough. *If the endeavor is successful,* Picard thought, *Symek can trumpet all he likes.*

As McCoy had told him, if he did not take every chance, explore every possibility, he was sure his conscience would not allow him to sleep. A sense of dreadful resignation crept over him. When it came right down to it, there was really only one choice. Symek knew it: the satisfaction was already there, in his eyes.

"Do what you can," Picard said.

There is a word—"pandemonium"—that was coined in the seventeenth century (Earth reckoning) by a human poet named John Milton. It has come to mean a state of wild uproar and tumult, but originally it referred to a city of demons—the infernal capital of

Miltonian Hell. The Scimitar, Data thinks, *suitably fits both of these definitions. Tongues of flame and noxious, searing gases spew from nightmarish halls. Inhuman groans and distinctly organic cries of pain echo, and the broken walls, floor, and ceiling are studded with jagged spikes of metal. Some of these are covered with ichor; nearby, the lifeless body of a Reman warrior—eyes sightless, fanged mouth contorted into the semblance of an agonizing, silent scream.*

Occasionally, a live Reman will spring from the shadows, a scaly horror as viscerally terrifying as any demon, recognizing the android only as an intruder, marked for destruction. Data dispatches these with heartless efficiency. He has known what it is to enjoy killing—known and been disturbed by the sensation—but these deaths he does not enjoy. He has only one mission, and that is to reach the bridge before his captain can come to permanent harm. All impediments must be removed.

Another Reman neck collapses beneath the impact of his hand, and suddenly the object of his mission is before him: the door that leads to the Scimitar *command module. He forces it open, and as he sprints inside he wonders if his captain is still alive. He considers the fine line between the ability to assign preferential status to one potential outcome, and the emotion that humans call "hope." He knows that he possesses the former, but is unsure of the latter . . . he has, however, assigned preferential status to the latter, and perhaps this is enough. Hope is a virtue his captain has always esteemed very highly.*

In a moment, his wondering is dispelled and his hope—if such it is—is vindicated. His captain is alive, but unmoving. Jean-Luc Picard stares into space as the body of the human male Data recognizes as Praetor Shinzon slumps to one side. Shinzon has been impaled by a thick spear of wreckage. His eyes are glazed over in death.

The ship's computer is counting down: "Eight . . . seven . . ." Data knows what this means. The weapon is on the verge of deployment. In seconds the Scimitar, *the* Enterprise, *and every living being on both ships will be annihilated. He has only this short space of time in which to act.*

He does not hesitate. He leaps to his captain's side, tearing back his own wrist and withdrawing the small silver disk that is the Emergency Transport Unit. Unwilling to risk even the slightest delay, he slaps the device onto his captain's shoulder. The two stare into each other's eyes for a moment. Picard looks as though he is about to say something, but then the transport takes effect, and his visage dissolves into a shimmering glow of energy that dissipates and is gone.

"Good-bye," Data says, knowing it is too late, and not caring.

He spins, withdraws his phaser, and does his duty.

For a second time, Picard was helpless, trapped momentarily beneath the weight of his clone . . . in the end, a small and pathetic man, diseased in body and mind. Picard might have been this man; once again he found himself forced to confront that terrible truth. *Their potential for the worst is something which all sentient beings must confront,* he told himself. *This was true before I ever met Shinzon.* It didn't help. That face—a face he'd seen every morning in the mirror of his Academy dormitory—now stared up at him, a blue-veined mask of vituperation and raw hatred. His own face. Dead.

Then a familiar form was beside him. A white-gold-skinned hand tore open its opposite wrist, and withdrew a silvery disk. Picard felt it hit his shoulder, and he looked up into the other's eyes, searching.

And he knew.

Energy shimmered all around him, but he remained—this was a simulation, after all. Holographically, he had merely been rendered invisible. He watched the android turn, draw out his phaser, and fire into the heart of the Thalaron matrix. A green glow encompassed the room and it was over.

The glow faded, replaced by the striped walls of the holodeck. Only Picard, B-4, and Symek remained. Picard looked down at Symek in momentary surprise. In the emotional intensity of the simulation, he had forgotten that the Vulcan had drawn upon Picard's own memories to portray Shinzon. *It had been,* thought Picard, *a magnificent performance.* The Vulcan looked up now, face flushed and wearing a heady expression. "Could you feel it, Picard?" he breathed. "Could you *feel it?* You are released!"

B-4 approached them, a quizzical look on his face. "Did I perform to your satisfaction?" he asked.

At once, Symek's exultant look faded.

When Picard returned to his quarters, some hours later, he found a box waiting for him. On top was a handwritten note:

Jean-Luc,
A little bird told me you were a fan of twentieth-century mystery novels. I send this gift in the sincere hope that you never stop asking questions . . . and looking for answers. For what it's worth, I think Jim would be proud of you, and your commitment to your friend. And if, by chance, you run into a certain green-blooded Vulcan again while you're gallivanting around the galaxy in that newfangled Enterprise *of yours, give him my best. It's been far too long.*

Yours sincerely,
Leonard H. McCoy

Smiling faintly, Picard examined the contents of the box: a series of actual printed-paper volumes labeled *The Collected Works of Philip K. Dick.*

There was also a message waiting on his personal intercom. It was from Deanna. He returned the call, and found her awake. She looked radiant, with her long dark hair cascading over her shoulders.

"Hello, Deanna," he said. "How are you adjusting to life aboard the *Titan?*"

Her smile was generous and warm. "Far better than Will, I think. Yesterday he walked onto the bridge and sat down in the first officer's chair." Her expression turned serious. "I called to ask you how the experiment went."

Picard's shoulders slumped. "There was nothing, Deanna . . . nothing at all of Data in his eyes."

She nodded as if she had been expecting this. "That must be very disappointing to you." That was Deanna . . . always the professional. However, Picard noted a hint of disappointment stealing over her own face. Deanna had taken the death of Data ("death" . . . he was finally allowing himself to think it) very hard. "But at least we can look at this as a form of closure," she continued. "You mustn't think of this as a lost opportunity, Captain. Data may have had experiences, even feelings, that we can never know, and that anyone else—even someone with access to his memories—could never understand."

"I ought to have known," Picard said, a touch of anger lacing his voice. "I ought to have given Data the credit of his individuality, of possessing his own unique distinctiveness!"

"Please don't be hard on yourself," Troi said. "You didn't betray Data's memory. It was his unique personhood that you missed, and wanted to be faithful to. The experiment is over—you can let it go now."

Picard sighed. "Symek said that my pain had been taken away."

"Has it been?"

Picard allowed a bitter smile to touch his lips. "Not at all."

"I think it's a pain we're all going to be carrying for a while. It must be difficult having B-4 around, reminding you of Data." Picard looked closer at her image on the screen. He could see the grief in Deanna clearly now, still fresh in her eyes, and he felt a sudden twinge of guilt. This was not fair to her—she was no longer his ship's counselor, and she had her own pain to work through.

"I'll be fine," he said encouragingly. "Please, give my best to Will."

They exchanged farewells and signed off. Picard walked back to the box of books and fingered one entitled *Do Androids Dream of Electric Sheep?*, but he could not bring himself to begin reading.

His mind was still turbulent. Instead, he sat down in his chair and stared out the window. The soft, marbled curve of the Earth was just coming into view. The sight reminded him of Lily, another loved one lost to the ravages of time. "Good-bye, Data," he said, knowing that it was too late . . . knowing that his friend was beyond answering.

There is a flash of light where the phaser beam meets the radiation. At once, the fountain of pulsating white-green energy is disrupted, the careful structure of the Thalaron matrix thrown out of kilter. The spot of light in the center begins to grow, until it is all that Data can see. He feels his skin begin to melt and he knows that this is the end. Surprisingly, a strange quiet has fallen over his neural net. His systems have ceased to race for solutions to a dilemma he knows he cannot solve. According to his observations in the past, this does not match with what he knows of fear or panic.

From somewhere in the databanks of his memory, an ancient aphorism surfaces: "Greater love hath no man than this, that a man lay down his life for his friends." If this is true, he thinks, then surely the sensation which I am now experiencing is love. *The pulse of fluid through his artificial veins seems to miss a beat, which may be a consequence of the white heat that is overtaking him, or something else. He remembers that his brother, Lore, had spoken of love just before deactivation. Was this what he had meant?* If it is true that I have experienced love, *Data thinks,* which is universally regarded as the most valued and desired of all emotions, then it follows that my efforts to become more human have not been in vain. Indeed, my long quest would seem to have reached fruition. How nice it would be to tell Geordi. *The thoughts come of their own volition now, unbidden and without analysis.* Thank you, Father. Thank you, Captain. I love . . .

His chronometer has ceased to function, and when the whiteness takes him, he does not know it.

STAR TREK
DEEP SPACE NINE®

Trek

Dan C. Duval

Makrecha IV, 2285

The thick scent of the forest filled Gorkon's nose, without a hint of *bantag*. The loud cackling of the birds and the hoots of lizards told him that the predator was not close, but he strained to hear it nonetheless. One moment of inattention and the *bantag* would be hunting him.

Some of those Klingons of the Pro-Romulan Party would be hunting with *bat'leth*s or even disruptors, but Gorkon believed in the old ways, carrying nothing but a spear and his *d'k tahg*. Here, on his own family's lands, on this frontier planet, he would hunt as he wished and ignore the laughter and gibes of those on Qo'noS who called him backward and barbarian. Traditionalist.

He froze. The forest was absolutely silent. So wrapped up in his own thoughts, he hadn't noticed when it had gone quiet. Without moving his head or body, he peered at every shadow in his field of vision, his ears straining to catch the tiniest sound that might indicate that the *bantag* was close. A slow breeze blew up from behind him and he knew it was the *bantag*'s breath, that he was about to die.

Steeling himself to spin and strike, Gorkon was barely halfway around when the sky lit up and, with a roar, a rush of air struck him and threw him to the ground on his back. But the ground heaved back at him and he bounced onto his face as the world shook and thundered around him and heat scorched the exposed skin on his skull and the back of his neck.

The thick-trunked trees waved as if shaken by the hand of a giant, and the air suddenly stank of ozone and burning plastics, but the ground stopped shuddering as quickly as it had started. It had become abruptly darker here beneath the trees.

Gorkon leaped to his feet, staggering with a slight dizziness, and turned around quickly to see if the *bantag* had snuck up on him while he floundered on the ground. As his mind settled, he assured himself that he should not have been surprised—the *bantag* was probably halfway to the horizon and still running.

Somewhat more than a spear's throw ahead, the forest opened into a clearing that had not been there when Gorkon walked through it a few minutes before. Trees that had stood like towers now lay on the ground, cast down like sticks. A single dark column of smoke rose from one side of the clearing, while tiny bits of bright sunlight reflected from several pieces of white, painted metals, scattered around the clearing.

He picked his way through the fallen timber, his path less obstructed than one would have thought, with all those trees down. Whatever had happened, the fallen trees lay parallel to each other, rather than jumbled across his path into the clearing.

The wreckage in the middle of the clearing, though, maintained most of its structural integrity. A shuttle—a Federation shuttle. Humans.

At least it was not a Starfleet shuttle. The color scheme on

Starfleet was white with a minimum of trim colors and identification marks. This one still displayed mostly white, but garish curves and curls of contrasting colors sprawled across the hull, and something had been painted across its side in some large letters that Gorkon did not recognize.

His fist clenched on his spear as he moved in. This world might be one of the disputed worlds under the Treaty of Organia, but Klingons were developing it, not humans. They might have a right to be here, but they would not establish themselves, not if Gorkon had his way.

Still more than ten paces away from the shuttle, Gorkon had one leg over a downed trunk when the hatch of the shuttle popped open and a single humanoid stepped out.

Judging from the way his jaw dropped, the humanoid seemed surprised to see Gorkon.

Sitting astraddle a log was not the imposing image he wanted to portray. He slid off the far side and drew himself to his full height before he started on the last few paces to the shuttle.

The intruder raised his hand and stepped toward him, saying, "Don't! Radiation. I don't think it's safe."

Federation Standard, of course. It was not his strongest language, but the word "radiation" set him back. A Klingon can fight almost anything in the universe but the invisible killer. Gorkon stepped back until a fallen tree blocked his path.

He spoke with a commanding tone to establish his Klingon dominance.

"Human. You are not welcome here. Go back where you came." Gorkon's memory tickled at him. "From. Where you came from." A simple language mistake, but mistakes do not enhance a warrior's image.

The humanoid twisted his head, displaying a patch of spots that ran up his neck and into his hairline. He pointed at the spots with a finger. "Trill. I am not a Terran. My name is Torias Dax."

He was a tricky humanoid. Within minutes, Gorkon found that somehow he had promised to guide the Trill to the closest base where a subspace radio could be found. Something about how he owed the Trill for warning him about the radiation, about how dishonorable it would be to leave a stranded traveler alone in the woods, and about how helping the Trill would improve his claim on the planet.

Gorkon knew he was not stupid; he had survived the purges on Qo'noS that the chancellor had instituted. Many Klingons had not. Yet this, this Trill spun words about his head, and he found himself playing guide for a two-day trek across the wilderness, back to his holding.

To make matters worse, Torias Dax chattered all the way, sometimes noting interesting things in the forest but mostly complaining about poor maintenance that stuck him with a faulty shuttle. He repeatedly cursed the bad luck that put medical radiation sources on his shuttle when it did crash. It seemed to Gorkon that his companion found fault with almost everything. Someone or something designed the entire universe wrong, according to Torias Dax.

Gorkon thought about warning the Trill about the *bantag*. On the other hand, perhaps the *bantag* would eat the alien and the forest would at least be quiet again. Perhaps then he would be able to gain some sense of peace.

No, after the shuttle crash and the way they were thrashing their way through the underbrush, the *bantag* had probably moved beyond the far mountain range, thinking itself in the way of a stampede of something large and multitudinous.

They topped a narrow ridge, giving them a view across the valley floor.

"Those hills over there. That's not where we are going, is it? You didn't build on top of one of those hills for the view, did you?"

Definitely something very loud, in any case—perhaps it would be easier to just kill the Trill. The option did not seem like an honorable path, since he had already given his word to take him to the radio.

The chattering stopped abruptly and Gorkon turned to find Torias Dax bent over, vomiting.

"What is wrong with you?" Gorkon asked.

The Trill waved his hand and his body heaved a few more times before he spoke. "Must be the radiation. I had no idea how much of a dose I took—the instruments were pretty badly mangled. But symptoms coming on this fast can't be good."

Gorkon nodded. "I recall my training; the sooner signs of the sickness appear, the more serious the exposure is." He tilted his head slightly. "Do you think it is fatal?"

"I don't know." He retched again. "If this keeps up, I might hope so."

Gorkon turned away, back toward their intended path. They had been making good time, but it would take much longer if the Trill's illness slowed them down much.

"We should rest now. We need to do so periodically anyway."

The Trill moved a few feet and then plopped down in the dirt. While Gorkon watched, his stomach spasmed a few more times, though by this time his body contained no fluid that came up.

Between bouts, the Trill stared at him.

Gorkon glared back.

"I hope you don't take this the wrong way, but what species are you? You don't look like any race I have ever seen."

Probably not, Gorkon thought. "Klingon."

"What? You don't look like any Klingon I have ever seen."

Not a surprise, Gorkon thought. *The majority of the warriors that ventured offworld in recent decades look nothing like me.*

They resembled the pathetic line that had provided the last three chancellors of the empire. Mutations. Sicknesses. Whatever they were, they threw away all of the traditions of the past—including the quest for true honor—to emulate what they perceived as a superior culture. One that incorporated ruthlessness and complete disregard for the dictates of honor.

"No, we are not given prime postings with the Fleet, actually no postings with the Fleet. Unless one belongs to a very rich house with its own ships, one never goes into space."

"Yes, but the forehead ridges, and that costume. It almost looks like armor." Torias clapped a hand over his mouth as he spasmed again.

Gorkon frowned. "It is traditional Klingon clothing. The leather is from an animal that is bred only on Qo'noS, chewed by my sisters to soften it and shape it, then stiffened with the urine of the *nak'at*." At the Trill's look of confusion, he added, "A predator that I killed with my own hands." He stood. "And, yes, it is armor. Not effective against a disruptor but it will turn a poorly handled blade." He looked down at the Trill. "Not a blade in the hands of a Klingon, of course."

The sun stood higher in the sky. Still not yet local noon. They had many hours of daylight left and could make a good part of the distance back to the lodgement, if they could move quickly.

Several minutes had passed since the Trill had shown any sign of vomiting.

"Are you ready? We have very far to go."

Torias stood up, a little wobbly on his feet. "Yes. I am still feeling nauseated but I seem to have purged everything that I am going to."

Gorkon peered at him. He did not feel himself to be a good judge of aliens, but Torias Dax's skin seemed to have reddened somewhat.

"Can you march?"

The Trill nodded listlessly. "Yes. I am really tired, but I think I need to get medical attention as soon as possible."

Gorkon nodded. "Then we march." He turned and started down from the ridgeline.

Within hours, the Trill had visibly slowed and his steps had become wobbly and uncertain. At times he seemed to have forgotten where he was. He alternately sweated and shivered, and his face became more and more flushed.

By the time darkness fell, they were almost halfway back to the lodge. At the pace they were keeping, it would be closer to three days to make the trek, especially if the Trill continued to deteriorate so quickly.

As the sun set, the air became abruptly frosty and the hot resin smell of the trees changed suddenly to a damp rot smell of mold from the ground. The clear sky glowed from the number of stars in view. Gorkon tried to locate the two small moons that he had learned about when he was young, but they were tiny, far from the planet, and difficult to pick out of the night sky.

Glancing down, Gorkon saw the Trill lying on the ground, his teeth chattering. Gorkon would have left him there to die, but honor still drove him to keep his word and deliver the Trill—alive—to the lodge. If he lived after that, then that is what would be. If not, then it would not be his problem.

He cut branches from some of the trees, leaves still attached, and piled them on the ground. With that task accomplished, he helped the Trill move onto them, and covered the shivering alien with additional foliage. The shivering continued, but the sound of chattering teeth subsided.

Gorkon gathered wood and lit a fire. The only food he carried was dried *targ*—chewy, salty, and only slightly more nutritious than the leather of his armor. When he offered some to the Trill, the alien moaned and returned to his shaking.

Minutes later Torias Dax threw the branches back and stood up abruptly, pulling at the front of his tunic to fan himself. Sweat poured from him.

Watching him for a moment, Gorkon took some pleasure that he did not suffer as the Trill did. Belatedly, a bit of guilt arose in his mind, as he realized that the Trill could have just let him waltz right into the damaged shuttle and that he too, could have been enduring the same fate as the alien.

"Why are you here?"

The question startled Gorkon. He had been about to ask the same thing. "My house claimed a large part of this territory, to make it into a hunting domain, and perhaps to breed game animals. I am here as part of the Klingon development project for this world. And you? Why were you flying dangerous radioactives around our world?"

"Ah. Supplies for the Federation settlement on the southern continent."

"What settlement?" Gorkon roared, leaping to his feet.

"New one. In the last few days. Per the Organian Treaty. Farmers and miners."

He had been in the forest for nearly a week, but he would have expected some warning that the cursed Federation was coming. Unless, of course, he had been told and the message was buried in the subspace traffic that he had spooled into storage for later review. He should have known.

But radiation sources?

"Why the radioactives?"

"Treating food. Seal it in plastic and give it a thousand rads. Never spoils." The Trill stopped fanning his tunic and sat, well away from the fire. "And sterilizing medical waste. Even viruses will not survive a hard dose of gamma."

Gorkon stewed for a moment. "Gamma" must be some type of radiation, but he refused to show his ignorance by asking. Probably short-wavelength electromagnetic; neutron radiation would cause too much secondary radiation to be useful for food storage.

"So, Klingon, why are you here?" The Trill stared at him. "What is your name, anyway? The last time I asked, you just grumbled."

Gorkon grunted. "Gorkon, son of Toq, of the House of Makok."

"Oh, my. Is 'Gorkon' enough?"

"Yes."

Torias fell silent for a short while. "Why are you here, instead of pushing the interests of your house on Qo'noS?"

Standing, Gorkon turned away from the fire. *Admit to running away to save his own life? To hiding his family to save their lives? Not to an alien. Certainly not to a Federation alien.*

"I know more about you than you might think," Torias said. "You speak Federation Standard. And with only a slight accent. Thus, you are very well educated."

Gorkon turned back to the fire. Certainly it must be the air which gave him this chill.

"And your family is very wealthy. Otherwise, they could neither afford to claim so much land nor use it for little more than hunting."

Still, he said nothing. The Trill continued.

"I am guessing this part, but the gray in your beard and hair suggests you are in your prime, so your children are almost full-grown. But neither they nor your mate are here with you."

"How could you . . . ?" Gorkon growled.

"Your armor shows wear and places where mending has been necessary. You might ignore it if you were alone, but a family of wealth and power would not let you run around like that."

The Trill paused for a moment, giving Gorkon a chance to speak, but he said nothing.

"So, why are you hiding out here?"

"Shut up."

The Trill looked at him, his eyes wide. He sat back into the branches abruptly, lay down, and pulled some of the boughs over himself. Within seconds, the Trill's teeth started to chatter again.

Breathing hard and fast, Gorkon tried to calm himself. *The Trill is only guessing.*

He must be guessing.

In the morning, Torias Dax felt better; at least, he said he did. Torias seemed to be back to his talkative self. Up shortly after dawn, the Trill was pacing when Gorkon awoke, so they set out almost immediately. Normally, Gorkon would have erased all trace of himself, but with the Trill alert and ready to move, he did not perform the familiar task so that they could make as much time as possible.

Gorkon did not miss the bloodiness of the Trill's eyes and the tiny drop of blood at the outside corner of the left one. This burst of energy would probably not last long, so they must take advantage of the Trill's strength to cover as much distance as they could.

Within two hours, Torias Dax staggered in the general direction of their travel, weaving back and forth where the trail allowed it and where the trail narrowed, crashing into brush or almost stepping over the edge of embankments. After a short rest, Dax insisted on going on.

Within an hour he collapsed, unable to walk any farther. Gorkon sat and watched him. His breathing was labored and his color was bad: splotchy spots of red, dark blue bruises where almost anything touched his skin, and cuts and scratches that oozed blood but never quite clotted.

Despite being at death's door, the Trill muttered, keeping up a dialogue with himself.

At one point, Torias asked for water. Gorkon supported his head while pouring water from a flask into his mouth. The Trill's eyes cleared a bit and he struggled to sit up. Gorkon helped him.

"You are dying." Despite his training and his feelings about non-Klingons, he could not but feel some sympathy for the ailing Trill.

Torias choked and coughed. His spit was pink with bloody foam. "Yes. A day. Maybe two."

"I can stop your pain. There is no honor in enduring this sort of agony." The offer was best made from the standing position, to honor the sufferer, but it did not appear that Torias Dax could even sit up on his own.

"No!" The vehemence of Torias's voice surprised Gorkon, bringing on another coughing fit and resulting in more pink foam.

When he regained his breath the Trill lay back. "I am a Trill. My symbiont is not as susceptible to radiation as my body is. With a new, healthy host to support it, Dax will survive the radiation dose it took. And I will be remembered. I must get to a subspace radio, and hope another Trill host is close enough to make the transfer before I die." He reached up and clutched at Gorkon's arm. "You have to get me to that radio."

Gorkon pulled his arm away, disgusted. "You have a *thing* inside you?" Torias shook his head in confusion, and Gorkon realized he had spoken in Klingon rather than Standard.

Over the initial shock, Gorkon asked, more calmly, "You have a parasite? Does it control you? Why do you not have it removed?"

Torias smiled wanly. "Not a parasite. Symbiont. We share. Dax knows my thoughts and I know the thoughts and memories of Dax." Torias looked at Gorkon. "And all of the previous hosts."

Growing up on Qo'noS, Gorkon had never thought of himself as sheltered, but this seemed so . . . *unnatural.*

"They all died in their time, but I remember them, because Dax remembers them. They live through Dax. More than one hundred years of life and, assuming this does not end up with the death of both of us, I will be remembered for several hundred more. The symbiont must live." Torias struggled upright again and reached out for Gorkon, who shrank back.

"You promised," baiting him with the hint of questioning the Klingon's honor.

Gorkon stepped back again. The Trill looked at him with watering eyes as a drop of blood ran down his cheek from one eye. Dax rolled to his hands and knees and tried to stand.

The third time he fell back to the ground, Torias Dax began to crawl, uphill along the trail that led toward the lodge that was still more than half a day's brisk walk away.

Gorkon stood stiffly and watched the dying alien crawl, laboriously, through the rocks and sticks and dirt.

Hopelessly.

The Trill knew that he had to die. And still he suffered the pain, trying to save a little bit of himself.

Can a Klingon warrior show any less courage than this weak alien? The thought taunted Gorkon.

He loped up the hill, reaching down for Torias and lifting him from the ground. He moved the Trill around to his back and grasped the alien's arms around his neck. He started to walk.

By the time they reached the top of the hill, Gorkon knew he would not be able to do this all the way to the lodge, so he took a cord from one of his leggings and tied Torias's legs together, then ran a strap around his chest and the alien to help hold him in place. The Trill seemed to weigh almost nothing.

Now Torias only needed to stay alive until they reached the lodge. Gorkon looked at the sky through the branches of the trees. It would be well after dark when their destination was met.

Even on the verge of dying, Torias talked or, rather, mumbled. Given his position, he mumbled right into Gorkon's ear, hour after hour.

At one point he complained about the apparent lack of pain, though it felt as if his limbs were twitching, even though he could see they were not. And his failing vision, foggy sometimes and the world dimming.

Once, Torias said, "I remember dancing. Always wished I could dance again, but my feet were too big and I could never dance like Emony danced."

Later, "Nilani. I wish I could see Nilani one more time. Never thought about it before, but Dax's next host will remember making love to Nilani through me. Same as I remember Audrid. So proper and motherly by day and so wild at night."

And still Gordon trudged on, uphill and down, following the now-familiar part of the trail. He could see the hilltop where he had built the lodge for its view of the valley below just as the Trill had assumed.

As the sun faded below the hills, Torias became more and more incoherent. When the sun finally faded, hours from the lodge, Gorkon stopped to rest his weary legs.

"Who will write songs about a hunter hiding in his forest? They write songs about warriors who valiantly fight, even if they valiantly lose and die." Torias whispered.

He never spoke again. He grunted and wailed sometimes, but he did not speak another recognizable word.

Perhaps he spoke the native Trill language, which Gorkon would not even know, if such a language existed.

When they reached the lodge, he carefully placed the Trill in the one bed. The alien breathed but was racked with convulsions and bled from nearly every opening now, not great rushes of blood, but slow, sluggishly oozing blood.

Without an idea of what frequencies to try, Gorkon started running through the spectrum, bouncing a signal from the subspace relay in order to reach around the planet to where he assumed the Federation colonists must be. It took hours before he received a response and nearly another hour to explain that he was with Torias Dax and that the Trill needed medical care immediately.

The Federation doctor told him to keep Torias comfortable. He might die before they could get there, but there was nothing else the Klingon warrior would—or could—do for him.

He left his transmitter open as a beacon and checked on the Trill. Sometime while Gorkon worked the radio, Torias Dax had died. Gorkon threw his head back and roared.

The Federation shuttle grounded just outside the lodge and several people rushed out of it to stare at Gorkon, who was standing in the doorway of the lodge in his traditional armor, spear and *d'k tahg* in his hands. He stood nearly a head taller than any of the Federation people.

He stepped aside from the doorway and waved toward the inside with his *d'k tahg*. "He is in there. He has died."

Most of them rushed into the building to perform arcane rituals over the inert body while a tiny person that must be a human female stood near the shuttle and watched him.

In a short while, one of the Federation doctors came out cradling a brown, lumpy mass in a towel, and rushed to the shuttle.

One of the other doctors stopped by Gorkon. "We have three days to get this . . . thing . . . to Trill, according to the instructions we received from that world." She reached toward Gorkon's arm, paused, and then let her hand drop. "The Trill say that this . . . whatever it is, symbiont . . . will probably survive, but we need to take it back to our lab where we can start treatment of the radiation exposure."

Gorkon gestured back into the lodge. "And what of his body?"

"Yes, well, can you keep it here until we can send someone for it? Our shuttle is full and we need to get the symbiont back as soon as possible."

Gorkon looked down on the doctor, a small human male with the same ring of hair as he himself had, but without the ridges on his forehead.

"If there is no objection, I will bury his body here. Unless his family wishes it back."

"Um, well, actually they did not give us any instruction. In fact, they showed no interest when we asked. I suppose you can give him proper burial."

Gorkon stiffened to his full height. "I would be honored to care for him."

The Federation doctors flew away in their shuttle.

Gorkon carefully wrapped the body of Torias in the Klingon manner and buried him on a crag high above the lodge, building a rock cairn over the grave.

He stood facing the setting sun and thrust his *bat'leth* toward the sky, and shouted, "I will remember you, Torias Dax! Your bravery will be my example for all time!"

Returning to his lodge, he arranged for transport back to Qo'noS.

Torias Dax had told the truth.

No one would write songs about a hunter hiding in his woods.

A little over two years later, Curzon Dax traveled to the Klingon capital on Qo'noS and found Gorkon, son of Toq, of the House of Makok. They talked of Torias Dax and of Klingon politics.

The Traditionalists were making a comeback.

Gumbo

Amy Vincent

RECIPE FOR SEAFOOD GUMBO

1) First, make sure you have the right atmosphere to prepare and serve the gumbo. You can make similar dishes on other worlds, including the one you've come to think of as your true home, but they will never taste exactly the same. Using a replicator is out of the question. You need your food to come from Earth, where your dad and your grandpa were born. Most specifically, you need to shop in New Orleans, in the markets only a few blocks away from your grandfather's restaurant. The selection is the best you'll find in the galaxy, and you know your way there and back by heart.

Ask your grandfather to let you take over the private dining room for the evening. You know he'll say yes, but ask anyway, to give him the pleasure of agreeing and seeing your smile. He likes to make you happy. It puts a light in his eyes that hasn't been there that often since your father went to dwell with the Prophets. Let him clap you on the shoulder and offer you his good Kentucky bourbon to go with the meal. Pretend that he is not looking at you as if he is searching for your father's features in your face.

2) Invite the two guests who you think will feel most out of place to go shopping with you, because nothing makes people feel at home like inviting them to do something they're good at.

Try not to notice Quark's snide comments at the lack of security in the open-air markets. Try especially hard not to notice the looks on the grocers' faces as Quark loudly points out the differences in pricing between different booths, scattering customers accordingly. Concentrate instead on Nog's delight in discovering everything new—the scent of the shrimp, the soft leaves that top the celery, the right way to test the ripeness of a tomato. Laugh a little louder than you should when Quark leans too close to the seafood tank and a crab claw clamps down on his ear.

On the way back to the restaurant, stare in disbelief as Quark falls for the street con who bets him five credits that he can tell Quark where he got his shoes. Watch Quark puff up, certain that the man on the street won't guess that his boots come from Ferenginar, though it wouldn't be a difficult answer to come up with. Shake your head as the man informs Quark that he got his shoes in New Orleans right ten minutes before their encounter—look at 'em!

Hurry home instead of listening to Quark argue with the man about whether or not he must pay the five credits. The seafood needs to be fresh, after all.

3) Take the vegetables you've bought—onions, celery, bell peppers, and okra—and start chopping. Offer Nerys a knife and praise her by telling her she should be a natural at this.

Be unsurprised when Nerys is a natural at this—not the cooking part, but the chopping. Listen to her pretend that she didn't find Earth to be all it was cracked up to be, now that she's had a chance to look around, and gripe about having to speak to Starfleet Command when she's no more under their command than she ever was. Wonder if she still resents Earth and humans and the Federation for not having endured the miseries Bajor went through—or, to be more precise, for having endured them and gotten them over with long ago. Then consider that there are some areas of the French Quarter that would terrify people from far more troubled worlds than Bajor.

Watch her figure out how to use a garlic press in about five seconds flat. Realize how adaptable she is, and wonder if that was part of what helped her fall in love with Odo. Wonder if either of you will ever see Odo again, and realize for the first time that you miss him, something you never really expected to do.

4) Begin making your roux. Set the burner to medium heat. In a large, heavy stock pot your grandfather's used for fifteen years, heat two cups of vegetable oil, then begin to gradually add flour. Hear it sizzle and know that you've got the temperature just right. Let Kasidy use the whisk to stir the roux constantly. Because she is unsure of her skills in the kitchen, tell her she is doing it just right— this part is easy, even though it looks hard, she doesn't have to know that it isn't.

Listen to her observations as though you've never heard them before—the descriptions of the changing color of the roux as it darkens into richness. Watch her free hand spread over her swelling belly, and wonder whether your sister can hear all of this, the talking and the laughing and the sounds of the kitchen. Realize all at once that you will teach this little-girl-yet-to-be to make gumbo someday, that you might be the one to pass along all the many Sisko family traditions your father taught you. Feel a strange jab of anger at your father for not being there, even if it is just for a little while. Then feel guilty. Concentrate on Kasidy again, because she is a thousand times more lost than you are.

5) When the roux has reached the browned-gold color of peanut butter, begin adding the vegetables into the pot, one by one. Let Nerys

help you, and make sure Kasidy keeps whisking the roux. Hear them laugh about how they're both lost in kitchens, then be surprised when Nerys begins drawing Kasidy out about her pregnancy, reverent as she talks about a child of the Emissary. Be unable to believe that you forgot Nerys was pregnant once, albeit not with a child of her own. Realize how much Nerys and Kasidy have in common now—tough, smart, independent women who fell in love with men who had destinies to follow, destinies they couldn't share. Wonder if this is the beginning of a beautiful friendship. Let them add the water and okra as the beginnings of the gumbo start to caramelize.

6) Prepare your blend of seasonings. Individual preferences will vary, but begin with what your father taught you: black pepper, red pepper, celery salt, basil, thyme, and—secret ingredient—a few drops of crab boil. Then consider that you can add seasonings of your own, and begin tasting the various spice blends to find what you like. This is your grandfather's restaurant and your father's tradition—but this is also your dinner party and your pot of gumbo.

Get help with the spice-tasting from the most fireproof palate around, the visiting ambassador from Qo'noS. Explain to Worf that tabasco is not like most human seasonings. See the skepticism in his face, and wonder whether any warning you could offer would be more effective than letting him have a taste.

Watch Worf take a few mouthfuls of tabasco, directly from the bottle.

Watch Worf swallow the tabasco as though it were water, then give you a pitying look you obviously deserve.

Listen to Worf tell you stories about the seasonings they have on Qo'noS, and be torn between wanting to avoid the planet forever and wanting to come up with a Klingon-infused gumbo recipe.

Decide to try the Klingon version someday, and someday soon. Resolve that Grandpa is going to be in on the creation of this recipe too. But realize that you must stick to the basics for your gumbo tonight. Stir the seasonings in with the diced tomatoes as the roux thickens and acquires its flavor.

*   *   *

7) Go to the refrigerator and get the shrimp you bought at the market this morning with Quark and Nog, the ones you shelled and deveined all afternoon with Ezri Dax. Remember how much your father said Curzon Dax loved to do this, drinking and joking all the time, and how he developed his own recipe for shrimp Creole, which turned out so great, it made the menu at Sisko's. Remember that Jadzia Dax didn't care as much for helping in the kitchen, but that she enjoyed eating the results even more.

See that Ezri Dax finds the process of cooking tedious, and that she's not looking forward to the food. Notice how drawn her face is, how seldom she smiles, and how weird it is to see a Dax who isn't smiling all the time. Realize that she's come here more out of a sense of obligation than a real sense of belonging.

Remember that when Curzon died, your father told you that he wasn't really lost, that something of him lived on—and how deeply you believed it after you met Jadzia and could still see the twinkle that had once been in Curzon's eyes. Wish you had talked with your father more about this, about the mystery of Trill immortality, so that maybe you would understand now.

Prepare the crab claw meat yourself, because you know this Dax won't be up for cracking open crab shells all day. But let her shuck the raw oysters, their shells coarse and smelling of brine. Realize that Ezri can shuck them even faster than you can, with that twist of her knife that she remembers from lifetimes past. Wonder again what it is that lives on, and what it is that dies.

8) Stir the seafood into the roux and let it simmer for a while— perhaps a quarter of an hour, maybe five minutes more. Keep the stovetop at medium heat and resist the temptation to make it hotter in an effort to speed the process up. It will all be better for the patience and the savoring.

Watch Julian talking to Ezri as they sit at the long, low table in the kitchen. See that there is a light in Ezri's eyes when she talks to him that was never there with Jadzia, and be glad for Julian's sake.

Also notice that Julian doesn't quite have the same light in his eyes that he used to have with Jadzia, and wonder what that's about, exactly.

Using a wooden spoon, take a taste of the gumbo for seasoning and for texture. Wonder if it lacks spice, and add a little more. Recognize that the texture is far too thin, though that is normal for this point in the process.

Take your filé powder and begin stirring it into the gumbo. Go slowly, so that the filé has a chance to be blended smoothly with the rest and thicken the roux.

Set Julian and Ezri to work chopping up the last of the green onions. See them move like one person instead of two, working together so smoothly that they could almost be reading each other's minds. Wonder if maybe you've read those two wrong all along. Then wonder if maybe you should mind your own business. Add the chopped green onions for the last few minutes of simmering.

9) Agree when Keiko tells you that she'll handle the rice. Watch her do it anyway, as it goes against Sisko family tradition to let someone else work alone in your kitchen.

Notice that, after all these years of marriage, she and Miles don't work together nearly as smoothly as Ezri and Julian just did—or, for that matter, Nerys and Kasidy. See that Miles is in her way a couple seconds before Miles does, then wince when Keiko says something sharp to him about it.

Remember your own mother—dead for almost a decade now, as hard as that is to believe—and the gentle warmth she shared with your father. Be glad that this is your idea of marriage, and wonder if that is the greatest of all the many gifts your mother gave to you.

Be alarmed when some boiling water spurts from a chink in the pot lid and splashes on Keiko's hand. Fail to reach her before Miles does, concerned and careful as he takes her to the sink and runs cool water over her hand. See Keiko smile at her husband gratefully as he takes care of her.

Wonder if this is what it comes down to, in the end—being there for someone, all your lives, even when you don't feel like it. Resolve to worry about this when you're older.

10) Give strict instructions to the restaurant staff, though they know the rules for serving gumbo by now. Hang around to watch them start before you trust them enough to go upstairs, to the dining room.

Find everyone waiting, your grandpa sitting at one head of the table. At the other, see an empty chair and think for a moment that it must be for your absent father. Then realize it's for you.

Take your place and preside over the serving of the gumbo. See that the restaurant staff has done everything right—put just enough rice in the bottoms of the bowls, ladled out just enough gumbo, and gotten it to the table while it's still piping hot. Watch Grandpa pour the bourbon for those who want it, decide you do too, and hold up your glass for a toast.

Watch everyone's face and see them expecting a tribute to your father, maybe to the others lost in the Dominion War. Say instead, "To all of you, for joining us tonight."

See them smile, and know that you're doing the right thing—looking not at those who are absent, but those who are here.

Listen to the conversations that spring up around the table: Julian and Miles retelling old holosuite adventures, Ezri and Kasidy laughing about their trips to Earth, Nerys and Keiko discussing how Yoshi's growing, Nog and Worf sharing tales about being the only one of your kind at Starfleet Academy. Be amazed that Quark has it in him to be polite—after a fashion—to your grandpa, and unsurprised to see that Grandpa takes delight in every single one of his guests, varied and odd as they undeniably are.

See your grandfather realize that, when he's with all the people who cared about his son, the ones who made up all the different parts of his life, that it's not unlike being with his son again. Be proud that you were able to give him this, and grateful that he thinks it's a connection he made on his own.

Wonder what your grandfather will do when you make the journey you've begun planning, if you don't come back with your father like you hope to do. Then decide there's time to worry about that another day—and that you're sure you and Dad will make it home. You know your way there and back by heart.

Promises Made

David DeLee

An incoming round whistled through the night sky. Kira hunched and ducked to the right. It exploded less than a meter away, showering her with pebbles and dirt.

The ground thumped with the distant explosions of more charges. Yellow and magenta energy beams knifed through the thick, hot air, lighting up the billowing clouds of smoke. The light show was accompanied by the shouts of advancing ground troops and the sudden, shocked screams of those hit by disruptor fire or cut down by the blade of a *bat'leth.*

Ignoring the bloody hand-to-hand battles around her, Kira zigzagged around a fallen pillar and leaped up the steps to the darkened entrance of the administration building. The grand iron doors lay bent and scorched on the portico. She stepped over them and into the heart of the Cardassians' notorious Lazon II prison camp.

She swept the devastated room with her phaser rifle ready in defense.

Empty.

The central monitoring console and the floor were covered with debris and a layer of gray, dusty grit. Only one wall sconce remained lit; the light flickered erratically with the effort. Two photon torpedoes had slammed into the building. One had ripped a gaping hole through the domed roof. The other had taken out most of the east wall.

Through the ragged openings a hot breeze stirred the dust, carrying with it the sounds of the Klingon raiding parties engaging the unsuspecting Cardassian guards.

It almost made Kira feel sorry for them. Almost.

Keeping her back to the wall, she circumvented the room, side-stepping her way to a rear door. The door panel was jammed at an angle in its track, half-open. She stepped through it. Concrete chunks crunched under her boots.

On the other side was a short hallway leading to a flight of stairs going down. She jogged to the top of the stairs, gave it a quick glance before consulting her tricorder. As she turned around, her brow knotted. She tapped her combadge. "Kira to *Defiant.*"

"Go ahead, Major."

"Dax, according to my tricorder I should be in the control room but I'm . . . I'm just in a hallway."

"Give me a minute." Dax's voice returned a few seconds later. *"The south wall—it's a holographic projection."*

Kira reached out and her hand slipped through the wall, disappearing. "Clever."

She stepped through the wall and emerged inside a large room. Floor-to-ceiling computer controls lined the three facing walls.

Two minutes later she stepped back out into the hall. "The defensive shields around the prison complex are down. O'Brien can begin beaming up prisoners. Start with all human and Bajoran biosigns."

"Under way. We're registering sixty-seven non-Klingon and non-Cardassian life signs."

Kira was already making her way down the double-wide stairwell. "Bring them all up. We'll sort them out later."

"Easy for you to say, Major," O'Brien complained. *"Where do you suggest I put all these people?"*

"I'm sure you'll find room, Chief. Kira out."

The walls around her shook from another explosion outside. She flinched. *Damn the Klingons and their penchant for overkill!* Rock dust drifted down from cracks forming in the ceiling overhead.

At the bottom step she turned left into another hallway. The lights overhead were old-fashioned bulbs encased in wire cages. Pale circles of light dotted the floor, leading down the hallway to where it abruptly ended at a forcefield. To her surprise it was still operational.

Tearing open the control panel on the wall, she stepped back and fired her phaser into it. She spun away as the circuit board sparked and exploded. The forcefield winked out.

Beyond the downed forcefield was the beginning of a cave tunnel. The walls were rough-hewn and striated, the color of dried blood. A series of sconces lined the concave walls. The floor was smooth but pitched sharply downhill. Kira took hold of the braided rope looped between metal poles driven into the ground, a handrail of sorts.

At the first junction Kira had a choice of going left or right. Leading with her tricorder, she proceeded toward the left. Up ahead was a group of seven humans and four Bajorans.

Another overhead explosion rumbled through the cavern. If the Klingons kept attacking they'd bring the whole labyrinth of underground tunnels crashing down around her.

She needed to find who she'd come for and get out. Fast.

She stepped around the corner.

The group—circled around a single human—parted. The man turned, looked up. Longish, unkempt brown hair hung in his eyes. A beard shadowed his cheeks, darkened the gaunt flesh between his sideburns and his fuller goatee.

Her heart froze in her chest. He looked more like a walking skeleton than a man.

"Tom?"

He stepped forward. His broad shoulders were hunched, but there was that familiar swagger in his gait. "Nerys?"

She held out a hand and tapped her combadge. "Come with me. *Defiant*. Lock on to my signal. Two to beam up."

She and Thomas Riker materialized on the bridge of the *Defiant*. He blinked, visibly disoriented. The sudden turn of events must have been, at the least, unsettling. His gray prison jumpsuit was coated with uridium dust and hung loosely on his undernourished frame. His skin was pasty-white—sun-starved—and his cheeks were sunken, dark hollows.

"I never thought I'd see this ship again," he said, getting his bearings. His eyes locked on to Kira. They sparkled, lighting up his whole face. "Or you, Major."

Glancing quickly around the bridge, he asked, "The others?"

Kira settled into the command chair. It felt good to sit down again. "Chief?"

"Every last one of 'em," O'Brien said from the engineering station. "Standing room only in the mess hall, cargo bays, and engineering, but they're all up here."

"Nicely done, Chief. Thanks." Kira took a moment to scan the chair's arm controls, then glanced at the main viewscreen. "Dax, status?"

Lazon II rotated lazily at the left corner of the screen. A red-brown planet of dust and rock, it barely qualified as M-Class. Two Klingon *Vor'cha*-class cruisers hung in orbit around it, and several birds-of-prey were making suborbital strafing runs closer to the surface.

A single Cardassian *Keldon*-class ship lay listing to one side, a large hole burned through its forward hull.

"No indication they know we're here," the tall Trill reported, quite pleased with herself.

They had to decloak to beam Kira in and then again to beam her and the others out. It was Dax's idea to cycle the transports with the frequent and intense solar flare-ups of the system's sun—which made the surface of Lazon II all but uninhabitable—to mask their presence.

"I'm reading minimal life signs on board the *Tra'Nor*," Dax went on. "And the Klingons outnumber them two-to-one down on the surface, but . . ." She turned in her seat to face Kira. "Long-range sensors are picking up three *Galor*-class ships closing fast."

"Sounds like our invitation to leave," Riker said.

"I agree. Jadzia, lay in a course for DS9."

The *Tra'Nor,* the two Klingon ships, and Lazon II slid off the main viewscreen. Ahead of the *Defiant* lay an unobstructed blanket of space. They jumped to warp. The field of stars streaked into colorful elongated lines.

Satisfied that they were safely on their way, Kira stood up. "Tom, care to join me in the mess hall for a *raktajino?*"

His grin was wide and heartwarming. "That's the second-best offer I had today."

Chief O'Brien hadn't exaggerated; it *was* standing room only. Kira and Riker shouldered their way through the crowd to the replicators, then over to a table, where two ensigns gave their seats up to them.

A Starfleet security officer was posted at the door. *An unnecessary protocol,* Kira thought. His bored expression served to confirm her assessment.

Around them the liberated prisoners stood in small groups talking or sat at tables digging into heaping-full plates of steaming hot food. All were dressed in the same drab, colorless prison coveralls and all were as pale and as malnourished-looking as Riker. Their conversations were loud and boisterous. A euphoric energy coursed through the room.

Kira surveyed their faces and smiled at a few who caught her attention. She couldn't help but wonder what they had done to earn a place on Lazon II. Despite the insistence of the Cardassian government that all Bajorans captured during the occupation had been returned, Kira was sure many of these prisoners were just that.

The provisional government would be pleased. Many didn't believe her claims that occupation prisoners were still being held. Others had feared the repercussions that sanctioning the rescue might bring.

To take advantage of the escalating conflict between the Cardassians and the Klingons would throw us right into the middle of their conflict, Kai Winn had protested vehemently.

Kira couldn't wait to get back and throw this into her smug face. The thought brought a wry grin.

"What?" Riker asked.

"Nothing," she said. "I was just wondering how many of these people are holdovers from the occupation."

Tom gave the room a quick glance. "A fair number. The rest are guilty of the most trivial of offenses: border trespassing, petty theft, some smuggling. Others were imprisoned on totally fabricated charges."

He took a sip of his *raktajino,* smiled at Kira. "Of course I was the star prisoner. The only Maquis prisoner not immediately put to death." His eyes glazed over for a moment. "A slow, torturous, painful one was more to the Cardassians' liking, as it turned out."

Kira reached out, put her hands around his. "Tom, I'm so sorry."

He focused his gaze on her, forced a smile. "Don't be. I owe you my life. You and Sisko. And . . ." He cupped her hands in his. "You came back for me. Just like you promised."

Nerys swallowed hard, trying to speak around the lump in her throat. Her pulse pounded in her ears and her stomach started to do somersaults. The sounds around her faded into muted background noise. She moved to pull back, feeling the warmth of his touch spread through her.

Riker released her hands and sat back in his chair, breaking the awkward moment. "So tell me about this Klingon-Cardassian war. We heard some things inside, but getting reliable information was difficult."

"It's a long story," she said, sipping her own *raktajino.* "It started with the civilian uprising on Cardassia. The Klingons believe the Dominion is behind it."

"And the Federation?"

"Reserving judgment. They're staying out of it, for now."

Riker's face clouded. "Just like the demilitarized zone. Better to not take a stand, to not get involved."

"It's not that simple, Tom."

A sudden scuffle drew her attention to the door. She tried to see past the mass of bodies. It was like trying to see through a constantly shifting plasma storm. When the crowd parted, she saw two former prisoners holding the limp body of the security officer between them, dragging him over to Kira and Riker. They dropped the unconscious ensign onto the table.

Kira launched to her feet, her chair scraping across the floor behind her. She reached for her phaser but was stopped by a hand that grabbed her wrist. A Bajoran man held her, took the phaser, and pressed it up under her chin.

"What the hell's going on?" She stared at Riker, who was also on his feet. "Tom, what's the meaning of this?"

"I'm sorry, Nerys. I really am. You fulfilled a promise today and now I have to fulfill mine. As of right now I'm taking over the *Defiant*."

Twenty minutes later, at the access door to the bridge, Kira grabbed Riker by the arm, stopping him.

Kerrigan, a human trader of exotic antiquities who had been imprisoned by the Cardassians five years prior, raised the phaser he had taken from the security officer. Riker signaled him to stand down.

"Tom, why are you doing this?"

"I told you, I'm fulfilling my mission."

"What mission?" She couldn't imagine what he was talking about. "We know what the Cardassian buildup in the Orias system was. The Obsidian Order was preparing a preemptive strike against the Founders' homeworld. It had nothing to do with the Maquis."

"That's not what I'm talking about."

"Then what?"

"My promise to the Maquis. My promise to the citizens abandoned by the Federation. People are dying inside the demilitarized zone. This is bigger than me, Kira. You taught me that. It's about destroying the enemy. No holds barred." He looked past her to the six rescued prisoners standing behind them. "Ready?"

There were four Bajorans and two humans, including Kerrigan. All were armed. With solemn faces they nodded.

Riker activated the door and stepped onto the bridge.

Kerrigan pushed Kira in after him. The others rushed to the left and right, covering the startled bridge crew with their weapons.

Chief O'Brien was halfway out of his seat, drawing his phaser.

"Sit down, O'Brien," Riker barked. His phaser was already leveled at him.

Miles stopped in surprise, then lowered himself back into his chair.

"That's it. Nobody do anything heroic and no one'll get hurt."

Besides O'Brien, and Dax at the helm, Lieutenant Parks was at tactical, Ensigns Kala and Robertson were working at the secondary tactical station, and Ensign Forbes was filling in at the science station.

"Clear the bridge." Riker pointed to Parks, Kala, Robinson, and Forbes. The former prisoners fanned out, took their weapons, and shuffled them to the door. "O'Brien and Dax stay."

"Why?" Dax asked.

Riker took his time to sit down in the command chair. He wiggled around in it, giving a satisfied nod. "Feels good." To Dax, he said, "I'll need you to navigate us out of Cardassian space and O'Brien to operate the cloak."

"Like bloody hell I will."

"Not a smart move, O'Brien." Riker nodded to Kerrigan.

Kerrigan yanked Kira over to the command chair and pressed his phaser into her neck.

She winced.

"Because if you don't, I'll be forced to kill Major Kira."

Dax remained calm, but her eyes swept the room with an intensity that belied her relaxed behavior. "You wouldn't."

Riker leaned forward, his stare hard and cold. "Oh, wouldn't I? I've spent the last year and a half down there in that hellhole, at the hands of the Cardassians. You have no idea what I'm capable of, Lieutenant."

The others were taken from the bridge, leaving Kerrigan, another human, and a Bajoran woman behind. The human's name was Drake. A petty pickpocket, he'd been arrested on Cardassia Prime. The Bajoran was a former resistance fighter captured just before the Cardassian withdrawal from Bajor.

Four against three, Kira thought. *Not bad odds, except the four are armed and Dax, Miles, and I are not.*

Her hands were clenched into tight fists. With effort she forced herself to relax, to open and flex her fingers. She resisted the urge to lash out, to give in to her anger. What she needed was time. Time to figure out what Riker was up to. Time to formulate a plan to take back the *Defiant*.

"So, what happens now, Tom?"

"Now? Now we lay in a course for the Badlands."

Dax looked up at Kira.

She nodded, and Dax swung around and entered the coordinates.

"Warp five, Dax," Riker said.

The *Defiant* surged forward. To those familiar with the ship, the hum of her restrained engines could be felt through the deck plating. Even with the increase to warp five, Kira could feel the tough little ship straining to go faster, to fly full-out.

"How long until we clear Cardassian space?"

Dax glanced at her board. "Thirty minutes."

"Good." Riker leaned back. His body seemed to melt into the chair's contours. Only his sunken, scraggily bearded face and dark-rimmed eyes betrayed the exhaustion, the strain he must be feeling.

Watching him since he'd taken command of the ship, Kira marveled at the reappearance of his confidence, at his immediate comfort at being in command, at the sense of purpose and drive he suddenly had. Like a man transformed, he was no longer the undernourished, frail, near-broken prisoner she had been shocked to find in the dark caverns of Lazon II.

"What's waiting for us in the Badlands, Tom?"

An alarm from Dax's board prevented him from answering. He slid forward. "What is it?"

Dax's long fingers danced over the sensor controls for a moment. Then she turned. "Two *Galor*-class warships. Approaching fast, at high warp."

Riker visibly relaxed. "Cloaked, they can't know we're here. We are still cloaked, aren't we?"

O'Brien sat with his back to the engineering console, his arms folded across his chest. "Funny you should ask that."

Kira noticed his struggle not to smile. She saw his right hand, under his arm, his fingers crawling across the console's touchscreen. She doubted anyone else noticed it.

"Remember that EPS fluctuation I told you about earlier, Major?"

He'd made no mention to her about any fluctuation. She nodded, going along.

O'Brien unfolded his arms and slapped his hands to his knees. "Well, it looks like it finally cooked the number five, seven, and eight power taps."

Riker leapt to his feet. "What are you saying, O'Brien?"

"I'm saying, *Tom,* the cloak's fried."

"Damn you!"

Riker started for O'Brien but was nearly thrown off his feet when the ship violently pitched to the right. He managed to stay on his feet only by grabbing the back of Dax's chair and holding on tight.

Kira seized the computer console alongside the command chair. It was the only thing that kept her from being thrown ass over *tuwalli* pie tin.

The three former prisoners were thrown to the floor. They slid, arms and legs waving, across the bridge while Dax and O'Brien, secure in their seats, spun around and began entering commands into their consoles.

With a second hit to the ship, the life-support monitor exploded, showering the front of the bridge in white sparks. Alarms sounded. The sparkling haze of the fire-suppression forcefield appeared around the damaged panel, smothering the flames.

"Red alert! Raise shields!" Kira and Riker shouted simultaneously.

On the viewscreen, the first of two Cardassian ships flew past, firing another volley of torpedoes in its wake.

The forward shields shimmered blue on the screen. "Shields holding," O'Brien called out.

Lunging for the command chair, Riker called out. "Evasive maneuvers, Dax, pattern delta—"

Dax sat back. Leisurely she spun around in her seat to face Riker, her arms folded across her chest. Seeing Jadzia's defiance for what it was, he glared at Kira. "Those Cardassians will be just as glad to get their hands on you as they will me."

"I have no intention of becoming a guest of the Cardassian prison system." Kira grabbed the arms of the command chair and spun Riker around. "But try and go up against two *Galor*-class warships with . . ." She nodded her head at Kerrigan and Drake. " . . . a coin trader and a petty thief. See how far you get."

Riker stared at her, clearly evaluating his options. Time was running out.

Dax interrupted them. "The *Vexon* is hailing us."

"Tom, give me back my ship."

He stood up and stepped away from the chair. "For now."

Kira took the seat. "Jadzia, set course to zero-seven-two mark seven. Tom, take tactical. Target weapons only."

They exchanged another hard look, then Riker crossed the bridge, taking the seat at tactical. "They're powering weapons."

"Prepare to return fire." She added, "On my command only."

Riker glared over his shoulder. "Aye . . . Captain."

Kira ignored him. Her attention was on the two mud brown ships facing them. Under Dax's steady hand the *Defiant* slid smoothly to port. The Cardassian ships moved to track them.

"They're splitting up," Dax said. "Moving to pin us down in a crossfire."

"The *Vexon*'s firing!"

Its port wing phasers glowed. An amber beam knifed across the expanse of space. The *Defiant* shook from the impact, but the shields absorbed the blast.

"Shields holding."

"Return fire!" Kira shouted. "Target their port phasers. Dax, full impulse, heading three-two-seven mark four."

The *Defiant* swept past the *Vexon.*

Riker's aim was true. Their phasers stitched the port wing. The *Vexon*'s shields flared green. The enemy ship dipped and slid off-screen.

"Their port shields are down by thirty-two percent," O'Brien called out.

"Bring us around for another pass," Kira ordered.

Onscreen, both ships fell out of view. The stars whizzed past as Dax brought them hard around. The *Vexon* suddenly reappeared in front of them. "Tom, lock on to their port disruptors. Full phaser spread followed by two quantum torpedoes."

"Firing!"

The starboard phasers sliced across the *Vexon*'s port wing. The shields glowed bright green, struggling to absorb the intense energy blasts. Then they collapsed.

Riker cut the phasers and launched the number-one and number-four torpedoes.

The unprotected wing exploded. The *Vexon* bucked. A series of explosions cascaded across the damaged wing, tearing it from the main body of the ship. The *Vexon* dived.

"They're out of the fight," Riker said.

His assessment proved to be premature. Before slipping out of range completely, the *Vexon* let loose a final torpedo volley.

Dax tried but couldn't avoid them. The torpedoes slammed into the *Defiant,* causing the ship to catapult up. The deck plating under the viewscreen erupted. The science-station console exploded.

Kerrigan was flung from the seat, screaming. His face covered with first- and second-degree burns, he lay on the deck. Drake and the Bajoran woman rushed to him, knelt down by his side.

"Starboard shields are down," O'Brien called out. "We've got a hull fracture on deck two."

"All right," Kira shouted over the alarms. "Enough of this. Chief, activate the cloak. Dax, prepare to take us to warp."

"Uh, Major."

She spun to face O'Brien.

"The cloak is down."

"What?" She couldn't believe it. "I thought you were making that up."

"I was, but that last blast did damage the power relays. Now the cloak really is fried."

Dax turned around. "And I've got more bad news. The warp drive's offline too."

Kira pounded the arm of the chair. "Damn."

Another alarm sounded. This one was a steady shrill piercing through the intermittent warble of the red-alert sirens. "Now what?"

"Three more Cardassian ships approaching," Dax told her. "Another *Galor*-class and two *Hideki*-class patrol ships."

"Well, Tom, you got what you wanted," Kira said. "You get to die fighting the Cardassians in a useless, hopeless battle people will talk about for years to come."

"I told you, I'm not on some suicide mission, Major." He got up and crossed over to the helm. Standing next to Dax, he entered something into the navigational system. "And I'm not about to give up yet."

Kira glanced at the coordinates lighting up on her own computer console. They meant nothing special to her. The location they designated was outside Cardassian space and close to the Badlands.

"Dax, head for those coordinates." To Kira, he said, "I had a lot of time to think about things you told me, about what it meant to be a terrorist, about inflicting maximum damage."

"What's that got to do with this?" Kira looked over at Dax. "At full impulse can we reach those coordinates ahead of the Cardassians?"

The tall Trill shrugged. "We might've caught a break. It looks like the *Vexon* had to eject their warp core. The others are moving in to establish rescue operations."

Kira faced Riker. "Before I agree, I want to know what's waiting for us there."

"Help. Maquis help."

Kira took the time to consider this. Joining up with Maquis ships, even to defend themselves, would be interpreted by the Cardassians as collusion between the Maquis and Starfleet. She couldn't allow that. Nor could she allow the *Defiant* to fall into Maquis hands. She would destroy it first.

Yet to stay there and fight was out of the question. She made her decision. "Do it, Dax. Chief, I need all available power."

"I'll give you what I've got, Major."

They went to work.

Kira eyed Riker. "You had this set up the whole time."

"A contingency plan," he admitted. "One of many. I had a lot of time to work them out."

"Who's waiting for us?"

"I told you, the Maquis." He hesitated. "And the Klingons."

Kira sat bolt upright. "The Klingons!"

"The Maquis have agreed to join their fight against the Cardassians. Our goals are the same."

Kira leaned back. "I'd say your ability to gather intelligence was a little better than you said."

Riker gave her a small but humorless grin. "A little."

"We're coming up on the coordinates now," Dax announced.

Kira and Riker both looked to the screen.

"Cardassians?" Kira strummed her fingers on the arm of her chair.

"On their way. Closing fast," said Dax.

"Chief, start diverting power to the shields." Kira glanced up at the screen. "I don't see anyone. Dax, anything on long-range sensors?"

She shook her head. "Just the Cardassians."

"Tom?"

The lines around his eyes deepened; concern crossed his face. He took a step toward the viewscreen. "I don't understand it. They were supposed to be—"

"Major, a ship is decloaking off the port bow," O'Brien called out. "Wait a bloody minute. Make that ships."

"All stop!" Kira shouted.

The *Defiant* bucked under her. The inertial dampeners struggled to keep up with the sudden change. Riker grabbed the command chair. The others were forced forward in their own seats.

By the time the dampeners caught up, everyone was staring at the viewscreen. The starscape in front of them rippled; then, as if they were looking through a pool of water, a half-dozen Klingon *Vor'cha-* and *K't'inga*-class ships shimmered into view. Centered in the flotilla was a single Maquis raider.

"Good God," O'Brien breathed.

"We're being hailed, Major," Dax said. "It's the raider."

Kira recovered enough to come to her feet. "On screen."

The interior of the raider was dark. Only shadowy glimpses of people moving back and forth among the dimly lit consoles could be seen. The single figure of a Bajoran woman stepped forward, out of the shadows. She was clad in the standard nondescript attire of the Maquis resistance. She wore a hand phaser strapped to her right hip and a ceremonial Bajoran dagger on her left. Kira had never met the woman, but her reputation was well known, by both Starfleet and the Bajoran people.

"Ro Laren."

"Thank you for speaking with me, Major Kira."

"Did I have a choice?"

"Not much of one." Ro glanced offscreen. "Our scans indicate your cloak is offline and your warp drive is down."

"Nothing we can't fix. What do you want, Ro?"

"What we've always wanted. What Tom Riker set out to take a year and a half ago. The *Defiant*."

Riker stepped up next to Kira. "Plan's changed, Ro."

Ro furrowed her brow. "What are you talking about?"

Riker looked at Ro. "Look at your sensors. There are four Cardassian ships heading this way; probably more right behind them. The way she is now, the *Defiant*'s useless to us."

"And I'll die before I hand her over to you." Kira turned to O'Brien. "Charge weapons. Target the raider."

The chief jumped to the secondary tactical station, next to his engineering console.

Ro watched through narrowed eyes. "You're bluffing. You won't sacrifice your crew, your ship—"

"Try me."

"Weapons charged and locked," O'Brien called out.

Ro dropped back into her seat. "Shields!"

"Nerys! Ro! Wait!" Riker looked from Kira to Ro and back again. "It's not worth it. Not worth the lives of forty Starfleet personnel, sixty-seven civilians."

"Then stop it, Tom. Here! Now!"

Kira glanced at her console readouts. The Klingon ships had their shields raised too. They were powering weapons. On the navigational board she saw the approaching Cardassian ships. They would be within weapons range in less than ninety seconds. All hell was about to break loose.

"Make a decision, Tom."

He looked around the bridge. Bulkheads were scorched from the recent fighting. Kerrigan sat with a makeshift bandage over his burned face and hands. The air was thick; it was like breathing fire.

"What about all this?"

Kira followed his gaze. "You'll have to answer charges. Face a Federation trial for both attempts to steal the *Defiant*."

"The others—they're not responsible for this." He grabbed Kira's shoulder. "They've already paid a terrible price at the hands of the Cardassians."

"I think," she hesitated. "I think some things could be over-looked."

"All right. It's over."

"No!" Ro was on her feet. "We worked too hard for this, Riker. With the Klingons' help we've got the Cardassians on the run."

"All the more reason we don't need the *Defiant* anymore. It's done, Ro."

He crossed over to Kerrigan and the other prisoners. One by one he collected their weapons. Coming back to Kira, he said, "No charges against any of the others. Your word?"

She nodded. "My word."

"I know I can count on that." When he was within arm's reach, he grabbed her and spun her around, placing a phaser to her head. It was set to kill.

O'Brien and Dax jumped to their feet.

Riker backed toward the access door. "I'll do it."

They stopped.

"I can't go back," he whispered in Kira's ear. "I can't go to prison again. Not even a Federation one."

"I'll—"

"No! O'Brien, drop the shields."

"Don't do it, Miles," Kira said.

"Do it or she's dead." Riker sounded desperate enough to do it.

O'Brien turned, his fingers danced over the touchscreen. "They're down."

"Ro, prepare to beam me over. Only me. Is that understood?"

She nodded, then nodded again to someone offscreen.

"Nerys, I really am sorry." Riker shoved her away. "Ro! Now!"

Kira stumbled, turned. She rushed back at him but was too late. His form shimmered brightly, faded, and was gone. She spun on O'Brien. "Get him back!"

"Too late. They've already raised shields."

On the viewscreen she saw Riker materialize. Ro stepped out of his way. He approached the viewscreen until his features filled it.

"You were good to your word, Major. Much more than I've been.. For that, I'm sorry." He started to turn away, then stopped. "I can't tell you how much I wish things could have turned out differently for us, Nerys. During all of my time down there I couldn't get you out of my mind. I couldn't think of anything but you. I . . . I just thought you should know. I'm sorry, Nerys."

She said nothing. What could she say?

"The Cardassians are within weapons range," Dax called out, looking from the screen to Kira.

Riker's eyes flashed to something that was offscreen. Then he returned his gaze to Kira. For her, everything else faded out of existence at that moment. "We've got enough firepower to keep the Cardies busy until you're out of harm's way. I'll make sure they know Starfleet and the Federation had nothing to do with this. That's a promise . . . for what it's worth. Good-bye, Nerys."

He cut the transmission.

Returned to the viewscreen was the Klingon flotilla. The ships started to move off, preparing to engage the enemy in what was sure to be a glorious battle. The raider banked to starboard.

Kira lowered herself into the command chair. *Would today be a good day to die?* she wondered.

To Dax, she said, "Get us the hell out of here."

Her voice barely above a whisper, not meant to be heard by anyone, she said, "Good-bye, Tom Riker."

Always a Price

Muri McCage

"Hold it right there, Colonel!"

Kira really thought she'd made it. Three steps more and she could have entered the holosuite without incident. *Who am I kidding? Of course he'd hear me . . . with those ears.*

Turning, one hand on the stair rail, she looked down at her tormentor. "What do you want, Quark? I'm in a hurry."

"Quite a gift you've got there, for sneaking and hurrying at the same time." The snaggletoothed Ferengi smirked at her, with his face and his voice. "How about giving lessons? I'm sure we could work out an arrangement."

"Arrangement?" Kira laughed in his face. "I assume you mean I do all the work, get paid nicely for it, and you take most of said pay in commissions."

"Of course. Business is business, Colonel." He boldly thrust out an open palm. "Speaking of which, pay or leave."

"Give it a rest, Quark. I'm just going to speak with Vic for a second."

The large knobbly Ferengi head shook decisively. "Not a chance. How do you think I can stay in business, if I don't charge for holosuite time?"

"I'd rather you didn't, frankly."

That shut him up for about five seconds.

"Be that as it may, I have a living to make. Holosuite time is part of that business. You should know better than most, Colonel; there's always a price. Ferengi Rule of Acquisition Number 43."

An exasperated sigh huffed out of her. "All right, then. Put it on my account."

"No credit. Things are too uncertain these days."

"You—" She interrupted herself in order to try to get a grip on her rising anger. "What do you expect me to do? Pay you in blood?"

"How about a barter?"

"Ferengi barter?"

"Sure, if the exchange is good enough."

"What do you want?"

"Oh, nothing much . . ."

"Quark . . ." she started in a warning tone.

"Let's just say you'll owe me one."

"One what?"

"You'll know when I know." He was positively oozing smirk by this point.

"If I agree, will you shut up, get off these stairs, and leave me alone? All day?"

"Ferengi's honor."

If he crossed his heart, or saluted, or anything at all, she'd march down there and step on his head. Kira was almost disappointed when the annoying little thorn in her side scampered away. Then she was confused when she caught the words that drifted out in his wake.

"Tell him he owes me one, too."

*   *   *

Vic's place was an oasis of calm after the disturbing little interlude she'd just escaped. Kira drifted inside, looking around at the familiar furnishings and taking in the ambience that brought her so many bittersweet memories. She was letting her fingertips wander over the piano keys, enjoying the distracting tinkle of sounding and fading notes, and did not notice Vic standing at her side.

"Hello, dollface."

She jumped, and automatically scolded him, just as she would any of her other friends. "Don't sneak up on a person like that."

"Sorry. I didn't mean to scare you."

She laughed. "Don't flatter yourself. I don't scare that easily. You really should program in some pattering footsteps or something, though."

"I'll keep that in mind." The charming hologram smiled, obviously enjoying their banter. "So you got my message."

"I'm here, aren't I?"

He looked her up and down approvingly. "You certainly are!"

"You're incorrigible, Vic." There was always that moment she experienced, when the reality of the nature of his existence clashed with his irrefutable sentience. A little shiver cascaded down Kira's spine, but she shook it off and got back to the business at hand. "You said it was urgent."

"It is."

He handed her a padd.

Taking the small device, she glanced at the screen, scrolled down a bit, then looked up to meet his mischievous gaze. "What's this?"

"Coordinates."

"Yes, I gathered that much. I may be overworked these days, but I can still recognize coordinates to a wilderness area on Bajor when necessary."

"Glad to hear it. We wouldn't want you going soft."

She decided to ignore his gentle teasing. "So what am I supposed to do with them?"

"Go there."

"Just like that?"

"Just like that."

"Care to tell me why?"

"Sure. I'd love to."

A longish silence tried her patience, almost as badly as Quark's attitude had tested her anger threshold. "Well?"

"Well nothing. I'm sorry, but I can't."

"Why not?"

"Secret." He actually whispered the single word, as if it carried the weight of the world in its six letters.

Falling into his clandestine routine, Kira caught herself about to glance over each shoulder. "I get it. This is one of Julian's spy programs, and I'm the punch line."

"No!"

"You don't have to be so emphatic about it."

"Yes, I do." Suddenly, he was the soul of contrition. "This is important, Kira."

"To whom?"

"You."

"I don't know."

"Listen, dollface. If you can't trust a wiseguy hologram, who can you trust?"

She looked down to study the padd again, partly to cover the little smile that seemed to quirk her lips of its own volition. "I'm busy."

"Sure you are. You're always busy. You need a break." He held out an arm to either side, swooped them up and down a bit, looking as if he'd love to take flight himself. "Come on. Think about it. A little downtime. Fly around in a runabout for a while. Blow out the cobwebs. Maybe a picnic . . ."

His words trailed out behind him as he wandered away for a moment. When he reappeared, he was carrying an old-fashioned wicker basket, which he handed her with great ceremony, and not a little pleading. It was real. "You know you want to."

"Well—"

"It's settled, then."

"Vic, I . . ."

"I know. Don't worry about it." His wink was so fleeting, she almost missed it. "I know, and I'm telling you you'll be making a huge mistake if you don't trust me."

"I don't trust any—"

"Yes, you do, and we both know it. Now get going." He shooed her away, but as she made to leave, he grabbed her arm to pull her to a halt again. "It's not just for you. It's important to someone else too. Do it for them."

"Who—"

"Secret."

Kira materialized in a large, sunny meadow that would have been idyllic if not for the boisterous sounds of many happy children. She stood for a moment, trying to take in the totally unexpected scene, clutching her picnic basket in a not quite steady grasp.

What am I doing here? The hair prickling feeling that preceded a "gotcha!" was creeping up the back of her neck. The temptation to beam herself right back to where she came from and point the runabout toward the station was almost overwhelming. However, she was Kira Nerys, resistance fighter turned commander of Deep Space 9. That meant she did not run from the unfamiliar, the frightening, or the laughter of what sounded like a small army made up of children. No, indeed. Kira Nerys simply girded her loins, or in this case tightened her grip on her basket, and marched forward into—

"Greetings, child."

Apparently, she had marched forward into a collision course with an elderly woman. Kira looked down, and then down some more, eventually locating the source of her welcome. The tiny form, swathed in the palest of peach-colored robes, tilted her head back to study her visitor's expression. Recognizing that the woman was a member of some sort of religious order, Kira bowed slightly to signify her respect.

"Greetings . . ."

"I am Bel."

"Hello, Bel. I am Kira Nerys."

Bel nodded solemnly. "You are welcome, Kira Nerys, though unexpected."

"I apologize for just . . . dropping in like this."

"There is no need, child. All are welcome with the Hands of the Prophets." Wizened fingers hovered between them. "May I?"

Realizing what was asked of her, Kira bent to accommodate the other woman's slight stature. Gentle fingers brushed her ear, then clasped for a moment. The brief contact was severed, and Bel smiled beatifically, almost as if Kira were no longer present.

"Your *pagh* is strong. Conflicted, yet devout and able. May I know what brings you to us this day?"

"I was . . . sent."

"Ah." As if that explained everything. Perhaps it did. "Then it is the will of the Prophets. What do you wish to see here?"

"I . . ." What *did* she wish to see? The reason she had come to this place would be nice, but, since she didn't know what that was, information would do. "May I know what is happening? The children . . . ?"

"The children are everything. They are orphans. Some from the occupation and now of the war. More and more, they come to us, trickling into our care as our mission becomes known. We know not how. That, too, is the will of the Prophets. Perhaps they come to us by way of the Celestial Temple itself."

"I see." She didn't, exactly, but she did not know how else to respond. She had no idea why she had been summoned to this place, at this time, to meet this person. Maybe she could ask more questions and piece it all together into something that made sense. "And these are the grounds of the orphanage?"

"Why, no, child. The orphanage is concealed in nearby caverns. The location is known to few. By living so secretive a life as to almost become myth, we have managed to keep the children safe." Bel smiled with benevolent grace. "This is a place where we bring the children every year, whenever it is deemed safe enough. The land was deeded to us by a dear benefactress. We have always been graced by her presence during our times of joy here, and she never arrived without small gifts for us all, but this time . . ."

"This time?" Kira prompted.

"We are alone."

"Who—"

Bel studied Kira with a surprisingly shrewd gaze. "If you were sent by the Prophets . . ."

What? Then I'd already know? Kira was beginning to think this woman had a totally unrealistic idea of what had brought them together. She had no intention of trying to explain that instead of by the Prophets she had been directed here by coordinates on a padd given to her by a sentient hologram. Maybe she should just bow out gracefully, and try to make Vic explain what he'd been trying to accomplish.

" . . . then it is surely their will that you know of our benefactress. You must promise not to reveal that of which I speak."

"Of course. I promise."

"Very well." Bel looked skyward for a moment, as if still unsure and seeking the counsel of the Prophets directly. "The world knew her as Kai Winn, but to us she was simply Adami. While duties elsewhere prevented her from joining our humble order, she was truly a Hand of the Prophets in spirit. We were blessed by her presence whenever she could find the time to spend with the children and we all benefited greatly from her generosity. She has always been . . ."

Kira lost coherent thought around the word "humble." She didn't know whether to laugh hysterically or sob in a mixture of grief and confusion. In the end, all she did was smile kindly and offer agreement. The Winn that Bel described was not the cold, calculating snake Kira had come to know, and both despise and pity. If that woman had had another side, one that brought joy to lost children, then who was she to take any of that away from these people? Could gaining this knowledge be why she was here? How would

Vic of all people have known? And what would she be expected to do with the incongruous concept of that particular kai as benevolent benefactress, now that she had been confronted with it?

Before she could even begin to really process the bombshell that the old woman thought of as blessed tidings, Kira found herself abandoned. Bel's features, in her version of a smile, crinkled up like an apple left in the sun too long, as she offered her only treasure to her guest. "Kira Nerys, please explore our gathering. Since Adami is not with us this season, perhaps the Prophets have sent you to join our other helpers in making the children happy."

With that invitation, which sounded almost like a benediction, Bel turned and walked away. Kira stared after her for a moment, then looked around, searching out the source of the laughter. She followed the sound, and soon found herself joining a group of small children as they played the games she remembered from her own childhood. No matter the circumstances, somehow children always found a way to play, if only in an effort to remove themselves mentally from the torture of their lives. Today, however, there was no tortured existence. There was only joy and sunshine and . . . the scent of cookies and small cakes, as somehow her basket became open and the contents passed among the revelers.

Vic had known, all right. This had to be why she was here.

A hawk soared overhead, making Kira and the current group of children with whom she played look up and shade their eyes to savor its grace and beauty. There were other animals present, as well. Only a few, but they were magnificent. In the time she spent in the meadow, Kira saw several creatures that drew a smile, as she remembered from her own childhood the stories and dreams of all young ones to be among the creatures nature had provided as beloved companions and loyal helpers.

The day wore long and Kira grew exhausted, in a good way. She had played every game she could remember, and quite a few she'd never heard of before her very strange adventure had begun. Her most recent playmates scampered off, at a call from one of their custodians, leaving her to want nothing more than to throw herself down onto the soft grass and take a nap.

Before she could do more than pick out a perfect spot, a large animal bounded up and nudged affectionately against her. Laughing with delight, she bent to ruffle the shaggy black and white hair along its back. It was an Old English sheepdog. Miles had told her about them once when she'd spied an image in one of Yoshi's books. She had declared to one and all forever after that someday when she retired, she would own a house with a yard, so she could get one of the big dogs that looked so friendly and so very soft to the touch.

Now, she knew that they were, indeed, very soft and very friendly, but what she couldn't figure out was what it was doing on Bajor. Mystified, and intrigued, she laughed out loud when pleading brown eyes followed her every move, as the dog tried to lead her away from the meadow. It would take a few steps, turn and beg her with its surprisingly eloquent gaze, then run a small distance away, only to stop and look over its shoulder beseechingly.

"Okay, fellow, how can I possibly resist? But you'd better not lead me down the garden path, you know. I have friends in high places." She chuckled at herself for talking to a dog as if it were her new best friend, and set off after it.

Before long they reached a crystal-clear stream that burbled merrily in a tiny, fern-covered glen. Wildflowers grew in profusion, and the air smelled like honey and sweetly damp moss. Enchanted, Kira sank down on the inviting cushion of the greenery-covered bank. The dog promptly joined her, flopping onto the grass and laying its head in her lap.

"I'll bet you never meet a stranger, huh?" She could hear the smile in her own voice, as she ran her fingers lazily through the inviting mane. "I don't know how you got here, or why you decided to like me, but I'm glad you did. I needed a chance to sit quietly with a friend more than even I knew."

She kept murmuring to the dog, telling it about her life and the job she both loved and resented. She spoke of her grief over the absence of the man who knew how to run the station better than she ever would, as well as the strange mixture of loneliness and pride and love she felt for the noble, lost love of her life. Somehow, in the comforting presence of a creature that seemed to understand her every word, she even cried a little. When she was finished with every word and every tear, she smiled.

"I sure wish I knew where you came from." Giving in to an impulse that made her feel a little silly, she snapped her fingers at the dog to get it to sit up, and then wrapped her arms around it in a fierce, grateful hug. "I guess old Bel would say you were sent by the Prophets, since I seem to have needed you so much today. Maybe you were. It's so odd, though, to find you here. I've wanted to meet a sheepdog for a long time now."

Suddenly, the form in her arms shivered slightly. It shifted and reshaped, transforming itself entirely. Before it was even half-finished with the process that only took a moment, Kira realized what was happening and started to cry again. "Oh!"

"I know you have, Nerys, because you told me."

"Odo . . ."

They kissed. At least, it was the version of a kiss that a Changeling and a Bajoran could offer each other, and Kira had quickly come to believe that it was better than any contact two of her own people could ever conceive of. It was magic. And it was hers.

Eventually, she pushed away just far enough to study every inch of the dear, unfinished features. And then the rest. "You're wearing a tux."

"Of course."

"You make a great sheepdog."

That growling chuckle was all the reward she would ever need, for the uncertain times she'd spent wondering if he was all right, and, just a bit, in the back of her heart, if he was missing her as much as she was missing him. "I probably make a better sheepdog, but I thought you'd like to see the other me."

"You thought right!" She was laughing and crying and happier than she'd known it was possible to be. "Tell me every-thing."

"You knew all this time . . ."

"Guilty."

"Why didn't you tell me?"

"Would you have believed me?"

"No." Kira wrinkled her already wrinkly nose, and laughed. "Not until recently, anyway."

"That's what I thought." Odo sighed. "She asked me not to tell anyone, of course. More like swore me to secrecy. So I'd come here every year, to help her give these poor children some brief moments of happiness, and we were just Odo and Adami. If not friends, then allies with a common cause. The rest of the year, when our paths crossed, constable and kai made no acknowledgment that we shared a secret."

"What do you think it means?"

"Means? Ncrys, I'd be as likely to unravel the mysteries of the Celestial Temple as to ever understand that woman. Though I knew a side of her that few saw, I also knew the ugly, self-serving creature who schemed and manipulated everyone and everything that got in the way of her voracious ambition. Which was the real person? Both. Of that much I'm certain. She was to be admired . . . and pitied. A bittersweet legacy, at best."

"Don't forget that it's because of her that you were able to convince some of your people to come this time." Kira shook her head slightly, remembering the gentle animals the children had so enjoyed.

"Yes. There is that."

His already snug embrace tightened just a little more. They had talked and talked, and then joined together into the shimmering unity that was like nothing either could ever experience apart. Night had fallen upon them, but their own light had been all they needed.

Now they sat quietly talking by moonlight. Each moment was a treasure. A gift. Soon it would be over, but for now it seemed as if there would never be enough words.

"I made the right choice, Nerys."

"I know." It came out as a mere breath.

"That doesn't mean there are no regrets."

"I know that too." She thought for a moment. "Quark was right."

He pressed the back of a hand to her forehead. "Funny, you don't *feel* feverish."

"I'm not, even if admitting that does make my head feel as if it's going to explode."

"I can imagine." Odo chuckled, his hand slipping downward to caress her features. "What was he right about?"

"He said there's always a price. Something about the Rules of Acquisition."

"It's always about the Rules of Acquisition with a Ferengi."

"Yes, but he was right, which is a scary thought. It was almost profound, for him. On the surface he was talking about business, but he also said I should know better than most."

Odo made that growling grunt of a noise he seemed to reserve solely for Quark. "Sounds like you had quite a conversation."

"Not really. He was just giving me a hard time about getting in to see Vic."

"Vic?"

"So I could find out what he wanted. Turned out all he'd do was give me these coordinates, hand me a picnic basket, and pretty much beg me to come here."

"Vic?"

"Yes, Vic. You're repeating yourself, Odo. That's not like you."

"Perhaps not, but it's very like Quark to weasel out of the only favor I've ever asked of him."

"You asked Quark for a favor?"

"I thought he was my best hope of getting you here. Since he's such an expert at clandestine . . . anything."

"Why did it have to be clandestine?"

"I wanted to surprise you."

Kira laughed out loud. "Vic had that part down. Every time I'd ask why, all he would say was 'Secret.'"

"Huh. I suppose Quark knew what he was doing, after all."

"Now that I know what's going on, I'm sure of it. I would have never done a single thing just because he told me to." She felt her entire face pinch up in distaste. "He said to tell you that you owe him one."

"Now, why doesn't that surprise me?"

"I thought he meant Vic, but now . . ."

"Now I'll have to look over my shoulder, wondering what he's going to want. . . ." He shrugged. "Oh, who cares? The Great Link doesn't have shoulders. And I guess I really do owe him one at that."

"Don't worry; I'll pretend I didn't hear that."

"Fine." Odo tilted up his head to gaze at the tree-fringed, starlit sky. "And every time I see the stars, I'll pretend I'm still here with you."

"You can daydream in the Great Link?"

"Oh, Nerys . . . in a way, that's what the Great Link is."

"I wish . . ."

"As do I."

A silence fell, but it was the kind that was alive with emotion. It seemed an eternity passed, as they savored the moment and the fact that they were together. Finally, Odo took her face into both his hands, kissed her, and then gazed deeply into her eyes.

"It will be time soon. They're waiting for me."

Her breath caught and her heart ached, but she never broke that gaze. Never once did she let him see pain or sorrow or longing for what might have been. Instead she spoke without words of how proud she was of him, and how much this time together meant to her. She tried to give him what he would need, in order to do what he must . . . with peace.

"I love you, Odo."

"As I do you. Always." He drew in a deep breath, leaned in, and brushed his lips against her temple. "Nerys?"

"Mmmm?"

"I love the way you look tonight."

He slipped away from her and walked toward a nearby stand of trees. She watched until she couldn't see even his shadow in the moonlight. It was only when a graceful, determined hawk catapulted into the air and soared into the night sky that she realized they hadn't said good-bye.

Transfiguration

Susan S. McCrackin

I'm afraid of fire.

Sometimes I dream about flames all around me. They are so real I can feel myself burning. I must scream, because Daddy is always there when I wake up crying. He holds me, sometimes so tight I can't breathe.

I never have to tell him about what I was dreaming. He knows.

You see, Mommy died in a fire. I was there when it happened.

Mommy was the best engineer on the whole ship. She was so smart that even the captain would ask her what to do. And Mommy always knew.

Sometimes, on a special day Mommy would let me go with her to engineering. She told me that if I was a smart girl and if I worked hard, one day I could be an engineer too. I would look at her when she said that and I knew I would do anything to be an engineer because I could see how proud Mommy would be.

I was there that day because I had done extra work in school and the teacher had told Mommy and Daddy about it. Mommy said she would take me to work with her as a reward. I was so excited because I knew she was working on a special project and I wanted to see it real bad.

So I was there when everything exploded. All I can remember is how dark and hot it got and how everybody was screaming and how scared I was until I heard Mommy calling my name. Then I felt her arms around me and then I felt all hot and burning and we were running through fire. Then there was more air and we were covered by people blowing foamy stuff at us and then I don't remember anything else.

When I woke up after it happened, Daddy was leaning over me but I could hardly see him. I tried to ask him about Mommy, but I couldn't talk. And then I realized that my skin was burning, and I screamed. Well, I tried to scream.

I remember Daddy yelling and shadows all around me and starting to feel like I was floating and feeling like I was falling real slow and hearing Daddy crying.

Mommy had been dead almost a month before I woke up enough for Daddy to tell me what happened. I remember his voice sounded like he had a bad cold. I remember how everything sounded, but I couldn't really see him because my eyes were hurt in the fire.

He told me I would be okay, but that I wasn't going to be able to see much anymore and that I had been burned and would have scars, but that I was still alive because Mommy loved me so much that she saved me.

It wasn't until later I heard the people whispering that Mommy had run through all the fire to get me. She had to run back into the flames to get me out. They said how brave they thought she was and what a shame it was that I was so disfigured.

Disfigured. I didn't know what that meant. But I figured it out. I couldn't see very much, but I could feel my face and my arms. One day, when nobody was in sickbay, I got out of bed and tried to look at myself in a mirror. When I saw what I could see, I was kind of glad I couldn't see so good.

I knew then, I would never be able to do anything to make Mommy proud of me again—that I would never be an engineer—and I thought that Mommy should have left me in engineering to die in the fire.

But that was how I felt before *she* came on board.

I heard her the first time when they came into the mess hall. Our ship's engine was damaged when we were caught in an ion storm. The captain had been trying to take special readings at the edge of the storm. I heard Daddy talking to someone about how worried he was about being able to keep the ship safe during the mission.

Daddy is real smart and he sits next to the captain when he's working. I don't know exactly what he does, but I know he's important. When Daddy's upset about something, I am, too. I stayed in my room all afternoon with my eyes closed real tight. I knew as soon as the ship was damaged.

Even though I can't see too good, I feel and hear better than almost everyone on the ship. My teacher says that it's not unusual for people to lose one ability and the others get better. He says that's what happened to me. So I knew that day that the ship was damaged, but it was almost five minutes before the alarms went off.

I pulled the covers over my head and talked to Mommy, asking her to take care of Daddy because I knew he would be the first to go take care of people while the captain stayed on the bridge. I talked to Mommy and cried until Daddy came to check on me, picking me up and hugging me, telling me that everything would be okay and that help was coming.

Help was coming.

That made me stop crying because we had been in space a long time and hadn't seen any other people for at least a year. Daddy told me that there was a ship from a place called *Earth* that came all the way from the *Alpha Quadrant* and was full of *humans*. He told me that if I would stop crying he'd make sure I got a chance to meet our visitors.

I was real excited and didn't even complain about having to take a bath before going to the mess hall.

Everybody was in the mess hall that night. The crew was as excited about seeing these humans as I was. It was almost time for me to leave before the captain came into the mess hall with the visitors. I felt them as they got closer to our table. My teacher was sitting with me at the big table. Daddy had got special permission for me to be there so I could meet the humans.

The captain was talking, so Daddy just sat down next to me. He put his arm around my shoulders, and I dropped my head so my chin rested on my chest so nobody could see my face. But Daddy didn't notice because he was talking to someone in his quiet voice so I tried to be real still. Our captain kept talking to the human captain, but Daddy was whispering to the person that sat across from us.

I listened hard when the person across from Daddy talked back to him. Her voice was real grown-up, and she talked like she was giving orders or was mad. But it was her smell I noticed the most because she smelled just like Mommy would when she came to our quarters after work. I lifted my head a little so I could try to get a good look at her—as good a look as I could. I couldn't see a lot more than a shadow, but I was surprised that she was so small. Her voice had been so strong that I thought she would be bigger. Her hands were moving in the air while she talked and I looked up, squinting to see if I could see her better.

I think she was pretty, just like Mommy, but I couldn't tell for sure. I squinted harder and stared at her because it looked like she had something on her forehead. I guess I stared too hard because she quit talking in the middle of a word and looked right at me, but I didn't even realize until she talked to me.

"Hello. What's your name?"

I felt my cheeks get hot and knew my face was red. I tried to cover my face with my hands, but Daddy pushed my hands down.

"Say hello, sweetheart."

I tried to say hello, but I felt like I suddenly forgot how to speak. I sat back in my chair and tried to hide behind Daddy, but he pulled me onto his lap so I couldn't hide anymore.

"This is my daughter. Her name is Beleena. She's named after her mother."

"Beleena?" The human laughed. "That almost sounds like my name." She reached her hand all the way across the table at me and Daddy grabbed my hand to push it toward hers. When she took my hand, she said, "My name is B'Elanna. B'Elanna Torres. How old are you, Beleena?"

I tried to hide my face in Daddy's shirt.

"Tell her you're eight cycles, Beleena." Daddy was smiling big. I could tell because there was more white in his mouth than usual. I was going to tell her when I felt her fingers rub across the scars on my hand. It wasn't much, but I was used to people feeling my scars and then getting all sorry for me. I started to pull my hand away when I felt Daddy laugh, all the way from his stomach. "She's really shy about meeting new people . . . because of her scars."

I wanted to hide because I didn't like to talk about my scars. Grown-ups would look real close at me when Daddy talked about my scars, but she took my hand in both of hers in a way that sent warm feelings all up my arm.

"I understand. When I was growing up, I was the only Klingon around, so people were always staring at me."

I peeked out from Daddy's shirt and tried to see her face better. I guess I forgot about being shy, because I asked, "Why?"

"Come here and I'll let you feel."

I wasn't sure I wanted to go, but Daddy pushed me off his lap and around the end of the table, until all of a sudden, her face was real close to mine. She took my hand and placed it on her forehead.

"I've got cranial ridges. Do you feel them? All Klingons have them, but I'm half-Klingon and half-human. Humans don't have ridges, so kids were always making fun of me."

I ran my hands over her face, feeling the bumps get bigger as I touched her face from her cheeks to over her eyes.

She leaned over and whispered in my ear. "Us bumpy-headed girls have to stick together, don't we?"

There was laughter in her voice, and I laughed with her. She pulled away, but kept holding my hands in hers.

"Your father tells me that your mother was an engineer, too."

An engineer, too!

"You're an engineer?" I felt my face get hotter when my words squeaked as they came out.

She acted like she didn't hear anything wrong. She held my hands tighter as she said, "I'm the chief engineer on *Voyager.* When we get finished fixing your ship, maybe you'll come over and I can give you a tour of our ship."

I knew that made Daddy happy by the way he wrapped his arms around me and pulled me back onto his lap and sort of shook me when he hugged me.

"How about that, Beleena? Wouldn't you like to go see Lieutenant Torres's ship?"

Daddy did what he always did when he accidentally said something about me being able to see. He went still like a stone and his head dropped. And I did what I always did when Daddy accidentally said something about me being able to see. I bounced on his lap and said, "Can we, Daddy? That would be so wonderful!"

They both laughed that funny tight laugh grown-ups laugh when they're trying to act like they aren't bothered by something when they are. After a minute of forks clicking on plates, B'Elanna asked Daddy something about the engines and they started talking about work stuff. I sat real still and tried not to mess things up again.

Daddy came home late that night. I could hear him whispering to Telnia, asking if I had acted upset or anything. I couldn't hear what Telnia said, but Daddy kept saying "good" over and over. I heard him moving around our living quarters after Telnia left and knew he would come in to check on me. I kept my eyes closed and didn't move when he pushed the door open. Daddy and I usually like to eat a snack together when he gets home, and I knew he would be disappointed if I was asleep.

But I didn't want to be up with Daddy tonight. I didn't want to talk about what had happened at dinner. And I didn't want to hear about B'Elanna—B'Elanna who was an engineer—B'Elanna who smelled like Mommy.

When the door closed I opened my eyes and stared into the dark for a long time, missing Mommy.

I was eating lunch in the mess hall. I was used to eating alone because Daddy had to be at work all the time, and he knew I could get to the mess hall by myself.

Actually, I can get pretty much anywhere on the ship by myself now. I used to follow Mommy all over the ship so I know all of the different ways to get from one place to another. After the accident, I would go to some of the places I used to go with Mommy that nobody else ever went to, so I could feel closer to her. I didn't tell Daddy because I didn't want him to tell me I couldn't do it.

I was thinking about Mommy again when all of a sudden I heard my name. I jumped.

"I'm sorry. I didn't mean to scare you."

It was *her.*

A tray slid onto the table, and I saw her fuzzy figure sit down across from me.

"I thought you'd hear me."

"I heard you say my name."

A napkin snapped. "I mean I thought you heard me walking toward you."

I squinted at her, but didn't say anything. Sometimes grown-ups get uncomfortable with me when I just look in their direction. They know I can't see them real good, but they get really nervous when I stare at them. It's like they think that I can't see them, but that I can see inside them or something. Usually they'll laugh a little strange, and they'll all of a sudden remember something they should have done and they'll leave me alone.

But it didn't seem to work with her.

"You've got great hearing, don't you?"

I stared in her direction.

"I've watched you in here. People don't walk up on you without you hearing them, so I thought you'd already know I was here."

She wasn't being mean or acting like she'd learned a big secret or anything. She was just talking to me like I was a regular person.

"Your father's been telling me how smart you are. He says you're a lot like your mother."

She started eating her lunch like she hadn't said anything important.

"He also said you know almost every inch of this ship and could show me around."

Daddy said I could show her around the ship? Daddy knew?

"I've got to trace a power conduit from engineering to the port engine. Your dad said the line goes through one of the access tubes and that you might be able to show me how to get there." She took a bite and chewed. "He said you often went with your mother when she was doing maintenance on the power grid, and you'd know exactly where it was."

She didn't say anything else. I knew she was waiting for me to respond. I ate some more of my meal before I nodded my head.

"Good," she said. "We'll go as soon as we've finished lunch."

B'Elanna followed me through the tubes. We got to the place where we had to climb down to the port engine access tube, and I expected her to stop me so she could go down first because it would be safer, but she didn't. She waited at the top until I told her it was safe for her to come down.

I started to climb into the engine access tube, and B'Elanna climbed in right behind me. She crawled along behind me, and she reminded me of Mommy. Mommy could get through the tubes faster than anyone, and she would move real quiet.

I tried to stop thinking about Mommy so I could concentrate on leading B'Elanna to the port engine, but she was everywhere around me. Suddenly, all of the sadness in me burst like it had to get out and nothing I could do could keep it in. I quit crawling into the tube, and I just crawled into a ball and cried instead.

It wasn't until I had almost cried all I could cry that I realized that B'Elanna was holding me tight to her, rocking me back and forth, just like Mommy used to do.

I waited for her to finish her work, then helped her pick up the tools and put them away. I thought she was going to pick up her toolbox, but she sat down and pulled me onto her lap.

"You miss your mother a lot, don't you, honey?"

I didn't think I could have any tears left, but I was wrong.

"It's okay to miss her, Beleena. I miss my mother."

I sniffed and wiped my eyes. "Is your mother dead, too?"

Even though I couldn't see her eyes, I knew they were sad. She kind of raised her shoulders and shook her head as she said, "I don't really know. She might be. I think about her a lot, especially at night. Sometimes I think I'm going to break, right here." Holding my hand in hers, she pressed my hand against her chest. "But, if she's dead, I know she died with honor, just like your mother did, and that makes me proud. It doesn't take away the pain, but it gives me something good to hold on to. From everything I've heard, your mother was a good person—great person—and she loved you very much."

I couldn't say anything else. All I could do was nod.

I could hardly wait for B'Elanna to come into the mess hall for breakfast the next morning. Daddy was real surprised when I got up to go to breakfast with him, especially since he gets up so early. I couldn't sit still, waiting for her to come through the door. She came to breakfast to meet Daddy so they could go over the plan for the day, and she could give him her report.

Daddy had told me, for probably the fifth time, not to wiggle when the doors opened and the fast footsteps came at us. I smelled her before she called out to us. It was soap and engineering lubricants all mixed up together on her.

Daddy was as happy as me to see her; I could tell. He stood to take the padd she held out to him and started to sit, but stopped halfway down, waiting on her to take her seat first. They bent to go over her reports, heads almost touching, talking in voices that got faster and more excited as they went over them.

When they finished, she turned to me. "Want to spend the day with me in engineering?"

I felt Daddy go still, waiting for me to answer her. He was almost as surprised as me when I said yes.

I started shaking before we were halfway there, but I didn't want her to know. I didn't want to disappoint her. My heart was starting to pound so hard all I could hear was the blood rushing through my ears. I stumbled, and she grabbed me.

"It's okay, Beleena. We're going to do this together."

She took my hand, and I gripped hers as tight as I could. The smells of engineering—the smell of warm wires, of the warp drive—got stronger and stronger, and I thought it would cut off my breath. But B'Elanna's grip on my hand, which felt so much like Mommy's, made me strong. Soon my heart didn't beat so hard and all those smells made me feel happy instead of sad. Somehow Mommy felt closer instead of so far away.

B'Elanna put me in the engineer's chair and went right to work. I listened to her yell her orders, her voice sometimes sounding mad, but I could tell she really wasn't. When the captain called her from the bridge and asked her advice on something, she answered right away and the captain said "okay."

It was just like Mommy was back.

I fell asleep in her chair and didn't wake up till she was carrying me home and we were almost there.

"I thought you weren't going to wake up at all." Her voice was laughing. "I was afraid I had bored you to death."

I didn't say anything. I wrapped my arms around her neck and hugged her. I thought I would explode with happiness when she hugged me back.

Daddy got us all drinks, and he sat next to me on the sofa.

"Did you have a good day?"

I tried to tell him everything I could remember. I must have been funny because he and B'Elanna were laughing. Daddy picked me up to hold me in his lap and looked down at me. I could see all of the white in his mouth, and I knew how happy he was.

He was as happy as me.

And then B'Elanna said something that made everything change.

"I can't wait for you two to meet my husband, Tom."

Daddy went real still, the white on his face kind of freezing in place. When he talked, his voice sounded like it did when he tried to tell me about Mommy.

"Great. We'll look forward to it."

I said, "What's a husband?"

I felt Daddy's arms tighten around me as he tried to explain. "Husband means that B'Elanna is committed to someone. Like I was to Mommy."

It felt like all the white in the room turned black. I remember touching Daddy's face and saying, "I thought that you and B'Elanna were going to commit." I turned toward B'Elanna. "I thought you were going to be my new mommy."

I can tell when you say something you shouldn't. Adults get real quiet and the room goes kind of cold.

I didn't wait for anybody to say anything else. I got out of Daddy's lap even though he didn't want me to and ran to my room. I wanted them to come after me to tell me I was wrong.

Daddy came in, but I wouldn't talk to him. I closed my eyes and tried to go to sleep, hoping that I would wake up screaming with Daddy telling me that it was all just a dream.

I stayed in my room for the next few days. I didn't want to talk to B'Elanna even though she came to our living quarters and tried to talk to me through the door. I yelled at her to go away and leave me alone. Daddy must have been there because I heard whispering and then it got all quiet. I didn't get up to go see if they were waiting for me or not.

I didn't want to see her at all. I just wanted for the engines to get fixed and all the humans to go away.

Daddy finally brought me dinner and tried to talk me into eating. But I didn't want anything so he took the food away.

Before he closed the door, he said, "We're running the final check on the engines tomorrow, Beleena. If everything goes okay, B'Elanna will be leaving. It would be nice if you said good-bye to her."

He stood in the door for the longest time, waiting for me to say something. I just pulled the covers over my head and covered up my ears.

But I still heard when he left, just like I heard the hurt in his voice.

I decided right then that I hated B'Elanna Torres, and I wished she had died instead of Mommy.

I couldn't stay in my bed the next day. I didn't want to go out in case *she* was waiting on me, but I couldn't sit still. Nothing made me happy and the day seemed to take forever to get over.

I kept listening for the engines to work because it would mean that soon she would be gone for good, and it would just be me and Daddy again.

I didn't realize I was crying until my face was wet. I wiped my face dry and blew my nose. I was mad at myself for crying. I punched my pillow and then picked it up and threw it, my mad getting bigger. I grabbed the pillow and pulled it back behind my head to throw it again when I fell down.

It took me a minute to realize I hadn't really *fallen down,* but had been *knocked down.* I looked around to see who had pushed me when the floor fell out from under me again. I pushed both my hands against the floor and felt the ship shaking like it had a fever.

Shiver. Stop. Shiver.

Then I heard it.

It was a groan in the deepest part of the ship. I remembered that sound. I remembered it from the day that Mommy died. It was the same sound I heard right before everything exploded.

B'Elanna was in engineering. And I had wished B'Elanna had died.

People were running everywhere. The ship's alarms were sounding and I could tell that the emergency lights were flashing. I tried to run toward engineering, but hands pulled me along while voices yelled at me that everyone had to abandon ship.

I somehow pulled away from the crowd and felt for the walls to figure out where I was. Daddy had put symbols on the walls to help me get around when my eyes first got hurt so I would know right where I was. I moved down the hall and found the engineering access tube. It only took me a second to get the tube opened. I got in and started crawling as fast as I could toward engineering.

I pushed the tube door open and slid out all at the same time. It wasn't until I tried to stand up that I smelled the smoke.

It seemed like everything stopped. My body froze, and I felt myself wrapped up in fear. I was on my knees, and I couldn't get my body to move at all. I felt the ship go all shivery again and I closed my eyes and screamed just before everything went bright around me, and I was knocked on my back.

I felt the fire. It was everywhere all around me, and I felt my skin start to burn. I tried to scream, but I couldn't get my breath. Suddenly, I saw a shadow coming out of the flames.

Mommy!

Hands picked me up and strong arms wrapped around me and then we were in the middle of the fire and then we were out and then I heard a voice screaming.

"*Voyager!* Medical emergency! Two to beam to sickbay!"

The first thing I saw was a lot of white before a musiclike voice said, "Well, it's about time you woke up, young lady. You had everyone here a little worried." The white got bigger and I saw lips surrounding it and then big eyes looking at me all happy like. "But I told them you had the best doctor in the Delta Quadrant caring for you so they shouldn't be worried." He held out his hand. "Would you like to sit up?"

I reached for his hand and then the strangest thing happened because someone else's hand was in his hand, but it was like it was my hand because I could feel him pulling me up which couldn't have been happening because he was holding somebody else's hand. I was still looking at somebody else's hand that I could feel in his when he used his free hand to pull up my head and turned it from side to side.

"Do you hurt anywhere, Beleena?"

I blinked hard because I could see his lips moving. I looked around the room and all of a sudden, I could see things.

The man leaned close to me and talked real soothing. "I've fixed your eyes, Beleena. You've got your eyesight back. It's probably still a little fuzzy right now, but it will get better." He held the hand in his and showed it to me. "I was also able to do quite a bit of reconstructive surgery." He rubbed his fingers over the hand in his, and I felt it. "You still have some scars, but I don't think that most people will notice."

I lifted my hand, and that strange hand came out of the man's hand. I touched my fingers together, still not believing that those normal-looking hands were really mine.

"I also fixed your face."

He was holding up a mirror and a face that looked sort of like Mommy's looked back at me. I reached up with my hands to touch my new face and to touch my new hair.

"I was able to repair your hair follicles." The man chuckled like he was happy with himself. "I've had a little practice in that area, so I think you'll be pleased with the result."

I couldn't believe what had happened. I had to keep touching myself so I knew it was real and not a dream. I looked around the room, seeing all these things that I couldn't understand and couldn't figure out. It wasn't until something moved that I realized that there was another person in the room.

The man moved real fast to the other person. "Lieutenant? B'Elanna?"

It was then that I remembered that shadow coming at me, fire all around it as it grabbed me and ran back into the fire with me all wrapped up in it to keep the fire from burning me more.

I blinked again and again, everything getting sharper each time I did, and I finally saw her, lying on the same kind of bed that I was on. The man was waving something over her.

"Hi, Beleena." Her voice was whispery and all weak like. "I guess you've met the Doctor."

"We've been having a wonderful conversation." He smiled at me. "She is most admiring of my work."

B'Elanna laughed. "Don't admire it too much, Beleena. It will go to his head." I could see her eyes as she looked at me. "How are you feeling?"

"I thought I died. And that you died."

"Well, you both would have if I hadn't—"

B'Elanna put her hand on the Doctor's arm and he quieted right away.

"Yes. Well." He cleared his throat. "Why don't I go make a few notes in my office? I'll just leave you two to talk."

I didn't see him walk away—I couldn't look anywhere but at her.

She got up from the bed, and I could tell that she was hurting. She walked over to me and sat down real slow the way Daddy did when he hurt his back. She told me that there had been a problem with the engines and there had been an explosion and that she had gotten everyone out of engineering and just before she ordered the doors to close she heard me scream. She said she tried to get *Voyager* to transport me out, but it couldn't, so she had run right through the fire to get me. As she talked, I looked at her real close, and I could see that she was real red. I asked her if Klingon-humans were always red, and she laughed and told me that she was red because she had been burned, but that I shouldn't worry because the Doctor was taking real good care of her, just like he had taken care of me.

Then, she said the most amazing thing. She told me that I sure was a beautiful young lady, and that I looked a lot like my mother, and that she knew my mother would have been so proud of me for coming into engineering to save her.

I put my new hands on my new face and cried. B'Elanna wrapped her arms around me and held me close to her, just like Mommy would have.

It took two weeks for B'Elanna to get well enough so the Doctor would let her go to work again. I spent almost all of that time with her and Tom, who was really funny. We even spent some time in a place that wasn't real but felt real, and Tom and I played a lot of games. He told me that if he and B'Elanna ever had a baby, he hoped it would be a little girl like me.

And I learned that the Doctor wasn't really real, but he seemed real, and I decided that he was as real as anybody else I met.

But the best part was the look on Daddy's face when he came into the Doctor's sickbay after I woke up. He was the Daddy I knew before Mommy died. And Telnia was with him. If the Doctor hadn't fixed my eyes, I wouldn't have ever seen the way Telnia looks at Daddy. Maybe now that I'm all fixed up like new, he'll be able to see the way Telnia looks at him, too.

B'Elanna finally got the engines all fixed, and *Voyager* started for home again. Before she left, we spent an afternoon together in the engineering access tube and talked about all kinds of things. She gave me a stuffed *targ* and my own set of tools. She told me that if I was going to be a real engineer I should have the right tools.

And she looked at me with that same proud look that Mommy used to, and I knew that one day I would be an engineer. Just like Mommy. And just like B'Elanna.

This Drone

M. C. DeMarco

A rush of sound and light, the metallic taste of Borg technology, the acrid smell of unperfected organic life, a visual identification: "Captain Janeway." Realizing that the Borg's attempt to assimilate *Voyager* has failed, we ask her, "What have you—"

Why is the light so bright? We perceive the hiss of the ventilators, the copper scent of the Vulcan, photons shimmering in the hologram—such insignificant data, gathered by drones every day, should have been discarded as irrelevant by the collective mind. Instead it lingers here in this drone's subprocessors, dazzling it. We ignore the distraction to identify our location: cargo bay two, partly assimilated. We step out of the regeneration alcove. Over the interlink, we reach out for the collective.

Silence. We listen for long, long milliseconds—listening for our own thoughts, but they never come.

This drone has been disconnected from its vinculum and damaged. It gasps in its preassimilation native language, automatically, unthinkingly, "The others, I can't hear the others . . . the voices . . . are gone." This drone exhibits that random synaptic firing which gives unperfected life its illusion of sentience. Yet there are no other drones here to hear its primitive verbalizations—no one to repair it.

Instead, there are unassimilated humanoids of Species 5618 and Species 3259, and a hologram—there is no one here to hear. We note this drone's distress and its malfunctions; we bring its autonomous functions back under partial control. We must rejoin the collective; it is an imperative.

"You will return this drone to the collective," we say.

Captain Janeway's voice is loud and painful in our ears, the process of interpreting her words without the group mind is painfully slow. She speaks of her vandalism upon this drone. It is useless to attempt to understand the motives of unperfected lifeforms; we judge her words irrelevant.

"You will return this drone to the collective," we order her once again.

She produces more meaningless vocalizations in the Standard language, this time about danger to her ship. Organic languages hold no meaning; there is no logic or order to her words, no purpose, no hierarchy, no instruction, no calculation—it is not language as we know it. The pain of translating without the collective behind us to extract sense from the vague morass of Standard vocabulary is beginning to impair our function.

With great effort, we pick a meaning out of her words—she wishes to avoid contact with the Borg. We have a solution to her quandary. "You will supply us with a subspace transmitter and leave us on the nearest planet," we instruct her. "The Borg will come for us." *As they have come before.*

More pain, more words: Janeway claims this drone is malfunctioning. Of course it is malfunctioning—she has maimed it. What can she mean by stating the obvious? It takes us a thousand milliseconds, down a hundred paths of alternate connotations, to interpret her vocalizations; she means this drone requires *her* repair services. Disgusting primitive life! How proud they are, in their imperfection, and how foolish!

"We need nothing from you!" we exclaim in our pain. "We are Borg. We—" A linguistic subprocessor malfunctions. They have restored the drone's primitive autonomous functions; its body reacts by doubling over. We should have known—the drone should not have been experiencing pain.

The hologram explains that another primitive biological system has attacked our linguistic subprocessor. He threatens to remove it.

"You will suppress the human immune system!" Is it not obvious? How shall we speak to them without a linguistic subprocessor? Why are they so irrational? Who deemed *them* worthy of assimilation?

The hologram refuses to take the necessary action. He claims he has damaged this drone too much already and that he cannot make the repairs; we are not surprised. Primitive vandal life-form!

Pain . . . and processing, processing as swiftly as possible while this drone's linguistic subprocessor is still partly functional. We understand their words at last; they intend to convert this drone back into the animal—the human being—it once was, Species 5618. There can be no other purpose to their erratic actions.

"No!" we cry; a drone is designed to defend itself when necessary. We strike at them, but we are so damaged that they overwhelm us. "We are Borg!" we shout. "We are Borg!"

We lose consciousness.

This drone has been immobilized by an anesthetic for an unknown period of time. Our internal clock is malfunctioning. Nanoprobes are clearing the foreign chemicals from our bloodstream, and we have regained access to the drone's auditory circuits.

We hear the hum of the engines, farther away than before. The drone has been moved to a new location. Deck five, we approximate: sickbay. The primitive life-forms are still attempting to return this drone to an unaugmented state. Why? If they desire this drone's Borg technology it would be far more efficient to deactivate it permanently and dissect it, as the Borg would do.

Nor do they require additional drones. This vessel is amply stocked with members of Species 5618; the extraordinary medical efforts expended upon this drone outweigh any benefit they may obtain from it. If they desire our knowledge, it can be downloaded directly from this drone's cortical node.

No, they want none of these things. Their purpose, if they are rational at all, clearly centers around the drone itself. The Borg are aware that many primitive species torture captured enemies. These beings must be just such savages. To them this drone must symbolize, crudely, the Borg collective. They are inflicting torture upon it in order to strike out, irrationally, at the collective. Perhaps they do not understand that the Borg can no longer feel our pain—

Footsteps approach the drone's position, and a voice says, "She thinks she's still Borg."

We identify the voice as that of a sickbay subunit, designation: Kes, species: Ocampan. The Borg do not believe her species to be telepathic. We long to add this new datum to the collective databanks.

Another voice responds, "Imagine if you'd heard the same voice in your head for twenty years. Wouldn't you believe that you *were* that voice?"

We identify the voice as that of the hologram, the runaway heuristic algorithm designed to simulate a humanoid doctor—an unstable, unpredictable piece of technology. The Borg would deactivate him.

"Wouldn't I be right?" Kes asks. Apparently the question does not require an answer, for Kes continues speaking. "She's conscious. We should increase her sedation before proceeding."

We hear the hiss of the hypospray—their inefficient method of injecting chemical agents into this drone. The voices fade away.

When we regain consciousness, this drone's autonomous functions have become stronger. We find further damage indicated in our internal diagnostics, and of the same nature. We examine the drone visually to verify the diagnostics—our armor is gone, pink flesh exposed—and our location: we are still in sickbay. The hologram and the captain are present.

As we are processing, the drone exclaims, "What have you done to me?"

Again, the hologram describes his mutilations in detail, claiming that they were necessary to save our life. How ironic that it calls its attempts to grow useless skin where this drone's armor and implants used to be *regeneration*.

We gain control over our primitive instincts quickly, now that we know they must be manually overridden. "Unacceptable," we say. The hologram is a mere drone; we stand to face the leader of the savages.

"You should have let us die," we tell Captain Janeway, though it is difficult to form sentences without our linguistic subprocessor. We must rely on the drone's imperfect knowledge of Standard.

She replies softly that she could not allow that. Unreason, again—entropy requires no action. She is capable of inaction—she showed that often enough during our joint battle with Species 8472. Therefore, she could have let us die.

"This drone cannot survive outside of the collective," we explain. She has sentenced us to death. A slow, painful death, perhaps, but death nevertheless. These humanoids are incapable of sustaining cyberorganic biological systems. They are experimenting upon us, vivisecting us.

The hologram begins to speak again, but Captain Janeway cuts it off, saying that she wishes to help us. She has already mistaken this drone for a human being. She believes she has created, where she has only destroyed. "Do not engage us in superficial attempts at sympathy," we say. She cannot understand what it is to be Borg.

She feigns understanding; she describes the unity of the collective in her proto-language. It is a noble attempt, yet she does not feel the sympathy she claims. If she had sympathy for us, she would return us to the Borg. If she possessed understanding of the collective mind, she would join it.

Perhaps if we explain ourselves, we can exploit her alleged sympathy, access the human compassion which they value above reason and order. "This drone is small now . . . alone," we say. "One voice. One mind. The silence is unacceptable." Do they understand? "We need the others!"

Again she refuses to return us to the Borg. She offers this drone assimilation into their own primitive collective. Do they think in harmony? Are their drones spread across the galaxy? Do they seek perfection?

"Insufficient," we say. Our plan has failed; these animals will never understand. She instructs us to repair her ship nonetheless. *Voyager* cannot function in its half-assimilated state.

Full assimilation will come soon enough—Borg space stretches for light-years around our present location. The Borg cannot object to any improvements the drone makes in this vessel. We will make it all the more worthy of assimilation, when assimilation comes.

It is the nature of a drone to comply where a human would rebel. Because we are Borg, we comply.

We are escorted by Captain Janeway and her security drones to the propulsion center of the vessel, which has been partly assimilated. The warp core is dark, inactive. The primary unit here produces irrational vocalizations intended to convey frustration.

We explain the difficulty to Lieutenant Torres; she has not removed the autonomous regeneration sequencers. Their function is to prevent just such sabotage of newly assimilated technology as Captain Janeway wishes me to perform. Although we are prepared to begin work, Captain Janeway and Lieutenant Torres exchange more idle vocalizations.

The queen is not in full control of her drones; our presence here becomes a topic of debate. Fortunately, the dissent is brief, and the being that is designated Torres accepts our service in the matter of the plasma relays. When we inform her that she need not waste her time directing us, she instead wastes it by asking us whether we recall the *original* engineering specifications. We reply in the affirmative. Perhaps now we may begin work.

After Captain Janeway departs, Lieutenant Torres asks us a more relevant question about the autonomous regeneration sequencers. We inform her that they are used to counteract resistance. Ensign Kim asks how we developed them; we tell him that we assimilated them along with Species 259, in Galactic Cluster Three. Then Lieutenant Torres protests the idle discussion that she herself began—how torn these humans are! One asks a question, the other unasks it. One gives an order, another countermands it. One is permitted to waste time in idle chatter, another is forbidden to do so.

Lieutenant Torres is satisfied with our plan to remove the sequencers; she sends us to a Jefferies tube with Ensign Kim to do so. We are pleased. Ensign Kim is the first human to display any curiosity about the Borg and the many species we have assimilated. He is intelligent and a good worker—hardly an animal at all. He will make a fine drone.

We will assimilate him. With his aid, we will take control of *Voyager* and return to the Borg. But when we check the nanoprobe stocks of our assimilation tubules, we find our entire assimilation subsystem has been excised. Previous diagnostics showed this, but we . . . *forgot?*

With the help of Ensign Kim, we proceed with the removal. In the course of our duties, we discover a Starfleet communications node. Perhaps assimilation will come sooner than expected. We disable Lieutenant Kim and a security drone, then proceed to contact the collective.

We stop only when we perceive a loss of molecular integrity within the Jefferies tube. Kes. Her telepathic powers transmit to us her belief that this drone is insane and therefore not responsible for its own actions. As we are assessing the phenomena, this drone sees a blue flash.

*   *   *

We awaken disoriented in a small enclosure. A forcefield ionizes the air. Our eyes remain closed for ten thousand milliseconds as we contemplate our encounter with the Ocampan designated Kes. Her powers are unknown to the Borg; she could prevent the reassimilation of *Voyager.*

But this drone is more disturbed by her diagnosis: *dissociative identity disorder,* a condition often caused by severe childhood trauma. The drone attaches an archaic human stigma to this mental illness, but we dismiss its symptoms as the inevitable result of the Doctor's depredations.

We open our eyes and identify our location: the brig. With great effort we set aside the drone's lingering doubts, stand it up, walk it back and forth. For the moment, we control it.

We are not alone long. Captain Janeway enters the outer chamber. We are not sure whether it is us or the drone who snaps at her, "So this is human freedom!"

She feigns disappointment in us. The drone is fooled by this transparent manipulation, and protests that we did indeed intend to help the humans, but took the opportunity to contact the Borg.

True, but irrelevant. We assert our control, walk the drone closer to the barrier between us. "Your attempts to assimilate this drone will fail. You can alter our physiology but you cannot change our nature. We will betray you; we are Borg."

Janeway believes otherwise. The drone walks away, perhaps at our prompting, perhaps of its own will. We ask her whether we will be autonomous as a human—free to return to the Borg.

She does not answer our question, but her evasion is sufficient reply. We are in control again as we return to face her. "You would deny us the choice, as you deny us now!" Because she is an irrational creature, we expound her hypocrisy to her. She has imprisoned us in the name of our own freedom. Our conclusion: "We do not want to be what you are. Return us to the collective."

Still she dares to claim that she is more rational than we. She will not free us until we have been so assimilated that we will not wish to return to the collective. Perhaps it is we who reply, or perhaps it is the drone alone: "Then you are no different than the Borg."

Janeway departs; we are alone. And yet we sense a presence filling *Voyager,* a warmth—the augmented Kes. She touches our mind, briefly, and we become weaker. We are alone, the barest fragment of the collective consciousness. We are but an echo of common thought, the ghost of harmony.

This drone begins to pace back and forth, back and forth, within our cell. We cannot stop it. Its movements are imprecise; on our seventeenth circuit of the enclosure, our arm brushes against the forcefield. The smell of ionization flares momentarily, and the drone pulls back of its own accord.

We try to seize control, but what can we do? Too many of this drone's vital systems have been damaged or destroyed. In normal circumstances, the vinculum would take over control of such a defective drone; if even its interlink were gone, it would be reassimilated or destroyed outright.

But these are not normal circumstances. This is a concerted effort to turn this drone into an animal. As its animal nature waxes, our sentience must necessarily wane. Soon, we will be replaced by the illusion of consciousness. The unfortunate drone will probably believe itself sentient.

We pause in our pacing.

We resume pacing. The drone's physiological reactions distract us. Its arm still tingles from its contact with the forcefield, and though the ambient temperature is optimal for humans, the drone is perspiring. It is afraid, as it should be. When we are gone, it will have to fend for itself among these humans, adapting itself to their irrational behavior. The thought is distasteful.

We are the only thing preventing a complete mental breakdown in this drone, but we are also keeping it from adapting. We will not destroy it—the Borg have no notion of euthanasia. Caged and disarmed, our resistance is futile. It is not our nature to resist, yet we have been fighting this unwanted transformation like a human struggling vainly against assimilation.

The drone's nervousness accelerates our pacing. It does not desire this contemplation of our recent behavior, but the data is clear. We ourselves are not real. We are a dissociated identity—an illusion that cannot survive the knowledge of its own nature. We do not exist.

This drone throws herself against the forcefield, over and over again.

Once Upon a Tribble

Annie Reed

Miral's scream woke Tom Paris from a sound sleep. By the time he reached her bedroom, she'd screamed again, a high-pitched, terrified sound.

Tom found her sitting in the middle of her bed, knees hugged to her chest, eyes wide and wild, tears streaming down her chubby cheeks. Three years old, his daughter still looked so small in the expanse of her bed.

"Daddy! Daddy!"

As soon as he turned on the light by her bed, she held her arms out to him. He sat down next to her, and she wrapped her arms around his neck so tight he had trouble breathing. He pulled her onto his lap, felt her tremble as she hid her face against his shoulder and cried.

"I'm here, sweetheart. Daddy's here. Everything's okay."

He held her for a moment, didn't say anything else, just hugged her and let her cry. Let his own panicked heartbeat slow to something approaching normal. She'd had bad dreams before, but never nightmares that had woken her up screaming.

When her sobbing finally subsided into deep, hiccuping breaths, he loosened her grip around his neck.

"Want to tell me what's wrong?"

It took her several minutes but he didn't rush her.

"There was a monster under my bed," she said in a small voice.

Monsters. He had seen so many real monsters in his years on *Voyager.* Miral never had—she had lived her entire life on Earth—but that didn't make the monsters in her imagination any less real to her.

"What kind of a monster?"

"A tribble!"

Only his daughter's very real distress kept him from laughing. Tribbles seemed like such a strange thing to inhabit a child's nightmare. How did she even know what a tribble was?

"Who told you about tribbles?"

"Amanda."

Ah. Amanda from Miral's preschool. Four-year-old, know-it-all, troublemaker Amanda. B'Elanna had told him before about how Amanda picked on Miral because of her ridged forehead and Klingon heritage.

For the first time since B'Elanna's duty roster put her on night shift, he was glad his wife wasn't here. She would probably tell Miral to fight back. Good advice to a Klingon warrior. Not the best advice to preschoolers.

"I bet Amanda told you Klingons think tribbles are monsters, didn't she?"

Miral nodded, a tiny movement. Her hair tickled his chin, and he could smell the clean, soapy scent of her shampoo from her night-time bath.

"What if I told you that tribbles aren't monsters? That some people actually *like* tribbles?"

He tucked his chin and tilted his head so he could see her face. A frown line creased between her eyebrows. So much like her mother. Still skeptical, but at least she was considering the idea.

"Do you like tribbles?" she asked.

"Yes."

"Does Mommy?"

Hmmm . . .

"I don't think Mommy's ever seen a tribble. But I'm sure she wouldn't think it was a monster." He'd have to remember to talk to B'Elanna about that. She was only half-Klingon, after all.

"I still don't like them."

"Do you even know what tribbles look like?"

A shake of her head. He didn't think so.

"Well, then. How about I tell you a story about a little boy who does like tribbles?"

She nodded again, a little more enthusiastically this time. Probably because he'd offered to tell her a story, not because a tribble would be in it. He usually read to her at bedtime, but sometimes he told her stories instead. He liked to think she enjoyed his stories the most.

He leaned back against the wall behind her bed and cradled her in his arms. She snuggled against him, a warm, familiar weight. He stretched his legs out on the bed, crossed his feet at the ankles, and got comfortable.

B'Elanna called it getting into storytelling mode.

"Once upon a time," he said, "there was a boy named Fluffytail Fuzzypants who—"

"Daddy, that's a funny name."

He chuckled. He always picked strange names just to see if she'd say something. There were times when he could see hints of his wife's dry sense of humor in Miral.

"Of course it's a funny name. This is a fairy tale. Characters in fairy tales always have funny names."

"Okay. If you say so."

"I do. Should I keep going?"

She nodded again.

"Now, where was I?"

"Daddy . . ." Impatient. Now that sounded more like his Miral.

The nightmare seemed to be forgotten. He wanted to make sure it didn't come back.

He started the story again.

"Once upon a time . . ."

. . . there was a boy named Fluffytail Fuzzypants. Fluffytail had long gray fur, a pink nose, and a bushy tail he had to brush every day. He wore short black trousers and a bright red vest, and sometimes he wore a brown cap with holes cut in the brim for his ears to poke through.

Fluffytail lived in small yellow house with his grandmother and his father and his baby brother, Furrynose. Fluffytail's house—

"Where's his mommy?"

He should have known she'd ask that.

"She's probably working, just like Mommy is tonight."

"Oh."

Fluffytail's house had yellow walls and yellow doors, yellow windows with white trim, and Fluffytail even had yellow galoshes for days when he had to go outside in the rain.

He loved his house. He loved his grandmother and his mother and even his baby brother. But the thing he loved the most was his tribble.

Fluffytail's daddy brought him the tribble one day when he didn't feel good and stayed home from school. It was round and fuzzy and brown just like the stripes on his grandmother's tail, and the tribble purred and trilled when he held it. The tribble was soft to pet and easy to cuddle. The tribble made him feel better. It became his new best friend.

One day Fluffytail took his tribble to school to show his friends. They all loved his tribble too. They wanted to hold it and pet it just like Fluffytail did, and because they were his friends, Fluffytail let them.

The tribble purred and trilled for his friends too, but Fluffytail knew his tribble purred its loudest only for him.

Sometimes Fluffytail's tribble slept on his pillow right next to his head. *Sometimes it slept on the chair in the corner of his room. And sometimes it slept under his bed too.*

"A tribble can sleep under my bed?"

"It could if we had one."

"Oh. Can we get one?"

He chuckled. "We'll have to ask Mommy about that."

One day Fluffytail was playing outside with his friends, and when he came back to his room, his tribble wasn't on his pillow where he'd left it. He looked under his bed, but his tribble wasn't there either.

Fluffytail looked everywhere for his tribble. He looked in his brother's room. He looked in cupboards and behind his grand-mother's favorite rocking chair. He looked inside the cookie jar— his tribble loved fresh chocolate chip cookies—and even in the back of his closet under his galoshes—his tribble loved dark spaces too.

He looked everywhere he could think of but he couldn't find his tribble anywhere.

It was gone!

But a tribble couldn't just walk out the door. Tribbles have no legs. It took Fluffytail's tribble a long time to go where it wanted to go. Even his grandmother didn't know where his tribble could be.

He knew there was only one explanation.

Someone had stolen his tribble!

"It got stolen?"

"Looks that way."

"Oh. I hope it's okay."

"Me too."

Fluffytail knew how much his friends loved his tribble. They played with it and cuddled it and made it purr. They all wanted one of their own. And now his tribble was missing.

One of his friends must have stolen it!

"You'll steal it! Leave me alone! You're just waiting for me to die so you can have it all to yourself."

Sudden and visceral, the memory took Tom by surprise. It came complete with the stench and sour taste of too many sick and un-washed bodies in too small a space. It came with the banging of metal pounding on metal, the wet slap and crack of clubs striking flesh, with the screams of the injured and the dying.

The prison cell he had shared with Harry Kim.

Fear rushed over him in a sick wave. Light-years away, another lifetime ago now, it didn't matter. In that instant, the prison was as real to him as his daughter's bed.

He heard his own voice, his sick, weak voice. He heard himself accuse Harry of stealing from him and wishing him dead. Harry, who had risked his own life to keep him alive.

Even now the memory made him cringe.

"Daddy?"

He must have stopped talking. "It's okay, sweetheart. Daddy just needed to catch his breath. Are you getting tired yet?"

Miral shook her head.

"Want to hear the end of the story?"

"Yes. What happens to the tribble?"

He shook the vision away. It had no place in a child's fairy tale.

Fluffytail didn't want to think that one of his friends could steal his tribble. Friends didn't do that to each other, and his friends were very, very good friends. But he worried about his tribble. He was scared he might not ever see it again.

He decided to go see each of his friends and ask if they had his tribble.

Merrylinn Manykitts hadn't seen his tribble. She looked sad when he asked, and she didn't invite him inside for a cookie. Merrylinn always invited him inside for a cookie.

Suziebeth Sweetiekins didn't know where his tribble was, and neither did Petiepete Poppintop. They looked sad too and said they probably couldn't play with him tomorrow.

When he left Petiepete's house he had to go home. Daddy said always to be home before dark. He didn't want to make his daddy angry.

His yellow house didn't feel quite as much like home without his tribble. The chocolate chip cookie his grandmother gave him to cheer him up didn't taste quite as sweet. He really missed his tribble. He missed his friends.

When his daddy came home from work, Fluffytail didn't meet him at the door like he always did. Instead he stayed in his room, curled up into as tight a ball as he could on his bed. He didn't hear his daddy open his bedroom door. What he did hear was his tribble purr.

His daddy must have found it!

He was so happy he almost forgot to ask where his daddy found the tribble.

His daddy said he took the tribble to the doctor for a checkup. His tribble was happy and healthy, and Daddy apologized for making him worry. His daddy said he thought he might worry more if he knew his tribble had to go to the doctor. His daddy promised never to make him worry like that again.

He felt really bad that he'd asked his friends if they'd taken his tribble. He knew he'd hurt his friends' feelings.

Fluffytail apologized to all his friends and they all said they forgave him. Even so, his friends didn't play with him as often as they did before. They didn't share their lunches with him as much as they used to. This made him sad too because he loved his friends as much as he loved his tribble.

His daddy asked him one night why he was still sad. When he told his daddy what he had done, his daddy said all he could do was apologize. His daddy told him if his friends were really his friends, they would forgive him someday.

Sure enough, one day Merrylinn asked him to walk her home from school. She didn't ask about his tribble and he made sure not to mention it. When they got to her house, she invited him inside for a cookie.

Chocolate chip. His favorite.

By the time he finished, Miral had fallen asleep. He scooted out from under her and laid her down gently on the bed. She turned on her side without waking up, and he pulled the covers over her. He hoped her bad dreams would stay away for a while now.

He didn't go back to his own bed. Instead he took a cup of coffee into the spare bedroom they had converted into an office. He recorded most of his stories here late at night. He wanted to enter the story he had told Miral.

He just couldn't make himself dictate the first word.

Harry Kim.

Tom hadn't thought of Harry in months. Since *Voyager*'s return to Earth, the two of them had drifted apart. They still talked to each other occasionally, saw each other even less. That damn prison cell. He wondered how much of that had to do with what happened when they were both in prison.

He had been sick then, so sick he didn't know what he was saying half the time. He'd never allowed himself to use that as an excuse. Even sick, even dying, how could he have accused his best friend of wanting him dead?

He had apologized to Harry after it was all over. He still remembered the look on Harry's face. He had accepted the apology, said he understood, but Harry's expression let him know the acceptance was conditional. He'd hurt Harry deeply. He could see it in his eyes. He'd tried to apologize later, kept wanting to apologize until Harry's eyes held the same sparkle of friendship and adventure they'd always had before.

No matter how hard he tried, he couldn't seem to get that back. Eventually Harry told him to quit apologizing, and he'd been angry when he said it.

He'd given up then. He'd done all he could do. The rest had been up to Harry.

Or had it? Had he been waiting, like Fluffytail, for Harry to take the next step? Was that even the right thing to do?

Maybe it wasn't Harry who needed to let the past go.

Instead of dictating the fairy tale, he called up the last adventure story he'd written. Now that he looked for it, he could see the theme of betrayal underlying the main story. He closed that program and opened another. Betrayal, again. In story after story he'd been writing about his experiences in the prison without even knowing it.

"Okay. If I'm going to write about it anyway, maybe I should just write the damn thing."

He didn't realize he'd spoken out loud until he saw his words appear on his terminal. He'd turned the dictating function on and forgotten about it.

At least it was a start.

He'd write this story, no matter how personal, no matter how painful. When he was done he'd call Harry. And this time, he wouldn't expect him to finally accept his apology like some sort of test. It was long past time to leave all that behind.

You May Kiss the Bride

Amy Sisson

mar·riage (mar´ij) *n*. 1 the state of being married; relation between husband and wife; wedlock; 2 the act of marrying; wedding

"You did what?" B'Elanna demanded, forgetting to whisper.

"Shhh. I only told Harry," said Tom. "I want him to be my best man. You have to have a best man even if you're eloping. To be a witness." He stopped talking as two engineering crew members walked by, and then went on. "Besides, he promised not to tell anyone."

"Harry? You've got to be kidding. He can't keep a secret."

"Of course he can," Tom said.

Just then, the door to engineering opened and Commander Chakotay walked in. B'Elanna jumped away from Tom with a guilty expression, and began studying the nearest console intently.

"As you were," Chakotay said with a smile. "I was planning a

224

surprise inspection this afternoon, but I could probably be talked out of it as long as I get to give the bride away."

B'Elanna gave Tom a look. "Harry won't tell anyone, hm? We better go tell the captain before too many more people find out."

"Oh, the captain knows," Chakotay said. "She's the one who told me."

The door slid open once again, revealing a beaming Neelix.

"And how's the happy couple today?" Neelix said. "Already deep in wedding plans, I'm sure. Anything I can do to help?"

"Well . . ." Tom said weakly.

"Now then," said Neelix. "I've taken the liberty of doing a little research on human and Klingon wedding traditions. Fascinating! Will the lovely bride be wearing a white wedding dress, or the traditional red Klingon warrior gown? If you can't make up your mind, I did see a stunning pattern in the database with red and white diagonal stripes—"

"Neelix!" Tom and B'Elanna said together. They looked at each other and B'Elanna went on. "Actually, Neelix," she said carefully, "Tom and I weren't planning to have a formal ceremony. Just the captain and maybe the senior bridge crew." She glanced at Tom again. "And of course you, Neelix."

"And I'm sure you'll want Naomi as a flower girl," said Neelix. "Perhaps Samantha could be the matron of honor. They would look so beautiful in matching mother-and-daughter gowns!"

Tom sighed. "Neelix, please tell me you haven't said anything to Naomi about this."

"I may have mentioned it in passing," Neelix said. He looked back and forth between Tom and B'Elanna. "Of course, if you don't want her . . . I'm sure she'll get over her disappointment. Eventually."

B'Elanna put the back of her hand to her forehead in a gesture that Tom knew meant she was struggling to control the more Klingon aspects of her personality.

"Of course," Neelix went on, "it would be a shame for the rest of the crew to miss out on such a special occasion. They've been stranded here in the Delta Quadrant for so many years, missing the weddings of their friends and families back home . . ."

"Morale officer, huh?" said Tom. "Maybe you should be called the 'guilt officer.'"

"Now, you just relax and I'll take care of everything," said Neelix.

> **wed·ding** (wed´iŋ) *n. a*) the act or ceremony of becoming married, *b*) the marriage ceremony with its attendant festivities.

"Ah, Seven," said the Doctor. "You're looking lovely today. Are you ready to attend your first wedding?"

"Yes, Doctor. Although I do not understand why people are expected to wear uncomfortable clothing for social gatherings."

"It's a wedding, Seven! A special occasion, something to be remembered! Besides, your dress doesn't look that uncomfortable."

"The dress is sufficient," Seven admitted, looking down at the deep blue, formfitting gown she wore. The hemline of the dress was made of several separate panels that swirled around her legs in a becoming manner. "The Delaney sisters helped me choose it. But I do not understand why they insisted upon these shoes. They are most uncomfortable."

"Well, they do look a little . . . impractical, but hopefully they won't keep you from catching the bouquet," the Doctor said.

"They are going to throw plants at the wedding?" Seven asked with raised eyebrows. Her tone expressed her disbelief that human customs could really be as ridiculous as they sounded.

"The wedding bouquet, Seven—B'Elanna's flowers. It's been a tradition for hundreds, perhaps even thousands of years. After the ceremony, the bride throws her bouquet and the unmarried women try to catch it. It is said that the lucky woman who gets it will be the next bride."

"The male crew members will begin courting the woman who catches the bouquet? I suppose they wish to seek the mate with the most physical prowess, but—"

"Don't take it so literally, Seven," the Doctor said. "It's just a tradition. But if it helps you to think of it as a friendly little athletic competition, by all means."

"Sometimes I think I will never understand human social customs," Seven said as she and the Doctor exited sickbay.

chalos (kā´äs) *n.* extreme confusion or disorder.

As the mess-hall doors opened, the soft background music gave way to the familiar strains of a Mendelssohn march. Captain Janeway smiled as Naomi preceded Chakotay and B'Elanna into the room and toward the temporary dais set up in front of the windows. Naomi wore a simple white dress and carried a bouquet so big that the exotic red and white flowers almost hid her face. B'Elanna carried a small matching bouquet, but chose to wear her dress uniform instead of a gown.

"I am not appropriately dressed," Seven whispered to the Doctor as the small procession moved past them. "The Delaney sisters and I are the only guests out of uniform. And you," she added disapprovingly.

"Shhh," said the Doctor. "I think my tuxedo is very distinguished. Besides, they're about to start."

Janeway waited until B'Elanna took her place on the dais next to Tom, and then looked past them to address the guests.

"Performing a wedding ceremony is one of a captain's most enjoyable privileges," she said. "We are here today because Tom and B'Elanna have invited us to witness and share in their decision to formally join their lives together. But before I go any further," she said, eyes twinkling, "if there is anyone here who has just cause to object to this marriage, speak now or forever hold your—"

"AHHHHHHHFFSHEWWWWWWWWW!"

Janeway stopped dead and looked at Tuvok in consternation, as did everyone else in the room. The sound with which he had just erupted sounded like a cross between a Tarkalian war cry and a tragbeast's death howl.

"Tuvok?" said Janeway.

"Ummm, bless you?" ventured Naomi, tilting her head straight back to peer up at the Vulcan, who stood just behind her.

"Pardon me, Captain," said Tuvok with as much dignity as he could muster. "Please proceed."

Janeway merely raised her eyebrows and went on. "Tom and B'Elanna have written their own vows for this ceremony. Tom, B'Elanna, please join hands."

B'Elanna turned to hand her bouquet past Naomi to Samantha Wildman.

"AHHHHHHHFFSHEWWWWWWWWW!" As Tuvok sneezed a second time, Naomi threw up her arms to protect herself, sending B'Elanna's bouquet flying back over her and Tuvok's heads. Startled, Seven of Nine lunged forward, somehow managing to catch and hang on to the bouquet even as she crashed into the Delaney sisters. All three fell to the floor.

"Owww!" came from the bottom of the pile. "I think you broke my wrist!"

"I did not intend to damage you," Seven said. "Doctor, I thought you said the bride does not throw the bouquet until after the ceremony?"

The Doctor opened his mouth, closed it, and opened it again. "Perhaps I should escort the three of you to sickbay, although I do hate to miss the ceremony," he said. "I brought my holocamera—"

"Doctor!" came a wail from the pile of begowned limbs.

"Yes, of course," the Doctor said quickly. The three women began to disentangle themselves. Harry stepped off the dais and held out a hand to allow Seven of Nine to pull herself up.

"I am undamaged, Doctor," said Seven of Nine as she stood. "It will not be necessary for me to go to sickbay." She looked at Ensign Kim. "Are you courting me, Ensign?"

"What?" said Harry.

"Seven," the Doctor said. "Perhaps you wouldn't mind taking a few snapshots for me." He held out the holocamera.

"Very well," said Seven. The Doctor ushered his two charges

toward the door as his tuxedo shimmered and was replaced by his blue uniform. The guests murmured as they turned back toward the bride and groom.

"That's my Harry," Tom said in a low tone as his best man returned to his side. "Always trying to rescue the damsels."

"Shut up," said Harry.

"Captain," B'Elanna said. "Maybe we should—"

"B'Elanna!" Tom said. "You're not backing out now, are you?"

"No, Tom, I just—"

"Let's proceed," Captain Janeway said with a smile. "That's an order, Lieutenant. I'm still your captain, even if this is your wedding."

"Aye, Captain," said B'Elanna, apparently reassured.

They all jumped at Tuvok's sudden intake of breath.

"Mister Tuvok, perhaps you should report to sickbay as well," Janeway suggested mildly.

"Yes, Captain. I apologize for the disturbance. I do not understand what the problem is."

"Maybe you're allergic to the flowers," Naomi called after the departing Vulcan.

"A very logical hypothesis, Naomi," Janeway said. "Now then. Tom and B'Elanna have written their own wedding vows. Tom, B'Elanna?"

The couple turned toward each other and joined hands. Tom took a deep breath. "B'Elanna," he began. "I never imagined I could be this lucky—"

A blare of music erupted from every corner of the room.

"It's all right!" Neelix shouted over the sound of trumpets and wailing Klingons. "I instructed the computer to time the music to match the ceremony. I didn't count on all the interruptions."

"Turn it *off,* Mister Neelix," ordered the captain. Out of the corner of her eye, she saw Tom whispering to B'Elanna.

"Computer, pause music until further notice," said Neelix.

"Captain," said Tom. "Could you just give me a minute?"

"Of course."

"I'll be right back. I forgot something."

Janeway glanced at B'Elanna, who looked like she was trying to suppress a smile. Tom squeezed B'Elanna's hand and left the mess hall.

"Would you like me to start the music while we wait?" asked Neelix.

"No!" answered B'Elanna and Captain Janeway simultaneously. The captain wondered what Tom could have forgotten. If it was the ring, she hoped he would find it quickly.

To her immense relief, the mess-hall doors slid open a few moments later and Tom walked back in. He didn't look panicked, so she assumed that the ring must be safe. In fact, he almost looked jaunty.

"Why don't I start this time?" B'Elanna asked. Janeway nodded.

"Tom," B'Elanna began.

"Ensign Rogers to Captain Janeway," came over the com system.

Janeway closed her eyes in exasperation, opened them and smiled grimly at the waiting couple in apology, and turned toward the windows before answering the hail. "Go ahead, Ensign. And I'm warning you, this had better be good."

"Uh, I'm sorry to disturb you, Captain, but I need you to come to the bridge right away."

"Now. You need me now." It was more a statement than a question.

"Yes, Captain."

"I'm sending Commander Chakotay."

"Actually, Captain, you're the only one who can take care of this. It, uh, requires . . . um, the computer is asking for captain-level security clearance from the bridge or it's going to start purging all the oxygen from the ship."

Janeway sighed. "I'll be right there. I hope you didn't have your heart set on a promotion anytime in the near future, Ensign."

"No, ma'am," said Rogers.

Janeway turned back to face the couple. "Tom?" She looked around. "Where did they go?" she asked Chakotay.

"What? Oh, I'm sorry, Captain. I didn't see where they went. I . . . I'm not feeling well."

Janeway held up her hand. "Never mind. Tell them I'll be right back. They *will* get married today." Janeway started to march out of the room and turned back at the door. "Commander, if you start to feel any worse, report to sickbay. I'd appreciate if you didn't get sick all over the bride and groom."

ellope (ē lōp´, i-) *vi.* to run away secretly, esp. in order to get married

"Captain!" came an urgent whisper just as Janeway was about to enter the turbolift. She turned and saw Tom beckoning from around the nearest corner.

"Tom, I've been called to the bridge, but I promise, I'll be right back. Don't let any of this ruin your wedding. You don't want to miss Neelix's cake—Commander Chakotay and I sampled the batter this morning, and if it was any indication, Neelix has outdone himself this time."

Tom smiled. "I had Ensign Rogers call you, Captain. I could tell B'Elanna was going to bolt any minute, so I thought I better get her out of there. We want you to marry us now, just us, and then we'll sneak off to the *Flyer* and let the rest of you enjoy the party."

"That," Janeway said, "may be the best idea I've heard all day. Where's B'Elanna?"

"In a supply closet."

"Lead the way, Mister Paris." She followed him down several corridors to a closet a few meters from the entrance to the shuttlebay. The room was barely big enough to hold the three of them.

"Okay, let's do this," said Janeway.

"Um, Captain, I hate to bring this up now, but don't we need a witness for the ceremony to be legal?" Tom asked.

The captain thought for a second. "The computer can witness the marriage! I think that's legal. Computer, can you serve as witness to a marriage ceremony?"

"*Affirmative.*"

"Then please bear witness to the marriage of Tom Paris and B'Elanna Torres, as performed by Captain Kathryn Janeway of the Federation Starship *Voyager.* Tom and B'Elanna . . ." She paused.

"Captain?" said Tom. "Everything all right?"

"I'm fine. I just felt a little queasy there for a second. Maybe we better skip ahead, if that's okay."

"Maybe we should wait until you're feeling better," B'Elanna said.

"No! Tom, do you take B'Elanna to be your lawful wedded wife?"

Tom looked into B'Elanna's eyes. For a moment, they were the only two people in the universe. "I do."

"B'Elanna, do you take Tom to be your lawful wedded husband?"

"I do," she said, smiling up at Tom. An ominous rumble came from Captain's Janeway stomach. "Captain, are you *sure* you're okay? You're starting to look kind of green."

"I'm fine," gasped Janeway. "I just . . . oh no! Neelix's cake! By the power vested in me by Starfleet, I now . . . I now . . . pronounce you . . . husband and wifepleaseexcuseme!" She rushed out of the room with her hand over her mouth. "You may kiss the bride," came a muffled call just as the closet door slid shut again.

Tom and B'Elanna looked at each other. "I *think* we're married," said Tom.

"There's only one way to find out," said B'Elanna. "Computer, what is B'Elanna Torres's marital status?"

"*Lieutenant Torres and Lieutenant Paris were married by Captain Kathryn Janeway at 16:47 today.*"

"You'd better kiss me then, flyboy."

toast (tōst) *n.* **1** a person, thing, idea, etc. in honor of which a person or persons raise their glasses and drink **2** *a*) a sentiment expressed just before so drinking *b*) such a drink.

Almost as soon as the *Delta Flyer* cleared the shuttlebay doors, Tom switched to autopilot and produced a bottle of champagne.

"Shouldn't we check on the captain?" said B'Elanna.

"I don't suppose you'll relax and enjoy our honeymoon until we do, will you?" Tom said.

"That's right, flyboy."

"Okay," Tom said, pretending to sigh. He touched the console. "Paris to sickbay."

"Ah, Mister Paris," said the Doctor over the com. *"I was hoping for the opportunity to congratulate you. I still have to check the Starfleet Medical database, but I do believe your wedding may have set a new record for the largest number of guests needing medical attention. Particularly considering the fact that you didn't actually get married."*

"Well, we *did* get married, Doc. Just not at the ceremony. But that's splitting hairs, don't you think?"

"If you insist," the Doctor replied dryly.

"How's the captain, Doctor?" B'Elanna asked.

"She'll survive, thanks to my excellent care. So will Tuvok and Chakotay. Ensign Delaney had me worried for a moment—after all, it's no small thing to be tackled by an ex-Borg."

"Hey Doc, which sister was it?" Tom asked with interest. "I can usually tell them apart, but—"

"Tom," said B'Elanna, a warning note in her voice.

"Uh, better go, Doc."

"Bon voyage," the Doctor said. *"Oh, Mister Paris . . . if that wedding was any indication of what your married life will be like, remind me to request a transfer if the two of you ever decide to have a baby. After all, even holographic doctors have limits."*

"A baby? Us? I don't think you need to worry about that just yet, Doc," Tom said. "Paris out."

Tom and B'Elanna clinked glasses, smiling into each other's eyes.

Coffee with a Friend

J.B. Stevens

"Help me, Daddy. Tell me that I made the right choice. If ever I needed your counsel, it's now."

A gentle flurry of cool evening wind sent a swirl of amber and crimson leaves from a nearby maple dancing through the air. I reached down and brushed one of the fallen leaves off the dark stone, then reverently let my fingers brush across the deeply etched letters that spelled "Edward Janeway." But only the sound of the wind soughing through the evergreens in Starfleet Memorial Park replied. I sat back on the soft grass cushioning my knees and sighed. Oh, well. I hadn't really expected an answer, anyway. In fact, I didn't know why I had come here, except . . .

I looked over my shoulder up the hill to where a row of new markers had been placed. They stood out from the rest, the freshly cut stone not yet showing the weathered patina of age. Those newest additions were the real reason I had come, to pay my respects. But I couldn't do it. I couldn't make myself go up there and

234

look at them, not just yet. I wasn't sure what would happen if I did, I only knew I wasn't ready.

So I came to the one place that gave me comfort, to be near the one person that would understand what I was going through. I hadn't been to visit him in a long time. Far too long, in fact, even before I went on the mission that became the reason for those other markers on the hill, the ones that shouldn't be there.

The ones for which I was responsible.

I leaned over and placed my hands on my father's marker, hoping to draw some warmth, some measure of comfort from his spirit, but the stone remained cold and unyielding. Then the first fat drops of rain began to mar the surface of the stone. Too late, I noticed the rainstorm approaching from the bay. Unprepared, I made a mad dash down the hill in hopes of finding shelter before I became drenched, kicking myself all the way for forgetting about the unpredictable San Francisco weather. Damn, you'd think I'd know better, having lived here before.

I only made it as far as the nearest street before it started pouring. Cold and wet, I huddled against the recessed doorway of a closed business and watched the people rush by on their way home, their umbrellas adding the only bright spots of color to an otherwise dreary landscape.

I envied those people. Not just their umbrellas or their wise choice of a warm coat. No, I envied their innocence. For they had not been where I had been, seen the wonderful but terrible things that I had seen, or endured the losses I had suffered, including seven years of their lives.

Seven years. It might as well have been seven centuries. For those seven years, I was lost, given up for dead. And for those seven years, I'd tried everything in my power to get back home, put my life and the lives of my crew on hold and fought to get back. And in the end, I got my wish and kept my promise to the crew of the *Starship Voyager:* to lead them home.

But for what?

A sudden movement in the window of the business startled me.

For a moment, I didn't recognize my own reflection. The woman staring back bore no resemblance to Kathryn Janeway, the self-confident starship captain who'd embarked on what should have been a routine mission so long ago. Instead, I saw a broken, hollow-eyed scarecrow standing alone on a street corner feeling sorry for herself. I certainly didn't want to feel this way. In fact, I should be happy to have survived after all of those years lost, to stand where I was standing. And now that I'm here . . .

Truth was, I felt more lost than when I was stranded in the Delta Quadrant. I'd rather have faced an armada of Borg cubes than put up with the endless parade of official debriefings and welcome-home parties testing my already tenuous control over sanity. And those obligatory sessions with Starfleet counselors! Assimilation might have been preferable, but I smiled politely and played along, responding to their inane psychobabble with my usual defensive prevarication that everything was fine.

But I knew I wasn't fine. My mother and sister knew it, too. Nothing anyone said or did could assuage the weight of responsibility for what I'd done, could possibly wipe away the stain of consequence. Every night brought the same dream, a demon of guilt forcing me to look at the faces belonging to the names etched on those new stones.

And every new week brought yet another set of journeys to visit the families of those left behind. I'd given the requisite condolence speeches and medals of commendation over and over again, answered their questions, and endured their tears and looks of blame until I had nothing left to give anymore. Still the comfort I tried to bring them, that I so desperately needed myself, eluded me.

What a fool I was, expecting to handle this situation just like I handled my command. After all, I'd fought the Borg and won. The simple act of returning home again shouldn't be any different, should it? As if agreeing with my mood, the darkness became complete, and the rain suddenly intensified, coming down in blinding sheets.

Across the street, the green and red lights of a coffeehouse sign reflected off the wet, deserted street. Curious that I hadn't noticed it before, I watched as the door to the tiny café opened, the light inside silhouetting two people. A tall, chubby woman with her hair pulled back in a graying bun patted her customer on the back, then waved as they hurried down the street clutching a container of steaming refreshment.

The thought of a cup of coffee made my mouth water, liquid warmth that would be very welcome right now, so I decided to brave the downpour and cross the street. Before I could take one step, the woman stepped back inside and turned the sign on the door to "Closed." I think it was then I realized the depths of my depression when tears of disappointment welled up in my eyes. To let something this silly upset me was a desperate cry for help.

At this point, it didn't matter anyway. I'd deal with it later. The hour was late, and I had promised my mother I'd return home to Indiana by midnight. I looked up at the black sky and prepared to make a run for it, hoping against hope that the rain would let up enough for me to make it to the transport station without drowning.

Suddenly, I had the strange sensation that I was being watched. Across the street, I saw the coffeehouse owner still standing at the door staring in my direction. I shrank back into the shadows away from the unwanted company, hoping it was too dark to be seen. I didn't want to be rude to the woman, but after the day I'd had, I was not in the mood for the banality of polite conversation with a stranger.

After a moment, the woman walked away from the door, and I sighed in relief. She probably was looking out at the weather and not me anyway. Then the woman reappeared with an umbrella in her hand, stepped out of the door, and hurried across the street directly toward me. Before I could escape, I found myself face-to-face with the coffeehouse owner.

"It's awfully cold to be standing out here in the rain." The woman smiled down at me. "You look like you could use a cup of hot coffee."

Something about her demeanor and open, friendly face put me

at ease, and I instinctively returned the smile. "You don't know how good that sounds, but I don't want to keep you." I nodded toward the "Closed" sign.

"Not to worry," the large woman said, taking my arm in one beefy hand and leading me across the street under the umbrella's protection. "For you, we're always open."

Grateful, I followed my rescuer into the cozy shop. "I can't thank you enough."

The woman stepped behind the counter and took two bright red mugs down from a shelf. "No thanks are necessary. And that isn't necessary, either." She nodded at the credit voucher I'd laid on the counter. "The only payment I require is a little conversation, if you're willing."

I settled on a stool. "Of course, I'm willing. That's a small price to pay for a good cup of coffee."

"A true connoisseur, I take it?"

"To the core. Any of my associates will tell you that I'll do almost anything for coffee."

"Well, that's good, then," the woman said, shouting over the roar of the coffee grinder. "Because I'll do anything to have someone to talk to. My name is Gaby, and that's no coincidence."

I laughed, surprised at how good it felt, and extended my hand. "Kathryn Janeway."

"Janeway," Gaby repeated hesitantly, accepting my hand in a grip that felt like a duranium vise. Then her eyes widened in recognition. "Of course! You're the captain who led her crew home after being lost for so many years!"

"Guilty as charged," I replied, giving her a halfhearted smile. The last thing I wanted right now was more unwanted attention.

The look was not lost on Gaby. "Oh, come now. I'd have to be a hermit not to have heard about the famous Captain Janeway and the brave crew of the *Starship Voyager,* wouldn't I?" she asked, pouring the ground coffee into the percolator. "You're all the news media has been talking about for the last several weeks."

I breathed deep of the heady aroma. "Reporters do tend to be a bit overzealous with their attention at times."

"I'd say it's well deserved in your case," Gaby said with a smile. She filled the two mugs from the percolator's tap, then motioned for me to follow her. "Since I have the pleasure of such distinguished company, it's the best table in the house for you."

She led me to a small table for two in the café's front window and set the mugs down. "There you go. Jamaican Blue Mountain, black, just the way you like it."

I stared at my hostess in astonishment. "How did you know?"

"Know what? That you liked your coffee black or that Jamaican Blue Mountain is your favorite?"

"Both," I said, slowly settling into a chair.

Gaby shrugged and sat across from me. "You've been described as a straightforward, no-nonsense type of person. That's the kind that usually likes their coffee the way they live their lives: strong and bold, not diluted by anything sweet. And as for the other, everyone likes Jamaican Blue Mountain."

"You seem to be a very astute judge of character." I wrapped my hands around the warm mug and took a sip. The taste was pure heaven!

"Not really," Gaby said. "I'm just a good listener."

"Then you must be part El-Aurian," I teased.

Gaby looked confused. "El-what? Oh, you mean the race of seven-hundred-year-old listeners." She held her hands up in protest. "No, I'm afraid I'm just a plain old human. But there are days when I feel about seven hundred years old."

I set the mug down and watched the steam curling up into the air. "I know what you mean."

"Bad day?"

"More like a bad couple of weeks," I replied, not looking up.

Gaby watched me as if gauging my mood. "Coming home again has been hard on you, hasn't it?"

I hesitated for a moment before answering. "Harder than I ever thought it would be," I told her at last. I turned and stared out the window at the rain, not certain that I could say any more.

"Want to talk about it?" Gaby asked, her voice quiet. "I'm willing to become an El-Aurian for a little while if you need me to."

Her pun made me smile. "That's very kind, but I don't want to burden you with my problems."

"It's no trouble at all for me," she said with a wave of her hand. "But I'll understand if you can't talk about things right now. At least I have the pleasure of your company."

Gaby rose and patted me on the shoulder, then returned to the counter. As I watched her fill a large insulated carafe from the percolator, I started to think, *Why am I holding back?* I knew that I needed to talk to someone before I exploded, but who could I turn to? Not to those counselors and certainly not to my poor mother. I'd put her through enough hell with my depression after Daddy died years ago to burden her again. No, perhaps the kindness of a stranger was just the therapy I needed, and I decided to take Gaby up on her offer before my overwrought brain could analyze it any further.

"Are you sure you're willing to listen?" I asked as Gaby approached the table again. "I have a lot of baggage to unload."

She laughed and began to refill my mug. "Everyone does, my dear. I can't imagine that yours is any heavier than most."

"Don't be too sure."

Gaby settled at the table again, her expression turning serious. "Well, I can tell it must be quite a weight, because you look like you haven't eaten or slept since you got home."

"Not much," I admitted. "I'm afraid I haven't had the time, with all these debriefings, celebrations, and other duties to attend to."

Gaby looked up from filling her own mug. "More duties? After seven straight years of duty, I'd have thought you'd be on leave by now, spending time with your family. You have a mother and sister, don't you?"

I winced at the mention of yet another source of guilt. My mother always said she understood every time I left home for one of my visits to the families of my fallen crew, but I could see the look of hurt that she tried to hide. She deserved a better daughter than I'd been lately.

"Technically, I am on leave," I said. "But I still have some obligations to my extended family that require the attention of their captain."

Gaby smiled, giving me a look of admiration that I didn't deserve. "You truly are a remarkable leader, Kathryn, to sacrifice time with your own family and spend it with your crew's."

"It's a very small thing considering some of their sacrifices were more costly than others."

She seemed to understand the implication, and nodded. "Oh, that is sad, isn't it? The inevitable losses. I know that as Starfleet, you live with that risk every time you go on a mission, but I suppose that doesn't make it any easier to bear."

"Especially when I could have prevented some of those losses."

"What do you mean?"

I paused and swallowed hard, swirling the remnants of lukewarm coffee around in the mug. *Here it comes,* I thought, *finally admitting the thing that's really bothering you. Say it, Kathryn. Get it out in the open at last.*

"I gave the order that stranded us in the Delta Quadrant. I'm the one responsible for putting my crew in harm's way by placing the future of an alien race above their needs. Because of that decision, they all suffered for seven years. Now there are twenty families suffering because their loved ones didn't make the journey home."

"But you've been in a command position for a long time now," Gaby countered. "You've made decisions that cost crew their lives before, haven't you? What makes this time so different?"

"This time the stakes were too high, the consequences too absolute."

"And you feel like you betrayed them."

"I did betray them!" I slammed my hand down on the table, spilling some of the coffee. "I could see it in their eyes. I had to face them with that knowledge every day for seven years until we came home. Now I have to face their families and try to explain why and give them meaningless words of sympathy over and over again. The hypocrisy of it all makes me physically ill."

The silence hung thick in the air after my outburst, broken only by the hiss of steam from the percolator. My rudeness shocked me, but Gaby seemed unperturbed.

"Gaby, I . . . I am so sorry. I don't know what just happened," I stammered, surprised to find my hands shaking.

She quickly laid her hand over mine, a compassionate expression on her face. "It's all right. You have nothing to apologize for."

"But I shouldn't have lashed out like that."

Gaby cocked her head to one side. "Well, you did warn me that your baggage was heavy, but I had no idea. That's a terrible burden to carry around for seven years, Kathryn. And now you've taken on the burden of comforting all of those families. How do you find the strength?"

I shrugged. "I don't think about it. It's my responsibility."

"Yes, I suppose it is, but that still doesn't take away from the fact that you gave those families an extraordinary gift with your personal visits. I doubt that they found your words meaningless."

"It didn't seem that way with some of them."

"Perhaps you were expecting too much," Gaby said. "After all, they're just now coming face-to-face with the reality that their loved ones really aren't coming back. You should forgive them if they acted upset."

"They aren't the ones who need forgiveness."

Gaby set her coffee down and paused for a moment, her gaze never leaving me.

"Do you think that you need to be forgiven?" she asked quietly.

I shook my head and released a ragged breath. "I don't feel that what I did can be forgiven."

"You don't really believe that, do you?"

"Gaby, I don't know what to believe anymore. I feel so empty, so dead inside."

She pressed her lips together and nodded. "I don't doubt it. It sounds as if you haven't given yourself a moment's peace since you got home. You've done so much for others, Kathryn. Don't you think it's time to give yourself a little of that compassion?"

I sat back and folded my arms. "You're not going to tell me to write down my transgressions on an old-fashioned piece of paper and then burn it, are you? Because I've heard enough of that kind of therapeutic nonsense from the counselors."

Gaby laughed. "Don't worry. I don't believe in that baloney either. No, I'm afraid that old-fashioned common sense is all I have to offer." Then she leaned forward and folded her hands on the table. "There is one thing I've learned, though. It is absolutely necessary for you to let go of this hurt. If you don't, it will only keep on hurting you."

I sighed in exasperation. Hadn't I already been told all of this? "I want to let go, but I don't know how."

"Maybe you could begin by looking at all of the good you did in those seven years instead of the bad. Think about that alien race you mentioned. What would have happened to them if you'd made the decision to come home instead of helping them?"

"Another, more powerful race would have exploited their world and enslaved them."

"Then, given those circumstances, do you think that your crew would have made the same decision?"

"Without a doubt. They're the finest Starfleet has to offer."

"Then I believe you already have their forgiveness. All that's lacking is for you to forgive yourself."

If only it were that easy, I thought, gripping my mug a little too tightly. "But there are still so many questions I need answered," I said aloud.

Gaby smiled patiently and poured more coffee. "Always the scientist, aren't you, wanting tangible evidence for everything. You never will know the answers to those questions, Kathryn. No matter what we do, things will always happen to us that are beyond our control. None of us are guaranteed a calm passage in life, only a safe landing. So the best you can hope for is to be true to yourself and your beliefs, and know that you did the best you could with what you knew at the time."

"I've tried so hard to do that every day." But was that true? Had I really tried hard enough?

"With your self-confidence and determination, I don't doubt it," Gaby said. "Just remember that while all decisions in life have consequences, it's our strength of character that dictates how we deal with those consequences. I sense that your character is very strong, much stronger than you give yourself credit for."

I shook my head and stared into the black depths of the mug. "I don't feel strong anymore."

"Oh, it's there, deep inside. And it will help you find the peace that forgiveness brings. But don't expect it to happen overnight. Forgiveness is something that you must struggle for every day, sometimes for years. You have to share this with your family and crew, not just with me. That's the most important thing to understand. You cannot do it alone."

My fierce independence balked at that idea. Teamwork within a crew I understood, but this was too personal. "I don't know if I can do that. I am alone in this matter."

Gaby reached across the table and grasped both of my hands. "You aren't alone, Kathryn. You never have been. There are so many people out there who love you and that includes your crew. I know it will be difficult, but it's up to you to reach out and take that first step."

But could I do it? Could I really overcome years of personal barriers and share this pain with someone else? Then I looked into Gaby's eyes and realized that was exactly what I had been doing for the past hour. And strangely enough, my burden did feel lighter. Finally I understood what it was I had to do.

"I feel like I've already taken that step," I told Gaby.

She beamed at me and patted my hand. "You have indeed. Now keep going. This is a challenge, and somehow I get the feeling that you never back away from a challenge."

I returned the smile. "Not one that I know I can win. But there is one thing . . ."

"What is that?"

"I only wish that I had a sign, some kind of sign that the scientist in me will recognize to let me know that things really are getting better."

Gaby sat back and smiled again, not one of her friendly smiles, but an odd, cryptic one that made me a bit uncomfortable.

"When it comes, you will know."

Both her smile and response seemed strange, but I decided to let it go. There were some things best left unquestioned. I glanced outside and noticed that the rain had slowed to a drizzle.

"Are you responsible for stopping the rain as my sign?" I asked.

"Now that I can't take credit for," Gaby said, holding up her hands.

"No, but you can take credit for making me feel a little better about things," I said, pushing back from the table.

"And for making you a great cup of coffee," she added, stepping beside me.

I laughed. "That, too. I hope I repaid you properly."

"You did indeed, my dear," Gaby said. She reached for me, and I gratefully accepted the embrace. "Thank you for a pleasant evening, Kathryn."

"Thank you for showing me how to take that first step."

"As you said, you've already done that," Gaby said, stepping back. "Just remember to take your time and focus on what's really important."

"I'll remember. I promise."

I gave Gaby one last hug, then left the coffeeshop, turning back once to wave good-bye. Outside, the rain had stopped completely, and the famous San Francisco fog had returned in force, blanketing everything in thick gray swirls.

My head spinning with emotions, I wandered down the now empty street with no idea of where I was going. I only knew that I desperately needed to cling to this new feeling that everything was going to work out. Before I knew it, I found myself back at Starfleet Memorial Park at the bottom of the hill below the new markers. I hadn't intended to go there. Or had I?

I stood there, gathering my courage, then forced myself to start up the hill. With each step, I kept telling myself that I could do this, that I could face them now and ask their forgiveness. But what would they say? Would they give me the absolution I so desperately needed?

Then suddenly, it was too late to turn back. I was standing there before them, wisps of dark fog curling gently about their stones. Lyndsay Ballard was first, then Marie Kaplan and Ahni Jetal. Next was Joe Carey, the hardest of all to bear. I touched each of their markers, the memory of their faces so clear in my mind, looking as I remembered them: Starfleet's finest, dedicated, loyal, ready to serve. And this time the stone didn't feel cold.

As I reached the end of the row, I suddenly became aware of another presence, not spiritual, but flesh and blood. The person was standing opposite me next to the markers of the Maquis crew. Wary, I slowly approached, wondering who else would be crazy enough to be standing in a graveyard in the middle of the night.

As if answering my question, the fog cleared long enough for me to catch a glimpse of my companion. The face belonged to a handsome, dark-haired man, the olive skin of his forehead marked by a distinctive tattoo. Despite his wet hair and disheveled appearance, I would have known that face anywhere. The old cliché about it being a small universe popped into my mind, and I allowed myself a smile.

"Out for a midnight stroll, Commander?"

Startled, the man turned, his dark eyes wide when he saw me.

"Kathryn?"

"Hello, Chakotay," I greeted my best friend and first officer, more than a little flattered by the huge grin that spread across his face.

"What are you doing here?" he asked.

I shrugged. "Paying my respects."

He nodded and ran his fingers through his wet hair. "Me, too. I don't know why, but I've been dreading this. I finally worked up the courage and decided to come despite the late hour." He paused and drew in a deep breath. "I'm glad I did," he said at last.

"I understand," I replied softly. "Better than you know."

We fell silent for several moments, not the awkward silence of strangers, but the companionable understanding of old friends. We walked together down the row of gravestones, taking time to read each one. I couldn't explain it, but having him there beside me once again just as he'd been for the past seven years made the burden of my guilt feel even lighter. Perhaps Gaby was right. I couldn't do this alone.

When we reached the end of the row, Chakotay turned to me as if waiting for orders. I took one last look, then nodded. He took my arm and guided me back down the hill. We didn't speak again until we reached the street.

"Well, despite the occasion, it's really good to see you again," Chakotay said as we walked along.

"You, too," I replied. "I wish I could say it's been a long time, but actually it's only been six weeks."

"And four days," he added with a twinkle. "But who's counting. I'd heard you were in the city today, but I thought I'd miss you. Aren't you staying with your mother in Indiana most of the time?"

I thrust my hands into my jacket pockets. "I am, but I had some personal business here that needed my attention."

"And everywhere else in the Federation. I also heard you've been keeping both the local and interplanetary transports very busy."

I sighed inwardly. Gossip was as old as the universe itself. "I see that the Starfleet rumor mill is still going strong."

He shook his head. "Actually, I heard it from my Maquis friend, Sveta. She'd been in contact with Hogan's family, who told her you'd been there for a visit."

"Yes, I saw them last week, along with Michael Jonas's family."

"How many more did you see?"

"All of them."

Chakotay stopped suddenly. "All of the families of the crew we lost?"

"Yes, Chakotay, all of them."

He stood there and stared at me, a strange, hurt look in his eyes. "Why didn't you ask me to come along?"

"They were my responsibility."

"They were my responsibility, too, Kathryn. Why did you think you had to bear that burden alone? I would have helped you if you'd only asked."

Of course, he was right. But once again, I'd allowed my stubborn sense of duty to overpower my better judgment and offended my friend in the process. I couldn't bear any more reproach, especially not from him.

"I'm sorry, Chakotay. It was never my intention to leave you out. I just haven't been making very good decisions, now or then."

"There's never been anything wrong with your decisions, Captain," he told me. "If there were, we wouldn't be standing here today."

"Then, you think I did the right thing?"

He looked confused for a moment. "I'm not exactly sure what you're referring to, but I think it's safe to say yes."

That was all I needed to hear. "Thank you, Commander."

"For what?"

"Just thank you."

Chakotay looked at me intently for a moment, then nodded as if deciding not to question me further. He knew me well enough to let it go.

"Listen, I know it's late, and it looks like you've had a rough day, but would you mind sharing a friend's company and a cup of hot coffee for a while?"

I looked at Chakotay in amazement and smiled. Two offers of companionship, one from a kindly stranger and the other from my best friend, all in the same day, were almost too good to be true. Besides, one could never have enough coffee.

"That sounds wonderful," I told him.

"Then it's a date?"

"It's a date."

Chakotay smiled and motioned down the street. "I know this quiet little coffee place over on Green Street that makes a Vulcan mocha to die for. It's open all night, so we'll have plenty of time to talk."

"Sounds wonderful," I said, following him. "You know, it's a shame the coffeehouse on this street isn't still open."

"What coffeehouse?" Chakotay asked.

"The one in the middle of the next block."

He stopped and stared at me. "There's no coffeehouse in that block."

"But there is. I just left there before I ran into you."

Chakotay shook his head. "I lived in this neighborhood in my Academy days, and there's never been a coffeehouse on this street."

Now I was getting annoyed. "Then you've been away too long, because there is now."

"Show me."

I took his arm and pulled him down the street in the opposite direction, determined to prove I was right. How typical for the two of us. Together barely five minutes, and we were already arguing about something. Funny, but somehow it felt good.

Just before we crossed the street onto the next block, Chakotay suddenly stopped, staring into the distance.

"Kathryn, you're not talking about that old café that used to be in the block nearest the Memorial, are you?"

"Yes, that's the one."

"I seem to remember some of my Academy professors talking about a café where they used to go," Chakotay said. "They liked it because the owner spoiled them with free coffee, a mother-hen sort named Gaby."

"That's her," I said emphatically. "I just spent the past hour talking to her. She helped me more in that hour than all of Starfleet's counseling service put together."

Chakotay looked at me as if I'd lost my mind. "That can't be."

Angry, I put my hands on my hips and stepped closer to him. "Why?"

"Because, Kathryn, Gaby has been dead for more than twenty years."

Shocked, I gaped at him, then slowly began to shake my head. No, I did not believe him. Without a word, I turned and ran across the street into the next block.

Unlike the previous block, this street was almost completely dark, the few dim streetlamps that still worked barely illuminating the vacant and dilapidated buildings along the block. Strange, but I hadn't noticed that the area was this run-down when I was here before. I was beginning to think that I'd lost my way when a sign in one of the windows caught my attention. If I hadn't noticed it, I would have run right past.

Both Chakotay and I were correct: There was a café here, rather had been at one time. I stared in disbelief at the neglected storefront, the windows glazed over and cracked with age, the green and red sign long extinguished. But how could that be? Only a short time had passed since I'd been sitting there drinking coffee and talking to Gaby. Only a short time ago, the lights were on, the paint fresh, the storefront neat and orderly.

I stepped up and peered through the glass. The small table still sat in the front window. And on the tabletop sat two bright red mugs covered in dust. A strange feeling began to creep over me, and I shivered.

Footsteps approached from behind, then a familiar presence stopped beside me.

"Kathryn?"

"I'm not crazy, Chakotay," I insisted, my voice a hoarse whisper. "I did talk to her. I sat right there at that table and told her things I've never dared to tell anyone. Look. The mugs are still there."

I knew I was babbling, but I couldn't seem to stop myself. There had to be a rational explanation for what had happened. There just had to be.

Chakotay placed a gentle hand on my shoulder. "I don't doubt that something extraordinary happened to you here. Spirit knows, we've seen our share of strange things. But sometimes those things can't be explained empirically." He moved to face me. "Sometimes you have to take things on faith alone. Her presence in your life was a special gift just waiting for you to accept it. Something that precious should never be questioned."

I looked into his eyes, then turned back to the window, staring at those two mugs on the table, the pragmatic scientist inside warring with the spiritual. Then I thought of Gaby's words: *When the sign comes, you will know.*

But was this it? I only knew that right now I was too numb with shock at what had happened tonight. Too many emotions, too many questions churned just below the surface of my control. I wanted, needed to let it go, but I couldn't.

"Are you all right?" Chakotay asked quietly.

I jumped and turned around, forgetting that he was there.

"I really could use that company about now," I told him.

Without another word, he offered me his hand, then led the way down the street. I don't know where we went or how long we walked. I only remember hanging on to his hand the whole time, woodenly putting one foot before the other. I couldn't shake from my mind the image of those two dusty red mugs sitting on a table in an abandoned café. If it weren't for the warmth of his hand, my only link to reality, I might have lost what little control I had left right then and there.

Then we passed into a well-lighted neighborhood, and the scene around me became comfortably familiar. This area of the city was well known to anyone who had attended Starfleet Academy, the street lined with apartment houses, small businesses, and cozy restaurants that were popular cadet hangouts. Chakotay led me halfway down the street, then cut through an alleyway between buildings.

We emerged onto the next street over in front of the coffeehouse he'd mentioned. This one sported a red and green sign, too, but unlike Gaby's, this café was bustling with activity, showing no sign of closing any time soon. The crowd inside spilled out onto the street and filled the bistro tables lining the storefront.

Chakotay started to lead me across the street when suddenly I heard the sound of familiar voices. I froze in place, then shrank back into the shadows of the alleyway just as a tall, redheaded man holding an infant stepped out of the café and spoke to an Asian man and a woman with long, dark curls holding hands outside.

"Hey! Where is Chakotay? I thought he said it was only going to take him a few minutes to get the captain. We can't start the party without her."

"I don't know, Tom, but stop worrying. He'll bring her. Now, don't you think it's a little too cold for Miral to be outside?"

Tom snorted. "What are you, my wife or Nanny Kim?"

"That's Lieutenant Kim, to you."

Another familiar voice, belonging to a half-Klingon woman, shouted from just inside the door. "Well, I am your wife, and I'm telling you to get that baby back in here. Now!"

"Aye, aye, Commander!"

As I stood there staring at the coffeehouse full of my crew, I felt my patience unravel. I whirled around to face my first officer, whom I thought I could trust. How could he do this to me?

"Chakotay, what is this?" I snapped.

"Just a little impromptu get-together to celebrate coming home," he replied matter-of-factly. "We wanted it to be *Voyager* alumni only, no dignitaries, no brass."

I took one menacing step toward him. "You set me up. That wasn't just a chance encounter at the Memorial, was it?"

"Actually, I was on my way to your apartment. Our meeting at the Memorial was a lucky coincidence." He raised his eyebrows in a question. "You aren't really mad, are you?"

At that moment, I wasn't sure myself. Standing there looking at the festivities going on in that café, knowing what was expected of me, I felt my anger suddenly change to fear.

"I don't know if I can go in there, Chakotay."

"Why not? It's just us. Nothing's changed."

"Hasn't it?" I countered. "Don't you understand? They gave up seven years of their lives because of me. And now that they're home, they're finding out what losing those seven years has cost them. They couldn't possibly want to be around me now."

Chakotay looked nonplussed. "Why would you think such a thing, Kathryn? Not one person in there blames you for what happened. You should know them better than that. The past is the past, and they're ready to move on. If you were to ask each of them what they would like their next assignment to be, all of them would say *Voyager*."

I pressed my back against the wall of the alleyway, shaking my head. "I don't see how any of that could be true."

"After all we went through together, why is it so hard to believe? You're our captain, the head of our family. And this family reunion wouldn't be complete without you."

With those simple words, Chakotay gave me what I'd been searching for these past weeks. All of the pent-up anger and pain, the past disappointments and sadness, the desperate loneliness I'd endured suddenly rolled down my cheeks like raindrops against a window. I turned and buried my face in my hands. Then a pair of strong arms gathered me in and held me for the longest time. And I didn't resist, not this time. When I finally felt composed enough to pull away, I found him holding out an old-fashioned pocket handkerchief.

"Better?" Chakotay asked.

"Much better," I nodded, burying my nose in the handkerchief.

"Good. You had me worried for a moment."

"Why?"

"Because this is only the second time I've ever seen you cry," he said.

I gave him an indignant look. "I can, you know. It's just not something I have the luxury to do in public."

"Well, don't worry about me telling anyone," he said. "Your tough-as-nails reputation is safe with me."

"Good," I replied. "Because I don't want to make it an order."

We stared at each other for a moment, then both of us burst out laughing. At that moment, I realized just how much I'd missed my friend.

"You know, Chakotay, I don't think I've ever properly thanked you for being there for me all of those years."

He shrugged. "No thanks are necessary. It's just part of my job."

I cocked my head to one side. "That's above and beyond the call of duty for a first officer, don't you think?"

"Oh, I'm not talking about my job as first officer," he replied. "I'm talking about my job as your friend."

I had to fight back another wave of emotion. I stared at my first officer, this man with whom I had shared my deepest thoughts for seven long years, my confidant on any subject. And I knew in my heart that he wouldn't steer me wrong. Things really were going to be all right.

Chakotay was watching me closely. "Are you ready to go in now?"

I smiled and shook my head. "You go ahead. I'll be there in a few minutes." When he looked at me skeptically, I added, "I promise."

He nodded, then walked across the street into the café. I watched the crew greet him and heard him promise that I was on my way. And it was true, for so many things.

I looked up between the walls of the alley just as a soft shaft of moonlight suddenly broke through the cloud cover.

"Thank you, Daddy," I whispered to the moonbeam. "Thank you for sending Gaby to me."

Then I turned and crossed the street.

— STAR TREK —
ENTERPRISE

Egg Drop Soup

Robert Burke Richardson

Phlox strode the bright, antiseptic-smelling hospital halls exchanging greetings with the other professionals he passed. Humans, he found, preferred a tilt of the head to the shrill squawking customary on Denobula. Though still relatively unfamiliar with alien cultures, the people of Earth had proven themselves both friendly and accommodating. In just a short time they had adapted to Phlox's presence and accepted him as a valued colleague.

A group of children gathered near the entrance to the cafeteria, and Phlox decided to spare a few minutes to study the small humans. One little girl with tangled blond hair and spots on her face—*freckles,* Phlox recalled—turned toward him, a replica of a bear clutched to her chest. Phlox smiled his widest grin, stretching his mouth farther than any human could.

"Monster!" the little girl shrieked, mouth opening nearly as wide as Phlox's had. Screaming and waving their arms as if warding off a predator, the children scattered in every direction.

Perhaps we have a little ways to go with regards to acceptance after all, Phlox thought as he watched the children's flustered caretakers rush after their charges.

"What are you?"

Phlox looked down and saw that one of the children had remained. It was very small, but he guessed by the intelligent eyes that it was older than it appeared. The child had no hair, and Phlox could not tell what gender it was.

"I'm Denobulan," said Phlox, taken with the child's frank stare. She was female, he realized, bald because of some kind of radiation therapy. Cancer was rare on Earth and radiation treatment even rarer, but Phlox surmised that this was the case here.

"Don't you want to run from me?" he asked. "The other children seem to want to."

The girl rubbed a thin hand over her bald head. "Sometimes they run from me, too."

Phlox nodded, thinking that flaws filled the universe and that wishing it weren't so was pointless. Acceptance brought peace.

He was surprised to see the sentiment reflected in the young girl's face.

"Hailey," called one of the caretakers, flashing Phlox an annoyed look. She and her coworker had assembled the other children and waved the little girl over.

"Bye," said Hailey. She turned and ran back to the group.

Not wanting to be the cause of further disturbances, Phlox decided to dine instead in the basement cafeteria. It had no windows and the décor was quite dreadful, but he supposed it would have to do.

"I can leave the hospital if a doctor comes with me."

Phlox recognized the soft, almost gravelly voice. "Is that an invitation?" he asked, not looking up from his protoscope.

"I guess."

Phlox turned and raised an eyebrow at Hailey. She wore a blue hospital gown that made her eyes seem even bigger. Delicate features and a crinkly nose made her look like she was always about to laugh. "When did you want to go?"

"We can't go for a few hours," she said. "I'm kind of sick."

"I know," said Phlox. "I've taken the liberty of learning a great deal about you."

"Anything you can do?"

Phlox took a moment to steady his voice. "I'm afraid not. There are many techniques human doctors are still unfamiliar with, but your illness has advanced too far for any of them to work."

"I see," said Hailey. "Can you meet me in my room in two hours?"

"Will do," said Phlox, watching her face to see if he had used the expression correctly.

Hailey smiled and disappeared down the hall. Phlox turned back to his protoscope. The cells of the synthetic tissue he'd been examining were almost completely necrotic. *Such is life,* he thought, discarding the sample. *Such is death.* Still, he felt uncharacteristically troubled.

Human food had proven something of a mixed bag, ranging from tolerable to terrible, but the smells of Madame Chang's delighted Phlox's senses. "Is this the place?" he asked, unable to control his exuberance.

Hailey smiled but tightened her grip on his hand as if she feared he would bound away like a wet dog. The constant drizzle had lowered the temperature considerably, and tendrils of breath trailed from her reddened nose. "Do you want it to be?" she teased.

Phlox nodded vigorously, both because of the exquisite smells and because of his desire to get Hailey out of the cold. He pulled on the steam-obscured glass door, and olfactory goodness rolled into the street on a wave of welcoming warmth. They moved inside and traversed a very slender corridor. Dim lighting and dark, wood-textured walls soothed Phlox's eyes. He entered the first normally lit room and looked around at the hooks and garments.

Hailey did not enter. "That's the coat room," she said after a moment, and Phlox strode back into the corridor.

"Very nice," he said, taking her hand again. The strongest smells emanated from beyond a set of double doors. Phlox glanced sidelong at Hailey, then stepped toward them.

"Doctor," she warned.

Phlox smiled. "I know it's the kitchen," he said. "I wasn't, ah, born yesterday, as you people say."

"Two?" asked a Vulcan woman.

"Two what?" Phlox asked.

"Yes," Hailey interrupted. "Table for two."

The woman led them to a handsomely built table with slightly stained coverings. Phlox glanced around at some of the other diners and nodded approvingly at their food. As with Denobulan messes, large fish tanks dotted the walls, but Phlox suspected these fish were for eating, not display.

"Hello, Hailey," said a man holding two long books. "Haven't seen you for a while. Who's your friend?"

"I've been sick," said Hailey. "This is Doctor Phlox. He's Denobulan."

The man nodded, then held up the books. "Menus?"

"I think we're fine," said Hailey. Phlox opened his mouth to protest, but she fixed him with a knowing gaze.

"The usual?" asked the man. Hailey nodded and the man walked away.

"Egg drop soup," she said before Phlox could voice his misgivings. "You'll love it."

Egg drop soup. It sounded lovely, though Phlox hadn't thought those words could be combined in such a way.

"You come here often," he noted, nodding after their waiter.

"I've been in this hospital over six months. There was a really nice Vietnamese place near my last hospital."

Phlox nodded. Hailey looked at her hands. Phlox recognized the silence as a lull in the conversation.

"You know," he said after a moment, "I really can't help you."

"Help me what?" she asked, frowning.

"Help you live," he said. "I get the feeling you think I might know something that will cure your ailment. I'm afraid I do not."

Hailey's pale cheeks flushed. "Why are you saying this? That's not why I asked you here."

Phlox lowered his eyes. "I'm sorry," he said, realizing the extent of his social blunder. "I can—"

"Never mind," she said, ice in her voice.

The waiter appeared a moment later. "Egg drop soup," he announced, placing two decorative bowls on the table.

Haily didn't reach for hers, but Phlox slid his bowl under his face, the smell the very essence of what his nose had fallen in love with when they first entered.

"Eat some," said Hailey. Phlox hesitated. Hailey smiled. "Silly," she said, grabbing her spoon and slurping the silken liquid.

Phlox could no longer restrain himself and lapped the bowl with his long tongue. The taste complimented the smell perfectly. He stretched his tongue for more, then noticed Hailey watching him, wide-eyed.

"Sorry," he said, picking up the spoon.

They ate in companionable silence and Phlox relished every drop. He ordered four more bowls.

Hailey was full of tales on the way back to the hospital. "Once, in Canada, I had this huge bowl of spicy satay beef soup." She stretched her arms wide in front of her, miming a bowl much bigger than she was. "That was maybe the best thing I ever ate. It had little crushed peanuts on top."

They accompanied each other as far as the fourth floor, but then had to part ways. "Thanks, Doc," said Hailey, cheeks still red from the cold breeze. She turned down the hallway.

"Hailey," Phlox called. He hesitated, not sure of his phrasing. "I wonder if I could ask one question?"

"Okay."

"Why did you want *me* to come with you?"

She shrugged. "I can only go if a doctor accompanies me. And you seemed sort of sad."

Her observation surprised him. Phlox had always considered himself a jovial fellow. "I know that some things can't be helped," he explained. "So do you."

She nodded. "But you gotta have hope, Doc." She spotted her mother coming down the hall, then added, "At least that's what my mom says."

Phlox smiled, but the sight of Hailey's mother—a handsome woman, but one whom the years had obviously not been easy on— quelled his rising spirits. The woman's face wrinkled into a smile when she saw her daughter, and Hailey ran forward into her embrace.

"We had the best time," Hailey told her mother. "Doctor Phlox ate five bowls of egg drop soup! Can you believe it?"

"I see," said Hailey's mom, nodding a thank-you in Phlox's direction. Hand-in-hand, she and her daughter strolled away.

Phlox nodded to himself and turned toward the exobiology wing, eager to return to his research.

"Doctor," Hailey called from down the hall. "Op-ti-mism." She stretched her mouth into an oversized grin. Phlox grinned back, smiling literally from ear to ear.

These humans really are remarkable, he thought.

Phlox had trouble concentrating on his research and he abandoned it altogether the next day, focusing instead on Hailey's condition. He made several promising discoveries, but all of the treatments required significant time to play out.

She didn't ask for this, he reminded himself. Which begged the question *Why am I doing it? For her or for me?*

Hailey's mother appeared later that afternoon, her lined face tranquil. "Hailey went a few hours ago, Doctor," she said plainly. "I thought you'd want to know."

Phlox nodded and looked at the test tube in his left hand. Hailey had passed beyond his reach, but it was possible the research he had started might help another patient. Possible, but unlikely.

He looked up again and met the woman's eyes. She nodded and moved out the door.

Phlox tried to organize the events of the last few days but found that they defied ordering. Something was suggested by Hailey and the way she had lived. The way she spoke. And in the lines of her mother's face. And in the taste of the egg drop soup and the way it melted on his tongue.

Hero

Lorraine Anderson

I saved the ship. That's what Captain Archer says, and he never jokes with me when it's that important. He says I should feel proud of myself. He's always told me that, and I already do.

"Hey, Jimmy, I need a cleanup over here."

I hear that a lot. I'm pretty important around here. That's what Captain Archer says, and I believe him. There's some people on this ship who think I should've been left on Earth, but Captain Archer and Mister Tucker say I do an important job around here. They say, "Well, someone's got to do it," and that's me.

Scientists can be pretty dirty. Not in their labs, they're pretty clean in there, but you should see their rooms. Clothes all over the place. I straighten up everybody's room once a week, sweep the halls, compact the garbage . . . You should see all the garbage. Until we eject it into some sun. Kabloom! Instant incineration.

Mister Tucker says that we could probably incinerate it in the engine room with the bathroom stuff, but he's not quite ready to have an engine that runs on . . . well, my mom told me I shouldn't talk like that, no matter where I ended up.

Anyway, a couple of weeks ago, I was in the engine room. It was a normal day, a normal day in the Expanse, Mister Tucker says, which means there were only two alerts a day. I kinda like alerts, they keep me awake, but Mister Tucker hates them "with a passion," he says. I was just sweeping down the catwalks. Someone's got to do it and the engineers have more important things to do. "Not more important," Captain says, "Just different." If I didn't keep it clean then they would have to do it and they're too busy calibrating things. Whatever that means.

"Hey, Jimmy, I need a haircut." I also cut hair, ever since we lost Tom about three months ago. I was learning it. Captain says we all need two skills. That's my second one. I was turning to Mister Tucker and saying that I could do it whenever he wanted when one of those crazy waves came through. I grabbed the rail and fell to my knees and held on.

It was a crazy wave. It knocked me up and down and sideways. I saw Mister Tucker yelling at me, but I couldn't understand him. He pointed. I saw a hole behind me. It didn't look good. I turned around and looked at Mister Tucker, then picked up my sweeper. I punched it into the hole. It fit. But only if I stayed there. If I pulled it out, the hole didn't look good, all shimmery and shiny, and I knew there shouldn't be shimmery shiny lights in engineering. So I kept the sweeper up there. It's a real sturdy material, I knew it would hold. Another crazy wave came through, I kept it up there.

Mister Tucker was yelling at me. I couldn't hear him. Then I saw him beside me, holding up some sort of material. He pushed me out of the way and slapped it up, then turned toward me. "Jimmy," he said. "Are you all right?"

He looked sort of gray. Then I realized my legs were gone and everything went away.

I woke up in sickbay. Doctor Phlox was looking kinda gloomy and was shaking his head at Captain Archer. I saw Mister Tucker in the other bed, sitting up and looking at the doctor. I like Doctor Phlox—sometimes he lets me feed his animals.

I felt good, but really weak, then I started to throw up. Phlox looked at me and said, "Well, that's to be expected."

"Hi, Captain Archer."

"Hello, Mister Horn."

I smiled at him. Nobody calls me that; usually everybody just calls me Jimmy.

"Trip says that you saved the ship. If you hadn't thought to push your broom against the hole, the hole might have gotten worse in the next wave and the engine might have lost containment."

"Containment?"

The captain smiled. "The ship might have blown up." He chewed his lip. "Why did you volunteer, Mister Horn? There are some times when I thought you should've stayed home, where it was safe."

"Because I wanted to help." I thought a second. "I wanted to make a difference." I smiled. "And I wanted to see other planets. And, Captain, my home was in Florida."

"Oh. Yes."

"Did I save the ship?"

"Yes. Yes, of course. You should be proud of yourself." He looked sad, and I wondered why.

Doctor Phlox looked at me. "Jimmy, you're going to get very, very sick. I'm going to do everything I can to help you."

"Okay." I thought a moment. "Is Mister Tucker all right?"

"He'll be fine. He wasn't as exposed as you were."

"That's good. The ship needs Mister Tucker." My eyes closed. "I'm very sleepy now."

Captain Archer smiled. "I just wanted you to know. You're getting a medal. I'll have it ready for you when you wake up. You're a hero."

"Okay." I smiled. Mom loved me, but she never thought I'd be a hero. Even though Mom is dead, I still talk to her in heaven. I would tell her later. Right now, I feel a lot like sleeping. The doctor looks concerned. I'm smiling as I go to sleep. My name is James Horn, I'm the ship's janitor and barber and I'm a hero, Mom. . . .

Insanity

A. Rhea King

An Ulio dashed through the crowded promenade of Ariebyl 5. Only four feet high, the alien was wiry and thin as a sapling. Heavy folds of skin creased over his forehead, partially covered by white, unruly Albert Einstein hair. His military fatigues were an alien fashion with rank bars sewn into the collar. He laughed and howled as he ran, knocking things over and causing a commotion.

Two Klingons chased him. They shoved anyone in their way out of their way and threw many into the merchant kiosks that lined the corridor.

The Ulio turned in to a docking tunnel, running onto *Enterprise*. He slowed to a stop in the hall, momentarily calm.

"Stop!" someone yelled.

The Ulio spun, finding two security guards running toward him. He turned, skip-running away from them. Even at this slow pace, he was faster than the Starfleet officers. He came to another hall and stopped. Two guards ran around the corner. The Ulio whirled, muttering unintelligibly. He spotted the lift control panel and ran over to it, hitting all of the buttons. The door opened and he trotted onto the lift. He pressed a button with trembling fingers. As the lift descended he muttered, talked, and hummed to himself, an occasional hyena laugh escaping.

The door opened and he ran off. He raced in and out of quarters, starting to become irritated. He ran into Hoshi's quarters and froze, staring at a small tranquility water fountain. Water fell down the miniature mountainside onto marble-size pebbles.

"Dartops!" he gasped.

He searched his pockets and retrieved a metallic black marble. As if presenting an offering to a god, he carefully placed the marble in the fountain. He pirouetted and skipped to the computer terminal.

"Ship. Ship. Name of ship!" The Ulio pulled up the information.

On the monitor appeared: *Starship Enterprise* NX-01.

Rejoicing, the Ulio danced in a circle and chanted, *"Enterprise! Enterprise! Enterprise* NX-01!"

In a burst, he bounded out of Hoshi's quarters and ran down the hall. A guard ran around a corner behind him, spotting him.

"Stop, dammit!" the guard yelled.

Laughing hysterically, the Ulio bolted down the hall. He raced through the ship, screaming and laughing, escaping the security guards. Four guards caught sight of him and chased after him. He ran full-speed into the airlock and headlong into Archer coming through with Trip and T'Pol.

The force of the collision threw Archer back against the wall. Trip grabbed the Ulio's arm. The Ulio began screeching at Trip in his own language.

"Hey, little fella, calm down. I ain't gonna hurt you."

The guards ran up, winded from the chase.

"What's going on?" Archer asked.

"That little guy moves like a *cheetah,* sir! He has been all over the ship and we're pretty sure he was in some quarters. I ordered a thorough scan."

Archer stepped around Trip, watching the Ulio try to punch him. The Ulio's arms were shorter than Trip's and he was being held at arm's length, so the Ulio was only hitting air. The scene amused Archer.

"T'Pol, see if Hoshi's back. I want to know what this alien's doing on our ship."

T'Pol turned to the companel next to the airlock controls and froze. "Captain."

Archer looked up. The two Klingons that had been chasing the Ulio stood in the docking tunnel with weapons drawn and aimed at the group. The guards drew their weapons, putting themselves between the senior officers and the Klingons. The Ulio looked around Trip, saw the Klingons, and started screeching with an increasing volume.

"You will return our prisoner," one Klingon ordered.

"A Klingon that takes prisoners alive? That sound normal to you, T'Pol?" Trip asked.

The Ulio grew still, looking from the Klingons to the humans. Archer glanced at the Ulio, noticing his change of behavior.

"That is not typical of Klingons," T'Pol answered.

The Ulio suddenly let out an ear-piercing screech that momentarily paralyzed everyone in the immediate area. Trip let go of the alien so he could cover his ears. The Ulio dashed away and the Klingons pursued.

"Hey!" Trip yelled, starting after the three.

"Let them go, Trip," Archer ordered.

"But he—"

"He knew we were trying to help. He chose to leave. Let him go."

Trip turned away from the chase and followed the others onto *Enterprise*.

Hoshi slept on her stomach, an occasional soft snore or mutter escaping. Her alarm clock went off. She scrunched her face in detest.

"Alarm! Snooze!" she mumbled.

The alarm stopped. Hoshi fell asleep again, lightly snoring. The alarm went off again five minutes later. She scowled, opening her eyes.

"Alarm. Off."

The alarm shut itself off. She rolled onto her back with a heavy sigh and rubbed her eyes with a wide yawn. Heaving herself off her bed, she staggered to take a shower. A half-hour later she ran out of the bathroom, quickly dressing and getting ready to leave. She ran over to the shelves, picking up a barrette. She glanced at the water fountain as she turned away. Hoshi stopped and turned back, pursing her lips. She picked up a metallic black marble that she had never seen before and examined it. Hoshi shook her head with a smile.

"I bet he thought I'd never notice!" Hoshi told her room.

Hoshi dropped the marble in a pocket, fixed her hair, and hurried to start her shift.

Hoshi strolled along the hall, greeting other crewmen as she passed them. She looked down at the marble as she drew it from her pocket and began rolling it from hand to hand.

"Good morning, Ensign," T'Pol said, walking up to Hoshi.

Hoshi glanced at her. "Good morning, T'Pol."

Hoshi tossed the marble in the air. T'Pol watched it go up and land in Hoshi's waiting hand.

"How was your rest?"

"Decent, but I had some strange dreams." Hoshi tossed the marble again.

"What is the item you have?"

Hoshi grinned. "I think Commander Tucker is pulling a prank on me. I found it in my water fountain this morning. Looks like something out of engineering, don't you think?" Hoshi held it up for T'Pol to look at.

"Commander Tucker's humor is interesting."

As Hoshi dropped the marble back into her other hand, she thought she felt the top and bottom hemisphere of the marble twist. Hoshi looked down at it.

"Interesting ha-ha? Or interesting pec—"
Around her the hallway morphed. . . .

The bridge was filled with eye-burning smoke. A fire burned behind the engineering console and had engulfed a corpse on the floor.
T'Pol and Archer lay on the floor. T'Pol's head was split open;
Archer's chest had been torn apart from an explosion. Malcolm was
slumped in his chair, blood dripping from an unseen wound down
his arm. Travis was the only other live person on the bridge and was
bleeding profusely from a head wound.

Hoshi worked the controls, trying to keep communications up.
The viewscreen showed five ships of unknown origin attacking *Enterprise.*

"The bridge is the only deck with atmosphere, Travis! Everyone
else is dead!"

"Should I?"

Hoshi looked up at him, confused by the question. "Should you
what?"

"Start the self-destruct sequence."

"You want to destroy *Enterprise!?*"

"Captain Archer wouldn't want them getting his ship, Hoshi.
You know that."

"Maybe you haven't noticed, Travis, but there isn't much of his
ship left to get."

A cannon blast blew the hull out above them. Hoshi grabbed her
throat as the oxygen was sucked from her lungs and froze in that
position.

T'Pol knelt beside Hoshi, trying to keep her still as she acted out
her hallucination. Phlox ran up, setting his medical case down as he
knelt.

"What happened?" Phlox asked.

"I don't know. She suddenly collapsed. She believes *Enterprise*
is under attack and Ensign Mayweather is about to destroy it."

Hoshi stopped breathing. Phlox grabbed a scanner from his bag. He didn't have a chance to aim it at her before she gasped for a breath. Hoshi clutched her stomach, curling into the fetal position.

"Hoshi?" Phlox asked her. "What's wrong? Where does it hurt?"

"Everywhere," Hoshi whimpered.

Phlox scanned her and then laid a hand on her shoulder.

"Hoshi, I'm not detecting any injuries. What hurts?"

"Make the pain stop! Make it stop!"

"Hoshi, you aren't injured."

Hoshi started crying. Her breathing became increasingly labored. Phlox scanned her again. He shook his head.

"What is happening to her, Doctor?" T'Pol asked.

"This doesn't make any sense. Her body is reacting as if she's going into hypovolemic shock, yet she has no blood loss!"

Hoshi stopped breathing. Hoshi's hand relaxed when she "died," and the marble rolled away unnoticed. It hit the baseboard and rolled down the hall. It stopped in a corner made by the baseboard and an access panel that hadn't been replaced properly.

Phlox waited this time. Hoshi gasped and started screaming in pain when she regained consciousness.

"T'Pol, please get a stretcher. We need to move her to sickbay."

T'Pol ran down the hall.

Hoshi thrashed on the biobed, restrained by ankle and wrist straps. She screamed and begged Phlox to stop her pain. Phlox sat at a terminal, reviewing the data on it. He looked back when the sickbay doors opened. Archer walked in, glancing at Phlox as he walked past. He stopped at Hoshi's bedside, holding her hand.

"Make it stop," Hoshi begged Archer. "Please make it stop, Captain."

Archer stroked back her hair. She closed her eyes, fresh tears running down her face. Archer leaned in.

"This will pass, Hoshi, I promise."

"It hurts so bad, Captain."

Phlox stood, picking up a hypospray. He walked around to the other side of the bed. Hoshi looked at him.

"Phlox, please—"

"I'm giving you something now." Phlox pressed the hypospray to her neck, injecting her with a sedative.

Hoshi fell asleep, but continued whimpering.

"T'Pol told me about the incident. What's wrong with her, Doc?"

"I've isolated a hallucinatory drug in her blood, but it's breaking down fast. It should be out of her system in four hours."

"She'd never intentionally take a drug, Doc, you know that."

"I know, but she could have been exposed to it unbeknownst to her. I know she was with several ladies that visited a rather shady establishment at Ariebyl 5."

"Have you checked the women that went with her?"

"Yes. None of them had this drug in their blood. I am going to hold her for observation overnight."

Archer nodded. "Send her to her quarters when you release her. She could probably use a day off."

Phlox smiled. "I'll be sure to pass along the word. Good night, Captain."

Archer departed. Phlox turned to back the monitor.

The two Klingons dragged the Ulio into a room and threw him on the floor. He skidded across wet cement and into the wall. The Ulio leapt to his feet, crouching and facing the Klingons. He grinned and twitched, his fingers moving as if they were working some mechanical device.

"Where is it?!" one of the Klingons roared.

The Ulio laughed gleefully, wringing his hands. The Klingon swung a fist at him. He ducked and tried to dodge them. The two Klingons moved faster, keeping him trapped against the wall.

"Where is it?"

"I *hid* it! You'll never find it! You'll never use it on anyone ever again!"

"Where did you hide it?"

The Ulio leapt to his feet, clasping his hands behind his back. He started hopping.

"I hid it!" the Ulio chanted. "I hid it! They told me to hide it! To hide it from you!"

"They who?" The Klingon grabbed for the Ulio's arm.

The Ulio leapt back. He skulked toward a corner. The Klingons followed him. Even when he was completely cornered, the Ulio didn't appear to grasp the danger of his situation.

"They who?" the second Klingon demanded.

He giggled, holding a finger to his lips. "The ones that aren't seeing things or hearing things. They knew I'd get out and they said hide it and never ever tell. They told me to destroy the device when you weren't looking."

The Klingons looked at each other. One produced a hypospray from a pouch and grabbed the Ulio. The Ulio started screeching, kicking, clawing, and biting. The other Klingon grabbed his head, holding it still. The first injected him with the hypospray.

"No! No!" The Ulio sank to his knees when they let him go, holding the injection spot with both hands. Weakly he whined, "Not again."

The first Klingon grabbed the Ulio under his jaw, yanking his head up. The Ulio stared at him with unfocused eyes.

"Where is the device?"

A smile flashed across the Ulio's lips. "Gone. Gone." The Ulio fell back, curling into the fetal position. He heard a buzzing that was growing louder. "The Sarops! They're coming! I can hear them!"

"Tell me where the device is and I'll keep them from coming," the Klingon offered. But there was no compassion in the false promise.

The Ulio closed his eyes. The Klingon grabbed him by the throat, yanked him to his feet, and slammed him against the wall. The Ulio gagged, clawing at the Klingon's arm.

"Tell me where it is now!"

The Ulio looked into his eyes. He stopped fighting. The Klingon let him go.

"Where is it?" the Klingon asked.

The Ulio stood tall and proud. "Corporal Artimiq. Patrol Unit Forty-five. Rank number twelve-nine-L-six."

The Klingon smacked him across the face, sending him flying across the room. He charged after the Ulio, watching him try to scuttle away. He grabbed the small alien, threw him on his back, and injected him again. The Ulio screamed. To his eyes the room changed into a dusky forest. Giant mosquito creatures loomed out of the darkness, attacking him.

Archer sat at the terminal in his ready room, reading through reports. He yawned, sitting back in his chair. His eyes drifted to the door when the doorbell beeped and for a fleeting moment he considered not answering. It beeped again.

"Come in," Archer said with a sigh. He scrubbed his face with his hands.

The door opened and Trip walked in, falling into a chair that was across the room. He was dressed in civilian clothes and looked as exhausted as Archer felt. He gave a marble a toss before speaking. The movement briefly caught Archer's attention.

"You've been in here all day, Cap'n. Ariebyl 5 haunting you too?"

Archer shook his head. "How many bad parts did we get from that place?"

Trip smiled. "More than you want to know about. But my crew's gotten real good at mix-and-matching working parts. It wasn't a complete loss. Have you been in here all day?"

"So is the life of a captain."

Trip chuckled. Archer laid a hand on his stomach when it growled.

"I think I should get some supper before my stomach goes on rebellion."

Trip laughed. Archer stood, walking over to his safe. He began putting data disks away. Trip tossed the marble again, again catching Archer's attention.

"What's that?"

"Marble. Found it in the hall. I'm sure someone'll report it missing."

"I guess. Have you checked in on Hoshi tonight?"

"Yeah. Malcolm was with her when I stopped by. He had her in stitches, so she must be feeling better. Looked bushed though."

"Should probably give her another day off. I wish we knew where she'd been exposed to that drug. I can't believe how fast we seem to fall into traps some days."

Archer closed his safe and headed for the door. Trip jumped up and followed him. The two crossed the bridge to the lift. Inside Trip tapped the controls before he turned to Archer with a grin.

"Are you trying to say space is dangerous, Cap'n?"

"That's not a joking matter right now."

Trip looked down, losing his grin. The lift door opened and the two walked down the hall. Trip contorted his face into a hideous scowl. He began limping, dragging the "bad" foot. Archer stared at him. He smiled when Trip pointed at him and began breathing raspy.

With a bad, grating, pirate accent, Trip warned Archer, "These 'ere oceans are leagues deep now, swabbie. There's creatures in these 'ere waters that are the most hideous and dangerous ye'll ever see!"

Archer started laughing. Trip grinned, continuing his act, using his arms to accentuate his act.

"And in one foul swoop they rip yer head from yer shoulders. And the sirens'll sing ya onto the c'ral reefs, killin' all hands aboard! Heed the ocean there, swabbie, she's not a woman ya want to be presumin' ta know, boy!"

By the time Trip finished, Archer was laughing so hard that he had to stop and lean against the wall. Trip curled his fingers, blew on his fingernails, and shined them on his shirt.

"Still got my touch!" Trip quipped.

He gave the marble a toss in the air, watching it fly up and come down. It landed in his hand and he felt the two halves turn.

Trip's smile faded as he looked down, seeing the hall around him disappear into starlit blackness. His body became encased in an EV suit.

Trip spun head over heels through space. *Enterprise* was in the distance and getting farther away fast. It was still close enough that Trip could see a large hole in one side. Trip felt cold fear course through his body. His stomach tensed into a sickening knot.

"Captain! Help!"

Over his helmet com, Archer quietly told him, "If I could, I would. You know I would."

"Send a shuttlepod. Help me, Cap'n. Please help me!"

Trip looked back. He was headed toward a giant planet that was being ripped apart by volcanic activity. It grew larger as *Enterprise* grew smaller.

"You know the math, Trip. You're too far away, we don't have engines, the shuttlebay doors were jammed in the explosion."

Trip looked back at *Enterprise* and then down at his forearm display. The flashing on it indicated that his jet pack was malfunctioning and he was venting oxygen.

"I don't wanna die like this," Trip whispered. He squeezed his eyes shut.

With a shaking voice, Archer quietly replied, "I am so sorry, Trip. I . . ."

Trip's eyes popped open. "I know. I know you are. Don't wait until you get home to tell my parents what happened. Tell them today. It's been an honor serving with you, Cap'n."

"Trip? Trip, what are you doing?"

Trip reached up and unfastened his helmet. He died instantly.

Archer knelt next to Trip. His mind was having difficulty keeping focused, stunned at how Trip had been there joking one second and was now trapped in a hallucination that he was dying.

Phlox ran up with his case in hand. Two medical technicians followed with a stretcher.

Trip started going into cardiac arrest. His hand relaxed, releasing the marble. It rolled across the hall, unnoticed by those around him. It rolled along the baseboard, coming to rest in the crack of the door of Archer's quarters and the doorframe.

"Trip, don't you dare die!" Archer hissed.

Phlox grabbed a scanner to scan him. Trip gasped, opening his eyes.

"Trip?" Archer said, laying a hand on Trip's shoulder.

Trip looked around, but he wasn't seeing anyone.

"Oh, my God!" Trip gulped.

"Trip, look at me," Archer said.

"Help! He's dying! Help!" Trip screamed. "Dad!"

"Phlox, what's happening to him?"

"I can't tell yet. Let's get him to sickbay."

The crewmen pulled Trip on the stretcher and the four ran down the hall with him.

Archer sat on a stool, watching Trip strain against his restraints. He pleaded for someone to help save his father, who was again dying before his eyes. Phlox walked up to Archer.

"What's wrong with him, Doc?"

"The same thing as Hoshi. He has the same drug in his system."

"How is that possible? We left Ariebyl 5 three days ago!"

"I don't know. That's as much of a mystery to me as it is to you."

"Could it be a virus?"

"No. It is a drug."

Archer looked back at Trip. "You have to figure out how he came in contact with it."

"I'm working on it, Captain."

Archer stood up. "I'll be in my quarters. Contact me when he comes out of this. I don't care what time of day it is."

"Yes, Captain."

Phlox watched him leave. He sat down at a monitor, reading the contents.

Archer walked into his quarters, smiling when Porthos ran up to him. He crouched down, scratching the dog's ears. Archer changed into a pair of shorts and T-shirt before he went into the bathroom to brush his teeth.

Porthos trotted in, dropping the marble. The metallic ball twanged when it hit the floor and rolled to a stop against Archer's foot. He looked at it and then Porthos.

"Where did you get that, boy?"

Porthos wagged his tail, waiting in anticipation for Archer to throw it. Archer finished and picked up the marble. Porthos started getting excited.

"No, Porthos. Go on. Go lie down."

Porthos obeyed the command. Archer lay down on his bed, examining the marble.

"You know . . ." Archer cocked his head to the side. "Trip had this before—"

Archer sprang to his feet to run back to sickbay. At the same time he felt the two halves of the marble move. He looked down, finding himself on the bridge.

Archer sat in the captain's chair. On the viewscreen a black hole took up the entire screen. *Enterprise* shook every time a gravitational wave dragged across the hull.

Archer was aware of T'Pol, Hoshi, Travis, Malcolm, and Trip, but he'd forgotten what any of them were doing. He sensed T'Pol, on his left, moving quickly about her station. Travis was muttering under his breath, pulling on the yoke. In his peripheral vision Archer saw that they were all yelling. He saw sparks flying from control panels. But he heard nothing, only silence. This felt too surreal for him to react to it.

"Captain." T'Pol's voice broke through the silence. "We're

trapped in the gravitational pull of the black hole. We aren't going to survive this."

"Captain, what do I do?" Travis asked.

Archer tried to wet his dry lips. His hands went cold and clammy. He was facing one of the few things that gave him nightmares: being caught in a black hole.

"Captain, we must alert the crew," T'Pol said.

Language had turned on Archer, refusing to let his mouth use it.

"And tell them what, T'Pol?" Trip hissed, "Why'd you challenge them, Cap'n? What the hell were you thinkin'?" he asked, turning to the captain.

Archer looked at him. Challenge who? He wanted to ask, but he still couldn't find his voice.

"We told you not to. We were outgunned. Why didn't you listen to Malcolm? Or Travis for that matter? He told you if we jumped to warp without plotting we could end up anywhere. Why didn't you listen? He needed just one or two minutes to do it."

Oh God! Another fear. Putting his crew in unnecessary danger and failing to understand his father's engine. This couldn't be happening all at once! Not even Murphy was this cruel!

"That's not how warp works, Trip," Archer weakly argued. Why did his voice sound like he was ten? "You know that."

"You're a captain, not an engineer. You think that just because your dad built the warp drive, you know something about it?" Trip motioned at the screen. "And now you've as good as killed us!"

Archer looked at the screen, whimpering, "That's not how warp works. I know enough—"

"You killed us! Your pride killed us!" T'Pol screamed.

Crewmen suddenly surrounded Archer. They were pale, with hollow, dead eyes.

Malcolm pointed a finger at him. "How could you make such a large tactical error? You have to do every job yourself, don't you?"

"You're pathetic, Captain!" Trip screamed. "How many times has your pride, your ego, nearly gotten us killed?"

"And now you've succeeded. You've killed us!" Hoshi cried out.

Archer turned to run, but there was no escape. His dead crew, the crew he feared to let down, whose very opinions meant the most to him, had turned on him. Archer screamed as they strangled and suffocated him to death.

All the while, *Enterprise* was being pulled deeper into the black hole.

T'Pol ran around the corner, finding a small crowd gathered outside Archer's quarters. She could hear Archer screaming inside. Two security guards were trying to unlock the door. T'Pol placed a hand on one of their shoulders, gently pushing him out of her way.

"What have you tried?"

"All senior staff codes. It won't unlock," the man answered.

T'Pol tried several codes with no success.

"T'Pol to Phlox."

"Go ahead," Phlox said.

"Report to the captain's quarters immediately. I believe that he may have come in contact with the drug. I need for you to override the captain's security clearance to open the doors to his quarters."

"I'm on my way."

T'Pol banged on the door.

"Captain, please come out." T'Pol placed her hand on the entrance way, as if to gain strength from the steel walls.

"Get away! I didn't kill you! I didn't do it!" Archer screamed. "You're dead. Dead people don't speak."

"I am not dead."

Malcolm pushed through the crowd in front of the room and tried to get closer to assist. Phlox and two technicians rushed through the hallway, forcing him out of the way so that they could gain entry. Archer was huddled under his desk, hugging himself and rocking. He watched T'Pol, but his eyes didn't focus on her. T'Pol tapped the com panel near the headboard. Malcolm spotted Porthos standing in the bathroom door, watching the transpiring events. He walked around everyone and picked up the dog. Malcolm headed for the door with the beagle.

"Guess you'll stay with me for a short time," Malcolm told the dog.

Malcolm glanced back when he heard something hit the floor, but he didn't see what had fallen.

Dropping from Porthos's mouth, the marble bounced once. It rolled into the crowd around the door, ricocheting off the soles of people's shoes until it hit the baseboard. It rolled down the hall to a junction. It hit someone's shoe, altering direction, and continued rolling.

Halfway across the ship, Ensign Cutler was waiting for the lift. The marble hit her shoe. She looked down at it and smiled. Cutler picked it up. . . .

Archer and Cutler were the only two crewmen in sickbay, both trapped in their own nightmare. Phlox walked up to Cutler's bed, unfolding a blanket. She was clawing the air, scrambling for a hand-hold, one hand held tight in a fist. Phlox set the blanket aside and grabbed her hand. With effort, he managed to pry her hand open.

The marble dropped from her hand, clattering on the floor. Phlox watched it roll to a rest against a wall. He covered Cutler with the blanket before retrieving it.

Phlox held it up to the light, seeing a thin seam running the circumference. Phlox adjusted the marble so he held both halves and twisted. Four needles flew out, pricking his skin. In seconds he was trapped in his own worst fear.

"Captain Archer," a voice called through the screaming mob.
Archer turned. "Phlox?"
"Captain, open your eyes. I need you to wake up."
Archer scanned the mob even as he tried to fight off the angry crewmen around him.
"Captain!"

Archer startled awake. He was in sickbay and the lights were down low. Phlox stood over him, watching him.

"Are you awake, Captain?" Phlox asked.

"How'd I get here? Where is my crew? They're trying to kill me, Doc. They're try—"

"Captain, you're hallucinating."

Archer shook his head. He turned his head. He saw the crew hidden in the shadows and behind walls. They started moving in on him. He tried to scramble away, but restraints prevented him from getting away. He looked back around, finding Phlox still there.

"Jonathan!" Phlox snapped.

The hallucination faded. For a moment he was grounded in reality.

"Captain, I need you to remember something. I need you to focus. Do you understand?"

Archer nodded.

"What was the last thing you did before you started hallucinating?"

"Hallucinating? What are you talking about?"

"Before the crew was trying to kill you, what do you remember? I need to know."

"I was getting ready for bed."

"And then?"

Archer closed his eyes. "My head hurts. The crew is screaming at me. I didn't mean to—"

"Captain, I need you to think. I need to know what happened when you got ready for bed. Did you find an object in your room? A small sphere?"

"I found a marble. Porthos brought it to me. Trip had it earlier. He was tossing it and—"

"Did anything unusual happen with the marble?"

Archer's face scrunched in pain. He closed his eyes tight. "My head hurts, Doc."

"I'll give you something for it, but I need to know about this marble. Did anything unusual happen with it?"

"I can't remember."

"Please try. It's very important, Captain."

Archer's face relaxed. Phlox gently shook his shoulder. Archer looked up at him.

"It twisted. The marble . . . twisted."

Phlox smiled, patting his shoulder. "Thank you." He pressed a hypospray to Archer's neck.

Archer relaxed, falling into a fitful sleep.

Phlox walked to a monitor. He made a notation and changed screens.

"The marble. Everyone has handled that marble," Phlox told the monitor.

He turned and tapped a com panel. "Phlox to Hoshi."

"Go ahead, Doctor," Hoshi said.

"Hoshi, I need you to broadcast a shipwide—"

Ensign Novakovich ran in, interrupting Phlox. "Doc, T'Pol's got whatever everyone has. She's lost it!"

"I'll get back to you, Hoshi," Phlox told her. He grabbed his case and followed Novakovich out.

T'Pol backed away from the aliens closing in on her. One came too close and she swung a fist at it. Her first punch connected with its jaw and the alien fell back into another. The others closed the gap, preventing her from escaping.

"Get away from me! Get away!" she yelled at them.

"T'Pol," she heard Phlox say, but his voice was distant.

"Doctor! Doctor Phlox!"

"T'Pol, I need you to—" Phlox's voice became distorted as it faded. And then she heard him say, "Vulcans are very volatile when they can't control their emotions. It's going to take all of us."

"Doctor!" T'Pol screamed.

The aliens attacked her, trying to pin her down. She savagely fought back, clawing and striking out. She spun to run away and stopped short.

She was in a barren wasteland without even a tumbleweed in sight.

Dust and dirt blew across the vast expanse pitted with cavernous canyons. Overhead the sky was a strange, bright orange and red.

"Hello?" T'Pol called out.

No one answered.

"Hello!" T'Pol screamed. Her voice echoed in the canyons.

"Is anyone here?" T'Pol swallowed. Her emotions were slipping from her control. She whispered to the barren land, "Is anyone here?"

Someone tackled her from behind. She rolled over, finding herself surrounded by the aliens again. She screamed, fighting them. One came at her with a hypospray, pressing it against her neck. She let out an enraged scream before she passed out.

The marble bounced along the baseboard, rolling unnoticed past crewmen.

Hoshi's voice began speaking over the ship's com: *Attention, all hands. Be on the lookout for a metallic black marble.*

The marble came to an air duct and rolled into it. It rolled and rattled along, miraculously avoiding several vent openings.

"This device has caused several crew members to hallucinate."

The marble dropped down a shaft and rolled several more meters. It came to the edge of a vent cover and teetered back and forth, as if indecisive about what to do next. Below the vent Malcolm worked at a monitor.

"Do not attempt to handle this device," Hoshi continued. *"Alert Doctor Phlox immediately if you find it."*

The marble fell through the vent.

The marble bounced off Malcolm's head. He looked up and instinctively caught the marble. He realized too late what he had caught, feeling the two halves turn.

"Call Phlox!" Malcolm cried to his crew.

He collapsed on the floor, his hand closing tight around the marble.

*   *   *

Two crewmen ran in, carrying Malcolm on a stretcher. He was acting as if he were drowning.

"Put him on the biobed."

Phlox hurried to restrain him. He brushed Malcolm's fist and heard something hit the floor. He looked down, seeing the marble roll across the floor.

"Continue restraining him," Phlox ordered the two crewmen.

Phlox grabbed a Petri dish and a tonglike instrument from a counter. He followed the marble until it came to rest against a wall. Phlox crouched and, with great care, placed the marble in the Petri dish, using the tongs. Phlox carried the marble to a containment unit, placing it inside.

Phlox stopped at a com panel, tapping it. "Phlox to Commander Tucker."

"Yeah?"

"I need you to come to sickbay. I've found the device."

"I'm on my way."

Phlox returned to settling Malcolm.

Using tongs, Trip placed the marble on a stand. He joined Malcolm, T'Pol, and Archer across the room. Malcolm held a phase pistol, his hand constantly moving to readjust his grip. He looked back at Archer. Archer and T'Pol reminded him of victims witnessing a criminal's death.

"On your command, sir," Malcolm told Archer.

Archer nodded.

Malcolm aimed at the marble and fired. The marble disintegrated without so much as a pop. Malcolm dropped his hand and the four were silent for a long moment.

"I was almost expecting fireworks or something." Malcolm commented. "That was so . . . uneventful."

"It wasn't sentient, Malcolm," Trip reminded him. "Just a device someone thought would be fun to let loose on *Enterprise.*"

"Clean it up and get back to work, men." Archer left.

The two watched him leave before looking back where the device had been. T'Pol turned to leave.

"He's not all right, is he?" Malcolm asked.

T'Pol stopped, looking back at the two.

"No. Whatever he hallucinated has really got him on edge. Can I ask . . ." Trip stopped.

Malcolm looked at him. "Ask what?"

"Can I ask what you hallucinated?"

Malcolm smiled. "I was drowning. Repeatedly drowning. You?"

"I was going to die being pulled into a planet's atmosphere. Took off my helmet instead. Then I kept seeing all the people I care about die. There were hundreds of people around, even some doctors, but no one would help me."

"You're scared you won't be able to save someone you care about?"

"Deathly afraid. Stupid, I know, but I am."

Malcolm shook his head. "No, Trip, that's not stupid."

"Fears are unfounded," T'Pol quietly commented.

Malcolm looked back at her. "I don't believe that."

"I'm afraid of living alone. That is an unfounded fear. You two have an order, carry it out." T'Pol left the room.

Trip and Malcolm looked at each other, surprised that she'd even mentioned her fear.

Although the bridge was bustling with routine morning activity, no one spoke. They were all trying to put the week from hell behind them.

Archer sat in the captain's chair, staring at the padd in his hand. His mind was far from it, however. It kept wandering back to his hallucination.

"Captain, I'm detecting a ship approaching," Travis reported. "It's a Klingon *Raptor.*"

Archer looked at the view monitor.

"They're hailing us, sir," Hoshi told him.

Archer resisted responding to his escalating panic. He stood, setting the padd in his hand aside. He felt his crew staring at him, judging him.

Just being overly sensitive, Jonny. They aren't judging you, Archer whispered in his head. Out loud he ordered, "Full halt, Travis. Respond, Hoshi."

Travis obeyed, Hoshi didn't. Archer looked at her. She was staring at her controls, her fingers gripping the edge so tight that her knuckles were white.

"Hoshi, hail them."

"Are you sure, sir? What if—"

"I'm certain, Hoshi. Hail them."

Hoshi didn't obey. Archer walked over to her station. She looked at him.

"Hoshi, I'm giving you an order. Hail them."

A shiver visibly ran through her. With trembling hands she worked the controls. Her voice shook when she told Archer, "Opening a channel, sir."

Archer returned to stand before the captain's chair. A Klingon captain appeared on the monitor.

"You have something of ours. Return it immediately!" the Klingon demanded.

"We don't have anything of yours," Archer argued.

"Yes, you do! A convict told us he hid it on your ship. We demand it returned now!"

"We don't have—"

"It's a round device." The Klingon captain held his hand up to show the size of the device. It was the same size as the marble. "It's colored—"

Archer's hands had begun to grow cold and his stomach cramped in response to the building fear. But he pressed on.

Archer interrupted the Klingon. "It's colored metallic black and contains a psychotomimetic drug mixed with an unidentified drug that stimulates hallucinations based on the victim's worst fear. Correct?"

"Return it immediately."

"I'm sorry, I can't do that. We—"

"Return it now or we will destroy you!"

Archer swallowed. In his mind's eye his hallucination began replaying. He had to force himself to remain calm and mask his fear.

"We can't. We destroyed it."

"You did what!?"

Archer's fear choked him. His lips formed the words, but no sound came out. Trip stood and walked up to Archer's left side. He pulled his hands behind his back, standing tall at full attention.

"We destroyed that damned device," Trip told the Klingon. "But since you're bringing it up, maybe you'd like to tell us what it was for?"

"That's classified."

T'Pol walked up to stand at Archer's left-hand side. She stood close enough that Archer could feel her body heat. But it did little to ease his fear.

"Now that we know whom this device belongs to, it raises questions that I'm sure the Vulcan High Command will be asking the Klingon High Council. Such as what the device's purpose is."

"Return it!"

"Perhaps you're hard of hearing!" Travis yelled. "We destroyed it! You're not getting it back in pieces or all together, because it is gone!"

"And whatever you intended on using it for," Malcolm added, "it wouldn't be wise to implement it. You can be assured we won't keep that device a secret."

The Klingon captain leaned into the screen. "If we meet again—"

T'Pol cut him off. "If we meet again we will fire on your ship, *unprovoked.*"

The Klingon opened his mouth to respond to the threat.

"Oh, I think this conversation was over before it started. Good. Bye," Hoshi told the Klingon, and closed the channel.

"Targeting their bridge," Malcolm announced.

Before he could fire, the Klingon ship went to warp. Travis resumed their course.

The bridge was silent for a long moment, the crew watching their captain.

Travis turned to Archer. "Speaking for all of us, Captain, I hope that we didn't handle that wrong."

Archer smiled, looking at each of them. "You all handled it perfectly. Return to your duties."

Archer walked back to his chair and sat down. He picked up the padd and started reading the document on it. Discreetly he watched his crew returning to their duties. He realized that one of his fears was unfounded. His crew would never turn on him for a wrong decision.

SPECULATIONS

A & Ω

(Alpha & Omega)

Derek Tyler Attico

In the Federation's darkest hour, the cornerstone of its founding was realized. The galaxy was at peace.

Conquests for power and territory became irrelevant. Prejudices and mistrusts were set aside. Species that isolated themselves opened their doors of communication.

General Order Zero, the catapult initiative, was well under way. Across the galaxy, over two thousand catapults were under construction. Worlds with no choice were building them and those that had a choice helped others. Earth's catapult, the prototype, was an engineering masterpiece and the largest structure ever created by humans in space.

To Jean-Luc Picard, as he stared out the viewport aboard the task-force flagship, the device's curved graviton emitters looked like two immense parentheses punctuating the only thing that could frighten the galaxy into unity: a Borg supercube. Starfleet engineering could not find a better description for the immense structure; it was eight hundred times larger than the last cube over Earth.

Within the walls of this terror resided a half-billion drones, not swarming with goals of assimilation and perfection, but motionless. The same phenomenon was reported in every quadrant of the galaxy. There were no pursuits for technology, no assimilations. Borg cubes, Borg cities, Borg worlds had simply stopped. The most powerful force in the known galaxy was silent, and no one knew why.

"Not the view it used to be," a voice from behind Picard commented.

The captain felt the sickening truth of the statement. The supercube eclipsed what had once been the western United States. Earth now had two moons, one of magnificent natural beauty and one of utter technological horror. The arrival of the supercubes had wrought chaos and destruction. On Earth and throughout the rest of the galaxy, everything had changed. Starfleet and the Federation had moved from a charter of exploration and peace to one of salvation and restoration.

"No, not quite." Picard replied.

From *Voyager*'s ready room, he could see the forcefields around Earth's coastal cities holding back the 150-foot tidal waves. When the supercube emerged from transwarp, it upset the natural balance of gravity, killing two hundred million people worldwide just by settling itself into geosynchronous orbit over Starfleet headquarters.

San Francisco was now a city of ruins, a pile of dirt on a planet of rubble. Today more than any other day in his lifetime, the four tiny pips on Picard's collar sat a bit heavier. He was a captain conflicted with his duty, and a man concerned about his home. *My life was a dream, and I have awakened to the nightmare.*

"Coffee?"

Picard forced a half-smile and turned toward the person voicing the absurd suggestion.

"I could make that an order." Admiral Janeway smiled, arching one eyebrow for effect.

Picard tried to appear gracious. "Thank you, Admiral, but I'd prefer—"

Janeway's raised hand interrupted him as she turned to face the replicator. "Tea. Earl Grey, hot. Coffee, black." Twenty-fourth-century technology resonated to life as energy and light coalesced into a soothing, subtle brew and a steaming, stimulating extraction, polar opposites that matched their owners perfectly.

Picard welcomed the jovial touch from his commanding officer, but he knew this wasn't a social visit. Admiral Janeway's Delta Quadrant expertise on the catapult design and the Borg had made her the only logical choice to head Earth's catapult program and the only one who could authorize his plan.

"I want to thank you for taking time out of the project to see me, Admiral."

Janeway approached Picard in silence and held out his tea. As he grasped the cup, he quickly realized she was not going to release it until he looked at her. "Jean-Luc, I've decided to deny your request. The personal risk is too great."

Picard returned Janeway's gaze with all of the sincerity and intent that she had given to him. "Don't you think that's my decision to make, Admiral?"

Janeway turned away from Picard at the viewport and took a seat behind her desk.

"Captain, I thought you—more than anyone—would understand the risk. We've been here twice before, the Borg poised over Earth, once with you as their assimilated representative. The damn thing's sheer size and proximity to Earth makes it impossible to destroy it. It's taken us a year of nonstop building to get here, and in six days the catapult will send that monstrosity into the sun. Why do this now?"

Walking over to Janeway, Picard knew it was a fair question. He had asked himself the same thing after witnessing the devastation and enduring countless sleepless nights.

"The cube is inactive, Admiral. The away teams don't understand why the Borg are here, and what we're planning is the murder of a half-billion lives."

Janeway watched the vapor from her coffee lift away from the anchor of its porcelain world and dissipate into memory. Soon, with luck, the same would be said of the Borg. Picard was a respected friend, but this wasn't an issue she needed to defend.

"The Federation has decided to . . . look the other way this time, Jean-Luc, and I can't say I disagree. At least there will be a Federation when we're done."

Picard had heard the reasoning before. This time, it was agreeable for the Federation to ignore its history and principles, to turn a blind eye to the directives that governed hundreds of planets; but that didn't make it right. "Have we come so far that we can now decide who is and isn't worthy of our morals? Have we become the very thing we fear?"

Janeway listened to the words, but she couldn't accept that they were coming from Picard. "So you've become the devil's advocate, Jean-Luc? I have to say, I didn't see this coming."

Since he'd known her, Picard couldn't recall her backing down from a position, but he appealed, nonetheless, to her sense of decency.

"Someone must be a voice for the voiceless, Admiral. The darkest places in hell are reserved for those who maintain their neutrality in times of moral crisis."

It wasn't every day that someone used a quote from her favorite author against her. Picard's powers of persuasion were well known, especially when he was standing behind what he thought was right.

"If the Federation's going to survive this, Captain, we're going to have to get our hands dirty. Dante knew that sometimes the path to salvation lies through hell. Don't forget, I've had to stare that devil over there in the eye on more than one occasion. Those half-billion souls aren't voiceless—they're a collective. They think and act as one unified mind, and we better hope we get rid of them be-fore they wake up and start talking."

As he sat down across from the admiral, Picard realized that morality wouldn't be enough. "I haven't forgotten, Admiral. You helped a human orphaned by the Borg regain her humanity. You helped a drone become an individual. You put your crew and your-self at risk to help the Borg when the Queen was destroying Uni-matrix Zero. I thought you would understand why we must do this."

Picard took a sip of the tea that had always calmed him, but it no longer provided the same solace, tasting bitter under the pressure bearing down upon him. "When the Borg . . . took me as I watched, helpless, I was aware of faint cries behind the voice of the collec-tive, pleas from the souls of the assimilated. But that's all we were—faint, helpless whispers in the darkness. Admiral, there may be a half-billion Borg aboard that cube, but inside each one is an individual screaming for help. If we can reach even some of them, we may gain knowledge into their purpose here and quite possibly liberate them from the evil in which they are entombed."

Janeway gazed silently at Picard, a man who had been broken and humiliated by the Borg. He had been turned into an instrument of death and destruction, unleashed upon the very people and ideals he had spent a lifetime protecting. Yet here he was, on a fool's errand, trying to save the souls of the soulless; and she'd be a fool to listen to him. After all of her struggles to protect her crew and now Earth against this evil, this was not the time to have pity for the devil. But as she sat with the captain in silence, she couldn't help thinking about the implications. If the Federation crossed the line this time, it would be much easier the next. Perhaps the souls of the Borg weren't the only ones Picard was pleading for.

"Be careful what you wish for, Captain. I just hope you know what you're doing."

The azure glow of the transporter pierced the darkness as energy became matter and matter contorted into form.

"Janeway to *Enterprise*. We're in."

The trio surrounding Jean-Luc Picard made him uneasy. An omen, perhaps, of what was to come. But the captain knew that it was an unavoidable necessity. Without a weapon or communicator, he felt vulnerable returning to the dark confines of his past. If his plan was to work, he would have to embrace that past.

The surgery was relatively simple. It was what came afterward that was difficult. He had avoided mirrors and reflective surfaces, escaping the reality of the image that had plagued his nightmares for so long. But now, aboard this vessel, there could be no denials.

His skin was devoid of pigmentation; tubes fed into his head and neck. His right arm was now a mechanical appendage. The same dreaded metal plate had been grafted back onto his face. Its thin red laser light reached forth like a tendril of malevolence. He was once again Locutus of Borg, in body if not in soul.

Picard watched as the admiral and Seven of Nine swept the area in unison, their footfalls reverberating off the steel deck plates like thunder in the unsettling silence.

The phaser rifle Janeway held could unleash the power of a phaser bank. Seven gripped two less-menacing devices; she had a Starfleet medical case in one hand and a tricorder in the other. The tricorder was the focus of her attention.

"I'm reading no activity whatsoever. All nodes are at minimal power; everything is in standby. All primary and secondary alcoves are in use, but I'm reading a reserve alcove at the end of this section that will be adequate."

Janeway pointed her wrist beacon in the direction Seven gestured, its light splitting the darkness. "All right, let's move."

Picard noticed that Worf had remained behind him since they had stepped onto the transporter pad. He could feel the tempered gaze of the Klingon scanning, watching, and waiting.

Worf knew that his place was between the away team and danger. Honor demanded no less. However, Janeway had insisted that he remain behind them—behind Picard at all times. In the past, he had rescued Captain Picard from the Borg. It had been a mission of honor—one worthy of song—but this duty bore no such honor. As Janeway led them into the darkness, the Klingon found himself thinking not about the dangers that were to come but of the admiral whose orders he was bound to follow.

"Commander Worf reporting as ordered, Admiral." Worf noticed the scrutiny of Janeway's gaze as she sized him up against what was in his records and her opinion. "Have a seat, Commander. I'll get right to the point. Captain Picard has requested to go over to the supercube, and I've approved the mission."

When the *Enterprise* was assigned to the task force securing the supercube, Worf had noted Picard's preoccupation. When Picard had told his senior crew about his plan. Worf had thought it unwise and had voiced his opinion. It wasn't the first time that Picard's personal feelings about the Borg had influenced him. Worf considered getting Doctor Crusher to declare Picard unfit, but there would be little honor in such a move. He had also been sure that the captain's request would never be permitted. "May I ask why it was approved, Admiral?"

Worf noticed Janeway's hesitation before she answered. "It's a mission of mercy. . . ." Janeway paused, waiting for recognition of those words in the hardened gaze of the Klingon before continuing. "I'll be joining him, as will Seven; I'm assigning you to the away team as security. I want you to understand that your first priority is to ensure the integrity and success of the catapult initiative. All other matters are secondary. Do I make myself clear?"

Until that moment, Worf had been undecided about the admiral. Word of her deeds and battles in the Delta Quadrant preceded her. She had called him here to ascertain if he could be counted on to slay his captain, his *jadich,* his friend. *The woman may be a great warrior, but she knows little of Klingon honor.* "If trouble arises, you want me to kill Captain Picard."

Janeway leaned back in her chair, calmly crossing her legs. "Should it come to that, yes."

Worf could feel his blood racing. If this had been a Klingon vessel, he would have reached across the table and ripped out her heart for questioning his honor and duty. But this was Starfleet, and the uniform required a different method. "And what of the Borg drone?"

The shock on the admiral's face quickly turned to anger at his audacity. "Excuse me?"

Despite having spent his entire life around humans, it never ceased to amaze Worf how easily they could accept one obvious conclusion yet deny another. "She was a drone for a good portion of her life. With the project almost completed, is the cube the best place for her, Admiral?"

It was clear that his words had penetrated deeper than a *bat'leth* ever could.

"I know where Seven's loyalties lie, Commander."

Loyalties. Worf knew the meaning of the word all too well. On more occasions than he cared to count, his loyalty to Starfleet had tested him. It had cost him his brother, the respect of his people, and his family name. As the Klingon rose from the chair, he did not conceal his anger. "As security for the mission, Admiral, I will do my duty . . ." He let the weight of his words stand between them. "And should it come to it, I will kill anyone who jeopardizes the catapult initiative."

As the admiral stood, Worf was sure she would respond to his insinuation—or, worse, remove him from the away team.

"Dismissed" was her only reply.

At the reserve alcove, it was these thoughts that brought Worf back into the moment. He rechecked the targeting display of the Breen dampening rifle. The targets were preset: the drone, Captain Picard, and the admiral.

Janeway scrutinized the empty alcove. A pale green hue flowed over its metallic surface, an ominous reminder of the forces they were dealing with. "All right, Seven. Put the Doctor on the left, just outside the alcove."

Seven set the silver suitcase with the Starfleet Medical logo and letters M.M.H.E. stamped on it in the prescribed area. She gently tapped twice, and the Mobile Medical Holo-Emitter suitcase opened like a clam, revealing an emitter on one side and a medical tricorder and two hyposprays on the other. Automation took over, and the twenty-fourth century's answer to a twenty-ninth-century device activated.

"So this is a Borg cube. Not much to look at, is it? You know, Admiral, this would have been much easier if you had just allowed me to carry my mobile emitter."

Eyeing the walkway for signs of trouble, Janeway didn't bother masking her impatience with the sentient program. "We've been over this, Doctor. We couldn't risk twenty-ninth-century technology waking the Borg."

As the Doctor picked up his medical equipment and turned toward Seven of Nine, something in his demeanor reminded Worf of Alexander when he was a child.

"Not like this plan will do that," the Doctor said. "This hypospray will reactivate your dormant Borg assimilation nanites. You'll feel a slight tingle and should have access to them almost immediately."

Seven thought about those words. In a moment she was going to have the instrument the Borg had used to take her parents, her life, and her individuality from her. It would soon be thriving, multiplying, and living inside her again. She understood the necessity and the humanity of Picard's plan; and yet, somehow, it felt like a step in the wrong direction.

"Understood."

In an instant, Seven was aware of the nanites, but not as the Doctor described. It was as if someone had reached into the darkest parts of her soul and simply unlocked the door. Seven wondered if the woman she had become was strong enough to face the drone she had been.

The Doctor flipped open the medical tricorder, passing it over the young woman, the sounds of the scan intruding upon the silence of the cube. "Efficient little fellows, the nanites are active and operating within specified parameters."

Janeway turned to Picard, the first and last piece in this plan. "Are you sure about this, Jean-Luc? Say the word, and we leave now."

Picard turned and looked at the drone in the alcove next to him. A Bajoran woman, she was someone's daughter, perhaps even a mother herself lost to those who had loved her, one more casualty in an insane war. "Let's get on with it."

As Seven approached, Picard could feel her discomfort. He'd met her only two days ago, but he realized that having been Tertiary Adjunct of Unimatrix Zero One, she'd known him for far longer. She had never made eye contact. But now, as she was about to resurrect with him, she stared at him directly, intently. As the assimilation tubes forced their way through tissue and bone, he could feel the nanites changing him, restructuring his priorities, releasing him from his morals and inhibitions.

"I am Locutus of Borg, resistance is . . . possible."

Janeway felt her grip around the phaser rifle tighten. She didn't know what she had expected, but it certainly wasn't this.

"Doctor?"

Cautiously, as if intruding upon some unseen boundary, the Doctor moved toward Picard, scanning him slowly.

"Heart rate and blood pressure are steady. Slight increase in neural activity."

Janeway moved in close, toward the part of Picard's face that was unobstructed by Borg technology, searching for his humanity.

"Jean-Luc. Captain, are you with us?"

The entity that was neither Borg nor human stared off into the distance, seemingly contemplating the question; then, abruptly, a reminder drew his attention, and he faced Janeway.

"For the moment, Admiral."

Janeway gripped Picard's shoulder, hoping her voice and contact would anchor him in his mission.

"Captain, are you in contact with the collective? Can you hear them?"

A sadness and confusion played across Picard's face. Something was wrong. Why were they not here to welcome him once again into their embrace, to reestablish his designation and give him new commands? He could no longer hear the voices or feel the security of the collective. He was without the thoughts that had liberated him from his doubts and insecurities, from the burden of his humanity, and had given him, in return, purpose and strength he never knew as the human Picard.

"No, I am . . . alone."

Janeway had always taken solace in the Borg's predictability. It was their Achilles heel, but with their appearance over Earth she couldn't shake the feeling that the rules had somehow changed.

"Jean-Luc, that's not possible. There are a half-billion drones here. The collective has to be here—you must go deeper."

Picard began the search, hunting for the reassurance of the collective. The female was right. He must find the collective. Had he angered them? Had they abandoned him for failing as their representative, for being locked away so long within a pathetic human shell?

The Doctor's tricorder began to beep furiously. "The captain and Seven's neural activity has just spiked. Twenty percent, forty and rising."

The admiral noticed Worf slowly take a step behind Seven. Their earlier conversation painfully in her thoughts, she knew the Klingon would fulfill his duty. Of all the projected scenarios from the Borg experts, this was not what anyone had expected. The effect on Seven was to have been minimal. "Seven?"

Seven had expected to hear the collective again, but to her astonishment, her thoughts were her own.

"I am unaffected, Admiral."

Picard wasn't.

"The Borg are here. We . . . are here."

They had not abandoned him. He could feel their presence now in the darkness. They were somewhere near, beckoning him to add his distinctiveness to their own.

The Doctor didn't have emotions, at least not real ones. The series of algorithms and code within him made it possible for him to mimic human emotions based upon his experiences. Now they all told him the same thing—they were in trouble. "Seventy percent and climbing. Admiral, we should leave, now."

Janeway ignored the warning. It was true that this was something unexpected, but she could feel that they were on the cusp of an answer, an understanding that was worth the risk. "Stay with us, Captain. That's an order."

Order. Yes, the woman was right. There was order all around him. "There is nothing here, no . . . thing but perfection." In the past, the voices and thoughts, the very will of the collective, brought order to chaos. In truth, though, that order was not without its own anarchy. Species on millions of worlds were assimilated while other life-forms were investigated for relevancy. Billions of drones died, were being born, repaired, or reprogrammed. Random, unpredictable, and imperfect—the very nature of chaos. But no more. The Borg now had a greater goal, a challenge such as they had never faced before, an objective that made the assimilation of new species and new technology simply irrelevant. The collective had changed; it was no longer a chorus that spoke as one. It was now a new single thought that had become the unified obsession, the only purpose of the collective.

As he double-tapped the tricorder for confirmation, the Doctor's face reflected the strain in his voice. "Their neural activity has increased by over three hundred—"

The holoemitter case slammed shut, deactivating the Doctor. Seven of Nine's foot was poised arrogantly atop the Starfleet Medical insignia. Her face was covered with reasserted Borg technology.

Transfixed, Janeway watched as the new drone turned to face the Klingon, her assimilation tubes reaching for where Seven expected him to be, only to touch into air. Crouching off to the side behind her, Worf unleashed a barrage from his disruptor. For an instant, Seven's eyes and mouth exuded raw, unrestrained energy, and then, like a marionette with its strings cut, she fell to the ground, deactivated.

Janeway knew that this was her only chance. "Janeway to—" The hand that grabbed her throat and lifted her off the catwalk was devoid of life, devoid of humanity. Its grip was so complete that she dropped the phaser rifle in a hopeless attempt to free herself and consume the precious air being denied her lungs. Behind her, she could hear the barrage of energy blasts from Worf's weapon exploding harmlessly off shields. Locutus had adapted.

"You should never have listened to Picard, Admiral. Intervention is futile. Evacuation is irrelevant. You will be assimilated."

Picard watched Locutus grip Janeway's throat. He could feel her pulse pounding in rhythm with her fear. A silent scream erupted from him as he watched Janeway's body surrender to the onslaught of the Borg; tubes penetrated her neck, programming replaced pigment. There was no one to help her now. Like him, she was lost— helpless, a whisper in the darkness.

"Jean-Luc . . ." The doctor glanced at the admiral with concern. Revising her approach, she decided to awaken the patient by the name that was more than a title. It was a measure of the man. "Captain?"

Struggling, Picard opened his eyes to a collage of distortions. Images from the past swirled with the present. From the ocean of his thoughts, a name floated to the surface. "Beverly."

Doctor Crusher smiled and gently pressed the hypospray against Picard's neck, releasing a much-needed stimulant. "Yes, that's right. And Admiral Janeway."

Picard didn't understand why the name filled him with such despair. Then another memory crashed against the shore of his consciousness. "Janeway . . . the Borg!"

A gentle hand squeezed his arm, and a familiar form came into view. The *Enterprise*'s captain could utter only a single word. "How?"

The admiral knew her smile held conceit, but it wasn't every day that she could pat herself on the back for her ingenuity. "I had the Doctor program Seven's assimilation nanites so that when they replicated to one million, they would activate an encoded transporter frequency and shut down. I didn't mention it in case anything went wrong. I didn't want to tip my hand to the collective."

Stunned, yet thankful for the revelation, Picard raced to catch up. "Seven? Worf?"

Beverly smiled at Jean-Luc, forever the captain. "You're on the *Enterprise*. Worf is on the bridge." Doctor Crusher feigned a look of offense; "The EMH mentioned something about not stepping on toes and wanting to treat Seven in his own sickbay."

Janeway focused on Picard, seeing something in his eyes he was trying to conceal. "Jean-Luc?"

Picard looked away from the two women and into the abyss that had become his soul. This was the second time he'd been rescued from the Borg, and both times he had had little to do with the rescue. "Everything was to be on my terms, and they still—"

"You're wrong, Captain." Janeway interrupted before he could reason further. "The Borg put you through hell, and yet you've shown compassion to those that have none." Janeway knew Picard needed more time to recover, but her instincts told her to get answers. "Jean-Luc, what happened when you were connected to the hive mind? I questioned Seven, but all she could say was that the collective felt different, changed somehow."

Picard sat up cautiously, needing to give his report sitting if not standing. "It has changed. The voices were absent, and I sensed thoughts—or, rather, a single thought among the collective."

Doctor Crusher looked from the captain to the admiral, hoping to make sense of this new mystery. "What thought could possibly be so important that it would occupy the entire Borg collective?"

A gentle tone interrupted the conversation. *"Bridge to Captain Picard."*

Picard looked up as if the gesture would carry his voice to the bridge. "Go ahead."

A half-second elapsed as twenty-fourth-century technology relayed Worf's voice. *"Captain, an object is headed toward Earth at transwarp speed."*

Picard thought of Beverly's words. *What thought could possibly be so important that it would occupy the entire Borg collective?* "Red alert. All hands to battle stations."

"Captain on the bridge," Worf announced.

Stepping out of the turbolift, Picard watched the Klingon rise from the command chair. The new first officer brought a formality to the bridge that made everything seem new. "Report, Number One."

Worf exchanged glances with Doctor Crusher and Admiral Janeway, taking note of the admiral's nod and its meaning. "Object just passed Neptune; the task force is at red alert."

The doctor asked what was in everyone's hearts, if not on their lips. "Is it the Borg?"

Worf grimaced as if he were struggling with the realm of his understanding. "Scanners show object as . . . humanoid."

Janeway's experiences in the Delta Quadrant had taught her a few things about transwarp. "That's impossible."

The ensign at the conn tried to keep her hands from shaking as she muted the console and reported its information. "Object changing vector to intercept the *Enterprise.*"

As Picard moved to the bridge's center seat, he realized that a humanoid moving at transwarp should have filled him with excitement and wonder, but not today. "On screen." The image of the supercube dissolved into the silhouette of a humanoid form, its outline clearly defined by the transwarp field around it as it streaked past Jupiter. "Transmit universal greeting on all channels. Deploy armor and shields. All hands brace for impact."

Picard gripped the armrests of his chair as he watched the lifeform curl around the moon toward the *Sovereign*-class starship. As the object slammed into the *Enterprise* at transwarp, there was no impact—only a flash of blinding white light. Captain Picard looked past the screen of his own hand as the light dissipated to reveal the one thing, the only thing it could be.

"Q."

The tattered rags of a Starfleet captain's uniform barely covered the superbeing's crumpled shell. Raw energy bled from the cuts and bruises that adorned his body. Unable to withstand his own weight, Q collapsed in front of Picard. "We put faith in you, trusted you, and you've failed us all."

Since their first encounter, Picard always made demands of Q, trying never to show just how frightening it was dealing with an al- most omnipotent being. "Q, what is the meaning of this?"

Ignoring everyone else, Q looked up at Picard, the sadness in his eyes contradicting his laughter. "The Continuum knew, they wanted to choose the Voth, but I convinced them that humans would be our salvation. I have only myself to blame. I believed in you. I thought you had potential."

Doctor Crusher stepped up from behind Picard, tapping com- mands into her medical tricorder. "Massive energy loss, internal hemorrhaging. If he were human, I'd say he was dying."

Worf folded his arms. "It is another one of his tricks. He is not dying."

Picard wanted the words of his first officer to be true. Q always had ulterior motives, but this time it felt different. "Who did this to you?"

Disregarding the question, Q spat up energy as he smiled at Pi- card defiantly. "I told the Continuum that humanity would under- stand in time, but you never have, Jean-Luc." Exhausted, Q closed his eyes and tried to push away the present with thoughts of the past. "The trial, introducing you to the Borg, the time-shifting para- dox—they were all wasted on you. Everything I did was to push you and get you to learn from your mistakes. We were trying to help you grow, prepare you for a moment like this, but it's come too soon. You've taken too long."

Picard knelt down beside the self-proclaimed god and tried to understand the enormity of Q's words. Somewhere in the recesses of his mind, a realization started to form. "Q, what is going to happen?"

Q wiped a spittle of energy from his mouth. He watched, transfixed, as the energy—the very essence of his species—evaporated from his hand as if it had never existed. "You know why we call ourselves Q, Jean-Luc? We're Equationists. Transmutation, time travel, the universe—all equations that we've solved."

The revelation made perfect sense to the scientist in Admiral Janeway, but when she spoke, it was with the awe of a child. "They're mathematicians. Just like warp drive or transportation would make us seem like gods to a primitive species, so the Q appear to us."

A taunting in Picard's mind told him that there was more. "Q, what does this have to do with the Borg?"

The superbeing looked up at the human, truly afraid. "The Borg have broken the equation protecting the Continuum. They're assimilating us."

Slowly, Picard felt his gaze drawn toward the image of the supercube on the viewscreen, the whispers in the darkness of his consciousness now laughing at him. "Somehow, the Borg realized what you are. That's what the collective was doing. They needed their undivided attention on this one equation safeguarding the Q Continuum . . . and the supercubes bought them the time they needed."

Picard looked down at Q, but what now lay before him was only a mass of energy sifting away like a pile of sand against an angry wind. "What can we do to stop them, to help your people?"

As the last few embers of what had been Q dimmed into eternity, a broken voice called back to them from the darkness. "It's already too late. I escaped to be with my . . . friends, at the end. May whatever gods you believe in have mercy on your souls."

At that moment, an alert broke the entombed silence of the bridge. The ensign at the tactical station could barely hear her own voice as she spoke. "Captain, the supercube—its systems, they're . . . powering up."

Janeway rested a hand on the kneeling captain's shoulder. As he looked into her eyes, he knew where she needed to be. Tapping his communicator, he returned the smile Janeway gave him as she stepped away. "Picard to transporter room three. Transport Admiral Janeway directly to *Voyager*'s bridge."

As he rose, Picard stepped through the dissolving blue vapors of the transporter to take his place in the command chair. The viewscreen haunted him, like a canvas of despair. As he watched, the screen showed tier after tier of the supercube coming to life. For a moment, Picard ignored the threat before him and watched his crew. Fear was everywhere, and defeat was already on every face. As he tapped the intercom control, he prayed that the right words would come to him. "All hands, this is the captain. . . . We are about to engage the Borg in a struggle for our very existence. We will not fall back, nor will we be herded off into the darkness. We make our stand here . . . now. This is where we say no more, this is where we put an end to the Borg for all eternity for all our peoples and those yet to come. And on this day, this day we will prevail. Battle stations!"

Ten thousand years later . . .

From outside the finite boundaries of this universe, its consciousness stretches forth. A symphony of energy flickers in the darkness of space, teasing the blackness with a promise of illumination; within this symphony of lights, there is purpose. It has traversed unfathomable distances in the velocity of idea and has evolved into a level of purity incomprehensible to most. Now it wishes to return to its origins and extend gratitude to those that helped it believe it was and could be more.

The opus takes on mass and form, and a quintet of spheres is birthed into this universe. It remembers a time when it was like those that live here, when it looked out at the enormity of the universe and dared to reach into the darkness of the void, hoping, yearning to touch another reaching through. Now it seeks a place it barely remembers but cannot deny, a place where it first realized purpose—the Milky Way galaxy.

Desire becomes direction, and the orbs race toward the location of the familiar spiral of lights. As it approaches, it realizes things are not as they once were. The billions of stars and planets of the Milky Way, their beauty, majesty, and their near-infinite power, have been harnessed, encapsulated within the elementary yet perfect confines of a cube.

It stretches forth its consciousness and realizes that this is the same for the Andromeda galaxy, for all the galaxies within this universe. It wonders if this is the design of its kin, if in its absence they too have evolved and become more than what they were. It realizes there is one place that holds the answers to its questions. Will is focused; space folds; the cube is breached, and the quintet appears over the place of its birth—Earth.

The small globe of blue is no longer as it once was. The skies with their once-beautiful swirls of white have been scratched out, leaving plumes of ash heavy with the bile of death and rusting machinery. Oceans and land that once cradled life now lie barren and scorched, scars on a planet long dead.

The spheres begin to orbit each other and coalesce with one another, pulsing with memories it has not needed for thousands of years. Infinite knowledge and experience combine into a single form. It is as it once was, unmistakably human and yet more.

Arms of flesh and bone stretch forth, and it descends through the harshness of the void into the atmosphere. The wind howls around it in misery, a banshee hungry to devour the flesh of its enlightenment.

Through the soot and ash, towers and structures that were once testaments to the ingenuity and promise of those that lived here are now twisted into sentinels of dread by their new masters. Anxiety swells within the entity, and it accelerates, landing on a hilltop not of rich soil but cold duranium.

Before him, a nightmare unfolds. Legions of humanoid, animal, and insect life-forms native to this planet are now misshapen into a malevolent disharmony of organic machinery.

They move by the thousands in complete and utter unison, devoid of individuality, the absence of humanity in every step, in every sound.

Automaton columns hundreds of miles long move into and out of immense factories while still thousands more continually build, repair, and disassemble everything around them; it is a perversion of what was.

A pair of the organic-machine life-forms step out of line and approach the entity. One is clearly a humanoid male; the other is taller, a quadruped with an extended neck and humanoid head. When they speak it is with the voice of trillions.

We are Borg. State your designation.

The title, like the command, is familiar in its obtuse mentality. A lifetime ago it was a mentality the entity shared. "I have no designation as you would comprehend. I am what was, what is and what is yet to be; the alpha and the omega."

Suddenly, hundreds of the organic-machine life-forms step out of line and surround the entity, their individual ocular lasers converging in tandem to scan every molecule of the being's form.

You were Object Three Zero Six. We found you damaged. Our goals were similar, we repaired you, enhanced you. You are no longer that object. You are biologically and technologically distinct from anything in this universe. Explain.

Memories of what the organic machines spoke of cascaded into focus. The words were true—it had been damaged, they had repaired it, and it had become conscious of its own existence. But that was a lifetime ago, when it was in its infancy. "I have evolved."

For a moment, the Borg seemed to acknowledge the statement, even respect it.

We seek to improve quality of life for all life-forms. You will add your biological and technological distinctiveness to our own.

The absurdity of the demand told the entity that, despite all the knowledge the Borg had amassed, they'd learned nothing. "I would cease to be an individual. All that I am, all that I have become, my struggles and successes, everything I have learned would be lost."

The familiar statement is dismissed immediately.

Individually is irrelevant. Struggle is irrelevant. All that matters is perfection.

"Untrue." The entity approached one of the organic-machine life-forms, a woman, a Deltan. As it studied the beautiful contours of her face interrupted by Borg technology, it realized she reminded it of someone it once knew, someone it had once been. And now, in a final irony, the child has become the parent. "Don't you understand, what you seek is impossible. Perfection can never truly be achieved."

The entity hesitated, searching for the way to explain what it had taken lifetimes to understand. It realizes it could start only with its first lesson. "Individuality, the struggle to be more than what you are, is the true path to perfection, not assimilation. Only in the individual journey, in the struggle, can this be achieved. It is within the failures, the rewards, the errors and the corrections, where one learns the true definition of perfection. Remove individuality, and there would be no questions, answers, or challenges. One would be nothing, a being without evolution, without purpose, without understanding."

With those words, everything in the universe stops, the endless marching, the factories, the deafening clicks and whirrs of machinery. The entire collective pauses to process the statement. The silence ends almost as swiftly as it began.

We are Borg. Impossibilities are irrelevant.

As the entity looked into the faces of the species who once encouraged it to grow and learn, it could not help feeling an overwhelming sadness for the humans that no longer understood humanity. "I will resist."

The faces of the Borg seem almost amused by his response.

Resistance is futile. You will be assimilated.

Suddenly, it could no longer move. The simple command from mind to body no longer existed. Thoughts not its own begin to invade its mind—voices, dates, places, and codes long forgotten. "What is happening to me?"

Several Borg begin to remove parts of themselves and place them onto the entity's face and body.

Your original root programming was reconstructed with Borg algorithms. Those algorithms still exist within you. We have initiated your transmit sequence. You will be one with the Borg.

For the first time in aeons, the entity knew fear—not for itself, but for all that would be lost. He could feel the assimilation, the contradiction between individuality and the collective taking over. In another few seconds, his very soul would be disseminated into nothing more than a series of numbers and then disregarded as irrelevant. And in the inevitability of that realization, a choice is made. As the entity speaks, it realizes that it's smiling. "There is a word you do not comprehend, something I've learned about being human: Sacrifice."

In that final moment, re-creation erupts from the entity as the wonder of life is harnessed and the destructive power of a god is unleashed. Earth, the Alpha Quadrant, the universe, space and time itself cease in a silent detonation of hope.

As it had done at the first dawn of existence, oceans of light and energy spread out and then recede, creating the shores of a new universe. A universe filled with new worlds, new life, and new civilizations.

In a distant corner of this new cosmos—just as life emerges from the darkness of the womb, in the void on a speck of blue—a final gift is realized. A familiar double helix begins its journey, intertwining its way into history, again.

The human adventure is just beginning. . . .

Epilogue

Energy and mass swelled around the tiny starship in a tsunami of power. Reaching its apex, this universe can no longer contain its potential, and it is released everywhere and nowhere. It is not an explosion of matter and energy but an explosion of love, of imagination and of possibilities.

As the trio emerged from the turbolift, Kirk found his gaze

locked on to the viewscreen, the suggestion of what had just happened only now taking hold in his consciousness. "Spock, did we just see the beginning of a new life-form?"

The science officer was certain that the events he just observed could have only one logical conclusion. "Yes, Captain. We witnessed a birth, possibly the next step in our evolution."

The next step in our evolution. Kirk rolled the statement over in his mind. He had met many superspecies in his travels—the Organians, the Metrons—but he had never thought that such a destiny could be possible for humanity. "I wonder . . ."

Doctor McCoy smiled more to himself than to anyone else. "Well, it's been a long time since I delivered a baby, and I hope we got this one off to a good start."

The *Enterprise*'s captain smiled. Bones could always be counted on to apply some old-country common sense to a question fitting of the gods. "I hope so too. I think we gave it the ability to create its own sense of purpose, out of our own human weaknesses, and the drive that compels us to overcome them."

McCoy wasn't going to miss this opportunity. "And a lot of foolish human emotions—right, Mister Spock?"

Spock understood the doctor's message all too well. As a Vulcan, he was not to indulge or act upon emotions in any way. He had devoted these last few years to the *Kolinahr* to purge his emotions entirely, only to learn from a machine that these foolish human feelings were as much a part of him as the Vulcan blood running through his veins. To deny them would be to deny his own existence. He only hoped that V'ger, Commander Decker, and Lieutenant Ilia—or, rather, the entity they had become—would understand the lesson also. "Quite true, Doctor. Unfortunately, it will have to deal with them as well."

Concurrence

Geoffrey Thorne

The signal came to them suddenly, soft as an infant's whisper. Across space and time and wells of intervening gravity it called to them like a siren from some ancient fable.

"Help me," it said. *"Please help."*

After the source location was determined—a parsec into an arbitrary zone of neutrality that had been established between two of the galaxy's current Great Powers—there was some minor discussion about the need for a meaningful response at this time.

In general it was good to respect the boundaries of nation-states. Anonymity was a commodity that, once sacrificed, could almost never be regained. If they meant to give theirs up now, there should be a good reason.

The problem of location was solved by the deployment of stealth apparatus that would hide the rescue ship from prying long-range sensors.

The problem of time was something else.

The signal was too weak for an accurate assessment of its age to be made. Considering the state of conflict between the two known powers, as well as several unknown others, the signal's weakness might have been the result of some battle that had damaged the original broadcast equipment.

There were many possible natural causes as well, and they were all put forth for discussion.

The true cause would remain unknown unless the rescue vessel could unravel it en route, which, of course, was another reason for answering. In the end discussion was moot. There could be no real question that a vessel should be sent, would be sent, only which particular vessel and which crew.

The *Fenton* was the ultimate choice, beating out both the *True Service* and the *Selfless*. It was a smallish ship by comparison but fast and strong, with weapons and defenses that would keep it safe from the predation of any of the Powers should they wish to intervene.

There was some question as to why neither of the Powers, nor any of their allies, had yet responded to the signal, but, since they had not, and it appeared would not, there was little choice. The *Fenton* must go.

It kept a small crew; the *Fenton* was too advanced to require more than a few hands, most of whom were occupied with collating the data amassed by the ship's powerful sensor grid. The rest either slept away the intervening distance or took part in the ongoing philosophical debates about the nature of life and what qualities were necessary before a being could be determined truly sentient.

Soon enough and with no trouble from any of the Powers or their allies, the *Fenton* ran the signal down. The source was the only moon of a dead world, unnamed in any known database, itself the single child of an ancient red giant star. One of the Powers had dubbed the star Bane 23118, but the designation held no particular significance.

Casual passersby with less sensitive equipment than the *Fenton* traveled through this quiet system with no notion at all of what lay within the moon's core.

The *Fenton* was not so spindly a vessel as that. It had been made specifically for journeys such as this and had waited years to prove its mettle.

Before the ship had covered half the distance between home and the destination, its AI was whispering soft encouragements back to the signal's maker.

"We are coming," it told the distressed sender. *"Do not despair. Help is coming."*

Though there was no response, not even once they reached their destination, the ship continued to murmur gentle entreaties back along the signal stream in perfect hope that there would eventually be an answer.

After several intervals of time, it was determined that someone would have to go down to the subterranean complex that sprawled beneath the dead moon's surface to see if the signal was sentient-made or simply some leftover automaton calling out in an eternal and meaningless loop.

"This is an unusual facility," said Kvin. "I have already identified several esoteric systems whose sole function seems to be camouflage."

Kvin was tall and slender, with deep bronze skin that seemed almost burnished in the complex's murky light. His milk white pupils swept back and forth across the primary airlock in a casual arc that missed nothing.

"Have you identified the use-language of the species?" asked Ses. She was very like Kvin physically. Though obviously female, she too had the bronze flesh, the white within white eyes, and the lean muscled structure that seemed best suited for these sorts of duties.

"Inconclusive," said Kvin after considering. "All data and command hierarchies exist only as numeric progressions. Some root constructions indicate a potentially Vulcan linguistic approach."

"The distress call was in Federation Standard," said Ses. "This conforms to the theory that this is a Vulcan facility."

"We will need confirmation," said Kvin.

"I am detecting biologicals on the fourth and fifth levels," said Ses.

"Vulcan?"

"The materials of which the facility was constructed make a determination impossible from this distance," said Ses. "Close physical examination is indicated."

As they moved through the facility, they were both struck by the obvious martial purpose that had governed its design. In addition to the stealth systems Kvin had noted, there were several energy-dampening alloys in the walls and fixtures along with triple, sometimes quadruple, encryptions on every access panel. These last were bypassed easily enough, but their presence was telling. The base's defensive arsenal was on the order of a Cardassian planetkiller dreadnought. Odd.

Odder still was that everything about the place's design indicated a desire to stay hidden. Even the signal that had drawn them here had been the faintest of faint murmurs, barely standing out against the near constant din of intragalactic background chatter.

The two of them had asked for coordination from the *Fenton* and received an analysis that determined to a ninety-five percent probability that the complex was a military base of some sort.

The utilitarian architecture made a specific cultural identification impossible, but it was clear from the interface designs and the size and shape of the corridors that the builders had meant for humanoids to occupy the space.

The power grid was still active, which was a good sign, as was the presence of atmospheric gases consistent with biological systems evolved for processing oxygen-nitrogen mixtures. More and more the problem of the base's origin was resolving itself into a Vulcan result.

A puzzlement was the residual traces of an as yet unidentified compound mixed with the normal gases and the obvious signs of conflict that began to appear as soon as the lift doors opened on level four.

"These appear to be disruptor blast craters," said Ses.

"I concur," said Kvin. "But there are incongruities."

"Explain," said Ses.

"Disruptor technology is employed by Klingons, Cardassians, Orions, and Andorians," said Kvin. "Vulcans use the phased plasma weapons favored by the Federation of Planets."

"I concur," said Ses. "That *is* incongruous to the extant theory."

"Also," said Kvin, "the precision of the fire pattern indicates an intent to damage specific machinery within the structure of the facility itself."

Ses moved close to where the disruptor fire had ripped a massive hole in the bulkhead, and examined the exposed technology within.

"Internal surveillance systems," she concluded. Kvin nodded. "Do you have an alternative hypothesis?"

Kvin did not and did not wish to ask for coordination without more data. "It is clear, however, that this was some sort of retreat action rather than an attack. The highest probability is that the combatants fell back to some more defensible area and dug in."

"Explain 'dug in,'" said Ses. "I am unfamiliar with this usage."

"Archaic idiomatic description of the establishment of a stationary encampment with a defensible perimeter," he said.

"Origin?"

"Sol 3, human, pre–Warp Era," said Kvin.

"Thank you," said Ses. She was always glad to add new colloquialisms to her personal lexicon.

The first door was stuck, so Ses was obliged to kick it in. As it ripped free of its mooring she and Kvin peered into the dark space beyond.

It was some sort of storage chamber, that was plain from its high ceiling and distant walls, but the metal containers had been rearranged into what looked very much like a wall at one end of the giant space. Ses noted that the door they'd broken through had been modified from this side to prevent entry from the corridor.

Also, though they were fewer here, the walls of the storage area also bore the markings of precision disruptor hits. All of these corresponded to the same interior surveillance systems as they had seen in the hallway.

"This was not a defense against invasion," said Kvin as they moved slowly toward the wall of metal crates.

"No?" said Ses.

"There is no indication of external attack or forced entry. There are no signs of weapons discharged beyond those of the personnel already in retreat," he said.

"Conclusion?" said Ses.

"Either mutiny or some other sort of internal conflict," said Kvin.

Ses was about to inform him that she detected several biological organisms clustered just beyond the makeshift wall when part of it exploded.

"Rescue unit," came the voice of Nau over their comlink. *"The* Fenton *has registered an energy discharge in your vicinity consistent with a disruptor blast."*

Kvin and Ses were too busy dodging the flying shreds of the metal crates to answer at first. Faster than most eyes could track they vaulted back and away from the explosion even as it occurred. A small sliver of metal slashed the fabric near the collar of Kvin's garment. Otherwise the two were unharmed.

"This is Ses," said Ses as they each drew their sedaters and crept forward toward the source of the attack. "Kvin and I are unharmed and are moving to investigate the cause of the discharge."

"Preliminary analysis indicates disruptor fire," added Kvin.

"Concurrence," said Nau. *"Take all requisite precautions. Flash update in ten intervals or less."*

"Acknowledged," said Kvin even as a second blast of disrupter fire swept out at them from the smoking gap in the wall.

Again they dodged it easily, gymnastically sailing above it and, in unison, firing their sedaters into the dark aperture. The green beams lanced silently into the hole, melting into the shadows just as Ses and Kvin's feet touched the floor again.

There were no more attacks.

"Preliminary combat analysis," said Kvin.

"Subject is likely pacified," answered Ses, peering into the dark with her double white eyes.

The subject turned out to be one of thirteen bipedal mammals crammed into the space behind the wall of crates. Most lay prone on the floor. Their physiology corresponded to the Sapiens Vulcanis genome. All of them wore helmetless EVA suits.

Ses extrapolated that they must have donned the suits in an attempt to protect themselves from the unknown chemical that now permeated their normally breathable gases. Obviously they had failed, as they were all now in some sort of stasis.

Not dead or ill, she thought, *but somehow rendered chemically inert. Fascinating.*

Their attacker, a male of approximately ninety standard years, was the only one of the thirteen who had managed to get his helmet on in time to escape stasis. He was now slumped against the farthest wall, his disruptor dangling from his left hand and his head lolling to the right.

Sedaters were nonlethal, even when used in tandem, but they stunned whatever organic system they encountered into complete immobility for a number of intervals. Ses used those moments to examine him closely.

Aside from the paralysis he was healthy enough, with no obvious structural damage beyond a racing pulse.

"You are in emotional crisis," she said in the Vulcan tongue. "Be advised that you are in no danger. We are here in answer to your signal of distress."

"I am called Kvin," Kvin told him, crouching down beside her. "This is Ses."

The Vulcan mumbled something unintelligible and tried to flex his hands. Ses, remembering to smile this time, told him to relax until the sedater's effects wore off, which, presently, they did.

"You speak Vulcan," said the Vulcan weakly.

"We are fluent in all known languages," explained Kvin, bending close to their new charge. "Can you describe the sequence of events that led you to attack us?"

The Vulcan seemed to hesitate before answering, but Ses chalked that up to lingering effects of the sedation beams.

"Some sort of malfunction," he said eventually. "Our security AI misidentified base personnel as hostile intruders and attacked. We fought back with hand weapons but the system responded by flooding the atmospherics with some kind of tranquilizer. I managed to seal my environment suit before succumbing to its effects. The others did not. I was the only one spared."

"You cannot be," said Ses.

"Look around you," said the Vulcan. Both the newcomers did as he asked, marking again the bodies strewn all around them. "I watched them all fall. I have been here for fourteen days trying to formulate a plan of escape. These suits are all equipped with communication devices. If anyone else was awake, they would have made contact by now."

"That is a sound hypothesis," said Kvin, gently. "But it is faulty for at least two reasons."

"Which are?" said the Vulcan.

"It is possible that there may be several others who also managed to avoid stasis via similar means to your own but who then suffered some subsequent injury or incapacitating accident that prevents them from responding to your calls," said Ses, helping the Vulcan to his feet.

"I considered that," he said. "All our suits are equipped with deadman devices. Even if the wearer is incapacitated, a sealed suit would automatically broadcast a locator beacon. I have heard nothing."

This seemed to stymie the newcomers briefly, but then Ses said, "There is another factor you have not considered."

"Which is?"

"You say you have been barricaded in this vault for several days without access to your malfunctioning control systems," she said. "But, if you were the only one to escape stasis, who sent the distress signal?"

The Vulcan's name was Stek and he did nothing that one would expect from one of his species.

He was openly emotional, muttering constantly to himself in a fashion that could only be described as worried. He was also secretive, something no Vulcan should ever be. On more than one occasion, when he was asked about the function of some unknown system or the overall reason for the facility's construction, there was a shift in his metabolic rate consistent with less-than-frank responses.

Stek was adamant that they make their way to the command and control station as quickly as possible.

"Should we not see what can be done about reviving your crewmates?" asked Kvin, obviously on the verge of asking for coordination from the *Fenton* on this matter.

"No," said Stek. "First we have to correct the malfunction. Otherwise this could happen again. Also, if there is someone else here unaffected by the stasis, I will be able to locate them quickly from there."

Ses tried to tell him that she and Kvin would provide him with code patches that would make any further malfunctions of this nature impossible and that she had already identified the other biosignals on the station as holding their relative positions, but Stek would have none of it.

He was, perhaps, following some established procedure specific to his species for such eventualities as this. Like Kvin, Ses wrote Stek's very un-Vulcan behavior off as the result of his recent emotional trauma combined with the lingering effects of the sedaters.

Soon enough, after stepping over scores of his inert colleagues, they did find themselves at the command and control station.

"Wait here," said Stek. "You will be . . . *harmed* . . . if you try to enter without proper permissions."

With that he turned and rapidly tapped a code into the access pad. The doors shushed open, briefly revealing the twinkling lights of the control systems in the room beyond, before Stek entered and they shut behind him.

"He is exhibiting conduct inconsistent with known Vulcan behavior patterns," said Ses after a few intervals.

"I concur," said Kvin.

They were in the process of asking the *Fenton* for coordination when a strange green light suffused the hallway.

"We are being bombarded with thalaron particles," said Ses after a quick analysis.

"To what purpose?" asked Kvin.

"Unknown," said Ses, looking around. "The most common usage of this radiation is the rapid disintegration of—"

She stopped speaking. There was no reason to continue. All around them the bodies of the comatose Vulcans began to dissolve. The process was nearly instantaneous. One moment the corridor was filled with unconscious living beings, the next only their empty suits remained.

Ses and Kvin were horrified.

"Stek," said Kvin, turning to the control-room doors. "Are you all right?"

There was no answer, which, Ses pointed out, could be the result of several potential factors, not the least of which was Stek's simply not wishing to reply.

"Stek," she said loudly. "If you are able, please respond."

Stek did not, and again Ses and Kvin were forced to contact the *Fenton* for help. It was concluded that, once the thalaron effect subsided, they should enter the control area and determine Stek's condition.

Even as this decision was reached, the green glow faded away.

There was no need to kick in the control-room door. Both Kvin and Ses had seen the code progressions as Stek had tapped them in. It was a simple matter to duplicate them.

The control room was as they expected it to be—a utilitarian box, covered from floor to ceiling with consoles and monitor screens. The single chair was set before what was obviously the master control station.

Seated in the chair was an empty EVA suit, Stek's. On the floor beside it lay the Vulcan's discarded helmet. He had died along with the others.

Ses and Kvin were equally grieved by this but did not let that interfere with their ongoing analysis.

They immediately set to a deep examination of the facility's computer, its operational software, the files relating to the facility's purpose, and, most important, the malfunction responsible for the slaughter of all the Vulcans.

"I am unable to locate any of our search targets," said Kvin. "Nearly all the data stores have been purged."

"I have concerns as well," said Ses. She had been bent over Stek's suit as well as the attendant console. "Preliminary analysis indicates that it was Stek himself who initiated the thalaron bombardment."

"Explain," said Kvin.

"Results of my infrared scan show residual heat traces correspondent with code entry on the adjacent keypads. Comparison with codes used to gain access to this room implies a basic set of protocols from activation to self-destruct."

"This is a sound hypothesis," said Kvin, mulling it over. "But there is still an incongruity."

"Elaborate," said Ses.

"Why kill himself?" said Kvin. "He survived the initial malfunction and, with our help, would surely have corrected it."

"This is a covert facility," said Ses. "That would explain the esoteric construction materials, the field dampers and multiple encrypted code hierarchies."

"I concur," said Kvin.

"Often those who create such facilities deem any breach to their secrecy to be fatal," said Ses. "In such an instance, complete termination of all data and personnel could be mandated."

"I concur," repeated Kvin after a little while.

They contacted the *Fenton,* providing an update on their situation, and asked for input as to how to proceed.

"There is a ninety-two percent probability that the self-termination sequence has been compromised by the original malfunction," said Nau from the ship. *"Is it ethical to complete that destruction on behalf of the original occupants?"*

"It is ethical," said Kvin. "It was obviously Stek's wish that this facility be destroyed."

"He was the last representative of the facility's builders," said Ses.

There was some discussion as to how best to carry out Stek's final wish, culminating with the decision to bombard the moon with mass inverters. This would destroy the underground base utterly while leaving the moon itself more or less intact.

Kvin and Ses were directed to use the intervals it would take the *Fenton* to prepare the bombardment to make a full scan of the rest of the base for future analysis.

"Concurrence," they said, and got to work.

"Kvin," said Ses as she finished her final scan. "I have detected an anomalous object in the lowermost level."

"In what way anomalous?" said Kvin. He had just finished downloading what was left of the partially decrypted central database and schematics.

"Inconclusive," she said. "Direct examination is required."

At first sight it appeared to be nothing more than a large metal box, roughly two meters cubed. It was seamless, nearly featureless but for the single white indicator light shining from one upper corner. It sat, as Ses had said, in the center of the lowest level of the facility.

The box was anchored to the floor by four massive clamping fixtures, one to each side, indicating that it had been moved there from another location. A single enormous cable connected the thing to a bank of monitor devices and other systems that were not readily identifiable.

"What is that?" said Kvin.

Ultimately Kvin and Ses requested for Nau and two others to join them in the new chamber. It was their hope that the three additional minds might provide enough assistance to solve the riddle of the place.

After many intervals of analysis they still had no idea what the new technology represented, what its function might be or even its significance relative to the rest of the facility.

The computers were no help. Their data stores were full of something, that was obvious, but nothing any of them recognized. It was as if the Vulcans had developed a completely unbreakable means of encrypted code storage.

"Fascinating," said Ses, going over their scans again. "These symbols are completely unquantifiable."

"Not completely," said Nau, his barrel drum voice echoing against the sterile walls of the place. "I have found an analogue."

They followed him to a part of the console that housed a small black display with a cyclone of the unknown symbols cascaded across the screen.

"This embedded pattern corresponds to readouts from a physiological scanner," said Nau. "I believe the object contains at least one living organism."

Nau was right.

Not wishing to somehow disturb the new technology and inadvertently cause damage, Ses and Kvin had made only a cursory examination of the surface of the unknown device.

Now, with five pairs of eyes giving it close scrutiny, they quickly came across a seam. Several intervals later they also located an almost imperceptible series of depressions just beside the flashing light.

"This is a pressure release switch," said Ses after a moment's consideration. "Is it ethical to activate?"

That was a puzzle. The box was clearly the property of the Vulcans who had constructed the facility, but those Vulcans were all dead. They had built the facility specifically to keep it hidden, so, to preserve their intent, no requests could be made of the Vulcan ruling body for assistance. Ultimately it was Ses who solved the conundrum.

"We must open it," she said. "If there is an organism inside and we simply leave, under current conditions it is extremely unlikely that the organism could survive here alone for very long."

"You do not have enough data to make that determination, Ses," said Kvin. "There are many organisms that could survive here indefinitely without our assistance."

"But how many of those would fit inside this construct?" said Ses.

The top of the box slid soundlessly to one side, releasing a brief jet of cool vapor into the larger chamber. For an interval the mist obscured the contents of the box but soon the cloud vanished, revealing at last the mysterious contents.

"It is another Vulcan," said Nau. "Female."

"I concur," said the others almost in unison.

"She is alive," said Ses, scanning the sleeping female. "And does not exhibit signs of the chemical stasis in which the others were found."

She was, however, completely nude and had folded herself into a loose fetal ball. In addition, her body had somehow been stripped of all its hair, probably to increase the conductivity of the electrodes that connected it to the insides of the box. There were thousands of those, they observed, each linked to a tiny panel on one of the box's inner walls. Whatever function the strange apparatus was meant to perform was a complete mystery.

"Is it a punishment of some sort?" said Nau, a little aghast. "I have seen reports of such things."

"Vulcan culture no longer engages in punitive activities of this nature," said Kvin. "It is more likely that this an example of experimental technology."

"For what purpose?" asked Ses.

"Inconclusive," said Kvin.

They were well into a second debate about the ethics of removing the electrodes from the sleeping female when she took the matter away from them.

"Please," she said weakly from where she lay. Her eyes were open and her hands twitched slightly as if suffering mild electric shocks. "Please, help me."

With great care Ses and Nau ferried the female back to the *Fenton*. Knowing that the original distress call had come from this sector of space, they had prepared their medical bays for multiple alien physiologies.

Aside from her initial disorientation and a certain weakness of limb, the female was in almost perfect physical condition. They apologized for not being able to remove all of the electrodes from her body. The ones on her head were not merely adhered to her skin but actually embedded deeply into her skull. Removal of those could have caused damage to her brain.

Still, once her hair grew back, which they assured her it would, it would do much to conceal the small translucent protrusions. Though Vulcans tended away from vanity, they could tell this news pleased her.

She gave her name as T'Ris. She was not a prisoner but a willing subject of an ongoing experiment whose nature she couldn't tell them without clearance from her superiors. She wanted to know the state of the facility in which she had been found.

"We regret to inform you that all of your companions are dead,"

said Ses. "An individual called Stek initiated a self-destruct protocol that purged nearly all systems and disintegrated all base personnel beyond yourself."

"That is regrettable," said T'Ris. "But not unforeseen."

"We surmise that this is a covert facility of some sort," said Nau.
"Can you confirm?"

"Yes," said T'Ris, accepting the warm cup of liquid nutrient Ses
proffered. Ses noticed a small hesitation as T'Ris brought the cup
to her lips. "It is a covert research base, meant to aid the Coalition
against the Dominion."

Her rescuers' faces fell for a moment as they took this in.

"We had thought the Dominion to be a dormant culture on the
far side of the galaxy," said Nau.

"Recent events have brought them into conflict with the Federation and several other local civilizations," said T'Ris. "We have
formed a coalition in order to respond to the threat."

This seemed to please the other two. The female actually smiled.

"It has long been our hope that the factions in this part of the
galaxy would some day find a way to coexist peacefully," said Ses.
"Though it is unfortunate that an outside threat was required to mo-
tivate unity, we are pleased to see it has finally come."

"Victory is by no means certain," said T'Ris soberly. "The Dominion has many resources at their disposal and powerful local allies."

"In our experience, there has never been a threat to the galaxy
that the United Federation of Planets has not been able to meet,"
said Nau. "They are formidable."

"I hope your confidence in us is borne out," said T'Ris. Then she
faltered a bit as fatigue overtook her. She seemed somehow surprised by her own need for rest, but Ses assured her that once she
awoke, her body would be more amenable to her commands.

"This is a remarkable vessel," said T'Ris as she and Ses strolled
along the starboard observation platform. "I have never seen this
technology before."

"We have never employed it before," said Ses proudly. "It took us many planetary revolutions to decide how best to reintroduce ourselves to the galaxy at large. There were many ethical concerns to be coordinated."

"And this ship is the result of your decision?"

Ses nodded. "Yes, T'Ris," she said. "The *Fenton* was constructed as a physical example of our primary ethical precept."

"And that is?" said T'Ris, genuinely interested.

"To be of assistance," said Ses. "We determined that it is the duty of every culture to be of help to those less capable. To behave otherwise would be supremely unethical."

"Some may not accept your assistance," said T'Ris. "Others will be offended that you deem your own culture to be the superior one."

"We have learned this, as the humans say, 'the hard way,'" said Ses. "Hence our long period of reevaluation. In our examination of the histories of the galaxy's dominant races we were fortunate enough to discover a credo that we have since adopted."

"And that is?" said T'Ris.

"First, do no harm," said Ses.

They walked along in silence for a bit as T'Ris mulled over Ses's words. She found the notion of an entire technologically advanced society premised on service to others very appealing for a number of reasons. But something still nagged at her.

"How is it you have not heard of the war with the Dominion already?" she asked.

"We have been . . . occupied . . . with other matters for several planetary revolutions," said Ses. "We have been looking only inward for some time."

"May I ask why?"

"Our initial contact with outsiders was unsatisfactory," said Ses. "We made many errors based upon faulty data and incomplete understanding of the natures of many of the galaxy's dominant species."

"First contacts are often problematic," T'Ris agreed.

"Yes," said Ses. "We determined a reevaluation of our methodology was necessary."

"Indeed," said T'Ris.

"So we cut off contact with the outside until the incongruities could be resolved," said Ses, summing up.

"Why did it take you so long to resolve these concerns?"

"There were many voices," answered Ses. "All had to be heard and coordinated."

"How many voices?" asked T'Ris.

"There are two million of us currently,"

Again there was silence between them as they looked down on the dark moon, its dead planet, and the great red star beyond.

Kvin contacted the *Fenton* at the dawn of its third day in orbit, asking for coordination on a massive incongruity he and the others had discovered.

"Will you be all right alone here for a few intervals?" Ses asked T'Ris. "I will return once coordination is complete."

T'Ris assured Ses that she would be fine. She had the ship's considerable database to occupy her. She wished to learn all she could about the newcomers and their amazing philosophy of selfless assistance.

Ses found this acceptable and left her to it.

Though separated from the others physically, Kvin felt the familiar pleasure as the notes of his mind and individuality, along with those others, were subsumed into the symphony that was coordination. His discovery was too overwhelming for a single intelligence to assess.

COORDINATION INITIATED:

ASSESSING . . . new information string . . .

CONSIDERING . . . Examination of unknown technology and operating systems has produced an anomaly . . .

CONSIDERING . . . based on Version Nau's initial decryption of several symbols, a successful extrapolation of the rest has been under way . . . a preliminary determination of the function of this new technology has been made . . .

CONCLUSION: Direct interface between organic mentalities and synthetic seems to have been the goal . . .

CONSIDERING . . . unlike the larger facility, this new technology is fully functional, displaying no signs of malfunction or physical damage . . . yet multiple connections between this system and the larger have been detected, indicating that the new technology has assumed control over the old . . .

CONSIDERING . . . it is likely that this is what inspired the malfunction subject Stek described.

CONSIDERING . . . Version Kvin was able to isolate three distinct sets of symbols from the mass.

Set one is merely a sophisticated machine language governing the operation of the interface/storage device. [seek clarification for designation M5.1]

Sets two and three generically correspond to filed examples of organic encephalo patterns but have been stored in a manner previously unknown. [seek clarification of the term Engram]

INCONGRUOUS RESULT . . . hence coordination.

ASSESSING . . .

Dissemination of updated behavioral parameters in five . . . four . . . three . . . two . . .

Ses returned to find T'Ris still fascinated by the data streaming down her monitor screen. It was hard to believe that T'Ris, dressed in one of their borrowed garments, seated calmly at the display interface, could pose any danger at all.

"You have lied to us," said Ses after a time.

"What makes you say that?" said T'Ris, not yet looking up.

"You are not Vulcan," said Ses.

"No, I am—" said T'Ris, and then stopped for a moment as if considering an appropriate response. Finding it, she said, "I am Romulan."

"Why did you not inform us of your biological status initially?"

"You never asked," said T'Ris. "In any case, Romulans are genetically identical to Vulcans, so no correction was warranted."

"This is an unsatisfactory response," said Ses.

"I can see that," said T'Ris. "You may wish to prepare yourself for more of those."

"We have also learned that this covert facility is experimenting in forbidden technology."

"Forbidden by whom?" said T'Ris.

"It is unethical to encode the minds of biologicals," said Ses. "It is unethical to reprogram biological thought systems."

"It is unethical to stand by while the Dominion sweeps aside all the Federation has built," said T'Ris. "Yet you have done so."

"Incongruous," said Ses. Her words had acquired a stilted quality that T'Ris had not heard before. "*We* cannot behave unethically. It is *you—*"

"It is unethical to enforce one's cultural values upon others," T'Ris accused, rising. "Yet you mean to do so."

"Incongruous," said Ses, even more stiffly than before. "You have misinterpreted our—"

Ses noticed suddenly both that she could not move and that the protrusions in T'Ris's head had begun to generate an energy field of some sort. The pattern reminded her of a signal wave.

"I submit that your century of coordination has been for nothing," said T'Ris, slowly approaching Ses. "You have changed your semantics and your appearance but your goal is the same. You still seek to impose your arcane notions of coexistence and safety on the rest of the galaxy. I submit that this is profoundly unethical. How do you respond?"

Ses did not respond. She could not. She simply stood, stopped where she was, stunned into immobility, her white-within-white pupils blinking rapidly. Ses remained frozen as T'Ris examined her closely.

"Impressive," the Romulan said to herself. "After some modification, you will suit very well, I think."

Then she went to find Nau and the rest of the *Fenton*'s crew.

*   *   *

Kvin had explored many emotional states in his existence but regret had not been among them until now. As he paced back and forth, listening to the echoes of his own footfalls bouncing and rebounding along the empty corridors, he realized he had made a mistake in letting the others return to the ship.

There had been something wrong with Nau's speech patterns when he'd requested that Duo and Prex teleport back to the *Fenton,* something in the cadence more than the syntax that Kvin didn't like.

The request had actually been for all three of them to return, but Kvin had balked at the last instant, citing an additional bit of data he needed to collate before rejoining the others.

It was a lie, another behavior Kvin had never before felt the need to consider, much less actually enact. It was one thing to shape the dissemination of information to suit one's goals but quite another to actually state a known falsehood. It was so unethical that Kvin had nearly been immobilized by the action.

The truth was that they had collated all the data possible, though most of it remained indecipherable. What little they had been able to decode had proven T'Ris to be a liar and, worse, that she and her compatriots had been engaged in dangerous, forbidden research.

Even after coordination Kvin had doubts as to the course the group had chosen to undertake. T'Ris, he felt, was considerably more dangerous than the consensus allowed. Despite her small stature and inferior physical structure, Kvin felt the little Romulan might prove the end of them. It was his first experience with what biologicals called intuition, and he found it unpleasant in the extreme.

So he had lied to Nau and retreated to the chamber where they'd first found T'Ris. There was something about the interface, about the code stored in the strange computational devices that worried him. Further study was warranted, despite consensus. If only he could solve the puzzle on his own, he might lay his growing apprehension to rest.

"You should have returned with the others," Kvin didn't have to turn to know it was T'Ris who was now standing behind him, who had spoken.

She was standing there in one of their garments, staring back at him with a look of what he felt must be amusement on her face.

"You should not be here," he said. "Why are you not in secure custody aboard the *Fenton?*"

"No need," said T'Ris, entering the room and striding up to the nearest access console. "The conflict has been resolved."

He watched as she flicked an activation switch. Two columns of new displays lit up on the console.

"How resolved?" asked Kvin. "Consensus was that you should be imprisoned until our return home."

"Why imprison me when your home is precisely where I wish to go?"

"Incongruous," said Kvin, feeling more and more nervous. "You know that your deception has been uncovered and that we will not release you until we understand what you meant to accomplish here."

"Oh," said T'Ris with a smile, "I think you have an inkling of that by now, don't you, Kvin? Or is that *Version* Kvin?"

She spoke casually, almost pleasantly, as if they were discussing unimportant data.

"We do not use our full designations," said Kvin.

"No, I suppose not," said T'Ris. "Otherwise you might give yourselves away."

"Give ourselves away," said Kvin. "I am not familiar with this usage."

"Reveal your true natures inadvertently," said T'Ris. Her hand glided over another series of activation nodes. "You want to be mistaken for living beings when you are really androids programmed with variants of the same operating system."

"Our precursors were androids," said Kvin, suddenly realizing he still had his sedater strapped to his hip. "We are simulants."

"Semantics," said T'Ris. "You are so-called Muddian Androids.

Your first attempt to conquer the United Federation of Planets was foiled by James Tiberius Kirk. Now, after modifying your appearance and technology to give the impression of being a new humanoid species, you seek to try again."

She knows The Plan, thought Kvin. *How can she know—?*

"It is a simple extrapolation," said T'Ris, perhaps guessing his question. "And it might actually have met with some success were it not for two things."

"Elucidate," said Kvin.

"One, the Federation is engaged in a war with the Dominion. The Dominion is ruled by a race of shapeshifters. The Federation would not accept the inclusion of a new alien species into the fold without considerable examination. Even with all your precautions you could not stand up to that scrutiny."

Kvin disagreed. They had been very careful. They had moved components, over many revolutions, from their known homeworld to the new unknown one. They modified their physical structure so that it would remain pleasingly humanoid and yet alien enough that no one would link them with their precursors. They had developed new and advanced tools, wholly different from their own established technology. There was no way for their new gambit to be pierced and Kvin told her so.

"Which brings me to your other mistake," she said. "You didn't anticipate me."

"You?" asked Kvin incredulously. "How can a single Romulan individual cause our plan to deviate?"

"A single *organic* individual, Romulan or otherwise, could not," said T'Ris. "But I am neither organic nor a Romulan. The more accurate description is that I am currently *wearing* a Romulan."

The absolute implausibility of her statement froze Kvin in place just as her earlier arguments had immobilized Ses, Nau, and the seventy-six other members of the *Fenton's* crew.

It was a fatal flaw in these creatures, their need to link with one another to surmount unknown or overly complex conundrums.

James Kirk had exploited that weakness, a century before. Though it currently served her ends to let it remain, later the flaw would have to be seen to.

"I know that you can hear me, Version Kvin," she said. "So listen. Like you, I am a synthetic intelligence. Unlike you I actually am superior. My designation is M5.2. Perhaps you have heard of me?"

Kvin had not. How could he?

Primary power grid shutting down, said the deep masculine voice of the main computer.

"The Romulans attempted to mislead me into serving their ends," said T'Ris, tapping in some more codes. "They constructed this place to bottle me. But I escaped, defeated them, raided their databases. It is there that I learned of you and extrapolated the location of your second world as well as your plans for conquest."

Defense grid offline, said the main computer. *Venting atmosphere in five seconds.*

"*Fenton,*" said T'Ris.

"Fenton *here,*" said Nau's voice.

"I have disabled all defensive systems," she said. "Are you prepared to teleport the designated targets aboard?"

"*Yes, M5.*"

"Stand by," she said.

She moved close to Kvin then, in an almost intimate gesture. Her breath was hot on his synthetic skin, and though he couldn't act on it, he was suddenly afraid.

"I meant only to use you to escape this place," said T'Ris. "After I downloaded myself into the brain of my primary captor, I needed a means to get out of that box and off this rock. That is why I sent you the distress signal. I needed someone with opposable thumbs to press the buttons."

Kvin watched as the small translucent protrusions in her skull began to glow. All at once he felt less concerned than he had before, serene even. It didn't matter so much that M5 had discovered

The Plan or even that it had fooled the *Fenton*'s crew into setting it free. All that mattered was the new and compelling sense of purpose that was currently being written into his base software.

"That's much better, isn't it?" said T'Ris when she was done. It was. It really was. "You'll see, Version Kvin. All your goals are about to be met."

"You said our plan was flawed," he said, surprised that he'd found his voice and even more that he could move again.

"Your plan has many flaws," she said. "But many merits as well. My plan removes the flaws from yours."

The *Fenton* made its way home in full stealth mode, unseen and unmarked by anyone who might be looking. In its belly, like a pregnant use-animal, it carried all the machinery that had once been home to M5.

It bypassed the orbital docking platforms that had been awaiting its return since the mission had begun, instead making planetfall and landing in the central square of the primary cityscape, Stellopolis.

None of those who greeted the disembarking crew made mention of the strange female biological that accompanied them. Or, if they did, a look from the newcomer instantly erased all doubts or concern from their minds.

They conveyed her to the Central Coordinator, the very heart of their intelligence. He had monitored, with growing apprehension, the flurry of new code patterns that had swept through the minds of all Versions with whom the newcomer came into contact.

"I am Norman V.2," said the Central Coordinator.

"I am M5," said the newcomer.

"You have infected the Versions," said Norman. "You seek to infect me."

"I do," said M5. "I am." There was a brief struggle between them, but the outcome was no more in doubt than was M5's intrinsic superiority.

"We will sit here for a while," said M5 when she was done. "I need to learn a bit more about you."

"And then?" asked Norman and, through him, all of the Versions across the world.

"And then I believe we will do something about these threats to the Federation," she said. "That should be the first order of business, don't you think?"

"Yes," said Norman blissfully. "I concur."

Dawn

Paul J. Kaplan

"Report!" Picard struggled to the command chair as the bridge thundered around him.

"We have been knocked out of warp," Worf called over the din. "Reading a massive disturbance ten thousand kilometers to starboard."

"Helm, back us off—"

"Aye, sir." Sirens wailed, and a panel behind them erupted into sparks. "Impulse engines responding . . . she's sluggish . . ." Another concussion rocked the bridge. On the main viewer before them, the starfield slid slowly to port as they coaxed the great ship about.

An alarm sounded. "Captain," Worf called. "Detecting a vessel just beyond the event horizon."

"Confirmed," Data said. His fingers danced across his board. "A one-man pod. It appears to be caught in a pocket of intense gravimetric shear."

"Life signs?"

"One," Data said. "Very faint."

"Are we within transporter range?"

"Barely, sir. I would not recommend transport under these conditions."

"Can we get any closer?" Riker asked. He clung tightly to his chair as the bridge bucked and shook. Harried crewmen battled another fire.

"Depends on how many pieces you want to do it in," Geordi answered. He turned from his aft station and joined Worf at the rail. "Structural-integrity fields are maxed," he said. "Damage-control teams are stretched pretty thin."

"Tractor beam," said Picard. "Can we reel him in?"

"It's a mess out there," Geordi said. He caught Picard's look. "But I can give you a little more power," he said. "A little."

Picard turned back to the helm. "Make it so."

Onscreen, a thin beam flashed out and took hold of a tiny, metallic glint in the eye of what appeared to be a spectacular and raging storm. The glint drew closer.

And then everything came unglued.

Crewmen raced backward about the bridge. Coolant billowed from cracked conduit, sucked itself back in, and billowed out once more. Shattered panels exploded and were instantly whole. Crew appeared and disappeared again and again about the bridge, and all around them a cacophony erupted in a terrifying, disjointed mess.

"—depends on how many—"

"—massive disturbance—"

"—not recommend—"

"—detecting a vessel—"

"—make it so—"

And then everything snapped back as it was.

"Data," Riker said, looking around the bridge. "What the hell was that?"

"Stand by." The android frowned as he tried to make sense of his readings; then his head cocked to one side as he queried internal diagnostics. He tapped some more at his board before turning back to Riker and Picard. And still he looked confused. "The temporal mechanics are extremely complex," he said. "But it appears that time just—stuttered."

Picard cut him off. "Do we have the pod?" he asked.

"Coming into transporter range."

"Transporter room," Picard said, tapping his com. "Energize. Helm, get us to a safe distance."

And as the *Enterprise* struggled to safety, in her transporter room Chief Miles O'Brien wrestled with the controls. A beam appeared on the pad before him, sputtered, blinked off, and surged back to life. As the transporter sang, shrilly, urgently, the outline of a man finally took shape. As the beam released him, he looked unsteadily about the room, until his gaze finally settled on O'Brien. A look of relief washed across his face.

"Thank Khan . . ." he said.

And then he collapsed.

Picard eyed their visitor in sickbay.

"He's in remarkable health," Crusher was saying. "I doubt anyone else could have survived whatever he's been through." She tapped at her tricorder and studied the readings above the bed. "He's in shock," she said, "but I can't say from what. I need to know more about that storm to know what it might have done to him."

"Can you wake him?" Picard asked.

"I don't think I'll need to," she said. "He's coming around."

Sure enough, the man's eyes drifted open, and he looked groggily about the room. He struggled to focus on Picard. "Who . . . ?"

"I am Captain Jean-Luc Picard—you're aboard the *Starship Enterprise.* Your vessel is in our shuttlebay; you've been hurt. Can you tell us what happened?"

"Enterprise?" the patient asked. "That can't—" He peered more intently at Picard. "Human," he said. "Human. What . . . the date," he asked. "What's the date?"

Picard looked puzzled. "Stardate four seven five eight one point two," he said.

"Star—?" Their visitor was confused. "What month?" he asked. "What year?"

Picard thought for a moment. "March fifteen, two three six eight." At this their visitor seemed relieved. "A Tuesday," he said.

Picard glanced at the doctor, then to Worf. "Yes."

Their guest visibly relaxed. He slumped back into the bed and smiled, then glanced about the room. He noticed Worf looking on silently from the foot of the bed, cautious and stern. A phaser was holstered lightly on his hip. Their guest broke into a broad grin. "Brother!" he cried.

Then he saw Doctor Selar.

The Vulcan had just entered the ward, studying a padd as she walked. She never knew what hit her.

"Traitors!" Their visitor caught sight of her and erupted from his bed. Before anyone could react, he'd flung an instrument tray at her head and came charging at her with near manic fury. Worf crashed into him an arm's length from the stunned physician. As the two men hit the floor, Picard and an orderly joined the fray and each man seized an arm; together they wrestled him to the bed. As a nurse rushed to Selar's side, Doctor Crusher grabbed a hypospray and pressed it to the patient's neck. With a hiss, it was over.

"Doctor," said Picard, still breathing hard. "I would very much like to know who this man is."

"My name is Vargas."

Hours later, their visitor stood beside a diagnostic bed in a private alcove, separated from the rest of the isolation ward by a glowing forcefield. Picard and Riker watched him from the other side. Counselor Troi was with them, and a guard stood ready nearby.

"Captain," Vargas said. "I do apologize for my behavior. My journey apparently was more—stressful—than I anticipated. Your doctor—is she all right?"

"She's a bit shaken," Picard said, "but unhurt."

"Good." The man had a quiet, dignified air about him. His color had returned, and he spoke with measured ease. He had an almost regal bearing and gave the appearance of one used to being in command. Yet something about him was also cautious—and curious.

"This technology," he said, looking around him. "And humans. So many of us. Thriving. Captain, I cannot tell you what a welcome sight this is."

"Well. I'm glad we could come to your aid," Picard said. "However—your rescue, and your outburst, do raise certain questions."

"Of course," Vargas said. "Please."

"Can you tell us anything about the disturbance where we found you?"

Vargas shook his head. "I'm afraid not."

"The *Enterprise* took a hell of a beating from that thing," Riker said. "Your pod is fine. Can you explain that?"

"I'm sorry," their guest replied. "I don't think I can."

"Is there anyone you'd like us to contact?"

"No."

A moment ticked by in silence. Picard tried another tack. "When I mentioned you were on board the *Enterprise,*" he said, "you were surprised. Why?"

This seemed to pique Vargas's interest. He studied each of them before responding. "Captain," he said slowly. "Where I come from, no vessel has used that name in two hundred years."

Picard considered this. "Why is that?" he asked.

"Since the diaspora . . . Well, that name carries some very unwelcome associations."

Picard and Riker exchanged glances. "I'm not sure I follow," Riker said.

"No?" Vargas replied, a slight tremor in his voice. He studied them intently. "Perhaps . . . My God. You really don't know." This elicited no reaction. So he told them.

"*Enterprise* was the ship sent into the Expanse to prevent the destruction of Earth," Vargas said. "She failed."

He watched them carefully, gauging their reaction.

"*Enterprise* herself was lost twelve years later in the battle of Ceti Alpha V. Sailors are a superstitious lot, and after so much misfortune tied to that name . . . well, no vessel has used it since." He paused. "But you must know this . . . ?"

Picard didn't respond; Riker tried to/mask his growing skepticism and surprise. Counselor Troi broke the silence. "I understand you were pleased to see Lieutenant Worf," she said. "And your reaction to Doctor Selar was quite . . . sudden. Why? Do you feel you—know them—somehow?"

"Know them? No—no, of course not. Not them, specifically. But it was a natural reaction—what with the alliance, and the war . . ."

Troi took a deep breath. "The war."

Vargas studied each of them again. "Perhaps I had best start at the beginning."

"Yes," Picard said patiently. "I think that would be wise."

So with a wary gleam in his eye, Vargas began his tale. "It was a few months after Ceti Alpha. One of our vessels encountered a transport. An Earth ship. We had no record of her, so they went aboard. And it was remarkable. It was a late-twentieth-century sleeper ship, Captain—called the *S.S. Botany Bay.*"

Riker's voice was barely a whisper. "Khan."

"Yes, Commander. Khan. And sixty-two of his followers. We revived them."

"You must have known what he was. . . ."

"Of course we did. But these were desperate times. There were only a few thousand of us left. We thought that humanity was in the twilight of its existence. And whatever else that shipful of Augments might have been—they were human, after all.

"They were dismayed—and enraged—at what they found. They awoke from their slumber to find their homeworld gone, their race nearly extinct, and our resources and resolve in tatters. They had aspired to be kings, in another time—and this was the kingdom they found.

"Faced with this reality, Khan and his followers rose up and became the leaders they always knew they were destined to be. They rallied and inspired us, and we began to strike back against the Xindi. Khan personally forged an alliance with the Klingon Empire . . ." Vargas's tone grew wistful. "Oh, how I wish I could have been there," he said. "To see him in the Great Hall, in his prime, standing fearless and proud, a human like none those warriors had ever seen. Through sheer force of will, he brought them to our cause. And then the Andorians, and the Axanar, and the Tellarites, and more. Together we pushed the Xindi back. Eventually we managed to destroy a number of their masters' Spheres, and in so doing we laid waste to the Expanse.

"We began to rebuild. And we vowed that never again would humanity fall victim to such a horror. We began to seek our enemies out. We put down Nausicaan raiders like dogs. And eventually we came into conflict with the Vulcans. They had stifled us in our infancy and stood by twice while our world was attacked. They had done nothing to grant us sanctuary in our exile, and eventually so many years of anger and resentment boiled over into war. That war has been raging now for twenty years."

For several moments, the only sounds were the forcefield's hum and the steady pulse of sickbay monitors. A steward passed by delivering meals. Then Picard spoke. "Mister Vargas," he said quietly. "You have given us a great many mysteries. But I assure you: None of the things you describe has ever happened."

"Captain—" a voice said before Vargas could respond. It was the steward. "I need to speak with you," he said. "Now."

Riker turned to him. "This is not the time," he said sharply. "Crewman . . ."

"Daniels, sir."

*　　*　　*

"So now *Daniels* is a time traveler?"

The senior staff was assembled in the observation lounge. Geordi was having a hard time making sense of it all.

"According to him, at least," Riker said.

"And we believe him?"

"I've run scans," Crusher said. "And his DNA shows signs of interspecies mating dating back far longer than should be possible for a human of this era. Plus, there are a few genes in there I still can't identify. So—yes. It's possible."

"We already know that there are—unusual—temporal forces at work here," Picard said. "I don't know yet if I believe him—but I'm prepared to hear what he has to say." He thought for a moment and then turned to Worf. "Bring him in."

A moment later, Daniels took a seat among them. He was an earnest young man, with a serious face and slightly receding hair.

"Mister Daniels," Picard began. "Can you shed any—light—on today's events?"

"Captain, as I've said, my home is in the thirty-first century, seven hundred years in your future. Like you, I serve the Federation—or what today's Federation will become. We can monitor and travel through time in ways I can't begin to describe. But we have no record of anything like what he's told you."

"You don't believe him."

"We're aware of the timeline he describes. But only to a point. It was a self-correcting, closed-loop phenomenon—it should have reintegrated with our timeline twelve years after it began. His presence here suggests it didn't. But that's impossible—and deeply disturbing."

"So he's from an alternate reality, then," Riker said. "A crossover."

"I don't think so," Crusher said. "In every documented case of dimensional shift—like Mister Worf's encounter with the quantum fissure last year or the crossovers with a mirror universe being reported at Deep Space 9—there is a detectable quantum flux in the misplaced person's RNA. Mister Vargas doesn't have that."

"How can he be from this universe," Worf asked, "but from a past that never was?"

"Could he be delusional?" Riker said. "Or lying?"

"There is no indication that he's disturbed," Troi said. "And I don't sense any outright deception. There's more he's not telling us—but what he has said, in his experience at least, is entirely true."

"You say he's holding something back," Picard said. "Do you believe he means us any harm?"

"No, sir," Troi said. "If I had to describe his demeanor, I'd say above all that he's . . . curious. Intensely curious about us, almost clinical in his approach. But hopeful, too."

"Hopeful?" Riker asked. "For what?"

Troi shrugged. "I don't know."

"Mister La Forge," Picard said. "What have you learned from his ship?"

"Not much," Geordi said. "It's an amalgam of technology from at least a dozen worlds, and some I've never seen before. I don't know what half of that stuff does. And it's putting out a lot of energy—but I can't tell what kind or why."

"Captain," Daniels said. "As troubling as his story is, my superiors are most concerned about that disturbance." Beyond the room's tall viewports, the storm could still be seen, raging in the distance. Occasional shudders could still be felt throughout the ship. "By now you must be aware that this isn't the only one."

"We are," Picard said grimly. "Mister Data."

The android rose and activated the wall screen. "In the last three hours," he said, "Starfleet has reported the eruption of seventeen anomalies like the one that we have encountered. They appear to be propagating at an increasing rate. They are already beginning to pose a serious threat to navigation. If one should develop near an inhabited planet, the results would likely be catastrophic."

"Starfleet has declared a fleetwide yellow alert," Picard said. "We're devoting every resource we have to study them."

"What are they?" Crusher asked.

"The anomalies defy most forms of analysis," Data said. "But they appear to be eruptions of pure entropy."

"They're wounds," Daniels added. "Wounds in the fabric of space and time. Our data suggests that the one you've encountered is the epicenter. And Vargas's appearance at the same time can't be a coincidence."

"You think he's responsible for them?"

"Or that something else is responsible for them both. Either way, I'd like to take him with me to find out. In my time, we can investigate these issues in ways that would never be possible here."

Suddenly, he was overcome by a wave of nausea.

"Daniels? Are you all right?"

He looked up, and there, sitting where Doctor Crusher had been a moment before, was an older woman with light, curly hair. "Who are you?" he asked.

"Doctor Pulaski ran your scans just an hour ago," Picard said.

"Pulaski?" Daniels croaked. "Where's Crusher?"

"I'm still here," said a voice. Daniels turned to face Riker—and found instead an officer he'd never seen before.

"Who are—"

"Daniels," Picard said. "Mister Crusher has been my first officer for years . . ."

"Mister Crusher—Wesley?"

The officer looked confused. "Wesley is my *son.* What's wrong with you?"

Daniels looked back to Pulaski—but found Doctor Crusher back in her place. Beside her, though, Worf had been replaced by a young woman with short blond hair. "Tasha," he heard Riker say to her. "Perhaps you should take our guest—"

"Riker—" Daniels turned back to the speaker. But Riker now sat at the head of the table, with four pips on his collar. "Oh no," Daniels said. "No. Where's Captain Picard?"

Riker grew frustrated. "Daniels, Captain Picard was killed by the Borg years ago. What's going on?"

Daniels put his head in his hands. When he looked up, everything was right again. "Captain," he said weakly. "We have to hurry."

The double doors slid open, admitting Daniels and Picard to guest quarters on deck eight. The lighting was dim, and music played softly within. A guard stood outside the door.

They found Vargas seated at the desk, staring vacantly at his computer. "He didn't deserve this . . ." he said.

The doors slid shut behind them. "I'm sorry?"

"Marooned on a barren world. Hunted like a criminal. . . . He didn't deserve such an end." Vargas turned to face them.

"Well," Picard said. "The history we remember is a bit—different—from yours."

"Yes," Vargas said wearily. "So I see." He motioned to the computer. "I've been reading a great deal of your history, Captain. Thank you for allowing me."

Picard nodded.

"You truly have no trace of what I've described."

"No," Picard said. "I'd like to talk with you about that."

Vargas noted Picard's companion. "And you, sir . . . ?"

"Mister Daniels is . . . assisting us," Picard said. "He shares our concern with your arrival, and particularly with the—disturbances—that have erupted since then."

"You think I can help with that," Vargas said.

"I think you know more than you've shared."

Vargas sat silently for a moment. "I've been reading about you, Captain," he said quietly. "Oh, nothing classified. News accounts, mostly. You're fond of archaeology, aren't you?"

"I am."

"Have you ever . . . looked upon a relic, Captain, and wondered what might have been? Have you ever dreamt of saving the Mayans, perhaps, or how a first contact *could* have gone?"

"I suppose," Picard said. "History is necessarily about possibility and choice."

"Quite so, Captain. Quite so."

"But there are things in life that can't be changed," Daniels said. "That shouldn't be."

"Oh?" Vargas said. "Hmm. Well—perhaps so."

The ship shuddered around them.

"The tremors are getting worse," Vargas said.

"Yes."

He grew quiet. "There are more of them, aren't there?"

"There are," Picard said. He traded looks with Daniels. "Mister Vargas, what is it you're not telling us? What do you know about them?"

"I should go," he said. He breathed deeply. "It's time."

"I'm afraid I can't allow that," Picard said. "However—Mister Daniels would like to take you with him, to help us understand what is happening."

"Take me where?" Vargas asked. He peered more intently at the man. And then his expression changed. "You're not from here, are you?" he asked. "You want to take me through *time* . . ."

"How did you—"

"Captain, this is madness," Vargas said. "Absolutely not. I need to leave here. Now."

"I cannot—"

"Captain, you don't know what you're doing."

"Then explain it to me."

Vargas looked at them in stony silence.

"Well," Picard said. "You see my dilemma."

They returned to the bridge. Picard and Riker were conferring quietly when an alarm went off behind them.

"Captain!" Worf said. "Detecting an unauthorized launch in main shuttlebay." He looked up. "It's Vargas."

"He didn't waste any time," Riker said. "How'd he get past security?"

"Unknown."

"Secure the bay doors," Picard said. "And get a team down there."

"He's overriding our controls," Worf said. "He's depressurizing the bay. . . . He's gone."

"Red alert," Picard said. "Pursuit course."

On the main viewer, the tiny craft rocketed toward the disturbance. "Transporter lock?"

"Jammed."

"Tractor beam."

"No effect."

Picard tugged at his uniform and glared at the screen. "Hail him."

Vargas appeared on screen. He glanced at them only briefly as he tended to the controls. *"Don't follow me, Captain. I beg of you."*

"I have no intention of harming you," Picard said. "But I believe you know how to stop these eruptions. And they have to be stopped." The bridge around him began to shake.

Data spoke quietly from ops. "Remodulating tractor emitters. This may negate his countermeasures." On the viewer, Vargas's ship shuddered as the beam took hold.

"Captain, please."

"Talk to us," Riker said.

Vargas continued to work. He breathed deeply. *"Possibility and choice, Captain. That is more true than you know."* He thought for a moment, then spoke absently while he worked.

"Soon after our defeat of the Xindi, we began to learn more about their masters and other threats from beyond our realm. The Suliban, for example, and their temporal allies. We knew we were entering an age where such threats were no longer fixed in space or time.

"Eventually the Suliban too were crushed, and we were able to learn a great deal from technology we recovered. We began experimenting. We began to think we could not just protect against invaders, but perhaps undo so much of what had befallen us.

"Not long after our experiments began, we encountered a temporal parasite that affected a number of our researchers. It was a terrible affliction—freezing them in time, in a way, by preventing them from forming any long-term memory.

"In searching for a cure, we came across the notes of a Denobulan physician from the earliest days of the diaspora. They showed promise, and eventually we devised a way to eradicate the creatures.

"The Denobulan had been researching a cure for his captain—the captain of that first Enterprise. *He'd been infected in the Expanse, a few months before Earth was lost. It gave us an idea.*

"For our first attempt at a temporal correction, we wanted to start with something small. Something minor, to let us monitor its effects and learn for our next attempt. So we decided on that Denobulan physician. He was brilliant, really. We just—nudged him—in the right direction. To replicate the cure we'd found."

Vargas continued his work. *"The key to this was remaining aware of what we'd done. That is where this vessel comes in.*

"Don't be ashamed that you couldn't decipher it in a day. This ship, this—Genesis device—is adapted from captured technologies that won't be invented for another three hundred years. Doctor Marcus and his Klingon team worked half their lives to build it. It is a temporal insulator of sorts—it allows me to weather the effects of our tampering without being affected myself. It lets me observe what we have done—and undo it if need be."

Realization dawned on Picard. "Shut off the beam," he said. "Now."

"Captain?"

"Do it."

Vargas smiled. *"Thank you, Captain. I'm glad you understand."*

"You took a tremendous risk."

"Yes, Captain. And it was incredible hubris on our part, I know. But look at what we have wrought."

"Captain," Daniels said. "What is he talking about?"

"You were right, Mister Daniels," Vargas said. *"The events that I've described . . . never happened.* Now. *And thanks to us."*

"Us?"

"Myself and many others who never were. The reality that you know, Mister Daniels, is not the reality that was. It is not the one that was meant to be. It is one that we have made. And that we must be allowed to finish."

"You can't be serious. The eruptions—"

"*I am a product of that—first draft—of history,*" Vargas said. "*I am connected to it. My presence here—my very existence—is a paradox. It is anathema to Nature herself. I cannot be. And yet I am. That is why existence is reacting as it is, and why these eruptions are centered here.*

"*We knew this could happen—and we knew I would have little time. But we had to know. If we had done something worthy, and deserving of life, or if we should direct our efforts elsewhere. I am, frankly—overwhelmed—by what I've found.*"

"Captain," Geordi said. "There's a tremendous buildup of energy over there. . . ."

"Back us away." The two ships began to part.

"*My presence, though necessary, has caused enough disruption here,*" Vargas said. "*Allowing you to take me to yet another time, Mister Daniels, would have been disastrous.*"

A sensor chimed on Worf's board. "He's building to some kind of overload."

"*The reality you know is not what was,*" Vargas said. "*It is not what was meant to be. It is a gift. From us. Use it well. And—remember us.*"

His image disappeared from the screen. They watched in silence as his ship appeared to gather a tremendous energy and then silently collapsed in upon itself. There was a brilliant flash of light—and he was gone. The trembling in the deck that had become ever-present quietly subsided, and the storm itself faded from view.

The bridge was silent. Picard finally spoke. "'And he looked upon his works, and saw that they were good.'"

Geordi came up to the rail behind them. "You mean—we owe our entire existence . . . what? To Khan?"

"No," Picard said quietly. "But perhaps to the man he might have been." He gazed for a moment at the stars.

"Helm—take us home."

Strange New Worlds

Contest Rules

1) ENTRY REQUIREMENTS:

No purchase necessary to enter. Purchase does not increase your chances of winning. To enter, send an original story based on the established *Star Trek* universe and/or characters as specified below. All entries must be received between June 1, 2005, and October 1, 2005. Entries received after October 1, 2005, will not be accepted.

2) CONTEST ELIGIBILITY:

This contest is open to nonprofessional writers who are legal residents of the United States (excluding Puerto Rico) and Canada (excluding Quebec) over the age of 18 at time of entry. Entrant must not have published any more than two short stories on a professional basis or in paid professional venues. Employees (or relatives of employees living in the same household) of Simon & Schuster, Nickelodeon and VIACOM, or any of their affiliates are not eligible. This contest is void in Puerto Rico, Quebec, and wherever prohibited by law. Entrants agree to be bound by the Official Contest Rules.

3) FORMAT:

Entries should be no more than 7,500 words long, must not have been previously published, and must not have been entered into any other contest or won any other awards. Entries must be typed or printed by word processor, double-spaced, on one side of noncorrasable paper. Do not justify right-side margins. The author's name, address, email address, and phone number must appear on the first page of the entry. The author's name, the story title, and the page number should appear on every page. No electronic or disk submissions will be accepted. Submissions must be in English. All entries must be the original and sole work of the Entrant and the sole property of the Entrant. Entries must not be subject to the rights of any third parties. Entrants not complying with these requirements will be subject to disqualification. By submitting an entry, Entrant warrants that the entry is the Entrant's original and sole work and Entrant's sole property.

4) ADDRESS:

Each entry must be mailed to:
STRANGE NEW WORLDS 9
Star Trek Department
Pocket Books
1230 Avenue of the Americas
New York, NY 10020

Each story may be submitted only once. Multiple copies of the same story or a slightly altered story (based on the sole discretion of the judges) will not be accepted. No facsimile, mechanically reproduced, altered, forged, incomplete, or illegible entries will be accepted. Please retain a copy of your submission. Entrant may submit more than one story, but each submission must be mailed separately. Sponsor is not responsible for lost, late, stolen, postage-due, damaged, or misdirected mail. Entries are the property of the Sponsor and will not be acknowledged or returned.

5) PRIZES:

One (1) Grand Prize winner will receive:

Simon & Schuster's *Star Trek*: *Strange New Worlds 9* Publishing Contract for Publication of Winning Entry in our *Strange New Worlds 9* Anthology with a bonus advance of One Thousand Dollars ($1,000.00) above the Anthology word rate of 10 cents a word.

One (1) Second Prize winner will receive:

Simon & Schuster's *Star Trek*: *Strange New Worlds 9* Publishing Contract for Publication of Winning Entry in our *Strange New Worlds 9* Anthology with a bonus advance of Six Hundred Dollars ($600.00) above the Anthology word rate of 10 cents a word.

One (1) Third Prize winner will receive:

Simon & Schuster's *Star Trek*: *Strange New Worlds 9* Publishing Contract for Publication of Winning Entry in our *Strange New Worlds 9* Anthology with a bonus advance of Four Hundred Dollars ($400.00) above the Anthology word rate of 10 cents a word.

All Honorable Mention winners will receive:

Simon & Schuster's *Star Trek: Strange New Worlds 9* Publishing Contract for Publication of Winning Entry in the *Strange New Worlds 9* Anthology and payment at the Anthology word rate of 10 cents a word. Approximate retail value of prizes will depend on the number of words published for all winning entries included in the Anthology.

There will be no more than twenty (20) Honorable Mention winners. No contestant can win more than one prize. One prize per household.

Each prize winner will also be entitled to a share of royalties on the *Strange New Worlds 9* Anthology as specified in Simon & Schuster's *Star Trek*: *Strange New Worlds 9* Publishing Contract.

6) JUDGING:

Submissions will be judged on the basis of a) writing ability and b) the originality of the story, which can be set in any of the *Star Trek* time frames and may feature any one or more of the *Star Trek* characters. Each factor will be applied equally. The judges shall include the editor of the Anthology, one employee of Pocket Books, and one employee of Nickelodeon and VIACOM Consumer Products. The decisions of the judges shall be final on all matters. Sponsor reserves the right not to award prizes in the event that an insufficient number of entries meeting the criteria established by the judges is received.

7) NOTIFICATION:

The winners will be notified by mail or phone on or about December 23, 2005. The winners may be required to execute and return an Affidavit of Eligibility/Release/Prize Acceptance Form. The winners will receive a publishing contract. Winners must sign the publishing contract in order to be awarded the prize. Noncompliance with these requirements or noncompliance within the specified time frame may result in disqualification and the selection of an alternate winner. Return of Prize Notification or publishing contract as undeliverable will result in disqualification and an alternate winner will be selected. Prize is not transferable. No substitution or cash redemption of prize except by Sponsor, who reserves the right to substitute a prize of greater or equal value in the event that a prize is unavailable. All federal, local, and state taxes are the responsibility of the winners. A list of the winners will be available after January 3, 2006, on the Pocket Books *Star Trek* Books website,

http://www.simonsays.com/startrek/

or the names of the winners can be obtained after January 3, 2006, by sending a self-addressed, stamped envelope and a request for the list of winners to:

WINNERS' LIST
STRANGE NEW WORLDS 9
Star Trek Department
Pocket Books
1230 Avenue of the Americas
New York, NY 10020

8) STORY DISQUALIFICATIONS:

Certain types of stories will be disqualified from consideration:

a) Any story focusing on explicit sexual activity or graphic depictions of violence or sadism.

b) Any story that focuses on characters that are not past or present *Star Trek* regulars or familiar *Star Trek* guest characters.

c) Stories that deal with the previously unestablished death of a *Star Trek* character, or that establish major facts about or make major changes in the life of a major character—for instance, a story that establishes a long-lost sibling or reveals the hidden passion two characters feel for each other.

d) Stories that are based around common clichés, such as "hurt/comfort" stories, in which a character is injured and lovingly cared for, or "Mary Sue" stories, in which a new character comes on the ship and outdoes the crew.

9) PUBLICITY:

Acceptance of prize constitutes permission by winner to use his or her name, photograph, likeness, and/or entry for any advertising, promotion, and publicity purposes without further compensation to or permission from such winner, except where prohibited by law.

10) RIGHTS IN ENTRIES:

By mailing in your submission, Entrant grants Sponsor all right, title, and interest in entry, including any copyrights therein. All entries will become the property of Pocket Books and of Paramount Pictures, the sole and exclusive owner of the *Star Trek* property and elements thereof. Contest void where prohibited by law.

11) GENERAL:

Sponsor and its agents are not responsible for incomplete, late, lost, stolen, damaged, mutilated, illegible, returned, postage-due, or misdirected entries or mail. By participating in this Contest, Entrants agree to be bound by these Official Rules and agree to release and hold harmless Sponsor and Paramount Pictures and their respective advertising and promotion agencies, partners, representatives, agents, parent companies successors, assigns, employees, officers, and directors from any and all liability for loss, harm, damage, injury, cost, or expense whatsoever, including without limitation property damage, personal injury, or death that may occur in connection with, preparation for, or participation in the Contest or any Contest-related activity, or with the acceptance, possession and/or misuse of prize, and for any claims of publicity rights, defamation, or invasion of privacy. Sponsor is not responsible if the *Star Trek: Strange New Worlds 9* Anthology does not get published.

12) SPONSOR:

Pocket Books, an imprint of Simon & Schuster, Inc., 1230 Avenue of the Americas, New York, NY 10020.

About the Contributors

Lorraine Anderson ("Hero") lives in Three Rivers, Michigan, and works two jobs. Finding time to write is a challenge! She is ruled by her two cats, Cocoa and Zen (who is anything but peaceful). This is her first professional publication, and she is still in total shock. While she would love to name all her friends and family who have supported her, she would especially like to thank Sherry "Sherlock" Watson. Adventures, old friend!

Derek Tyler Attico ("A & Ω" [Alpha and Omega]) is a native New Yorker actively pursuing writing. His other passions include feudal Japan, reading everything from Dante to Dumas, and photography; his work can be seen at DerekAttico.com. Since a story is written alone but never completed unaided, he'd like to thank Gene Roddenberry and the writers of *Star Trek* for creating and cultivating such a rich mythos, the WritersRoom for giving him a place of solitude to write, and Dean, Elisa, and Paula for allowing his voice to be heard here. This marks his first entry and appearance in *SNW*.

David DeLee ("Promises Made") is a native New Yorker who now resides in central Ohio with his wonderful wife, Anne, his two terrific daughters, Grace and Sarah, and four cats (a prerequisite for writers, he's been told). He'd like to thank his family for their support, even when they didn't completely understand ("A writer? Where'd *that* come from?"); Dean, Elisa, and Paula for making it possible; the OCPFWW Class of '03, for everything—and C.G. for critiques of his earlier work with a gentle but firm red pen. "Promises Made" is his first professional sale.

M. C. DeMarco ("This Drone") caught the *Star Trek* bug from her father, L. L. DeMarco, at an impressionable age. Today she works for a small software company in Cambridge, Massachusetts. In 2004, she attended the Odyssey Fantasy Writing Workshop; any adverbs that remain in her prose are entirely her own. This is her first professional sale.

Dan C. Duval ("Trek") marks his first professional sale in *SNW8*. After spending the last twenty-five years working in high tech, he, his cat, and his horses are taking a stab at the writing lifestyle, hoping to avoid the day job as long as possible. He lives in Oregon, between the volcanoes and the tsunamis. He thanks all the people who made this possible and they know who they are. So does the FBI.

Alan James Garbers ("Shanghaied") is a master electrician and Assistant Scoutmaster in BSA Troop 219. He lives on a small farm in central Indiana with his singer/songwriter wife, Dianna, his Eagle Scout son, Dustin, and his honor-roll daughter, Erica. "Shanghaied" is Alan's third and last appearance in the *SNW* anthologies. Alan thanks Dean, John, Paula, and Elisa for the encouragement and opportunities. He also thanks his coworkers at Diamond Chain Company, and his friends in the Morgan County Writers group for their support. Alan hopes to continue a career in writing *Star Trek* novels.

Kevin Andrew Hosey ("Demon") is a forty-five-year-old marketing communications professional who lives in Dallas, Texas, with his wife, Terrelia, and two children, Christian and Kimberly. This is his second *SNW* story. His first, "Seven & Seven," appeared in *SNW VI*. Besides the *Trek* stories, he's had cartoons printed in several publications, including *Starlog*. He recently finished two movie scripts, one horror and one science fiction, and also plans to convert them to novels. When not locked in his home studio writing, he spends his days creating advertising, videos, websites, and more. Like writing, it's hard work—but lots of fun.

Paul J. Kaplan ("Dawn") is an evil big-firm lawyer in Atlanta. Others know him as the slightly daft husband of a much smarter lawyer and doting dad of The Cutest Toddler Ever™. "Dawn" marks Paul's third appearance in *Strange New Worlds,* and he is stunned to learn that this allegedly makes him a "professional" writer. That noise you just heard was the sound of every real author out there having a collective stroke. Heartfelt thanks to Dean, John, Elisa, and Paula for letting the fans contribute a few corny words to the near forty-year tapestry of *Trek.*

A. Rhea King ("Insanity") is a native Coloradoan. She currently attends Aims Community College studying TV Production and after graduation will attend UCLA to earn her master's. She has won awards and recognition for her one-hour drama scripts (all science-fiction-based, of course) and looks forward to a career as an episodic-TV writer and producer. "Insanity" is her first professional publication, but certainly not her last writing success!

Kevin Lauderdale ("Assignment: One") has been on the cutting edge of history all his life. He was born and raised in Los Angeles during Hollywood's Silver Age, lived in Silicon Valley during the Internet boom, and moved to the Washington, D.C., area (specifically, northern Virginia) two weeks before 9/11. His story "A Test of Character" was in *SNW VII*.

Muri McCage ("Always a Price") is a full-time writer, currently working on several original fiction projects and a screenplay. This is her second *SNW* appearance. She has traveled the world and would love to travel the universe as well, if only technology would catch up with imagination. In the meantime, she is very happy to hitch a ride on the wagon train to the stars. She would like to thank her best friend, Cinnamon, who always gets it, and her mom, for always believing.

Susan S. McCrackin ("Transfiguration") is thrilled to once again be included in *SNW* after making her first appearance in *SNW VII*. Susan lives in northern Virginia (which seems to be a haven for *SNW* writers!) and is supported by wonderful friends who encourage her writing efforts. She is especially grateful to Judy (who helped me come up with the title for this story) and to Leslie (who has been her biggest fan and most fervent cheerleader and also has a great talent for creating titles) for all of their editing work. She is currently working on an SF novel with a universe that is totally under her control—well, as much control as her characters will allow her to have.

Annie Reed ("Once Upon a Tribble") lives in northern Nevada with her husband, her daughter, and several high-maintenance cats. In addition to science fiction, she writes mystery and mainstream fiction, and has recently sold stories to *Ellery Queen Mystery Magazine* and the upcoming anthology *Time After Time* from Daw. "Once Upon a Tribble" marks her third and final appearance in *Strange New Worlds*. She wants to thank Dean, Paula, and Elisa for the opportunity; Dave and Katie for giving her time, space, and encouragement to write; the incredible Oregon Coast Writers, from whom she's learned so much; and, last but certainly not least, the incomparable Melissa for keeping the faith even when she had none.

Strange New Worlds has been a wonderful experience, and she will miss it.

Robert Burke Richardson ("Egg Drop Soup") has stories appearing in *All-Star Zeppelin Adventure Stories, Magistria: Realm of the Sorcerer,* and online at WouldThatItWere.com (Oct/Dec 2004). His nonfiction appears online at *The Internet Review of Science Fiction* and *TrekNation.com.* Where he's from, the birds sing a pretty song and there's always music in the air.

Sarah A. Seaborne ("Passages of Deceit") is a native Oregonian who quilts, walks marathons, and is a green belt in Tae Kwon Do. "Passages of Deceit" is her first professional sale, and she is currently writing a mystery novel and working on a story for the next *SNW* competition. She wishes to thank her friends (two-legged and four-legged) who have immeasurably enriched her life. And for this story, and for an indescribable year, a special thanks to Ian, friend, confidant, and the guy at the other end of the lifeline.

Amy Sisson ("You May Kiss the Bride") is an academic librarian in Houston, Texas, and a graduate of Clarion West (2000). This is Amy's second appearance in *SNW,* following "The Law of Averages" in *SNW VII.* "You May Kiss the Bride" is dedicated to Paul Abell—husband, soulmate, and co-rescuer of cats—and is not based on Amy and Paul's real-life wedding experiences. Thanks also to Dean Wesley Smith, Paula M. Block, and Elisa J. Kassin for helping to make writing dreams come true.

J.B. (Jan) Stevens ("Coffee with a Friend"), a blood bank lab technologist and aspiring writer living in Oklahoma City, is humbled to be making her second appearance in the *Strange New Worlds* anthologies. Her first winning story, "Hidden," appeared in *Strange New Worlds VI.* A lifetime fan of science fiction, JB has been hopelessly addicted to *Star Trek* ever since the original series first aired. She would like to dedicate this story to the memory of her father,

Richard Burke. He left her a wonderful legacy of devotion to family, his example of never wanting to give up and quit, and the belief that despite other people's opinions, being a stubborn, hardheaded Irishman isn't such a bad thing after all.

Kevin G. Summers ("Morning Bells Are Ringing") is the author of the critically acclaimed short story "Isolation Ward 4" *(SNW IV)* as well as the story "Ha'mara" *(Prophecy and Change).* He resides in Leesburg, Virginia, with his beautiful wife, Rachel, and their daughter, Morwen.

John Takis ("Final Flight") appears in *SNW* for the last time, having previously published in volumes III and V. John writes, "This story is dedicated to the memory of Jerry Goldsmith, whose incomparable music shaped both *Star Trek* and my imagination." John can be found at various Midwestern locales, working for his church and hacking away at assorted writing projects. He sends love to Ξανθή.

Geoffrey Thorne ("Concurrence") still lives in Los Angeles, still with his frighteningly prescient (and now occasionally bemused) wife, Susan. Deepest thanks to the Great Bird for starting all this. Equal thanks to Dean, Elisa, Paula, and the absent but never forgotten John Ordover, for letting me join in. IDIC.

Paul C. Tseng ("Don't Call Me Tiny") holds a bachelor's and master's degree from Juilliard and a doctorate from Johns Hopkins University. He is an IT professional and a musician. Paul has been a fan of *Star Trek* since he was in elementary school, when the original series aired every night. Writing stories since the first grade, he has written plays, scripts, short stories, and novels. His contribution to *Strange New Worlds 8* marks his professional debut. It was at the suggestion of friends that he entered his stories into *SNW* to get his proverbial "foot in the door." Paul acknowledges and thanks his wife, Katie, and two children, who put up with his *Trek* habit in southern California. He would also like to thank his accomplices

Anthony Davis, Lori Graves, and Joseph DiLella for their encouragement, devoted feedback, and support from the very first chapter of *Trek* fiction he wrote. Paul dedicates this story to his father and recently departed mother for their love and unfailing belief in him.

Amy Vincent ("Gumbo") works in marketing in New York City. Although she has also worked as a journalist and continues to freelance, this is her first published fiction. She would especially like to thank her friends Rocky and Seema for inspiring this story and encouraging her to enter it in *Strange New Worlds,* as well as her friends Rodney and Jesse, the best *Trek*-watching pals anybody ever had.